Light filled the mirror, bright as the sun.

The light spread into the library. Snow White felt as though she were falling into the glass. She grabbed the mirror's frame with both hands. Wisps of fog curled from the glass. She peered into the light, trying to follow Beatrice's soul wherever it had gone.

Snow's blood battered her head from within as though straining to crack the skull. Her body felt numb, and she clung to the mirror to keep from falling. Through the pain, a part of her marveled at what the mirror had done, reaching out so far in pursuit of the dead.

"Come back to us, Bea." Silence swallowed her words. Snow wasn't even certain she had spoken aloud. She could no longer make out the library around her. Nothing existed save the light and the place that lay on the other side. The place Beatrice's spirit had gone.

With her hands clenched around the frame, she felt the glass shift ever so slightly. Pain exploded behind her eyes as she tried to focus not on the light, but on the mirror's surface, where a white line now curved across the center of the glass. Lines spread in a starburst from her hand. Fragments of glass no larger than pebbles fell to the floor. Blood dripped down the frame, though Snow hadn't felt the cuts.

The magic surged like a living thing. How many times had Talia warned her against bending the laws of the universe too far? Push hard enough, and things were going to snap. Even her mother's mirror had limits. Snow tried to end her spell, but it was far too late. . . .

DAW Books presents these delightful fantasy novels
by Jim C. Hines

THE STEPSISTER SCHEME
THE MERMAID'S MADNESS
RED HOOD'S REVENGE
THE SNOW QUEEN'S SHADOW

***

Jig the Goblin Series:
GOBLIN QUEST (Book One)
GOBLIN HERO (Book Two)
GOBLIN WAR (Book Three)

***

Magic ex Libris
LIBROMANCER*

*Coming in 2012 from DAW Books

The Snow Queen's Shadow

Jim C. Hines

DAW BOOKS, INC.
DONALD A. WOLLHEIM, FOUNDER
375 Hudson Street, New York, NY 10014

ELIZABETH R. WOLLHEIM
SHEILA E. GILBERT
PUBLISHERS

www.dawbooks.com

Cover art by Scott Fischer.

Cover design by G-Force Design.

DAW Book Collectors No. 1553.

DAW Books are distributed by Penguin Group (USA) Inc.

First Printing, July 2011
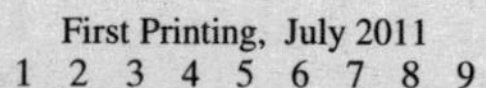
1 2 3 4 5 6 7 8 9

DAW TRADEMARK REGISTERED
U.S. PAT. AND TM. OFF. AND FOREIGN COUNTRIES
—MARCA REGISTRADA
HECHO EN U.S.A.

PRINTED IN THE U.S.A.

To Skylar

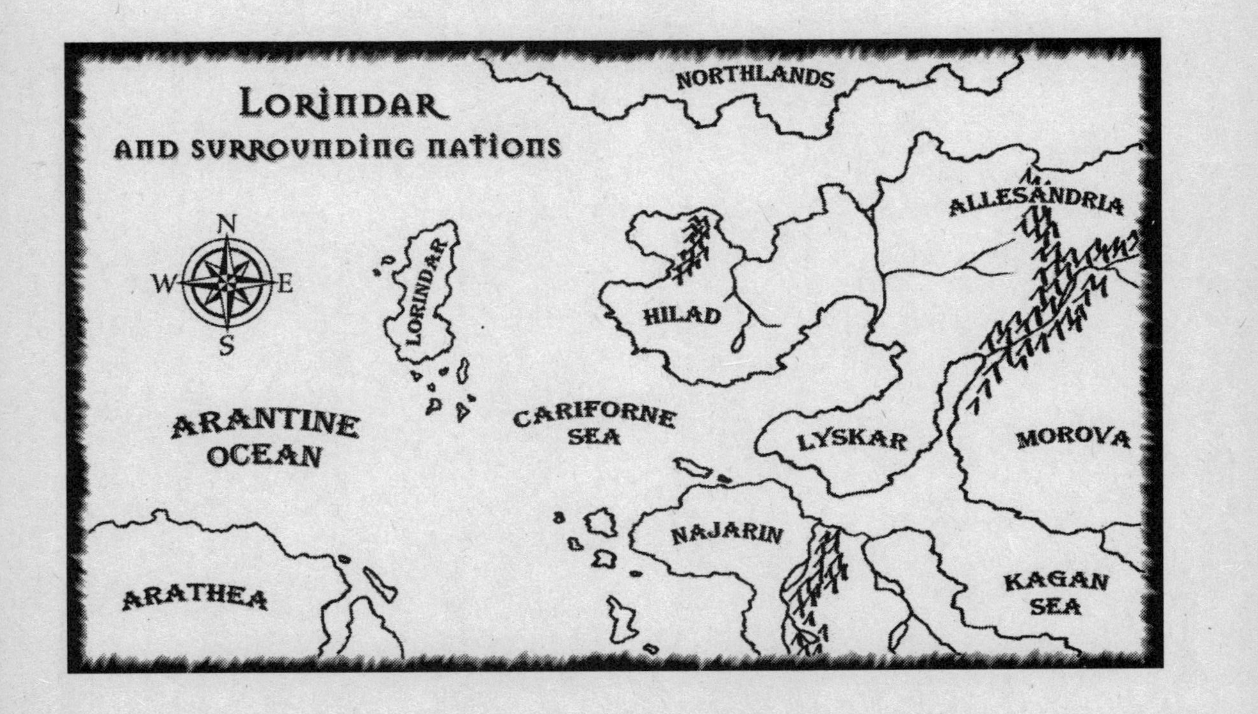

LORINDAR
AND SURROUNDING NATIONS
NORTHLANDS
ALLESANDRIA
N
W
E
S
LORINDAR
HILAD
ARANTINE
OCEAN
CARIFORNE
SEA
LYSKAR
MOROVA
NAJARIN
KAGAN
SEA
ARATHEA

The Snow Queen's Shadow

Chapter 1

THE PLAN HAD BEEN SO SIMPLE. An hour or so before sunrise, Snow White and Talia would sneak into the Sailor's Bone Inn. Talia would "persuade" the innkeeper to tell them which room held the two fugitive witchhunters who had recently snuck into Lorindar. Snow would cast a spell of sleep upon their quarry, who could then be brought to Whiteshore Palace to face trial.

The universe rarely cooperated with Snow's plans. She should have been halfway back to the palace by now, not staring down the pointy end of a silver-tipped arrow, wielded by a man known to have murdered at least sixteen witches, while fire spread through the inn's upper story.

It went without saying that this was entirely Talia's fault.

Snow's would-be prisoner went by the name of Hansel. He was middle-aged and built like a bear, with shaggy blond locks that hung just past his shoulders. He wore heavy furs over a thick leather vest, studded in brass. Knotted braids of hair dangled from his belt: trophies of his kills.

Hansel jabbed his longbow at Snow. "Call your witch friend. Tell her to bring my sister back."

"Talia's not a witch." Snow searched the empty tavern for anything she might use as a weapon. The occupants had fled into the cold right around the time Snow sent Hansel tumbling down the stairs. His sister had escaped onto the roof, with Talia close behind. "Besides, she never listens to me. If you'd like to put down that bow, we could head to the palace to wait for them."

"No, thank you," he said, his expression half sneer, half smile. "I've better things to do than be executed by your witch-loving king and queen."

He stepped around a broken table, wincing as he put weight on his right leg. Blood darkened the area around the sharpened steel snowflake stuck in his thigh. Hansel had some sort of protection against her spell, but nonmagical weapons worked just fine. Had her aim been better, she might have ended things at the top of the staircase. On the other hand, then Talia never would have let her forget how brute force had triumphed where magic failed.

At least if Hansel killed her, she wouldn't have to worry about Talia's teasing. Snow knew the only reason he hadn't fired was because he might need to bargain with Talia to get his sister back, but she had no idea how long he would wait. He didn't strike her as the patient sort.

"Take off that necklace of yours," Hansel said. "Slowly."

Snow touched the back of her choker. Gold wire unraveled, and the choker fell into her hand, its small oval mirrors clinking together. She glanced at the largest, searching for Talia, but it was dark outside, and Talia was moving too quickly to make out any details. Snow concentrated, maintaining the thread between her choker and the mirrored bracelet Talia wore. If nothing else, Talia should hear their conversation and know what had happened.

"Toss it to the floor."

Snow obeyed, throwing the choker so it landed at his feet. She moved sideways, putting another table between herself and Hansel. He stood so he could see both Snow and the door, and he was rumored to be good enough with that bow to put an arrow through her knee should she try for the stairs.

She heard shouts outside as neighbors worked to organize against the fire and keep it from spreading. The flames had reached the top of the staircase, and smoke darkened the ceiling. "That was an interesting charm you used to protect yourselves from my spell," she said brightly. "The one that burst into flame when Talia ripped it from your neck? So you kill witches, but you'll use witchcraft when it suits your purposes?"

He scowled. "You're Allesandrian, aren't you?"

"I am."

"So you're old enough to remember the Purge."

Snow's smile vanished.

"I see that you are. You've seen the damage such power can do. How many people did Queen Curtana murder?"

"Officially? Forty-seven." Unofficially, the tally was far higher. Forty-seven men, women, and children were known to have been executed for treason during the weeklong purge, convicted only by the secrets Snow's mother had plucked from her magic mirror. Snow forced the cheerfulness back into her voice. "Two years ago, a man from southern Lorindar murdered twelve people with an ax. Should we kill all the woodsmen? And what of you? You shoved a witch into an oven when you were younger. Obviously we should hunt down and destroy all bakers!"

As she finished speaking, she waved a hand at her choker. Sunlight flashed from the mirrors. Snow crouched low and upended the table between herself and Hansel. She heard the snap of Hansel's bow, and an arrow punched through the wood a handspan from her face.

She pulled a long knife from her belt and thumbed a hidden catch on the hilt. A circular plate with an engraved snowflake swiveled open at the center of the crossguard, revealing a small mirror. Through the mirror, she saw Hansel stumbling toward the door, one hand shielding his eyes.

Snow jabbed her knife at the door and spoke a quick spell. The door slammed shut.

Hansel merely lowered his shoulder and smashed his way through. Cold air rushed into the tavern.

Snow swore and hurried to retrieve her choker. Her head throbbed from the magic she had used tonight, an old injury warning of worse to come if she continued to push herself.

She shoved the pain aside as she followed Hansel onto the street. Sixteen witches dead, in Lorindar and elsewhere. Like Snow's mother, Hansel killed indiscriminately and without remorse.

Snow had been too young to stop the Purge, but she'd be damned before she let Hansel murder another witch.

She squeezed through the gathering crowd, diverting a part of her attention to her choker and her connection to Talia's mirror. "Where are you?"

"On my way back to the inn." The choker relayed Talia's voice as clearly as if they were running side-by-side. Talia didn't even sound winded. "Are you all right?"

"I'm fine!" Her boots splashed through slush and snow as she ran. The sky to the east was just beginning to brighten, but the streets were still dim. Her mirrors enhanced her vision, helping her spy Hansel limping up Mill Street. Snow cut through an alley, hoping to intercept him. The snowdrifts were higher here where the three-story buildings protected the streets from the sun. "He's making his way toward Holy Crossroads."

"Probably heading for the gates."

Snow bit back a yelp as her feet skidded on the cobblestones. A rain barrel had frozen and split, and ice covered much of the alley. She slowed, chafing at the delay, but she would never catch Hansel if she slipped and snapped an ankle.

The crowds had already begun to fill the streets at Holy Crossroads, eager to hear the preachers and their daily performance. The preachers' garb had grown more flamboyant over the years, as had their rhetoric, as each shouted and condemned his neighbor to eternal damnation.

Even if Snow had been able to spot Hansel, the crowd

shielded him from both magical and mundane attacks. She slipped into the crowd, elbowing her way past the gawkers. "Danielle, are you listening to this?"

Princess Danielle had remained behind at Whiteshore Palace. "I'm here. Did you really set the Sailor's Bone on fire?"

"That was Talia's fault! And if they get that bucket line organized, I'm sure they can save part of the building."

A priest of the Fairy Church stepped into the middle of the street, blocking her way. He raised a hand to her. "No mundane errand is more important than your immortal soul," he shouted. "Enter the house of the fairy saviors. Confess your sins and receive their blessings!"

Snow smiled. "I like my sins."

The priest looked to weigh twice as much as Snow. Had he stood his ground, she would have been hard pressed to move him. But Snow had spent years working with Talia, and had picked up a number of tricks. She lowered her shoulders and ran, showing no sign of slowing. The priest stepped back. That move cost him his balance, and moments later he was tumbling into the slush on the side of the road, earning shouts from his followers and cheers from the other churches.

"What was that?" Danielle asked.

"Nothing. Can you get word to the guards at the southern gate?"

"It will take time, but I'll see what I can do."

A splash of red drew her attention to a snowbank on the left. She plucked her steel flake from the snow where Hansel had discarded it. Droplets of blood marked his path toward the gate. Snow ran around a mule-drawn wagon, then stopped to search the intersection in front of the gate. The main avenue was broad enough for three carriages to pass side by side. Two other roads branched away from the gate, parallel to the wall. There were too many people and too much space.

The stone wall wasn't as impressive as the one surrounding the palace, but Snow doubted Hansel could have scaled it with his wounded leg. The barred iron gate was wide open, though. Danielle's message must not have gotten through. Snow approached the closer of the two guards on duty. "Have you seen a witchhunter pass through here? Shaggy and bleeding, carrying an enchanted bow?"

He stared. "Are you all right, miss?"

"I've had better days." Snow sighed and turned away, just as Talia came running up the far street.

"Don't tell me you lost him."

Despite her annoyance, Snow grinned at the sight of poor Talia, bundled tight against the winter cold. Talia had grown up in the deserts of Arathea, and viewed snow as a punishment delivered personally by vengeful gods. She wore a thick wool cloak, and a knitted scarf covered her mouth and nose. Only her hands were bare, so she could better grip the various weapons hidden about her person. At the moment, she had one hand tucked beneath her arm for warmth while the other held her hood low to protect her face from the cold.

"I haven't lost anyone." Snow crouched to scoop a handful of slush, crushing it into a ball. She tilted her steel snowflake, allowing a single drop of blood to fall onto the slush. Tucking the weapon away, she whispered a spell to harden the ball to ice. "I just thought it was more sporting to give him a head start."

Her head pounded as she cast another spell. She blinked back tears, turning it into a wink when she caught Talia watching her. She switched the ice to her other hand and hurled it into the air. At its peak, the ice jerked to the east as if caught by the wind, though the air was still. It plummeted back to earth, the blood magically guiding its flight more than a block past the gate. The crowd at the gate hid Hansel from view, but Snow heard the impact, followed by loud swearing.

More shouts followed. By the time Snow and Talia made their way past the crowd into an alley between a butcher's shop and a tavern, Hansel was ready. He aimed his bow at Snow, the string drawn back. "Where is my sister?"

"I don't know," Snow said. "Let's go ask the nice guards at the gate if they've seen her."

The bow didn't waver. Snow glanced at Talia.

"She fell off a roof and broke her leg." Talia stepped sideways, away from Snow. "I tied her up at the hitching post a few blocks over. Danielle said she'd send men to collect her."

"Wait, you just left her there?" Snow asked.

"I had to make sure you didn't get yourself killed," Talia shot back.

Snow jabbed a finger at Hansel. "I found him all by myself, thank you."

"And now he's got a bow aimed at you!"

Snow shrugged. "We can't all throw people off of rooftops."

"I didn't throw her!"

A brown shape swooped from the wall. A small hawk flew through Hansel's drawn bow, its claws neatly plucking the arrow from the string. He jumped back, releasing the string so it snapped against his arm.

Snow smiled. Her choker flared to life.

Hansel turned to run, but his feet slipped on the magically-slick ice. He rolled over and pulled a knife from his boot.

Snow gestured, and an icicle snapped from the eaves overhead. It shot down as if launched by a crossbow, piercing his arm. He screamed, and the knife dropped to the road.

Talia had her own knives out now. She kept one raised as she approached, as if daring Hansel to try something.

Snow leaned against the wall, closing her eyes against the pain throbbing beneath her skull. The worst should pass soon, but it would be at least a day before she fully recovered. She wiped her face. "I assume the hawk was your doing?"

"Oh, good." The cheerfulness in Danielle's voice carried quite well through Snow's choker. "I was afraid he wouldn't reach you in time."

Talia sheathed one of her knives and tossed the bow to Snow. Hansel grabbed her wrist, but Talia took his fingers in her hand and twisted, flipping him onto his stomach and eliciting another shout of pain. By the time the guards arrived, she had taken an array of blades from Hansel's person.

Snow plucked one of the mirrors from her choker and tossed it to the closest guard. "Talk to your princess. She'll explain."

She waited long enough to make sure the guards had everything under control, then grabbed Talia's hand and tugged her away. "Come on. The bakery should be open soon. I want cookies."

"What about your mirror?" Talia asked.

"It will find its way home eventually."

Talia shook her head, smiling despite herself. "You enjoyed this."

"Didn't you?" Snow asked, giving her a sidelong glance. Talia had tugged her scarf down beneath her chin. Wisps of black hair framed a stern face, but amusement crinkled the corners of her eyes. Snow grinned. "It reminds me of the time Queen Bea sent us out to find that frog who was impersonating a prince to harass young maidens."

"I still say you should have let me cook him," said Talia. "Fresh frog legs, soaked in butter and sprinkled with nadif spice—"

"I'll take the cookies, thanks." Snow made a face. "You keep your frog."

"Snow? Talia?" The urgency in Danielle's tone caused Snow's stomach to tighten.

"What's wrong?" Snow yanked the largest mirror from her choker, rubbing the glass clean with her sleeve. It was hard to make out much detail in the tiny glass, but Danielle looked like she was fighting tears.

"It's Beatrice."

* * *

Snow had foreseen this day a year and a half before, when a mermaid stabbed Queen Beatrice in the chest with a cursed blade. Snow had done everything she could, magically stitching the wound and using every potion and poultice she could think of to help the queen heal. Her efforts had given the queen an extra eighteen months of life, but even magic had limits, and death could only be denied for so long.

"We're here," Snow whispered as they reached the palace, counting on her mirrors to send her voice to Danielle. "Is Bea—"

"She's still alive," Danielle said.

Snow allowed herself one moment of relief before turning to Talia. "There's something I need to take care of."

Talia whirled, her eyes wide. Snow had seen Talia angry before, but rarely had that anger been directed at her. Not like this. "Whatever it is, it can wait."

"No, it can't." Snow stepped away.

"Beatrice is dying." Talia's rage slowly shifted to disbelief. "What could possibly be more important?"

Snow shook her head. "Tell Beatrice . . ." Bea would have understood, but not Talia. No words could make this right with her, and the longer Snow stood here, the less time she would have.

Talia grabbed Snow's arm. "Beatrice took you in. She gave you a home after you fled Allesandria. She cared for you like her own daughter."

"You think I don't know that?" *And now it's my turn to care for her.* Snow twisted away. Anger she could take, but the pain and disappointment in Talia's eyes were too much. Talia would understand soon. "I'm sorry."

Talia's lips moved, as though she were searching for words. Instead, she turned her back and hurried down the hallway, the soles of her boots echoing on the tile floor.

"Talia—" Snow started after her, but forced herself to stop. Years of spellcasting had given her practice at pushing her own emotions and turmoil aside when she needed. Growing up with a mother who punished her for the slightest transgression, whether real or perceived, had only strengthened her self-control.

Most of the time, she simply chose not to use it.

Word of Bea's condition had obviously spread through the palace. Voices were muffled, the cheerful gossip of the servants replaced by somber whispers. Snow heard more than one woman weeping quietly behind closed doors.

She made her way through the palace toward the royal bedchamber. Given Beatrice's state, the room should be abandoned. Bea had been moved to a room on the ground floor after she became too weak to climb the steps, and King Theodore would be with his wife.

Once Snow reached the bedroom, she shut the door behind her and checked to make sure she was alone. She stepped past the bed to the fireplace, where a few coals glowed within the ashes. Taking an iron poker, she jabbed a brick in the back of the fireplace, opening a hidden panel in the wall. She squeezed inside and yanked the panel shut behind her until it clicked into place.

Sunlight shone from her choker as she made her way down a narrow stairway to the secret rooms hidden beneath the palace. Her light gleamed from weapons of every shape and size as she hurried through the armory toward her personal library and, most importantly, her magic mirror.

Tall as Snow herself, made of flawless glass and framed in platinum, the mirror dominated the wall where it stood. As she strode into the room, the glass responded to her will, showing her Queen Beatrice.

The library was a mess, with books strewn about the floor and falls of hardened wax dripping over the closest shelves where her candles had burned themselves out. Snow grabbed a discarded cloak of white fox skin from the floor. These rooms were refreshingly cool in the summertime, but come winter they grew cold enough she could see her breath.

A mummified cat was tucked away in one corner. A

bundle of roses hung from one of the shelves, their petals dried and wrinkled. She had rolled the carpet up against the wall, and the stone floor was covered in chalk scribblings. For months now, every time Danielle came down, Snow had watched her fight the urge to scrub the library clean from top to bottom.

Pulling the cloak over her shoulders, Snow eased into the wooden chair in front of an old, heavily stained table. In the mirror, King Theodore sat beside the queen, holding her hand. His eyes were shadowed and shone with tears, but he had forced a smile for his wife. Danielle and Prince Armand sat on the opposite side of the bed, while Talia stood in the corner. It appeared as though Tymalous, the royal healer, had already retired from the room.

Snow wasn't certain Beatrice could even see them anymore. Heavy blankets buried her from the neck down, almost hiding the faint rise and fall of her chest. Her skin was like wrinkled parchment. Her hair had thinned, and her body was little more than a shadow of the woman who had rescued Snow from Allesandria seven years ago.

In all of Snow's planning over these past months, her one fear had been that she wouldn't make it in time. That Bea would die suddenly, before Snow could reach her mirror.

Snow turned sideways, keeping the mirror in the edge of her vision. Her table held a single fat beeswax candle, dirty yellow and brittle from the cold. To one side sat a bronze mug, half-full of fairy wine. She took the candle in both hands, checking the silver wick that curled from the wax.

A quick spell ignited the candle. She wrinkled her nose as the initial puff of smoke carried the smell of burning hair through the library. She had spun Beatrice's hair into the wick more than a month before.

A puff of breath guided the smoke toward the mirror. "Mirror, mirror, proud and tall. Mirror, mirror, seeing all. Help me reach the dying queen. Help Beatrice to hear my call."

Talia would have teased her. Snow had never been much of a poet, but the clumsy rhymes helped her focus her magic. She blew again, and again the black smoke dissipated against the glass. Snow closed her eyes, pushing back against the pounding in her head. The third time she tried, the smoke passed through the mirror into the queen's room.

Snow carefully returned the candle to the table. She watched the mirror closely. The smell of burnt hair had mostly faded, and neither the king nor the queen appeared to notice the thin trail of smoke drifting over their heads.

She reached over to pick up the mug of wine, finishing the contents in three swallows. Everything was prepared. Now there was nothing to do but wait.

The candle had lost a quarter of its height when Beatrice's breathing changed, becoming strained. Theodore's fingers tightened around the queen's hand. He kissed her knuckles and knelt beside her, whispering so softly Snow could barely hear. On the other side of the bed, Danielle, Armand, and Talia crowded close. Armand's cheeks were wet as he put his free hand on his father's shoulder. Danielle called for Father Isaac, who stepped into the room, praying softly.

Snow swiped tears from her cheeks with the back of her hand. Between one breath and the next, Beatrice's body appeared to relax. For the first time in months, the tension left her face.

The candle flame flickered higher, becoming a deep red. Snow pressed her fingers to the mirror. The pain in her skull flared as her spells responded to the queen's death. "Follow the trail, Bea."

The smoke, nearly invisible in the shadowed room, should have shone like a beacon to Queen Bea's spirit. Snow had tested the spell dozens of times over the past months, calling the souls of mice, rats, birds, even an old hound she had discovered half-frozen in the streets . . . but never a human.

The flame began to shiver. Bea had discovered the trail. "It's me," Snow whispered. "Stay with us."

The mirror would hold Beatrice for now, though it wasn't an ideal solution. It was one thing to trap and hold a soul; the true challenge had been teaching herself how to create a body. She glanced at the discarded books, tomes that described everything from the making of fairy changelings to a spell that could form a new body from flowers, of all things. Snow had combined the different magics into her own—

The flame stilled.

"Bea?" Snow stood, toppling the chair. "Don't turn away."

Bea would be disoriented, like most souls newly freed from their bodies, but the touch of Snow's magic should have been familiar. She brought the candle closer to the glass, thickening the thread of smoke passing into Beatrice's room. "I know you can hear me."

King Theodore straightened, sniffing the air, but Snow ignored him. Her heart pounded against her ribs as though fighting to escape. This was taking too long. In every test, the soul had moved into her mirror as the body exhaled its last breath. Either Beatrice was unable to find her way . . . or else she was choosing not to follow. "Think about your grandson. This is your chance to stay, to be a part of his life and watch him grow up."

Nothing. Snow passed her fingers over the candle flame, which doubled in size. Every spirit for miles around should have been able to see it. "Beatrice, please. We need you. Don't—"

The flame quivered and died.

"No!" A thought was enough to renew the flame, but it was too late. The trail had been broken.

Beatrice Whiteshore—the woman who had saved Snow's life, who had given her a home and purpose and a family—was gone.

Snow pulled her hand from the mirror. Her fingers were numb, and cold enough to leave frost outlines on the glass.

She stumbled back. Her hip bumped the table. Her vision blurred, and she closed her eyes against the stabbing pain in the back of her head, the price she paid for overexerting herself. It was nothing compared to the pain of her failure.

It should have worked. It *had* worked, in every test she had performed. So many spirits roamed this world after death, refusing to heed the call of whatever followed. Snow had encountered them again and again: jars enchanted to hold the souls of the dead, ghosts who moved from one body to the next . . . she had once seen an entire army of the dead rise to serve their master.

Danielle's mother had remained with her, surviving in the hazel tree Danielle planted in their garden. She had gifted Danielle with a silver gown and glass slippers, allowing her to attend the ball where she met Armand. She continued to defy death to this day, living on in the enchanted glass blade of Danielle's sword, all for the love of her daughter.

What of Snow's own mother, Queen Rose Curtana? Rose's ghost had lingered for years, searching for a way to regain her power. She had plotted with Danielle's stepsisters, hoping to possess the body of Danielle's child.

But Beatrice had turned away.

"Why didn't you stay?" Bea had been more of a mother to Snow than Rose Curtana ever was. If Bea had died naturally, taken by the ailments of age, that would have been one thing. But she could have lived for many more years. She should have lived. Would have, if Snow had been skilled enough to save her. If she had been strong enough.

Snow stared into the mirror. The glass showed only her own face. Black hair dusted with white. Red-veined eyes, swollen and shadowed. Faint wrinkles around the eyes, and laugh lines at the corners of her mouth. With every year, she looked more like her mother.

She picked up the candle. Clear wax burned her fingers as it spilled onto the floor. She should leave. Find Danielle and Talia.

The thought made her wince. Danielle would forgive her for not being there with Bea, but Talia was another story. Talia was angry and hurting. She had known Beatrice a long time. Almost as long as Snow had.

"You're safe now," Beatrice had said on that first journey to Lorindar. Snow had woken from a nightmare in the middle of the night, screaming loudly enough to wake half the crew. The smell of burning flesh had been so real. She had thought she was back in Allesandria, reliving her duel with her mother. Beatrice had held her, running her hands through Snow's hair and whispering softly, *"I'll look after you."*

Snow flung the candle away. It broke into pieces, splattering hot wax over the stone wall.

She stared at the broken chunks of wax for a long time. There were other spells. Spells her mother had known, magic Snow had never tried. Slowly, she reached down to take the largest piece of wax from the floor.

She pressed the wax directly to the mirror, drawing a simple circle. She adjusted her hold, using a corner to sketch the more detailed symbols of binding. A modified summoning circle soon took shape on the glass. She finished the final characters, working Beatrice's name into the runes, and tossed the wax aside.

"Mirror, mirror, on the wall. Let Queen Beatrice hear my call. Seek her out where e'er she be. Mirror, find my queen for me." The words spilled forth without thought. The mirror changed, once again showing Queen Beatrice's lifeless body. Armand and Danielle knelt together at her side. Tears spilled freely down Danielle's cheeks.

Snow scowled and pushed beyond the image. That was but the body. Where was Beatrice's soul?

Light filled the mirror, bright as the sun. Snow squinted but refused to turn away. The light spread into the library. She felt as though she were falling into the glass.

She grabbed the mirror's frame with both hands. Wisps of fog curled from the glass. She peered into the light, trying to see what lay beyond, trying to follow Beatrice's soul wherever it had gone.

Never had the mirror responded so easily to her will. She felt as though she flew through the sky. In Snow's hands, the mirror could pierce Heaven itself if that was what it took to find Beatrice.

Sweat made her grip slippery. She tightened her fingers until they cramped. The wax runes began to flake away from the glass.

They didn't matter. The reflection of the runes remained in the mirror, their power pouring forth in pursuit of the queen.

She blinked to clear the tears from her vision. Her blood battered her head from within as though straining to crack the skull. Her body felt numb, and she clung to the mirror to keep from falling. Through the pain, a part of her marveled at what the mirror had done, reaching out so far in pursuit of the dead. If only she could see beyond the light.

"Come back to us, Bea." Silence swallowed her words. Snow wasn't even certain she had spoken aloud. She could no longer make out the library around her. Nothing existed save the light and the place that lay on the other side. The place Beatrice's spirit had gone.

The first crack made no sound. With her hands clenched around the frame, she felt the glass shift ever so slightly. Pain exploded behind her eyes as she tried to focus not on the light, but on the mirror's surface, where a white line now curved across the center of the glass.

Beatrice was there. She was so close. Snow could feel the pressure from beyond the mirror, as though Bea was pushing to escape back into this world.

Another crack grew from the center of the mirror, curving up and to the right to create a triangular shard that might have fallen if Snow hadn't moved her hand to hold it in place.

Lines spread in a starburst from her hand. Fragments of glass no larger than pebbles fell to the floor. Blood dripped down the frame, though Snow hadn't felt the cuts.

The magic surged like a living thing. She imagined she could hear Talia's voice, chastising her. How many times had Talia warned her against bending the laws of the universe too far? Push hard enough, and things were going to snap. Even her mother's mirror had limits. Snow tried to end her spell, but it was far too late.

This was a hell of a time for Talia to be right.

The light faded as the cracks spread through the rest of the mirror. For a moment, Snow saw herself in the reflection, her features distorted by the broken glass. Herself, and something more.

"Oh, Mother. What did you do?"

Chapter 2

DANIELLE SQUEEZED HER HUSBAND'S hand. "The first time I ever saw her was at the ball," she whispered. "Beatrice was watching the two of us dance."

"I didn't notice," Armand said, a sad smile on his bearded face. His hair was a rumpled mess, and his eyes were shadowed. Here in this room, away from the world, he allowed the mask of prince to slip, revealing the son who longed for just one more day with his mother. He wiped his cheek, never looking away from Beatrice's body. "I never wanted a ball in my honor, but she insisted. I never found the words to thank her."

"She knew," whispered the king. "Seeing you both, seeing your happiness, was enough."

Father Isaac folded the queen's hands together on her chest. The nails were short and chipped. Her wedding ring hung loose on her finger.

"My own stepmother didn't recognize me," Danielle said. "My stepsisters glared at me all night long without ever realizing who I was. But Beatrice knew. She knew me the moment I set foot in the great hall. I nearly fled the palace."

"As I recall, you *did* flee," said Armand.

"Not until midnight." Danielle gave her husband a mock scowl. "Beatrice smiled at me. A small kindness, but enough to tell me I was welcome."

Even at the end, when pain and weakness imprisoned

Beatrice in her bed, she had always smiled with genuine love and affection when Danielle stopped by to visit, or when she brought Jakob to see his grandmother.

Father Isaac straightened and clasped his hands. His fingers moved stiffly, the skin scarred and wrinkled from burns he had received months before. It was strange to see him in such formal black robes. His blood-red collar was starched as stiff as boiled leather. The ruby-capped crucifix around his neck shone like glass. If not for the disheveled curls of his beard and hair, and the compassion in his eyes, he would have appeared a different person altogether.

He bent to address the king. "Chancellor Crombie can make the announcement, if you wish."

King Theodore shook his head. Standing silently in the corner behind him, Talia pursed her lips in distaste. She and Crombie had never gotten along.

"It was her choice," the king said softly. "Beatrice's injury was the result of her efforts to help another in need. She never resented that choice."

Danielle would have to send word to the undine. Beatrice had saved the life of the mermaid queen Lannadae. Lannadae would want to know of Beatrice's passing.

Armand's hand tightened around Danielle's. "Where is your friend Snow? She deserves to be here as well."

Talia's scowl deepened. "Snow had . . . other duties to attend to."

"What duties?" Danielle asked. The prisoners had been taken care of, and Snow had no further responsibilities. Even if she had, Snow would have ignored her duties without a second thought to be here with Beatrice.

Distant crying from the hallway drew her attention toward the door.

"Jakob," said Danielle. The sound was coming closer.

"He's supposed to be napping." Armand opened the door and peered into the hall. "Nicolette has him."

"He knows," she said. Even as a baby, Jakob had shown signs of inheriting his grandmother's visions, seeing things he couldn't have possibly understood. He had cried the day the mermaid stabbed Beatrice, refusing to settle down until Danielle and Armand returned to the palace with the queen's unconscious body.

Servants had already begun to gather in the hallway, waiting for news. When Danielle stepped out to take her son from Nicolette, Jakob kicked and twisted in her arms, trying to peek into the room.

"He kept asking about the queen." Nicolette was making an obvious effort not to peer past Danielle. "When he wouldn't go back down, I thought perhaps—"

"It's all right," Danielle said. Jakob had awoken only a short time ago. His hair was a sweaty mess, and red lines from the wrinkles in his sheets marked the right side of his face.

"I want Gramma," Jakob said.

"I know you do." Danielle moved him to one side, resting his head on her shoulder.

Nicolette shifted her feet. "Is there anything you need, Your Highness?"

Danielle heard the unspoken question. Nicolette knew Jakob well enough to trust his gifts. It wasn't Danielle's place to announce the queen's passing, so she let her tears speak for her. "No, thank you."

"God watch over her." Nicolette bowed and turned away.

Danielle carried Jakob into the room. He squirmed in Danielle's arms until he faced the bed. "I want Gramma," he said again.

"So do I," Danielle said softly. She started to say more, but a flash of light caught her eye. Something silver had fallen from the stained glass window on the far wall.

Armand followed her gaze. He stepped past the bed and picked two small fragments of glass from the carpet.

"A mirror," Danielle said. The square pane had been the size of a small coin before it broke. This had to be one of Snow's mirrors. She glanced at the window. A simple illusion would have concealed it as just another colored pane.

"Snow?" Armand sucked air through clenched teeth and switched the mirrors to his other hand. He stuck his index finger in his mouth, but not before Danielle saw a thin line of red where the glass had cut his skin.

Danielle had never seen one of Snow's mirrors simply break before. Snow could use her magic to destroy them when necessary, but this was something different. She glanced at Talia. "Other duties?"

"She wouldn't say anything more." The concern on Talia's face matched her own.

Armand set the broken mirror on the windowsill, then reached over to take Jakob. "Go."

Danielle kissed him and Jakob, then stepped into the hall. The servants parted, clearing a path. For once, Danielle didn't stop to greet them.

Talia caught Danielle by the arm after only a few steps.

"What is it?"

Talia held up her wrist, showing a copper bracelet with a small mirror in the center. A tiny web of cracks covered the mirror. Talia pushed back Danielle's sleeve. Danielle's bracelet had suffered the same fate. Talia carefully removed both bracelets, slipping them into a leather pouch at her belt.

Danielle's heart pounded harder. One broken mirror was unusual, but for three to crack at the same time? "Something's wrong."

"Are you armed?" Talia asked.

Danielle reached beneath her overdress, pulling out an ivory-hilted dagger. Talia grunted her approval.

"Where was Snow going?" Danielle asked.

"She didn't say, but she kept looking to the northwest tower." Talia began to run. "She could have been heading for the royal bedchamber."

"The secret passage in the fireplace?" Danielle guessed.

Talia glanced back. "So you found that one, did you?"

"Snow's not as careful as you are. She leaves ash fingerprints on the hidden door leading into the armory. Who do you think ends up cleaning up after you two, anyway?"

"What about the hidden tunnel in the courtyard?"

Danielle frowned. "You're making that up."

"Maybe."

Danielle did her best to keep up as Talia dodged a page, then shoved her way past an older man who was loitering in the hallway. He cursed them in passing, then gasped and bowed, begging forgiveness as he recognized Danielle. She was already past, heading for the spiral steps of the northwest tower.

When they reached the royal bedchamber, Talia flung open the door, eliciting a yelp from the chambermaid who was sweeping glass from the floor by the window.

"You realize that was Lord Grimsley you plowed through downstairs?" Danielle squeezed past Talia. "Catherine, could you please excuse us?"

"Of course, Your Highness." Catherine whisked the last of the broken glass onto a metal shovel. "Second mirror I've cleaned today."

Danielle forced a smile, working to steady both her breathing and her composure as she escorted Catherine toward the hallway. She slid the bolt into place the moment the door closed.

Talia was already ducking into the fireplace, jabbing the bricks at the back. A panel to the side of the fireplace slid open.

The stairway was short and narrow. Talia hadn't bothered to bring a light, but the passage was so cramped it would be difficult to fall. Danielle hunched her head, keeping one hand against the stone ceiling.

They couldn't have been more than halfway to the bottom when Talia whispered, "Wait."

Below, the orange glow of candlelight slowly brightened, illuminating Talia's silhouette. Talia had a knife in each hand: one held by the tip to throw, the other low and ready to strike.

"I know you're there." It was Snow's voice, soft and weary. "Toss those toys at me, and I'll turn you into a toad."

Talia's knives vanished into her sleeves as Snow stepped into view. Talia's breath caught. Danielle moved closer, peering past Talia's shoulder.

Her first thought was that Snow had been attacked. Bloodstains covered her white cloak. Bandages bound her palms, and Danielle could see cuts on her legs and torso as well. Her face was the worst. A gash across the side of her nose still oozed blood, and a large cut slashed the skin from her left eyebrow down to her cheekbone. The white of her eye had turned pure red.

Talia took the candle from Snow's hand. "What happened? Who did this?"

"I did." Snow examined her hands. "I was careless."

Danielle waited, but Snow said nothing more. "Your mirrors—"

"Broken." Snow lifted a clinking leather sack. "Shattered into a million pieces."

"How?" demanded Talia.

"Nothing lasts forever." Snow smiled, but it was a forced expression. "A spell went wrong. My own fault. I was too distracted."

"What spell?" Worry and anger deepened Talia's words. "What could be so important?"

"I thought I could save her." Snow's voice was flat. She sagged against the wall. "I thought . . . I was wrong."

"'Save her?' You mean Beatrice?" Talia caught Snow's arm. "How?"

"I failed. What does it matter?"

"We have to get you to Tymalous," Danielle said, cutting off Talia's response. She should have guessed it was something like this, but she had been so focused on Beatrice, and on Armand. Whatever Snow had done, they could discuss it later. "Those cuts need to be cleaned and stitched."

"Don't bother the healer on my account. I can tend my own wounds." Snow dabbed blood from her chin, her good eye boring into Danielle's with such intensity that Danielle took a half step back.

Talia looked past Snow to the darkness below. "What about the mirror? We should—"

"You should stay away until I've had a chance to clean up. There was . . . there could be . . ." Snow's voice trailed off. She looked confused. "It's a mess," she said weakly.

"You're in shock," Danielle snapped. "You look like you can barely walk, let alone treat your injuries. You will let Tymalous help you. If I have to, I'll order the guards to carry you."

Snow smiled, but it was a forced expression. "That won't be necessary."

"Will you be able to rebuild the mirror?" Danielle asked as she and Talia guided Snow up the steps. So much of Snow's magic was mirror-based. She must feel as vulnerable as Talia would without her fairy-gifted grace. Snow had smuggled that mirror onto a ship when she fled Allesandria. It was the only thing she had kept from her former home.

"I don't think I want to." Snow tilted her head to one side, as though surprised by her own words. "My mother created that mirror. I've spent half my life relying on its power. On *her* power." She touched her throat. Thin red lines showed where the mirrors of her choker had cut her skin when they broke. "So long as I used her mirror, I was chaining myself to her memory. But now, after all these years, I'm finally *free*."

The following day left Danielle little time for grieving or for worrying about Snow. Nobles from throughout Lorindar were beginning to arrive to pay their respects. Chamberlain Dennen and his staff handled much of the arrangements, but tradition required that a member of the royal family greet each visiting noble in person. It was one of the many duties Beatrice had performed, duties which now fell to Danielle.

By midday, she wanted nothing more than to throw away the crown of braided silver and gold that pressed upon her brow, and to trade the formal black gown with its layered skirts and satin lining for something—anything—that allowed her to bend at the waist.

Her mood lightened somewhat as a herald announced John and Heather Jeraldsen. For the first time all morning, her smile was genuine. She waited for them to approach, waving a hand as they started to bow. "None of that from you. Welcome to Whiteshore Palace, my old friend."

John touched a hand to his graying hair. "Not *that* old, I hope."

Danielle had known John for most of her life. Her father had crafted the glass replacement for his right eye. John came from a good family, and had married into the nobility only a year before, but he had always treated even the poorest souls with respect. Danielle gestured to one of the pages waiting in the corner. "Andrew will see that your belongings are taken to your room in the guest wing."

"Thank you, Princess." There was genuine pain in his wife's voice as she said, "I was sorry to hear of the queen's passing. I remember when she and King Theodore were married, though I was only a child."

Everyone had recited some variation of those words, but Heather was one of the few who truly appeared to mean them. Others were more interested in taking Danielle's measure as the future queen, or figuring out how Beatrice's death would affect their own fortunes in Lorindar.

"It's good to see you both again," said Danielle. Looking at the two of them momentarily eased her grief. John and Heather stood so close that no light passed between them, holding hands like newlyweds.

"Princess Whiteshore?" A girl in the green cap of a page bowed to Danielle and the Jeraldsens both. "Please forgive the intrusion, but Lord Montgomery wishes to meet with you and the prince tonight to discuss an extension of tax relief for the coastal towns."

"Tonight?" Danielle shook her head in disbelief. "Elaine, do I look like the Royal Treasurer?"

Elaine flushed. "No, Your Highness."

Danielle yanked off the crown and rubbed her forehead. "I'm sorry. Please go on."

"Lord Montgomery said, since the tax exemption was given to help the towns recover from the merfolk's attack, and since you knew the situation better than most . . ." Elaine took a step back, like a rabbit preparing to bolt.

"Please tell Montgomery that he can take his petition and—" No. A funeral should be an opportunity for friends and family to comfort one another and remember the one they had lost. Not a time for political squabbling.

Heather cleared her throat. "Your Highness, it occurs to me that most of Lord Montgomery's fortunes come through trade and fishing."

"That's true," said John. "I wonder what would happen if someone were to warn the fish to avoid his waters."

Heather tilted her head. "Or simply send rats to warm his bed?"

Danielle fought a smile. "I can see why you married her," she said to John. "How long did you search to find a woman as evil-minded as yourself?"

"Forty years," said John. "And it was worth every one."

To Elaine, she said, "Please tell Lord Montgomery I would be happy to consider his request. Please also inform him that we will need to conduct an audit of his finances to determine his needs. A *thorough* audit, including all shipping logs and cargo manifests."

"Yes, Your Highness." Elaine bowed again and disappeared.

"You suspect him of padding his treasury?" John's words were playful, but there was a glint in his eye that gave Danielle pause. No matter how friendly John and Heather might be, they were also nobles of Lorindar, with their own agendas.

"No," Danielle said. "Lord Montgomery can be . . . difficult, but he's never struck me as dishonest. His men, on the other hand?" She shrugged. "Who can say? If I'm fortunate, this will keep him busy reviewing his own affairs to make certain there's nothing for us to find. And John?"

He raised an eyebrow.

"I know you. If you sneak alum into Montgomery's food like you did with Bette Garnier that time—"

"You have my word," John said. "Though Montgomery *would* be hard-pressed to voice his complaint with his mouth pickled shut."

"What about a nice senna seed tea instead?" offered Heather. "He'll have to bring a chamber pot to any meetings."

"Leave the man in peace. That's an order from your princess."

John was the only person she knew who could convey laughter with a simple bow. As the two of them left, Danielle heard Heather saying, "*We* have to leave him alone, but what if a third party were to sneak in and coat his codpiece with lard?"

Danielle met with three other noble families before finally escaping at midday. She grabbed a quick meal from the kitchen and made her way to the chapel, where Beatrice's body had been laid out in preparation for the funeral.

Honor guards stood to either side of the entrance. Danielle greeted them in passing and ducked inside. Sunlight shone through the stained glass windows at the tops of the walls. The air smelled of incense, a mixture of lavender and cypress, which rose from silver thuribles, incense burners suspended from the ceiling behind the altar.

At the front of the church, Queen Beatrice's body rested upon a waist-high platform to the right of the altar. Her hair had been left loose, framing her face in gray. She wore a formal blue gown, and her gold crown rested upon her chest.

Danielle wiped her face. Beatrice never wore her crown when she could avoid it. She had always been happier in a sailor's jacket, her hair catching the ocean winds. It was as though an imposter lay in Beatrice's place, as if this were all some cruel jest.

Armand and Jakob stood beside the body, talking to Father Isaac. Jakob looked like a miniature version of his father. Both wore tailored black jackets, dark trousers, and polished boots. But where Jakob was sniffling and wiping his nose on his sleeve, Armand's face was stone.

"She looks so fragile." Danielle scooped Jakob into her arms. Loose threads hung like the legs of an insect where he had managed to lose the top button of his jacket. His small fingers gripped Danielle's cloak.

"Why won't Gramma wake up?"

Danielle kissed him, unable to answer.

"Because your grandmother is dead," Armand said.

"Why?" Jakob burrowed his head into Danielle's shoulder. "Why is she dead?"

"Your grandmother was sick for a very long time," Danielle said. "She was hurting, and she was very tired. She's not hurting anymore. She's at peace."

Jakob turned his head, peeking at Beatrice from the corner of his eye. "Will you die?"

"Yes," said Armand. "Everyone dies."

"But not for a long time," Danielle said sharply. "Armand, what's wrong?"

"You'd prefer I lie to my son?"

"I'd prefer you remember he's not yet three years old. He doesn't understand—"

"What is there to understand?" Armand stepped away, turning his back on the queen's body. "These empty rituals we perform to comfort ourselves? We will spend these days paying our respects to a broken husk. We will share pleasant memories, ignoring her flaws and making her out to be a saint called back to Heaven. We will cry false tears, though all knew she was dying. We will 'celebrate her life' and pretend death doesn't wait to take us all at any moment."

There was no compassion in his voice. He spoke as though to a stranger. Momentarily speechless, Danielle turned to Father Isaac. Isaac had known Armand for years, long before Danielle came to the palace

"Your Highness, your son looks to you for strength," said Isaac, his words ever so slightly chastising.

"He looks for lies." Armand barely even glanced at Jakob. "We dress death in its finest garb, arrange it to appear restful and calm. Let him see the world as it truly is."

"As it truly is?" Isaac's bushy brows lowered slightly.

Danielle reached toward Armand's shoulder. "Armand, that's enough. What's the matter?"

Armand pulled away. "My mother is dead. I'll thank you not to harangue me with foolish questions." With that, he walked out of the chapel, leaving Danielle to stare in silence.

"What's wrong with Papa?" Jakob asked.

"He's upset." Danielle squeezed him tight, planting another kiss on his sweaty brow. Had Armand been anyone else, she might have suspected him of drinking, but Armand rarely indulged these days. "Sometimes it's easier to be angry than sad."

Isaac placed a hand on Jakob's back. "Your father loves you. His anger is not toward you."

"Mad at Gramma?" Jakob asked.

"He's not mad at anyone," Danielle said. "He's just mad."

"I don't like this papa."

"Your father loves you, Jakob." Danielle hugged him. "And he didn't mean to upset you."

Isaac stepped away, twirling his crucifix between stiff fingers as he looked up at the stained glass windows.

"What's wrong?" Danielle asked, watching him closely.

"I'm not sure. For a moment, when Armand left . . . the windows have whispered to me today, but their warnings are too faint." Father Isaac's magic might not be as powerful as Snow's, but he had spent years working spells of peace and protection into those windows.

"You think something could be wrong with Armand?" Danielle kept her voice steady so as not to upset Jakob. "Something magical?"

Isaac shook his head. "It may be I'm simply on edge myself. Or perhaps it's an effect of Snow's broken mirror. That much power released in the palace . . . How is she?"

"I've barely seen her today," Danielle admitted. Snow certainly hadn't acted hurt as she flitted through the palace, retrieving the rest of her broken mirrors. Tymalous had clearly taken good care of her.

"I never saw Snow's mirror, though she told me of it once," Isaac said. "Given its power, I'm surprised its destruction didn't have more of an impact on my own magic. She did well to contain the damage." He turned away from the windows and tucked his hands into his sleeves. "She's not been by today. We each grieve in our own way, but I know she and Beatrice were close. She should take the chance to say farewell in private, before the funeral. As should you."

Danielle nodded and set Jakob down. Keeping his hand in hers, she stepped toward the queen's body. As she knelt, she glanced at Father Isaac, who had gone back to studying the stained glass windows. Worry furrowed his brow.

Danielle bowed her head and prayed.

Chapter 3

TALIA STOOD IN THE SHADOWS BEHIND Danielle, letting the low murmur of dinner conversation wash past her. Danielle was stiffer than usual. She had spoken only a handful of times since arriving from the chapel, and hadn't yet told Talia what was bothering her.

Armand appeared equally lost in his meal. Occasionally one of the nobles from Eastpointe, Dragon Lake, or Norlin would try to engage him in conversation. His responses were short and abrupt, and they soon gave up their efforts.

Talia's gaze kept returning to the empty chair at the king's left. For years she had waited on the queen, acting as both servant and bodyguard. Earlier tonight when she first entered the hall, she had moved without thinking to her usual position, as though Beatrice would at any moment come hurrying through the doors to join them.

She shifted her weight, trying to ease the stiffness in her legs. Strange to think that only yesterday she had been chasing witchhunters through the icy streets. Only yesterday Beatrice had still been alive.

Talia wrenched her attention upward to the ancient wooden beams that supported the arched ceiling. Oil lamps burned brightly on the walls between tall, arched windows. She searched the shadows for any shapes that didn't belong. This many strangers meant many more opportunities for "accidents."

The responsibility gave Talia something to focus on. Few nobles would risk acting directly, but each had brought his or her own retinue. If something did happen, it would likely be someone in his or her staff who did it. Someone most people would overlook, who could be disavowed if caught.

Lord Oren of Dragon Lake was a possible candidate. The man was paranoid enough to bring his own personal food taster, despite the implied insult to King Theodore's hospitality. Oren and his wife ate with their own utensils of pearl-handled silver. Such fears revealed much about the mind that harbored them.

Another man to watch was Anton of Eastpointe. Anton was an older man, one who gave every impression of contentment with his lot. But his son was known to harbor a grudge against Jessica of Emrildale, who had spurned a marriage proposal. When the delegation from Emrildale arrived, Talia would have to watch them all.

Then there was the pixie Febblekeck, recently-appointed ambassador from Fairytown. Febblekeck was a pretentious rag doll with wings who shed glittering orange dust everywhere he went. He sat cross-legged on the table, sipping a noxious drink of salted honey water from a thimble-sized cup as he leered up at Oren's wife Yvette.

Febblekeck was unlikely to be involved in any assassination attempt, at least directly. The treaty between Lorindar and Fairytown prevented Febblekeck from harming humans. But Talia had watched too many fairies snake their way around the stipulations of that treaty. Though Yvette appeared ready to stab him with her fork, which would take care of any fairy threat for the moment.

"Humans have a peculiar attraction to all things fairy," Febblekeck was saying. "To this day, there are those who smuggle pixie dust out of Fairytown, to be used as a drug. I'm told the effects on a human are quite . . . potent."

Yvette wrinkled her nose. "I can't imagine inhaling that filthy stuff."

Febblekeck's smile grew. "Inhaling. Yes, let's say that's what they do."

If Snow were here, she would be whispering crude comments to Talia regarding the mechanics of pixie/human relations, trying to crack Talia's composure and make her laugh. But Snow had been spending all her time cleaning the debris from her broken mirrors and repairing the damage to her library. Given Snow's vanity, Talia suspected she would try to keep to herself until her wounds healed.

Talia stared at one of the windows, trying to push the image of Snow's bloody face from her mind. Had the glass cut any deeper, or if one of the shards had struck her throat. . . . Snow could have bled to death, and it would have been hours before anyone found her.

"What did you say to my wife?" Lord Oren struck the table hard enough to rattle his plate, jolting Talia's attention back to the conversation. The room fell silent.

Febblekeck's wings blurred, raising him to eye level with Oren and showering the table in glowing pixie dander. "I merely asked if she might join me for breakfast tomorrow. I've a bottle of syrup from Fairytown that's far too much for one pixie." Glittering eyebrows wagged. "Tapped from the maple of a dryad, with all of the associated . . . *benefits* that come from a nymph's magic."

"You miserable little insect!" Oren kicked back his chair and stood. Talia was already circling the table.

"Lord Oren, stop." Danielle's tone was the one she used when Jakob refused to listen, and it cut through Oren's bellowing as easily as a sword. "Would you play into the pixie's hands?"

"If he'd keep those hands where they belong—"

"He's not touched your wife," Danielle said. "He's committed no crime." She glanced at Febblekeck. "There's no law against behaving like an ass. However, if you were to attack him—an ambassador from Fairytown—"

"What kind of ambassador dishonors the very people he's supposed to work with?" Oren demanded. By now,

Talia was in position behind them both, ready to seize human or pixie should the need arise.

Danielle gave Talia a slight nod of appreciation before turning her glare on Febblekeck. "The kind who's more interested in leverage than peace. The kind who views politics as a game, seeking to score points for himself and his masters."

Febblekeck flashed a disarming smile. "I humbly beg your forgiveness, Princess. And yours, Lord Oren. I was overcome by your wife's attractiveness, and forgot myself. It's a flaw of the fairy race. We're far too susceptible to beauty."

Prince Armand snorted. Without looking up from his meal, he said, "Pixies have an unfortunate sense of beauty."

Talia froze. Even Febblekeck appeared taken aback.

"Excuse me, Your Highness?" Lord Oren appeared torn between anger and uncertainty. "I . . . believe I misheard you."

Armand took a drink, then returned his cup to the table. "Lady Yvette has the complexion of a plucked boar, and her voice grates the very soul. Febblekeck might as well seduce one of the hunting dogs from the kennel."

Oren's cheeks went blood red. His hands balled into fists. Talia swore softly and moved to the left, to better intercept him if he forgot himself and lunged for the prince.

"Forgive my son," said King Theodore, speaking for the first time since dinner began. He stared at Armand as though seeing a stranger. "Beatrice's death has been a strain upon us all, but grief is no excuse for such behavior. My apologies, Lord Oren."

Armand stood. "Do we now beg forgiveness for speaking the truth?"

"Armand, sit down." Danielle grabbed his hand, but he pulled away.

"I take no orders from commoners."

Danielle jerked back as though struck. Lady Jeraldsen started to speak, trying to intervene, but Armand ignored her.

"You've nothing to fear," he went on. "Oren is a fat old coward, no threat to anyone."

Oren snarled and started toward the prince, one arm pulled back to strike.

Talia hooked her arm through Oren's and yanked him off-balance. A kick to the back of his leg spilled him to the floor. "Would you assault the Prince of Lorindar in his own hall?" Talia whispered.

Oren shoved her away and pushed himself upright. His hands were shaking and his face was red, but he made no further move toward the prince. Armand stood with arms folded, an expression of boredom on his face.

Talia glanced around thc table, making sure nobody tried to take advantage of the chaos. Most of the assembled nobles had risen and backed away, distancing themselves from the fight. Danielle was talking to the king. Febblekeck had flown up to the rafters.

"Have you suffered humiliation enough?" Armand asked. "If being knocked down by a servant doesn't satisfy your need to look the fool, perhaps I could summon a young child to trounce you next."

Oren moved before Talia could stop him. She couldn't tell which of the two men struck first as they crashed together. Oren punched the prince in the jaw, even as Armand buried his fist in Oren's stomach. Talia jumped onto the table, dancing between plates and platters as she grabbed a silver pitcher of wine and emptied the contents over both men.

Oren sputtered and reached for Talia. She swung the pitcher, which rang like a gong against his knuckles. He howled and spun away.

"Enough!" King Theodore's voice thundered through the hall. "If either of you so much as sneer at the other, I will have you *both* locked away. Is that clear?"

Armand gave his father an exaggerated bow. "If you'll excuse me, Your Majesty." Without another word, he spun and left the hall.

Oren was clutching his fist. The knuckles had already begun to swell. "My deepest sympathies on the death of your wife, King Theodore." He stared after Armand. "I hope you'll forgive me if my family chooses not to attend the funeral. We will be departing tonight."

Talia returned to Danielle's side. "What just happened?"

"That was not the man I married." Danielle shook her head. "I've seen him angry, but never cruel."

Oren and Yvette were already leaving—through a different doorway than the one Armand had used, thankfully. The rest of the people slowly settled back into their seats, all save Febblekeck. The pixie remained overhead, giggling to himself as he sipped his drink.

"Armand has insulted you like that once before," Talia said. "When he was under your stepsisters' spell."

"Get Snow." Danielle left to follow her husband.

Talia palmed a roll from the table as she slipped away. She glanced back to make sure Febblekeck's attention was elsewhere. There was one last thing she needed to attend to.

Febblekeck squawked as the roll struck his head. He fell in a cloud of glowing dust, nearly striking the table before he recovered enough to take flight. He whirled, glaring from one human to the next. Talia smiled and pulled the door shut behind her.

Snow walked slowly along the northern edge of the courtyard. The roof extended overhead, sheltering her path. Icicles as thick as her arm hung from the copper gutters. The evening air was chillier than usual, and the sun had dipped low enough that the castle wall blocked its light.

At the woodpile, she dropped to one knee to retrieve the broken fragments of another mirror. She tossed the pieces into the sack she had carried since yesterday. The leather was thick enough to keep the sharp corners from jabbing her, though she could see a small hole near the bottom where the glass had cut the seam.

She sat beside the pile, leaning against one of the iron

rods that held the logs in place. Old spiderwebs stretched from the bottom logs to the base of the wall, though the weavers of those webs were nowhere to be seen. Deep within the woodpile, she could sense the warmth from a family of mice.

With a touch of her mind, she summoned one of the mice to her hand. The magic flowed so easily, with no pain at all. The mouse shivered in her palm, a filthy, fat rodent with bulging black eyes and yellow teeth. She could crush it in her fingers, and it would neither fight nor flee, bound by her spell.

Were humans so different from animals? Fighting for food and a safe place to sleep, doing their best to avoid the dogs and the owls. The Whiteshore family talked of peace while hiding behind walls of stone and magic.

There was one difference. Snow raised the mouse higher. "Animals never lie, do you?"

Danielle had deceived everyone, disguising herself in order to enter the ball and win Prince Armand. Talia lived every day pretending to be a mere servant instead of the rightful ruler of Arathea. Even Beatrice had lied, secretly sending Snow and Talia out on one mission after another to manipulate her kingdom. King Theodore lived in blissful ignorance, never knowing the plans his wife concocted from the darkness beneath the palace.

Beatrice's lies had killed her. Her secret meddling in the politics of the merfolk. And what was politics but the art of smiling through deception? What was civilization but a mutually agreed-upon facade, ever on the verge of cracking and exposing the ugliness beneath?

Kingdoms and treaties, palaces and boundaries, all lies. Talia's family once ruled all of Arathea until a fairy curse destroyed them. King Theodore believed himself the ruler of Lorindar, but how many years remained until death robbed him of his crown? There was no kingdom here, only an old man struggling to hold on to his power, to delay the inevitable.

Her own exile from Allesandria, another lie. Queen Curtana had ordered a hunter to cut out the heart of her own daughter, yet when Snow killed her mother to defend herself, it was Snow who was condemned for murder. Snow who was banished from her home, clearing the path for others to seize power.

For half her life, Snow had pretended it didn't matter. Just as she had pretended not to care that day when she was arrested for murdering her mother. Battered and exhausted, she hadn't fought the Stormcrows, the magical guard of Allesandria. They had locked her in chains and dragged her to the city to face trial. She remembered standing before the Nobles' Circle as they debated when and how she should be executed.

Every man and woman in that room had known what Rose Curtana was. They had seen her cruelty, the torments she visited on enemies and allies alike. Even upon her own husband. Even her own daughter.

She touched her neck, remembering the way the links of the magic-inhibiting chain had pinched her neck, leaving raspberry-colored lines.

Beatrice and Theodore had worked a bargain with Laurence, a minor noble from one of the southern provinces. They used their influence to help him gain the throne, and in return he spared Snow's life. Snow came to live in Lorindar, and Beatrice placed both the new king and Snow White in her debt.

And for years, Snow had smiled and flirted and laughed and pretended none of it mattered. She had lied to herself, and to all she encountered.

"No more lies." Her fingers tightened around the mouse's body. Its heart pounded as fast as the beating of a hummingbird's wings. With a sniff, she lowered her hand, allowing the mouse to scamper back into the woodpile.

She rubbed her left eye. The irritation had faded quickly enough, though she could still feel the lump beneath the surface where the splinter from her mirror had lodged. She had feared at first it would steal the vision from that eye, but instead her sight had grown clearer. She could count every pimple and scar on the groundskeeper's face from across the courtyard. When she looked to the sky, she could make out every swirl of gray in the dark clouds.

She wasn't alone. Armand had also begun to see the world's true ugliness. When Snow concentrated, she could peer through his eyes, just as she had done with her mirrors before they broke. She had shared his disgust in the chapel earlier that day, as he gazed upon the wrinkled body of his mother. She had felt his hatred of the fat, greedy nobles who sat with him at dinner.

Snow rose. The muscles of her arm and shoulder throbbed from carrying the heavy sack. She ignored the pain. She had retrieved most of her mirrors, but a handful of pieces yet remained.

She started with the throne room. Now that Danielle and the rest were busy elsewhere, it was a simple enough matter to reclaim a mirror where it had fallen unseen behind the dais. She whispered a spell, calling every speck of broken glass to her hand, then carefully brushed the pieces into her sack.

Next was the private dining room used by the royal family. Smaller and less formal than the great hall, the dining room was a warmer place, with brightly painted windows and a fire burning in the hearth. Jakob and Nicolette sat at the long, wooden table, arguing over a plate of mashed cod.

"No fish!" Jakob pressed his lips tight.

"No fish means no pudding," Nicolette said wearily. Her face was worn, though she always donned a mask of cheerfulness, to the point where it made her appear addlebrained. Her blouse was stained, her hair a thinning nest.

Jakob gave her a crafty smile. "Pudding first. *Then* fish."

"Nice try, Your Highness. You can't— What is it, Jakob?"

The prince was staring at Snow, his dinner apparently forgotten. "Aunt Snow?"

Snow didn't bother to answer. Her mirror remained where it had fallen in front of the fireplace. Snow had lost a dozen to overzealous servants, all infected with

Danielle's need to clean. Snow picked up the pieces of glass, dropping them into her sack before turning around.

Jakob's chair clattered to the floor. He ran toward the door, arms flopping like rags, but Nicolette intercepted him before he could escape. "What are you doing, Jakob?"

"Bad Snow!" Jakob pointed.

Snow frowned and studied Jakob more closely. She slipped a hand into her sack, carefully pulling out a narrow triangular shard the length of her finger.

"Pay him no mind," Nicolette said. "You know how the prince gets spooked sometimes for no reason."

"He has reason." Snow approached slowly, and Jakob's eyes grew wide. He squirmed and kicked, drawing a grunt of pain from Nicolette. "What do you see, Jakob?"

Jakob bit Nicolette's hand. She yelped, and he dropped to the ground. He fled, his clumsy movements making him look like a damaged marionette.

"He's really scared." Nicolette was slow, a useful trait in one whose life consisted of such drudgery, but she watched Snow more closely now. She stepped to the left, putting herself between Snow and the prince. "I should take him back to his room to let him settle down."

Snow struck almost absentmindedly, slicing Nicolette's cheek with the broken mirror. Nicolette gasped and grabbed her face.

Snow could sense the tiny sliver working its way deeper into Nicolette's flesh. Snow gave a mental push, helping the mirror's magic to clear Nicolette's mind and vision. For an instant, she saw as Nicolette did. Saw the bloody lines carved across Snow's face, the way Snow squinted through her rheumy left eye. Age had wrinkled the skin by her eyes, and the gleaming ebony of her hair had begun to fade, replaced by strands the color of a dirty mop. Even her mother had never appeared so ugly.

She pushed Nicolette aside, doing the same with the images in her mind. Jakob had run toward the kitchen. She hurried after and yanked open the kitchen door, releasing a wall of hot, humid air. Woodsmoke darkened the air from the brick oven burning on the far side of the room. Coals smoldered in the larger fireplace to her right. A half-butchered lamb lay upon the wooden table in the middle of the room.

The kitchen staff stood like slack-jawed statues. Jakob was here, hiding behind one of the cooks, but they couldn't tell whether he was playing another game or if there was some genuine threat. Snow licked her lips, wincing as her tongue touched one of the cuts left by her mirror. Nine people, not counting the prince. Most with knives or pots that could be used as weapons.

Snow slipped a hand into her sack and pulled out a larger shard of glass. The edges cut her fingers, but she paid the pain no mind. She slammed the glass to the stone floor, where it exploded into a silver cloud.

Snow pursed her lips and blew. Tiny fragments flew up, speckling skin with dots of red. In the time it took to draw a breath, her power spread into everyone in the room. Everyone save Jakob.

Snow stepped around the table, past the oven. Jakob was squeezing into the corner between the oven and the wall. He tried to push her away.

She pulled another shard from her sack and placed it directly against Jakob's forehead. A drop of red welled from his skin where the glass had kissed it, but unlike the others, he appeared unaffected by her magic. He trembled and pressed harder against the wall.

"Interesting." Snow held no illusions about her own power. Any magic could be countered . . . just as any counter spell could be overcome. Jakob was a sniveling brat, with no magical training, meaning his ability to resist her mirror was something inherent. Something in his very blood. "What do you see when you look at me, Jakob?"

He shook his head.

"You saw it in your father, too, didn't you?" She thought back to that conversation, heard through Armand's senses. "Not as strongly, but you saw."

A servant boy of ten or so years peeked in through

the door. "The princess would like desserts served soon . . ." His voice trailed off as he took in the kitchen staff standing dumbstruck, and Jakob whimpering in the corner. "What's wrong, Jakob?"

Snow frowned. The boy was familiar . . . that dark skin, the long reddish hair . . . "What's your name?"

"Tanslav, ma'am."

Tanslav. Ah, yes. Snow had helped to rescue this boy from Rumpelstilzchen earlier this year. He had been one of many children taken by the filthy fairy thief, but Danielle and Beatrice had been unable to locate his family. So Tanslav had made the palace his home. "You're friends with the prince, right?"

"Yes, ma'am."

Snow waved a hand, and specks of glass peppered Tanslav's face. He started to cry out, but Snow's power clamped down, tightening his throat. "Pick up that cleaver, Tanslav."

Blood trickled down Tanslav's cheeks as he obeyed.

"Cut your arm."

Jakob covered his eyes, but Snow yanked him around, forcing him to watch. "I can make him slash his own throat. I could do the same to your father. Do you understand?"

Jakob tried to tug free, but Snow merely tightened her grip. He whimpered, then nodded.

"Come along," said Snow. "I've a great deal of work to do, and you're going to help."

Chapter 4

TALIA HURRIED THROUGH THE CORRIDOR toward the private dining room. According to a page named Andrew, Snow had been seen heading in that direction a short time ago. But when Talia entered, she saw only Nicolette standing beneath the window, blood dripping from her cheek.

"What happened?" Jakob's food sat unfinished on the table. One of the chairs lay on its side.

"I've always hated these windows," Nicolette said, her voice distant. "So garish."

"Was Snow here?"

Nicolette turned. "Did you know your skin is almost the exact shade of cow dung?"

"What?" Talia wasn't sure she had heard correctly. Nicolette had never insulted anyone that she could remember.

"Maybe that's why Beatrice kept you," Nicolette continued. "Like an exotic pet."

Talia's fists clenched. "How did you cut your face?"

Nicolette absently touched two fingers to her cheek. "Perhaps it was to prove that you Aratheans could be civilized. Don't worry; I'm sure Danielle will keep you on now that Beatrice is dead. She's always had a weakness for animals."

Talia stepped forward, sinking into a low sik h'adan fighting stance, her body straight, her weight slightly forward. "Where are Snow and Jakob?"

"Might as well invite ogres into the palace." Nicolette jabbed a finger at Talia's chest. "Princess Cinderwench might consider you a friend, but I—"

Talia caught Nicolette's finger and twisted, lifting Nicolette to her toes, then bending her backward. Nicolette yelped and grabbed Talia's wrist, but she was off-balance. The slightest pressure and Talia could dislocate the finger.

Nicolette swung her other arm. Talia slapped the blow aside with ease. She swept Nicolette's feet and twisted her about, bringing her face-first to the floor. Nicolette spat and swore as Talia switched her hold, clamping wrist and neck to pin Nicolette in place.

Armand had been cut picking up one of Snow's broken mirrors. Nicolette's cut could have come from glass as well, judging from the smooth edges. "Snow was here. Where did she go?"

"I'm not her keeper. How should I know?"

"No, but you're Jakob's." Talia pressed harder. "Where are they?"

Shouts drew Talia's attention toward the kitchen. She bounced to her feet. Nicolette started to rise.

"You should stay down." Talia pushed her way into the kitchen to find a riot. Two people lay unmoving on the floor. The rest were shoving and punching everyone they could reach.

Talia grabbed the closest, a boy named Tanslav who held a bloody knife in one hand. He started to swing at her, but she struck the wrist of his knife hand with her forearm. The knife clattered on the counter. A kick to the inside of the knee took his balance, and she tossed him to the floor. She grabbed a half-carved lamb from the table and yanked it down on top of him.

She backed away long enough to shout for the guards, then waded back in. She saw no sign of Snow or Jakob.

A woman swung an iron pan at Talia's head. Talia ducked and waited for the next swing. When it came, Talia stepped close, hooked her arm, and flung her out of the way, stripping the pan from her grip in the process. Talia hefted the pan, nodded with satisfaction, and moved toward the next combatant.

By the time the guards arrived, Talia had left five of the staff strewn about the kitchen. All were alive, though they would be in pain for several weeks. She moved back, allowing the guards to separate the rest.

She crouched by the head chef, who was groaning and clutching his head. Talia grabbed his ear and tilted his face toward her. In addition to cuts and bruises from the fighting, bloody speckles covered his face, making him appear diseased. She had noticed similar marks on the others. "What happened?"

"This is my kitchen," he spat. "*I* say when the meat is done. *I* say how much spice is too much."

"Too much? Food in this country is tasteless!" She caught herself. "Were Snow and Jakob here?"

"They left."

"I passed them on the way here," said one of the guards. Like the others, he was dressed more formally in a bright green tabard over a polished breastplate. They clanked like church bells wherever they walked. "Snow was taking the prince toward the northeast tower."

Talia pushed back her sleeve before remembering her bracelet was still sitting in her room, along with the broken mirror. She grabbed the guard's arm. "Find Princess Whiteshore. Tell her to get to the tower."

"Is something wrong?"

"Probably." Talia hurried away. First Armand, then Nicolette, now the entire kitchen staff. And Snow had been cut worse than anyone else by her broken mirror.

She checked with a passing laundress to confirm that Snow and Jakob had indeed entered the tower. A single guard stood at the base of the staircase, but Talia was a familiar figure, and he allowed her to pass with nothing more than a nod of greeting. She ducked beneath the brightly dyed green plume that sprouted from his helm. Lorindar's fashions were strange.

Once on the stairs, she slowed. Her shoes made no sound on the tiled steps. She walked sideways, keeping her back to the inner wall.

She checked each door as she passed: first a darkened storeroom, then the weaving room where two girls worked on a half-finished tapestry stretched across the loom. Talia scowled at the spinning wheel tucked in the corner before quietly pressing the door shut. The next room was the candlemaker's workshop, and that door refused to budge.

There was no lock on the door. If someone had barred it from within, she should at least be able to rattle it in the frame. She pressed her palm against the edge. The wood was warm to the touch. She could hear Jakob crying on the other side.

If she climbed down the outside of the tower, she could enter through the window. But that would take time, not to mention she'd be scaling the tower in full view of everyone on the walls and in the courtyard.

Forget subtlety. Talia backed away, clenched her jaw, and slammed into the door. It gave ever so slightly. Ignoring the pain in her shoulder, Talia tried again. Each time the door edged inward. It didn't seem to be blocked. It was more like the wood had swollen into the frame.

On the fourth try, the door swung open and crashed against the wall.

"I wondered how long it would take you to get here," said Snow. She sat on a wooden bench in front of a small fire pit in the center of the room. A metal grate covered the pit. The air smelled of beeswax and dyes. Dipped candles hung from pegs in the walls and from beams crossing overhead, making the room feel crowded. Thicker rolled candles were stacked on shelves behind Snow.

Frederic, the candlemaker, stood at the window like a statue. Only the shallow rise of his chest and the occasional blink told Talia he was still alive. He had been cut along the side of his neck.

Prince Jakob sat on the floor, his back to a small water barrel, knees clutched to his chest. Blood oozed from a cut on his cheek.

Snow waved a hand. Talia jumped to the side, barely avoiding the door as it slammed shut behind her.

"What did you do to the prince?" Talia asked. The only light came from the moon outside the window, and the coals glowing faintly orange in the fire pit.

"Nothing." Snow sounded genuinely puzzled. She turned to study Jakob, and her forehead wrinkled. "Nothing at all."

Talia stepped forward.

"Don't do that." Snow lifted a shard of mirrored glass as long as her forearm and pointed it at the prince. Red cloth was wrapped around the base of the glass to form a makeshift hilt.

Talia froze. "Jakob, are you all right?"

Jakob shook his head without looking up. "Aunt Snow hurt me. She hurt Tanslav and Papa."

"That's not Snow. When the mirror broke, it did something to her."

"Oh, Talia." For an instant, Snow sounded like herself, both amused and exasperated. "My mother created that mirror because she wasn't strong enough to contain its power herself. I am. I don't need it anymore. Look at me. For the first time since that mermaid flung me against a wall, I'm casting spells without pain. You should be happy for me."

"You're casting them on your friends," Talia said. "On the people who love you."

Snow brushed her nails through Jakob's hair. Jakob tensed, and he held his breath until Snow pulled away. The moment he relaxed, Snow's hand flicked out, and a second cut appeared on the prince's cheek.

Talia lunged forward, but Snow placed her blade beneath Jakob's chin, halting her in midstep. "Such a strange child," Snow whispered. "Armand was mine with a single cut, yet Jakob sits here untouched by my magic. Don't you want to know why?"

"Not particularly." Talia folded her arms, slipping two fingers up her sleeve to reach the flat throwing dagger sheathed on her arm.

"That's always been your problem. You've no curiosity, no sense of wonder." The hand holding the glass dagger never moved. "He's not casting any spells, nor is he warded. It's not human magic, at least none I've ever seen. I'd love to cut him open and see how he does it."

It was Snow's body. Snow's voice. Even the lilt in her words was Snow's, teasing and taunting as she pointed her knife at the prince.

Talia stepped sideways. "What did you do to Armand and the others?"

"I helped them to see."

"To see *what?*"

Snow's smile raised the hair on Talia's neck. "The world as it truly is."

"You sound like your mother."

Snow frowned, her confidence flickering so quickly Talia nearly missed it.

"Is that it?" Talia pressed. "Your mother's spirit—"

"Is long gone." Snow flicked her free hand, dismissing the idea. "What will you do now, Talia? If I were anyone else, you'd already have thrown that knife you palmed."

Talia grimaced and adjusted her grip on her knife.

"Can you do it?" Snow asked. "Can you kill the woman you love?"

Sarcasm dripped from her words, twisting in Talia's chest. "That woman would never torment a child."

"If I'm not Snow White, then who am I? A fairy changeling, perhaps? Or a witch wearing your friend's face?" Snow smiled. "I was the one who helped Queen Bea find you in that nasty cargo ship where you were hiding. I got drunk with you the night you first realized Bea was dying. You sang that ridiculous Arathean song about your old god, the one with the three extra heads."

Talia took another step, trying to get close enough to interpose herself between Snow and the prince. "Don't worry, Jakob. You'll be back with your mother soon."

Jakob shook his head.

Snow's smile returned. "He knows better, Talia." She tilted her hand, digging the point of the glass shard into Jakob's skin. "If you care to test your fairy reflexes against me, keep moving." Moonlight quivered on the ceiling, reflected from her blade.

Talia raised her hands. Whatever was influencing

Snow, she wasn't as confident as she sounded. Otherwise she would have already struck. "You can't hide here forever."

"I don't intend to. But before I depart, I had hoped to leave a gift for King Theodore, to thank him for his hospitality these past seven years. A single scratch, and his grief will end."

"You're leaving?" The question slipped out before Talia could stop it.

Snow leaned forward. "I could do the same for you, Talia. I know the pain of leaving your home, your lover, everything you've ever known. Tell me, does your heart still ache for the twin sons you've twice abandoned?"

Whatever was manipulating or controlling her, this was still Snow. Only Snow knew Talia well enough to cut her so keenly. "I had no choice."

"Another lie." Snow sighed and shook her head. Her weapon never left the prince's throat. "There are always choices, my dear Talia. Nobody forced you to flee, to turn your back on your throne. You surrendered your birthright. How many generations did your family rule Arathea?"

"Stop this," Talia whispered.

"They murdered your family and stole your throne, but to hear the stories of Sleeping Beauty, the man who raped you was a prince and hero. They raise your children on those same lies. And you . . . what lies help you to live with your choices, Talia? That your sons are better off without you? That your presence would only bring pain and chaos to Arathea? I could help you, Talia."

Talia lowered her knife. "Go ahead and try."

"Oh, stop it. We both know you love me too much to kill me."

"I do love her," Talia admitted. She swallowed, trying to push down the knot in her throat. "And I know her well enough to know what she would want."

Talia slid forward, her front foot snapping into a kick that struck the outside of Snow's wrist. The mirrored blade flew into the wall and shattered. "Jakob, run!"

Snow gestured, and the fragments of her blade floated from the floor. Talia dropped flat, and broken glass shot over her head. She rolled and kicked the bench out from beneath Snow, who yelped as she fell.

Jakob was young and unsteady, but he ran to the door and stretched to grab the handle. The door wouldn't move. Snow's magic kept it stuck tight.

Talia bounced to her feet. She flipped her knife to throw, and then Frederic crashed into her from the side. The candlemaker was middle-aged and overweight, but he fought like a mother griffon protecting her nest. He wrapped his arms around Talia and slammed her against the wall. Candles tumbled from the shelves.

Talia stomped her heel onto the arch of his foot, then brought both legs up and kicked off from the wall.

"Aunt Tala!"

Sunlight gleamed from three more spinning shards, floating in front of Snow. Talia wrenched Frederic around as Snow launched the shards through the air. They buried themselves in Frederic's back, earning a startled grunt. He staggered, one foot dislodging the grate from the fire pit. His foot sank into the coals, and he howled.

Broken glass clinked onto the floor as Snow emptied her sack. She clapped her hands, and the glass rose into the air, spinning around her like a glittering whirlwind. "I'll shred you both to ribbons before I let you leave this room. Please don't make me kill you, Talia."

There was a hint of genuine pain in Snow's words, but not enough to suggest she wouldn't do exactly what she threatened. A single cut, and Talia would be as much a slave as Frederic. Talia stepped to the right and threw her knife.

Snow's wall of glass knocked the blade aside, but Talia was already moving. She grabbed the grate from the floor with both hands. The muscles in her back strained to toss the iron grate through the window. Talia followed an instant later, her arms held tight to her chest to keep from slashing herself open on the broken glass.

Talia twisted in the cold air, but she was falling too

fast to completely control her landing. Tiled rooftop rushed toward her. She hit hard, her hip and shoulder slamming into the roof of the kitchen. She was too far away to catch the chimney, so she grabbed for the gutters, but they were frozen over. As she slid from the roof, she glimpsed people shouting and pointing from the courtyard below, and then she was falling again.

Chapter 5

DANIELLE PACED A CIRCLE AROUND TRITtibar. "I know my husband, Tritt. This wasn't him."

"I agree," said Trittibar. The former ambassador from Fairytown wore his usual cacophony of clothes, including a loose shirt that fountained rainbow ribbons for sleeves, knee-high trousers, and sandals the color of spring buds. He had braided tiny gold bells into his white beard for good measure.

Until recently, Trittibar had lived in a mouse-sized hollow in the southern wall of the palace. After his exile from Fairytown, he had been cut off from the fairy hill, the source of his magic. The loss of his magic trapped him in human form. Snow had been able to rescue some of his belongings, but she hadn't been able to change their size.

Danielle looked past Trittibar, to where his entire library sat on a shelf no wider than a saucer. The large glass lens and tweezers he used to read the books hung from a peg beside the shelf.

"I've been friends with Armand since he was a child," said Trittibar. "I've seen him at his best, and at his worst. Never have I known him to act the way he has today."

"Maybe Father Isaac was right. Maybe this is just grief."

Trittibar's beard jingled as he cocked his head. "If you believed that, you wouldn't be wearing your sword."

Danielle touched the hilt with one hand. She had retrieved it after dinner. "We need Snow." She hesitated.

With her mirror destroyed, how much magic had Snow lost?

"If it's magic, Father Isaac will find the source." Trittibar combed his beard with his fingers. "Where is the prince now?"

"In his study. He wanted to be alone. I asked Aimee to let me know if he leaves."

Someone rapped at Trittibar's door. He jumped to his feet. "Still not used to having a real door," he muttered. Outside stood a single guard.

"What is it, Stephan?" asked Danielle.

He gave a quick bow. "Talia asked that I find you, Your Highness. She said to meet her at the northeast tower. Snow was taking Prince Jakob there."

"Why would Snow . . . ?" If Stephan had known anything more, he would have said so. She saw Trittibar grab a slender rapier from the wall. Her own sword bounced against her hip as she ran past Stephan into the cold night air.

A small crowd had gathered in the corner of the courtyard. Danielle's heart thudded in her chest, and she ran faster, jumping over the low stone wall around the garden.

"Move aside!" Her shouts cleared a path for herself and Trittibar. Two guards were holding Talia near the base of the tower. Her nose was bleeding, and she appeared dazed. Danielle spun, searching the crowd. "What happened here?"

Talia pointed toward a broken window in the tower. "Snow took the prince." Her words were terse. She tried to wrench free. "I couldn't get to him. She attacked me. The guards have already gone to check the room, but they didn't find anyone except Frederic. They're taking him to be checked by Father Isaac. I don't know where Snow took Jakob."

"Let her go," Danielle commanded. The guards jumped back. Talia swayed, but kept her balance. "Get Tymalous."

"I don't need a healer." Talia wiped her nose on her sleeve.

Danielle didn't have time to argue. She ran inside, taking the steps two at a time. The door to the candlemaker's workshop was open, the latch splintered. She stared at the empty room. Cold air gusted through the broken window. She spotted a shard of silvered glass half-buried in a candle on the wall.

"Whatever happened to Armand, it began with Snow and her mirror." Talia moved to retrieve the candle with the broken shard. "She must have collected the rest of the pieces. Anyone who has been cut by one of her mirrors needs to be placed under guard at once."

Danielle braced herself. "Was Jakob hurt?"

Talia hesitated. "Snow cut him twice that I know of. The magic didn't appear to affect him."

Shock and disbelief held Danielle in place. The wind played over her as she repeated Talia's words in a whisper. "She cut him?"

"Small cuts only," Talia said quickly.

Danielle spun to face the guards who had followed them up the stairs. "Seal the palace. Stephan, get to the king and tell him what's happened. Take him someplace safe, and don't let anyone else near him."

Locking the gates wouldn't stop Snow. She could be anywhere, or anything. Her magic could change her and Jakob into mice, or it could create an illusion to disguise them both. "We'll need hunting dogs. Trittibar, get the hounds and give them something with Jakob's scent. Nicolette can—"

"Nicolette was cut, too," Talia said softly.

Danielle nodded, refusing to let the news affect her. "She'll need to be watched as well." She touched her bare wrist where her mirrored bracelet had rested. Yesterday, a single kiss to that mirror would have conjured an image of her son. "Get Armand to Father Isaac."

Isaac's magic wasn't as powerful as Snow's, but of everyone in the palace, he had the best chance of reversing whatever Snow had done. She waited until the others hurried from the room, leaving her alone with Talia. "Why would she take my son?"

"I think . . . I think she was curious." Talia was staring

at the overturned bench. "She wanted to know why her mirror didn't affect him."

"Do you think she'll . . . what will she do to him?"

Talia looked away. "I don't know."

Danielle could feel the fear pushing up from her chest. She put one hand on her sword, but even the touch of her mother's final gift couldn't quell that terror. Snow had taken her son. "Tell me the truth. Are you well enough to fight?"

"Always," said Talia. The blood trickling from her left nostril made her assurance less convincing, as did the obvious stiffness in her arm, but Danielle took her at her word.

"Search Snow's library. I doubt she'd take Jakob there, but whatever happened started with the destruction of her mirror. Be careful."

"What will you be doing?"

Danielle was already on the stairs. "My husband was one of the first to be cut. With Snow missing, perhaps he'll hold some answers."

Talia took the bronze rungs two at a time as she descended the narrow passage hidden in the room Danielle shared with her husband. When she neared the bottom, she loosed her grip and dropped silently to the cold, hard-packed earth. The impact jolted the bruises in her side and reawakened the throbbing pain in her shoulder.

There was no light here. She stepped away from the ladder and did her best to slow her breathing. She heard nothing but the pounding of her own heart.

Talia moved from memory, taking two steps and reaching out to touch the smooth wood of the door. She pressed her ear against it, listening for several heartbeats before pulling it open and stepping inside.

She ran one hand along the whitewashed wall to her right, seeking the lamp and tinderbox stored there. She pulled the tinderbox from its oiled leather pouch and retrieved the steel striker and flint. Dropping to one knee, she placed the box on the floor, arranged the char cloth, and scraped flint to steel. The equipment was well-tended, thanks to the vigilance Beatrice had drilled into them all. Moments later, the lamp was lit.

Black tiles littered the floor before her, each one carved in the shape of a sailing ship. Snow's magic had bound those tiles to the map of Lorindar on the ceiling, allowing them to track various ships through their waters. Now the lapis lazuli seas were empty.

Weapons shone on the walls to either side. Talia took a curved Arathean dagger, sliding it through her belt, then turned to light another lamp.

A set of sharpened steel snowflakes, each one about the size of a playing card, rested on a small shelf in the corner. The original snowflakes had been a gift from Talia, years before. Snow kept losing the things, which meant Talia had to commission a new set at least once a year.

There was no movement in the library. She retrieved a steel-banded Hiladi war club before stepping through the doorway, just in case. Light glinted from the empty platinum frame of Snow's mirror, which lay on the floor. Dark smears of dry blood showed where Snow had tried to grip the frame, perhaps to keep it from falling. Talia brought the lamp to the floor, searching for the telltale glitter of broken glass. Nothing. Snow had reclaimed every speck.

Broken chunks of wax littered the floor. Another candle sat in the middle of the table, melted wax pooled around the base. Drops of blood, now dried to a rusty brown color, were scattered over the table and floor.

Talia crouched to study the blood. The thickest drops led to a cedar chest in the corner. Snow would have walked there for bandages. Talia was all too familiar with the contents of that particular chest. There had been no blood in the armory, so Snow must have bandaged her wounds before leaving.

But she hadn't done so right away. Dark lines and smears of blood covered the table. Talia touched one of the black lines. Ash rubbed away at her touch. The lines were too regular to be random. A spell of some sort, though Talia couldn't follow the pattern. The ashes were stuck in the surface of the congealed blood, meaning Snow had worked this spell after her mirror broke, but before tending to her own wounds. Charred stems, perhaps from flowers, were sprinkled through the mess. "What were you doing down here?"

Talia stepped away, searching the room until she spied a dark smudge on the bookshelves. Snow had tried to wipe the leather clean, but faint smears showed where she had grabbed a particular book on dwarven architecture. That book was the trigger mechanism to open the seawall passage down through the cliffs. The seawall passageway was meant to be an escape route of last resort. Why would Snow—or whatever had taken control of her—have bothered opening it if not to flee?

Talia set her lamp on the table. A quick tug of the book triggered the mechanisms in the wall. Talia crossed the room to grab the far set of shelves, which hid the passageway. Keeping her club ready, she swung them inward.

Cold, damp air spilled into the room. Little light penetrated the passageway, but it was enough for Talia to make out the woman huddled on the stone steps.

Talia raised her club. "Snow?"

The woman was the right size, with the same pale skin. Talia snatched the lamp from the table. The light revealed a woman younger than Snow, with dark red hair and a pale, frightened face. She was naked, shivering violently from the cold. Her lips and ears had a bluish tinge.

"Is she . . . is she gone?" Her words were slurred.

Talia tossed the club behind her and reached to take the woman's hand. Her fingers were cold as ice. "Who are you? How long have you been down there?"

"Don't know." The woman tried to walk, but her legs gave out. "Maybe a day?"

Talia pulled the woman into the library and kicked the shelves shut. She fetched an old wool cloak from another chest and wrapped it around the woman's shoulders, but wasn't sure what other aid to offer. Snow was the healer, not Talia. Growing up in Arathea, Talia had learned the symptoms of sun poisoning by her fifth year, but she knew much less about treating half-frozen women. "What's your name?"

"Gerta." She pulled her body into a ball, squeezing her hands beneath her arms.

Talia set the lamp on the floor in front of Gerta, who eagerly cupped her hands around it. Gerta wasn't a name common to Lorindar. It was possible, if unlikely, that Gerta had discovered the concealed opening in the water at the base of the cliffs. Perhaps a runaway, or an escaped prisoner of some sort, someone desperate enough to brave the rocks and waves? "Your full name?"

Gerta was shaking so hard she had to try three times to answer. "Rose Gertrude Curtana. But I prefer Gerta."

Talia yanked her dagger from its sheath. "Rose Curtana is dead."

"I know. Snow destroyed her." Gerta's cracked lips managed a weak smile. "I'm Snow's sister."

"That's impossible. Snow had no sister."

"Half-sister." Gerta shivered again.

There *were* similarities. Rose's hair was shorter, but it framed a face with the same narrow features and high cheekbones as Snow's. Gerta's large brown eyes were almost a perfect match for Snow's own. She was attractive, though not as beautiful as Snow. "She would have told me."

"There are many things Snow preferred not to remember," Gerta said.

"A forgotten sister? One who happens to arrive in Lorindar this very night?" Talia kept her dagger ready as she backed away to retrieve another blanket. She tossed it to Gerta, who wrapped it around herself with shaking hands.

"Our mother, may she burn forever, sent me away when I was a baby," Gerta said. "At least, that's the story Snow liked to tell herself when she was older. When she was young, she believed I was her true mother, come to save her from Queen Rose."

If this was a trick, Talia couldn't begin to guess its

purpose. "Get to the point where you explain who you really are and how you ended up here."

Gerta shrugged. "I'm who she made me. In the beginning, Snow wanted a mother who would protect her. Later, she longed for a friend. She used to lie awake at night, imagining what it would be like to have a sister. She made up stories. We explored the woods together, having marvelous adventures. Fighting evil dwarves, rescuing cursed princes, and doing everything she was forbidden to do."

"Imagining . . . so you're not real?"

"Don't I look real?" Another faint smile. "Would you like me to prove it to you, Talia?"

"I hate magic." Talia circled Gerta. "You know who I am."

"I have fragments of Snow's memories. She gave them to me before she pushed me through that door."

"She pushed you . . ." What in the hell had Snow been playing at? "She *made* you?"

"I think so." Gerta glanced around the room. "It's hard to remember. There was pain. Pressure, as if my body was being kneaded and shaped like wet clay. My first clear memory is of Snow looking down at me. She was frightened and hurt. What happened to her?"

Talia remembered her first view of Snow on the staircase, blood still dripping down her face. "We don't know yet. Can you find her?"

Gerta shook her head. "I'm sorry. I'm not powerful enough. In her fantasies, she was always the stronger sorceress."

"Why did she leave you here?"

"I could feel her fighting against something, trying to hold on to herself." Gerta turned toward the empty frame of the mirror.

Talia's throat tightened. "I know."

"She told me to help you." Gerta stared at the wall. "I could feel her ripping memories from her own mind. She hid me from herself as she closed the door, sealing me into the darkness. Even through the door, I felt her lose the battle. She stayed down here for a long time. I couldn't use magic to warm myself until after she left, for fear of drawing her attention. I waited as long as I could, and then . . . the door wouldn't open. I tried climbing down the steps, but the cold grew worse."

Talia sheathed her knife. Keeping Gerta in her vision, she retrieved a small, locked chest from the corner of the room. She pulled a silver key from a chain around her neck and opened the lid to reveal a dirty red cloak lined in wolf fur. She bundled the cloak under one arm. "I should get you upstairs where it's warmer."

"Thank you, Talia. I wouldn't have survived much longer."

"Come on. You can tell Danielle and Father Isaac what you've told me."

And hopefully Isaac would be able to tell them all exactly what Gerta was.

Danielle had spent her childhood learning to shield herself from the torments of her stepmother and stepsisters, building armor that their cruelest jabs failed to penetrate. But exhaustion had weakened that armor, and Armand shattered what remained without even raising his voice.

His hands were shackled, and two armed men stood watching him. Father Isaac's magic would prevent him from physically harming anyone so long as he remained inside the chapel, but it couldn't stop his verbal assaults.

"Without my mother to guide you, you're lost. You allowed our son to be stolen from within your own home. You've failed, *Your Highness*. Both as a princess and as a mother."

Danielle was tempted to order him gagged. Instead, she turned to Father Isaac. "Whatever magic infects my husband, it came from Snow's broken mirror. Can you use that same magic to find her?"

Isaac shook his head. Neither he nor Trittibar had been able to explain Armand's behavior, let alone find a way to counter it. Everyone else cut by Snow's mirrors had been moved to the dungeons, by Danielle's orders.

Twenty-two people were now locked in the dark, cliff-side cells, many of them her friends. But it was the only way to keep them from harming anyone else.

She had ordered Armand brought here to the chapel. The smell of incense was stifling. The grassy smoke was enchanted to dampen violence within the church. The air was warmer here, as though each of the candles mounted along the walls was giving off the heat of a much larger flame. But so far, the magic of the church hadn't been strong enough to free her husband.

Nobody had seen Snow or Jakob since they entered the candlemaker's workshop, and thus far, no magic had been able to locate them. The gates were locked and guarded, and Danielle had ordered every available man and woman to search the palace, but given Snow's power, she held little hope.

"He's not possessed," said Trittibar.

"Or if he is, it's no form of possession that we've ever heard of." Father Isaac tapped his crucifix against his chin.

"It's the mirror." Talia strode into the church, side by side with a barefoot girl in a wool cloak. Danielle had never seen the girl before, but something in her walk was familiar. "With every cut, a tiny splinter breaks off and enters the blood. Snow took the worst of it when her mirror was destroyed, but Armand and the rest each suffer from a smaller portion of that same power."

"It's how mirror magic works," said Talia's companion. "Even the smallest piece can channel the power of the rest."

"Who is this?" Danielle asked.

"I was hoping Father Isaac could answer that." Talia beckoned Danielle closer, away from Armand. In a low voice, she explained how she had discovered Gerta below, as well as the girl's claim to be Snow White's sister. For Gerta's part, she appeared more interested in Armand than anything else.

Danielle cut Talia off. "Gerta, if you know what happened to my husband, can you reverse it?"

Gerta approached the prince. Danielle signaled with

one hand for Talia to stay close, but Gerta merely studied Armand.

"Keep away from me, you filthy witch," snapped Armand.

Danielle tightened. This wasn't her husband. He would never speak so to anyone.

Yet even as she defended him to herself, she wondered. Did some part of Armand believe those words? Was this cruelty merely an aspect of himself he kept hidden . . . an aspect that reminded her so much of her own stepmother?

"Look at his hand." Gerta pointed to a pair of dark bruises on the back of Armand's hand. "You'll find others where the sliver cut him from the inside as it moved through his body."

"Can it be removed?" asked Danielle.

Gerta chewed her lower lip as she stared at Armand. She moved away from him, out of earshot, and gestured for the others to follow. "It would be dangerous. The splinter isn't the problem. It's what that splinter carries."

"Tell me."

"Have you never wondered where the mirror's power came from?" Gerta looked from one face to the next. "All magic has a cost. Minor spells like your priest's incense take most of their strength from the ingredients of the potion. He can prepare a new batch and feel no more fatigued than a man who spends an afternoon chopping firewood. But an artifact like our mother's mirror, one with the ability to show anything its master commands? Not even Rose Curtana was powerful enough to create such a thing on her own."

"So where did it come from?" asked Danielle.

"I believe our mother enslaved something within the mirror. Forced it to serve her."

Something which had broken free when the mirror shattered. "Snow never spoke of this," said Danielle. "You told us Snow created you, formed you from her own thoughts and memories—"

"She never spoke of it," Gerta agreed, "but she used

to lie awake at night, wondering about the price of Mother's magic. As she grew, she learned not to question such things. Much of our mother's magic was best left to the shadows. Snow was a child. Had she allowed herself to dwell on the torments our mother inflicted, the rituals she wove, it would have consumed her. So Snow locked those fears away, burying them so deep they couldn't reach her even in dreams."

No wonder Snow had imagined a companion for herself. For a child to face such nightmares alone . . . the thought made Danielle wish she could somehow go back and whisk Snow away when she was first born. "And then yesterday, the mirror broke."

"Releasing what?" Isaac asked.

"We once encountered a mermaid who trapped human souls and used them as slaves," said Danielle. "Could the mirror have done something similar?"

"No human soul would be powerful enough." Gerta shook her head. "If any were so strong, my mother never would have been able to enslave them."

"A demon." It was Father Isaac who spoke. "No minor fiend, but a true denizen of Hell."

"Snow didn't know," Gerta said quickly. "Even had she tried to discover the truth, it was impossible to be certain, short of shattering the mirror." She gestured toward Armand. "She never intended any of this."

Talia whispered a curse in Arathean. "Snow gathered up every last speck of glass. If each splinter is a reflection of the demon's power, she could infect half of Lorindar."

Danielle was watching Father Isaac. "Is Gerta telling the truth?"

"I believe so," said Isaac. "Strange . . . in some respects, she appears a construct, yet her flesh *is* human."

Gerta reached out and tugged the curls of his beard, earning a yelp. "Is that real enough for you, Father?"

"From the moment Snow emerged from her library, she carried a demon within her," said Talia. "Why did nobody detect it? What good are these damned wards and spells if—?"

"Snow created many of those wards," Danielle pointed out. "She avoided Father Isaac, and Tymalous tells me she never came to see him, either." She looked to Gerta. "Can you use the glass in Armand's blood to find Snow?"

"I already asked," said Talia.

Gerta turned away. "Snow always imagined me as the weaker sister. Someone she could impress with her own spells. I am as she made me. If I use magic to touch the splinter, it's likely the demon could take me as well."

Despair swelled in Danielle's chest. She would continue the search until every corner of the palace had been checked, but she knew deep down it was futile. Snow was gone, and she had taken Jakob with her.

Laughter pulled her attention to her husband. There was nothing pleasant to the sound, only mockery, like a bullying child. "You've lost them both. How long before you accept your failure, Cinderwench?"

To her surprise, Armand's use of her old nickname helped her regain control. This sort of hate was familiar, easier to brush aside. She strode toward him. "The man I love would never call me by that name."

"The man you love?" He laughed again. "They say love is blind, but in truth love is blinding. You've no more love for me than I had for you. You looked upon me and saw salvation. I was nothing but a way to escape your stepmother and stepsisters."

"You know that's not true."

"Just as I looked upon you and saw . . . simplicity. A child with no hidden schemes, a girl trained to obedience. A bride fit for a prince. Love is the lie we feed ourselves when we're too weak to accept the truth. You warmed my bed and kept to your place."

Gerta stared. "You're married to *him*?"

"Yes."

"He's an ass."

Trittibar coughed and covered his mouth.

Danielle clasped Gerta's shoulders. "You claim Snow created you."

"That's right."

"When Armand was stolen from me, Snow used my unborn son to find him. As Jakob grew into his own person, that connection faded. But you were ripped from Snow's mind less than a day ago. Can you use that bond to find her?"

Gerta shook her head. "Not without exposing myself to her power."

"Damn," Danielle whispered. That left but one other option, one she had prayed she could avoid. "Thank you for your help. Please stay with Trittibar and Father Isaac. There has to be a way to remove the glass from Armand. Work with them to find it."

"There might be, but—"

"Try." Danielle started toward the doors. "I'll be in my chambers. Send a page to fetch me if anything changes."

"What will you be doing?" asked Talia.

"Finding my son."

Chapter 6

SNOW PAUSED WHEN SHE REACHED Fisherman's Canal, the narrow waterway that ran along the base of the white cliffs. The foulness of fish and old bait permeated the air. Half-finished sailing ships huddled like rotting corpses in the shipyard to her right. To her left, buildings crowded the rocky land closest to the cliff. Most were stilted on columns of wood or stone, protecting them from waves and high tides. Taverns and inns competed with warehouses and shops. All were built with steep, reinforced roofs to protect them from falling snow and ice in winter.

A single rockslide would crush half the harbor. Snow squinted, searching for the spells that protected the buildings below. Her vision was sharper than before. With only the moon and stars, she could still discern details that only a few days ago would have eluded her in full sunlight: a nest tucked into a crag of rock, a slender sapling clinging desperately to the cliffside close to the top. The magic shone as if aflame: strong charms, but someday their power would decay. All magic failed eventually.

Even in winter, hours before dawn, the harbor was a place of chaos. One overweight captain in a garish green jacket shouted orders to the men unloading his ship. Farther along, a younger man in the uniform of the Harbormaster's Office guided a fishing vessel into the docks. Beggars crawled like lice along the edge of the canal, competing with the gulls to collect fish guts to sell for bait. The cries of the gulls sounded like the mocking laughter of children.

"Look at them," Snow said. "Cawing and racing about as though their lives were in any way meaningful."

Jakob didn't answer. He walked beside her like a pet, his hand clamped in her own. He hadn't tried to run away, not since she threatened to fling him into the ocean. The crying was another matter. Her magic had silenced his whimpering, but couldn't penetrate his mind. He had cried throughout the carriage ride to the harbor. Dried tears and snot covered his face.

She scooped Jakob into one arm, carrying him in a way that might from a distance be mistaken as caring. His body was taut, and he wouldn't look her in the eyes.

"You could burn it all, and who would notice?" Snow asked. "Ten years from now, their names would be forgotten. Twenty years, and the fire would be but a story told by old men. Even you, little prince. Your death will be nothing but a note in a forgotten history of the royal family."

Jakob whimpered.

"I was to be queen," she continued, looking out over the water. "My mother wouldn't live forever. All I had to do was survive, and one day I would have earned my reward. When I met Roland, I dreamed I would make him king, that we would rule Allesandria together. But the world cares nothing for dreams."

As she walked, she marveled at her strength. The mirror's magic had infused her blood. She hardly noticed Jakob's weight. She could toss him into the sea or dash him against the rocks without straining, and spellcasting came as easily as breathing. She briefly considered ripping the cliffside apart, merely because she could. Perhaps this was Beatrice's final gift, giving Snow the power to take back what was hers.

"All my life, my mother's magic dwarfed mine. It was only anger and desperation that allowed me to defeat her, and even in defeat she destroyed me. I should have been queen, but her poison had already spread through Allesandria, corrupting those in power. They were afraid to confront my mother, but once she was dead, they turned their loathing and their fear upon me."

She adjusted the strap of her sack. The rope dug into her shoulder, but the pain didn't bother her. "The world is broken, Prince Jakob. A place of chaos and madness that can never truly be controlled. Your parents believe they will one day rule Lorindar, but they cannot control her people any more than a beggar can command those gulls."

She smiled and stretched a hand toward the birds. With barely a thought, one of the gulls cried out and fell, bouncing off the roof of a warehouse with a wet thump.

She slowed, glancing at the road behind her. It would be a shame to abandon her library at the palace, but Lorindar was a small, insignificant nation. And what need did she have for old books and scrolls? Though there was something . . . a spell she had been working on? Something to do with Beatrice's body. Her experiments to save Beatrice had been a failure. The potions and charms she had created over the years were of no use anymore.

The memory slipped away, retreating down into the darkness.

The presence of magic pulled her attention back to the docks. As a child, she had always been able to sense her mother's spells. Now the magic hummed through her body, a silent tune that rose and fell with her surroundings. This latest chorus of spellcasting originated from the four people hurrying up the road toward her. The Harbormaster himself led the group, if Snow's eyes didn't lie.

"Master Francis." Snow should have foreseen this. The Harbormaster was responsible for all incoming and outgoing ships, which meant checking those vessels for illegal enchantments. A simple illusion had allowed her to stride out of the palace and steal a carriage, but Francis would be able to see through such tricks. She slid the sack from her shoulder, dropping it to the road. A single fragment of glass, no larger than the cap of an acorn, spilled out. "Is there a problem?"

"Princess Whiteshore sent word to watch for you and the boy." Francis' men spread out behind him. "Set Prince Jakob down and surrender."

"What gives you the right to command me?" Snow stepped forward, crushing the glass beneath her heel. She lifted her boot from the pieces and blew softly.

She could feel Francis' magic circling her, trying to contain her without hurting the prince. She shredded his spell as easily as cobwebs.

Frost spread over the glass shards on the road. Tiny frozen spikes grew from each splinter, spreading into paper-thin panes of ice.

From behind the Harbormaster, a grunting bull of a man lunged forward to grab Snow. Francis shouted an order, but it was too late. The man's fingers dug into her forearm, trying futilely to pry her grip from the prince. Snow put her other hand over his and squeezed until she felt the bones snap.

Snow pointed to the broken shards. Wings of ice twitched, then fluttered to life. Insects of snow and glass, no larger than wasps, swarmed toward the Harbormaster.

He cast another spell, knocking two of the wasps back. One of his men destroyed a third, but there were too many. Soon the rest were crawling over their bodies, jabbing stingers of mirrored glass into their skin.

Snow glanced around. She had created close to twenty of the wasps, more than she needed to deal with the Harbormaster and his men. There was no point in letting the others go to waste. She called the rest, allowing them to settle into her hair, a living crown of ice and glass. "Come, Jakob. Let's find ourselves a ship. I've so much to do."

Danielle maintained her composure until she reached the room she shared with Armand. She shut and locked the door behind her, then pulled her sword from its sheath. She collapsed against the door, pressing her forehead to the flat of the blade. The glass sword was liquid smooth, save for a handspan near the hilt where it had once broken. Snow's magic had fixed the sword, but that part of the blade was frosted.

Jakob was gone. Armand, too, for all intents, unless Isaac or Gerta could free him of Snow's spell. Snow, Beatrice . . . it was too much.

Snow had taken her son.

No matter how hard she tried to focus, thoughts of Jakob returned. His confusion yesterday as Danielle pulled him from his father. His laughter the week before at the performance of a tumbler who juggled as many as seven eggs at a time, only to break them all in the end. His small hands digging into her nightgown in the mornings, demanding she wake up.

She forced herself to rise. Clutching the sword in both hands, she made her way to the edge of the bed, thinking back to the first time she had felt Jakob moving within her womb. Danielle had been a prisoner of her stepsisters at the time, trapped deep in the Duchess' domain below Fairytown. She remembered the cold touch of fairy hands, the tightening of her skin as magic aged her flesh and the unborn child within.

The Duchess was no fairy noble. Centuries ago, she had been a lowly servant, a spy who betrayed the king and queen of Fairytown. On the way to her execution, she had tricked her freedom from the king, bargaining for the right to see one final sunrise. When he agreed, the Duchess fled to the chasm at the center of Fairytown, hiding deep underground where sunlight never penetrated. There she had built her own small kingdom, forever protected from fairy interference by her bargain. Until she looked upon another sunrise, the rulers of Fairytown wouldn't touch her.

"When you wish to contact me, simply call three times." Danielle could remember every detail of the Duchess' face as she spoke those words. What had the fairy known, to create such certainty that Danielle would one day come begging for aid? Had she foreseen this day, or had her words been mere boast?

Danielle wrapped one hand around the hilt, the other around the blade. The sword had never once cut her skin. Her mother's magic saw to that. A part of her wished it would, if only so the physical pain would distract her from the emptiness inside.

Danielle licked her lips. She had learned enough from Snow to know it wasn't the name alone that worked fairy magic, but the intention. The need of the caller.

Thinking of Jakob, she whispered "Duchess" three times.

The carpet sagged at a spot between the bed and the door, as though the tile floor beneath had been cut away. Individual fibers unraveled, sinking into a hole illuminated by sickly blue light.

Danielle stood, watching the hole expand until it was the size of a serving platter. The surface shimmered like water, blue lights dancing along the ripples.

"Princess Whiteshore. How lovely to hear your voice once again." The Duchess' face was little more than a shadow on the water, but Danielle's mind painted the details. Short silken hair the color of bleached cotton. Slender ears, the pointed tips rising just past the top of the head. Overlarge eyes and narrow lips that seemed ever quirked in a predator's smile. "I wasn't expecting your call. Particularly so soon after you sent your ambassador to demand my arrest."

Danielle wasn't at all surprised to learn the Duchess had ears in the fairy courts. The spying and intrigue of Fairytown made human politics look like the simple squabbling of children.

Danielle did her best to remain calm. The Duchess had tricked a fairy king. She would do the same to Danielle in a heartbeat. "That was months ago, and I made no demands. I merely asked Fairytown to investigate your role in the death of my stepsister Charlotte."

"I was saddened to hear of her passing. The girl should have stayed in my care. She was unprepared for the harsh realities of the world. But she wished to leave, and as a kindness, I chose to grant her freedom. Had I known—"

"And the gown you provided her?" Danielle asked. "Enchanted to carry a fire sprite. I watched as it burned her to death."

"The fire sprite was to provide warmth only," the Duchess said. "As you know, my domain is a cold place, without the luxuries enjoyed by those on the surface. I've no idea why the sprite turned upon her. Your stepsister was not the most pleasant woman. Perhaps she said something—"

"I've no time for pretty lies." Danielle moved to stand at the edge of the pit. "You sheltered my stepsisters when they kidnapped my husband. You conspired with the Lady of the Red Hood against my friend, murdering Charlotte in the process. Had I any proof you did these things knowingly, I would find a way to see you punished."

"But you have no such proof." The Duchess' tone never lost its smothering politeness.

"No." Danielle fought the urge to drive her sword into that shadowed face. "I wish to speak to you about another matter. My son Jakob has been taken from me."

"If you intend to accuse me, you're wasting your time, Your Highness. Believe it or not, my people aren't responsible for every child you humans misplace."

"I know who took him. I want you to help me find him."

The Duchess was slow to respond, as if savoring Danielle's words. "You must be devastated. Please accept my sympathy to you and your family."

"You told me once that I would need your help. Can you find my son?"

The Duchess' smile grew. "You would bargain for my aid?"

Danielle could hear Talia's warning as clearly as if she were in the room. *Never bargain with fairies. Not if you wish to keep your future, your joy, your very soul.* But what if the bargain was the only way to regain those things? "Yes."

The ripples cleared, bringing the Duchess' pale face into focus. She wore a circlet of platinum, inlaid with flakes of jade. A high, silver collar followed the contours of her cheekbones. "I may be able to help you track him. Your son is marked, both by the human magic in his father's bloodline, and by fairy magic."

"Thanks to your darklings."

"You still don't know what he is, do you?" The Duchess laughed. "Danielle, do you think it normal that the animals obey your every wish? That your mother lived on after her death, that she watches you to this day, imprisoned in that magic blade you carry?"

"She loved me."

"And your father did not? I don't see you carrying his soul around in a sword." The Duchess leaned closer. "My darklings did nothing but awaken the fairy magic already within your son's blood. Judging by your mother's trick with the hazel tree, I'd guess dryad magic, perhaps three or four generations removed. Your son is a rare creature indeed. One with the ability to manipulate both human and fairy magic. The only question was who would be first to sense that potential and try to steal it."

"Impossible." The anger in her voice startled her, but she didn't try to suppress it. The idea that her mother, that she herself carried fairy blood . . . "Jakob is human. Snow examined him many times after we escaped your cave, and she never found anything unnatural."

"What could be more natural than fairy magic?"

Danielle shook her head. "I would have known."

"Is our kind so horrible? Rest your mind, Princess. You and your son are human in every way that matters. But, like your friend Talia, you're also something more."

"You knew."

The Duchess spread her hands. "I suspected. Human blood dilutes our own. Even a fairy of the pure caste might not recognize one of our descendants after a few generations."

"Why did you never—?" Danielle backed away. There were many reasons to keep such secrets. A better question was why the Duchess was telling her now. Was it simply a way to keep Danielle off-balance? "What do you want?"

"I can help you find Jakob. In exchange for that help,

you will send him to me in Fairytown for six months of each year. I give you my word to raise him like my own son. He will be protected from all harm. Given everything you've said, he'll be safer here than in your own palace."

"You can't be serious," Danielle breathed.

"Isn't this better than losing him altogether?" The Duchess softened her words, never losing her smile. "I can teach him to understand his fairy blood, to use his magic to protect himself."

For Jakob's sake, Danielle refrained from telling the Duchess what she could do with her bargain. "Choose another price."

"Why ask me, Princess? Why not your friend Snow White?" Amusement danced in her eyes. "Could it be she has finally overreached herself, that she's fallen prey to her own power?"

The Duchess knew Snow was behind Jakob's kidnapping. It shouldn't have surprised her. Febblekeck was the obvious candidate for the spy, but by now word had likely spread.

"As I understand the story," the Duchess said, "Snow's mother ordered her killed. She intended to dine upon her own daughter's heart. Gruesome, but not unknown."

Danielle kept silent, unsure where the Duchess was leading.

"Ancient wizards believed you could consume another's magic in such ways. I hope whoever stole Jakob away doesn't believe as Snow's mother did. I hate to imagine him suffering such a fate because his own mother was too weak to protect him."

"I won't save him from one evil only to give him to another."

"Very well." The Duchess' image began to fade. "When you change your mind, you know how to reach me."

Danielle's blade rang against the floor where the Duchess' face had mocked her only a moment before. Her strike cut the carpet and gouged the tile below. She relaxed her grip, allowing the sword to fall to the floor.

The Duchess was fey; she would keep her word, protecting Jakob and raising him as her own son. Raising him to be fairy. Shaping him into God only knew what. Given the Duchess' own magic, how difficult would it be to turn Jakob against his own kind?

She stepped to the window. Tiny flecks of silver and iron were worked into each pane of glass. Fairy glass, said to protect against magic, though only the weakest of charms would be repelled by such. The Duchess had answered Danielle's summons easily enough.

A quiet squeak made her jump. A lone mouse stood in front of her wardrobe, balanced on his hind legs. The animals had always known her mood, coming to comfort her in the darkest times of her childhood. Danielle thought them friends sent by her mother's spirit.

She dropped to one knee as the mouse darted closer. Drawn by friendship, or by some instinctive fairy allure? "The Duchess is right about one thing," she whispered. "Every moment I waste, Snow takes my son farther from here."

The mouse jumped back and waited, whiskers quivering. Its pose reminded her of a soldier awaiting orders.

"Thank you, but I'm afraid you can't help me in this." She grabbed her sword and headed for the chapel. Nobody stopped her as she crossed the courtyard. Perhaps something of her mood showed upon her face, because while several people started toward her, each one swiftly turned away.

She yanked open the chapel doors, taking in the scene in a single glance. Armand lay asleep on the altar. Gerta and Father Isaac had stopped talking in mid-sentence with Danielle's arrival. "How is he?"

"Unchanged," said Talia. She appeared disheveled, her hair a mess, her clothes rumpled and sweaty. A glance at the bench beside her explained why. A red cape, lined with wolfskin, sat in a pile on the bench. The cape had once belonged to the assassin known as the Lady of the Red Hood. Talia must have tried using the cape's magic to track Snow and Jakob.

"Did you find anything?" Danielle asked.

Talia glanced at the cape. "Snow's scent vanished from the workshop. I picked her up again near the main gate, but lost her outside the palace. I think she took a carriage, but I couldn't say where she went."

"Damn."

Talia was studying Danielle's face. "What's happened?"

"Nothing." This wasn't the time to talk about the Duchess' revelations. Danielle marched past, toward the altar. Gerta took a step back. Was Danielle's frustration so apparent? "What have you found?"

"Very little." Gerta was clearly exhausted, her eyes red and shadowed. She had nearly frozen to death below the palace, and hadn't gotten a decent night's sleep since . . . ever, really. "Neither exorcism nor summoning rituals have helped. Everything is coming from within the prince. As far as we can tell, the demon isn't controlling him. It's simply changing the way he sees the world. It's fascinating, really."

Father Isaac cleared his throat, and Gerta blushed. Her enthusiasm reminded Danielle of Snow. Her eyes shone with the same excitement when she talked about magic. "We have to remove the splinter from his body."

"It moves each time we try to examine it," said Father Isaac. He had unbuttoned the prince's shirt, and pulled it open to show new bruises along the right side of Armand's chest. "I've kept him asleep, but the splinter acts like a living thing. I'm afraid if we try to cut it from him, we'd only send it deeper into his body."

"Where is it now?"

Gerta pointed to Armand's lowest rib on the right side. In a soft voice, she said, "Had it remained in his arm, we might have been able to amputate."

Danielle forced those images away. "Snow could destroy her mirrors at will, reducing them to powder. Can you crush this splinter?"

"Even if we did, the pieces might still carry the curse," said Father Isaac.

Gerta chewed her lower lip as she studied the bruises

on Armand's side. "If we bled him as soon as the glass was crushed, we might be able to remove most of it. Like sucking poison from a wound."

"Or we could spread the poison throughout his body," Isaac countered.

Danielle turned away. "A single sliver took my husband from me. My father was a glassmaker, but never have I seen a mirror as large as Snow's. What we've seen in the palace is only the start. We have to know if this infection can be cured."

"There are others we could attempt to free," Isaac said. "I could have one of the prisoners brought from the dungeon—"

"They're not prisoners, they're people. Friends. You mean to tell me their lives are less important than Armand's? That their families will grieve less over their loss?"

"He means you don't risk the Prince of Lorindar to unproven magic," said Talia.

"I could trap it," Gerta said suddenly. She brushed her fingers over Armand's chest. "Crushing the splinter isn't enough. I need to isolate it from the prince . . . bring me a pearl."

"Why a pearl?" Danielle repeated.

"Pearls are formed to protect the oyster from irritation," Gerta said. "If I can do the same to this splinter—"

"Sympathetic magic." Father Isaac moved toward the prince. "Yes. We can use the pearl as a focus to encase the glass."

"Assuming we can trust her," Talia said sharply. "We don't know what she is, and now you mean to let her work her magic on the prince?"

Gerta jerked back, her brow furrowed with unguarded hurt. "Have I lied to you, Talia? Tried to trick you in any way?" She turned to Danielle. "I don't know how Snow created me, or why, but she's my sister. She wouldn't want this. Let me help you."

Not for the first time, Danielle wished Beatrice were here. The queen had always been able to see through deception. She would have known whether Gerta could be trusted, whether they should allow her to help Armand. "How long would it take?"

"Armand is asleep. We've isolated the splinter. I could begin now." Gerta shrugged. "Bring someone new, and it will take longer."

"Snow's magic has already robbed Lorindar of its prince. And every hour gives Snow more time to escape with my son." She whispered a quick prayer to her mother, and to Beatrice. "Father Isaac will help you."

Isaac stepped sideways, away from the altar. "Perhaps we should consult King Theodore first, just to be certain—"

"No," whispered Danielle. "He's already lost his wife. Would you burden him with this choice?" *Or with the consequences, should things go badly?* From Isaac's expression, he heard her unspoken words. "Do what you can for Armand."

Chapter 7

GERTA APPEARED OBLIVIOUS to everyone's attention as she pored over Armand's body, her face so close to his skin that the hairs on his chest brushed her nose. If Danielle was wrong about her, it would be so easy for her to kill Armand.

Danielle banished that thought, as she had so many others. Father Isaac stood beside Gerta, his expression intent as he split his attention between Gerta and the prince. Talia paced behind the altar, her face a mask of distrust.

What *was* Gerta? Could Snow really have created a true person, an individual with her own mind and soul? Snow had never hinted that she could cast such magic. Or was Gerta's life mere imitation, perhaps a fragment of Snow herself, broken from the whole?

Danielle could see glimpses of Snow in Gerta. The way she whispered absently to herself as she traced runes onto Armand's arm, the set of her lips when she concentrated, her obvious excitement over the workings of magic.

How many years had Snow spent imagining a sister, sculpting every last detail with her mind, trying to ease her loneliness? Gerta wasn't quite as attractive as Snow, which made sense. Snow's vanity wouldn't allow her to imagine a more beautiful sister. Gerta was taller, with a more prominent nose. Her teeth were perfect, but slightly too large. Her eyes were a muddy brown, reminding Danielle not of Snow herself, but of Snow's mother.

If they were unable to stop whatever demon had taken Snow, Gerta might be the closest Danielle ever got to seeing her friend again.

Gerta's scream filled the chapel. Talia lunged to grab her arm, but Gerta shook her away.

"Let her work," Isaac shouted. Danielle had never heard him yell before.

"What's happening?" Danielle asked.

"Give me the pearl." Gerta reached blindly toward the silver communion cup that held a single perfect pearl. Talia shoved it into her hand. Gerta began to chant in another tongue. Sweat beaded her nose and forehead. Danielle could hear the pearl rolling about, though Gerta held the cup perfectly still.

"The demon," said Isaac. "As Gerta's magic touches the mirror, she also touches Snow." He took his crucifix in both hands and began to pray. Gray smoke billowed from the thuribles, the incense strong enough to make Danielle's eyes water. His voice grew deeper, filling the church. "Depart. You are not welcome here."

"She sees me." Gerta was trembling.

Danielle stepped closer, putting her hand over Gerta's on the cup. "Focus on the mirror. You can do this."

Gerta grabbed a small jar of oil and poured a circle onto Armand's chest around the freshest of the bruises. The skin turned pink where the oil touched. Gerta pressed her fingers into the center of the ring.

Danielle could see a tiny lump beneath Armand's skin. "Is that it?"

Gerta took the pearl from the cup and pressed it onto the lump with her thumb. "She's trying to break it. I can encase one sliver, but if it fragments further . . ."

Armand's eyes opened. Talia jumped forward, catching his arm and pinning it to the altar. Danielle did the same on the other side, using her full weight to keep him from reaching Gerta. He was so strong, his fingers pinching and ripping the skin of Danielle's arm as he struggled to break free. He kicked at Isaac, who stepped out of the way without interrupting his chant.

Isaac gestured with one hand, and Armand fell back, though he remained awake.

"I've almost got it," said Gerta.

Armand's eyes narrowed, and his lips drew together in a smile.

"Be careful," Danielle warned.

The cracking sound was so quiet Danielle almost missed it. Gerta screamed and yanked her thumb back. The pearl had split in two, and blood beaded from the center of Armand's chest.

Isaac caught Gerta's wrist and reached out with his other hand. "Knife!"

Talia slapped a dagger into his hand. Isaac pressed the blade to Gerta's thumb and cut a shallow line. Gerta shrieked again, but didn't fight. Instead, she grabbed the dagger and pushed it deeper.

"The cup," Gerta said.

Danielle grabbed the cup from the altar. Blood dripped from Gerta's thumb, along with a sparkle of glass no larger than a grain of sand. "Is that—?"

"She broke the splinter in two." Gerta stuck her bloody thumb into her mouth. Her whole body was shaking. "She tried to shove the other piece into me."

As the pounding of Danielle's heart slowly calmed, she noticed another sound: Armand, laughing softly to himself.

"I could feel her reaching for me," said Gerta. "Like her magic was a weed, digging its roots into my veins. If Father Isaac hadn't cut it free, she would have taken me as well. I'm sorry." Gerta wiped her face as she turned to Talia. Isaac grabbed a cloak and wrapped it around her shoulders. "She was surprised. She wasn't expecting anyone to try to remove one of the slivers, but she'll be prepared now. She'll be watching for me to try again."

Isaac set the cup and splinter onto a small shelf, whispering a quick blessing over them both before returning to the prince. He placed a hand on Armand's chest and began to pray.

"Not even our mother could do such magic," Gerta whispered. "Snow ripped through Isaac's protections, threw off my spells, all through such a tiny fragment of glass."

"You're still here," said Talia. "That's what matters. We'll find another way."

Armand laughed again. A thin line of blood dripped down his stomach, staining the waist of his trousers. "Do you tell such lies to comfort yourself, Talia? Or are you foolish enough to believe them?"

Danielle stepped away from the altar. Armand hadn't moved since that one aborted attempt to reach Gerta. "Father, will your magic hold him?"

"His body," Isaac said, stepping away from the altar. "For now."

Danielle gestured for the others to follow as she strode to the far side of the chapel. In a low voice, she said, "Thank you for trying, Gerta."

Gerta managed a crooked smile. "So *now* do you trust me?"

Gerta might be a stranger, but she spoke with weary familiarity, so much like Snow that Danielle couldn't help but smile in return. "It's a start."

"Will Snow come after you?" Talia asked.

"I don't think so." Gerta checked her thumb. Blood welled from the cut, and she wrapped it in the hem of her cloak. "She hid me from herself, ripping the memory from her own mind to protect me from the demon. She knows someone tried to free Armand, but she doesn't know who I am."

Danielle turned away. What had Snow intended for Gerta? Gerta wasn't strong enough to fight a demon. Was she a merely a way for Snow to save some part of herself?

"What now?" asked Talia. "Half the palace is out hunting for Snow and the prince, but we don't know where she intends to go next."

"She's at sea," said Gerta.

They turned to face her.

"As Snow tried to take me, I . . . I think I glimpsed her as well. Her whereabouts and her thoughts. Like a nightmare, trying to swallow me into darkness, but I saw water, and I felt the shift of the deck."

"She's going home," whispered Talia. "To Allesandria."

"How do you know?" asked Gerta.

"She spoke of the pain of leaving your home. Of surrendering your birthright." Talia stared at the floor. "'Nobody forced you to flee, to turn your back on your throne.' She was talking about me, but . . ."

"But herself as well," Danielle finished. "If the winds are favorable, we might be able to intercept her before she reaches Allesandria."

"Do you know how to stop a demon?" asked Gerta. "She took your son and swept through the palace as though neither guards nor wards even existed."

"Accounts of such creatures are rare," Isaac said, hooking his thumbs through his necklace as he paced. "The church teaches that demons are beasts of Hell. By their nature, they spread pain and chaos, and they do not stop until they are destroyed or returned to Hell."

"There are theories that Hell is simply another world," Gerta said. "Albeit one less hospitable to beings such as ourselves."

"Perhaps." Isaac turned to Danielle. "Like the devils of old, this one works through lies and deception. It seeks not to control Snow, but to corrupt her."

"Snow's mother bound it into the mirror," said Danielle. "If we could do the same—"

"Once trapped, we could find a way to destroy it!" Gerta nodded eagerly. "There was a witch named Noita. She lived by the river near the winter palace in Kanustius. My mother went to her on occasion, when she required assistance with certain rituals."

"Would she know how your mother controlled this demon?" asked Danielle.

"She might. Not even my mother could have worked such magic alone."

"We'll take the *Phillipa*," said Danielle. "She's the fastest ship in the Lorindar navy. If we can intercept Snow before she reaches Allesandria, we'll try to rescue Jakob. If not, we find Noita."

"How do you plan to steal Jakob away from her?" Talia demanded. "She took Jakob from the heart of the palace. When I faced her, I barely escaped with my soul intact."

"So don't face her," Danielle snapped. "While we engage with Snow, you sneak onto her ship and find my son. Snow might be too powerful for us to stop, but you've had no trouble dealing with her other victims."

Unspoken between them was the fact that they had no idea how to save Snow herself. Talia dug her nails into her palms, but nodded once. "The *Phillipa* was Bea's ship. Captain Hephyra's oath was to her, not to Lorindar. With the queen dead, she might already have left."

"Not yet." Danielle was already hurrying toward the door. "Her crew were men of Lorindar. She would need time to raise a new one. Pack your things. We leave at high tide today."

Talia found Danielle in her quarters a short time later, stuffing clothes into a brass-studded carriage trunk. It was a measure of Danielle's distress that she wasn't bothering to fold them.

Talia coughed softly so as not to startle her. "I've asked the kitchen to search for some of that tea mix Snow used to make, to help your seasickness."

"Thank you." Danielle stifled a yawn as she shoved a jacket and a pair of boots into the trunk, followed by a thick brown cloak.

Talia glanced at the second trunk sitting beside the bed. "Armand?"

Danielle's shoulders tensed. "Still in the chapel. Father Isaac will continue to search for ways to free him from the demon's influence."

Talia pressed the door shut behind her. "When I

faced Snow, the things the demon said . . . you can't parry words. To hear those taunts from the one you love lodges the barbs deeper."

Danielle bowed her head. "Snow makes for Allesandria because, deep within her heart, some part of her longs to return home, to regain those dreams. That longing is real. What does that say of Armand's heart? Deep down, did he choose me not for love, but for simplicity? Because I was *safe*?"

"Perhaps some part of him did." Talia shrugged. "Just as a part of you wanted him because he could help you escape your stepmother and stepsisters."

"I love him," Danielle insisted, turning away from the trunk.

"I know." Talia leaned against the doorframe, arms folded. "You love him now. What was it you loved that first night, when you knew nothing but his name, his looks, and the fact that he danced like a drunken ox?"

A smile tugged briefly at her lips. "He wasn't that bad."

"You should have seen him when he was learning. He nearly crippled three of his mother's handmaidens." Talia sighed and joined Danielle, helping to gather her things into the trunk.

Danielle was holding up thus far, keeping her emotions under control while she dealt with the crisis at hand. Talia had seen her like this before when Armand was kidnapped, and again a year later when Beatrice was attacked. But she didn't know how long Danielle could keep going with both Armand and Jakob endangered. Danielle was exhausted, her body tight with the strain, as though the next blow might shatter what strength she had left.

"Danielle, are you certain about this? Whatever this demon is, it will fight us. Perhaps you should remain behind to keep Lorindar from falling apart. I know Theodore would appreciate the support."

Danielle yanked a pair of trousers from Talia's hands and refolded them. "She has Jakob."

"So you would give her the future queen of Lorindar as well?" Talia kept her voice soft. "A single cut from her mirror and she'll own you, just as she does Armand."

"Then I'll trust you to keep me safe, as always." Danielle rose. In addition to her sword, she wore a long dagger on her belt. Talia nodded her approval. "Talia, I have to go. I can speak to the animals of the sea, ask them to help us."

"What of your husband? If Jakob— If we can't stop Snow . . . you and Armand—"

"I know what you're not saying," said Danielle. Her cheeks were wet. "I know my duty. Chancellor Crombie has already expressed his 'concerns' over this voyage. He feels as you do, that I should remain here while others search for my son. Should Jakob be lost, my responsibility is to bear another heir, to protect the Whiteshore line."

Talia made a note to punch the chancellor in the face at the next opportunity. "You know how I feel about Jakob. I'll do everything in my power to—"

"There will be no other heir, Talia. We've tried. Whatever magic the Duchess' darklings performed on me, it left me unable to bear another child. Snow confirmed it two months ago. I asked her not to speak of it."

Danielle spoke without inflection. From the weariness in her face, she had already shed her tears over the news. Talia stood mute, uncertain what to say. Of all the arguments she had prepared for, this one had never occurred to her.

She understood why Danielle had asked Snow to keep this secret. Once it became known that the future queen was unable to bear another child, it wouldn't take long for certain individuals to suggest Armand turn elsewhere "for the good of Lorindar." This would only encourage those who condemned the prince for marrying someone they considered beneath his station. From the expression on Danielle's face, she knew this all too well.

"I'm sorry."

"You didn't know." Danielle rubbed her face. "I don't need sorrow or sympathy. I need you to help me find my son."

"You know I will. But you should—"

"You know better," Danielle said. "Tell me, what words could make you stay behind? What responsibilities could keep you off that ship while others search for Snow and Jakob?"

Talia tilted her head, acknowledging the point.

"We'll get them back, Talia. Both of them." Danielle turned away to resume packing.

"Do you truly believe that, or are you trying to convince yourself?" Talia asked softly.

Danielle didn't answer.

Danielle jolted awake as the carriage hit another pit in the switchbacked road that led to the harbor.

"We're almost there," Talia said softly. She sat on the opposite bench, a small hand crossbow on the seat beside her.

Danielle fought the impulse to ask the driver—again—for greater speed. The roads were too slick, a result of their exposure to the ocean winds. Slush and snow had frozen into the cracks between the paving stones. Any faster and they risked the carriage sliding from the road.

"Hephyra is going to be furious," said Talia.

"I know." Danielle had once seen Captain Hephyra fling a man almost twice her size from the deck of her ship. She rubbed her eyes, trying to scrub away the fatigue and the lingering remnants of her dreams. "Trittibar says this should work."

"Easy for him to say. He's not the one who has to protect you from a pissed-off dryad. We should have brought an escort."

"And make it look like we're threatening her?" Danielle shook her head. Bad enough an extra garrison of the king's soldiers had been dispatched to the harbor. King Theodore had ordered them dispatched around sunrise, after news reached the palace that the harbor-master and several of his men had fallen to Snow's magic.

The rhythm of the carriage changed as they left the frozen dirt-and-stone road for the wooden planks of the docks. The driver called back, "Keep the shutters drawn, Your Highness."

Danielle double-checked that the shutters were latched. "What do you think of Gerta?"

Talia sighed and leaned back. "She's a magical construct created by a woman who was fighting demonic possession."

Gerta was currently waiting back at the palace. She would follow as soon as Danielle sent word. If all went well, they could be off in less than an hour, just in time to catch the high tide at midmorning. "You don't trust her."

"We don't even know what she is. I've seen Snow cast incredible spells before, but to create a new human being . . . it seems impossible."

"I created Jakob," Danielle pointed out. "With a little help from Armand."

"That took nine months. Snow did it in nine heartbeats. She's the one who always says magic has a price."

Danielle's thoughts had followed a similar path. What was the cost of creating a new life? "Gerta claims to be a part of Snow."

Talia nodded. "A part which Snow ripped from herself. The part she tried to protect from the demon."

"So what happens to Gerta if we succeed?" Danielle knew little of magic, but if Gerta was incomplete, a fragment of Snow White, would Snow eventually need to reclaim that fragment? How long could Gerta even survive on her own?

"I imagine she's asked herself the same questions." Talia's jaw was tight. "Gerta didn't ask for any of this."

"I know." The carriage slowed. "Watch her. She's done nothing to earn our suspicions, and I'm grateful to her for trying to save Armand, but she's not Snow. It would be easy to forget she's a stranger to us."

Talia quirked an eyebrow. "Princess, I've made certain she was under guard from the moment I found her."

"Of course you have." Danielle gave a faint smile as she wrapped her cloak around herself. The carriage sheltered her as she stepped down, but as soon as she moved past it, the air buffeted her toward the white cliffs that rose behind her.

They had passed the commercial ships, rounding a bend in the cliffs to reach the part of the harbor used by the Lorindar navy. Banners fluttered from the signal tower built into the cliffs a short distance ahead. Tall ships aligned in the docks like horses in their stables.

The road here was raised against the tides, but a salty mist still filled the air as waves broke against the rocks. Chimneys from the buildings packed along the base of the cliffs spread lines of smoke across the sky.

Danielle spotted the *Phillipa* at once, docked about a third of the way down the harbor. Unlike the other ships, the *Phillipa* was unpainted, a narrow double-masted ship of fairy design. Silver sails were furled tight to the yards. A carved swan extended from beneath the bowsprit. The *Phillipa* carried fewer guns than most naval vessels, but she was as tough as any warship.

"Princess Whiteshore!" Captain Hephyra stood at the rails. Even from a distance, Danielle could see the fury on the captain's expression. "Was it you who ordered the harbor closed?"

The order had come from King Theodore, but Danielle doubted that would matter. She cupped her hands to her mouth. "I would speak with you, Hephyra."

Hephyra jumped from her ship, not bothering with the gangplank. She landed hard enough that Danielle feared the impact would shatter the planks of the dock, but things of wood obeyed different laws for Hephyra.

Captain Hephyra was a dryad, exiled from Fairytown for crimes against her queen. She was taller than most humans, dressed in a fashion that gave no consideration to the cold weather. Her black trousers were tied off at the knees, leaving her lower legs and feet bare. A matching black shirt exposed her midriff and her arms from the elbows down. A green bandanna swept auburn hair back from a face both severe and beautiful.

Her stride swallowed the distance between them. For a moment, Danielle thought Hephyra meant to simply toss her into the water. But she came to an abrupt halt half a pace in front of Danielle. Suspicion filled her cold, gray eyes. "Beatrice is dead."

"Yes," said Danielle.

Hephyra rubbed her wrist. The last time Danielle had seen the dryad, a golden tattoo had circled her wrist, a sign of her bond to Queen Beatrice. Today, Hephyra's skin was bare. "The fairy queen gave my ship to Beatrice. With her gone, you've no hold over me or the *Phillipa*, and no right to keep me here."

Danielle held her ground. "I need you to take us on one final voyage. To Allesandria."

"And back," Talia added. "No stranding us across the sea."

Hephyra snorted. "Good to see you again, Talia." To Danielle, she said, "This is about your witch friend, isn't it? The one who sailed from here like a hellstorm earlier today."

"You saw her?" Talia asked.

"She took a merchant vessel. Not one of those gut-heavy cargo ships, but an escort, fast and armed." Hephyra jabbed a finger at the sea. "She stood at the bow, hair and cloak flapping in the wind. Even I could feel the magic she wove as she raced from the docks. She passed through the chains at the harbor mouth like they were mist. I'd have done the same, had I her powers."

Danielle's throat knotted. "Was Jakob with her?"

"I couldn't say. Sorry, Princess. Best of luck finding the little sapling, though. I liked him."

"I saved your ship, almost two years ago," Danielle reminded her. "You owe me."

Hephyra snorted. "You made no bargain with me. I appreciate what you did for the *Phillipa*, don't get me wrong. But it was your quest that put us in danger to begin with. Yours and Beatrice's. I owe you nothing, and my answer is no."

"I told you," Talia whispered.

"I know." Danielle had hoped it wouldn't come to this. "I didn't *ask* you for your help, Captain. The fairy queen gave your ship to Beatrice Whiteshore as a gift."

"And Beatrice is dead," Hephyra spun on her heel and began walking back to the *Phillipa*.

Danielle raised her voice. "The queen left a will."

Hephyra stopped.

"A short document," Danielle went on. "One which lays out her wishes for those few belongings she claimed as her own. Including the *Phillipa*."

Hephyra touched her wrist. "I'm free. You can't—"

"I've spoken to Trittibar." Danielle kept her face cold. "Your ship, and by extension yourself, belonged to Beatrice Whiteshore. By fairy law, she has every right to pass you to her heir." She held her ground as Hephyra stormed closer.

"Now you've done it," Talia muttered as she shifted, moving into position to better defend Danielle.

"So I'm to belong to the prince now, is that it?" Hephyra's shout drew stares from the closest ships.

"To me," said Danielle.

Hephyra blinked. "You can't get within ten paces of a ship without turning green as spring grass. Why would she leave the *Phillipa* to you?"

"Maybe because she knew I would need your help one last time. Or maybe because she knew I'd be willing to free you once this journey ended." Danielle moved closer. "Give me your word as a fairy to help us save Snow and Jakob. Carry us until they're safely returned to Lorindar, and you will be free."

"And if they're beyond saving?" Hephyra asked.

"Three months." Danielle refused to feel shame for the tears that slipped down her cheeks. "If we're unable to save them in that time, I'll free you to do as you wish."

"Allesandria isn't that far. One month."

"Two," Danielle countered.

"So be it. My word to serve you for two months, or until Snow and Jakob are safely returned to Lorindar." Hephyra spat. "You've changed. The seasick princess I remember wasn't one for enslaving innocent fey."

Danielle allowed herself a small smile. "This must be some new use of the word 'innocent' with which I'm unfamiliar."

"Ha! True enough." Hephyra gave a slight bow. "You bargain like a fairy, Highness. Cold and ruthless." She spun away and began shouting orders to the *Phillipa*'s crew.

Neither Danielle nor Talia spoke until Hephyra was back on board. The dryad's hearing was sharp as an owl's.

"A fairy bargain indeed," Talia said softly. "I don't think she meant it as a compliment."

"She's more right than you know."

Talia was already moving to unload the carriage. "How so?"

"Hephyra is a living, thinking creature. Do you really believe Beatrice would have passed her to me like some trinket?"

Talia's eyes widened. "You bluffed her?"

"The *Phillipa* is the fastest ship in Lorindar. We need that speed." Danielle stomped her feet, shaking slush from the soles of her boots. Guilt and shame warred with that need, and once again, need won out. "I secured her help the only way I could."

With that, she called to one of the hawks that hunted from the cliffs. The hawk swooped down to land atop the carriage, black talons gouging the wood. Danielle carefully tied a message to the hawk's leg with a silver ribbon. She had prepared the note before they even left the palace. "Gerta will be on her way shortly. We leave as soon as the *Phillipa* is ready."

Chapter 8

TALIA SAT ON THE STARBOARD RAIL OF the quarterdeck, one leg hooked through the rail for balance against the swaying of the ship. Danielle stood at the bow, illuminated by the brass lantern hanging from the foremast. Steam rose from the tin mug clutched in her hands. The overly strong tea was Snow's own recipe, a blend designed to ease Danielle's seasickness. But the tea could only do so much, and the white-capped waves below promised another miserable night for the princess.

A pair of dark shapes surfaced in the water ahead. She tensed, even as she recognized them as two of the dolphins Danielle had been chatting with off and on since leaving Lorindar two days ago. Talia's cape was making her jumpy.

The assassin known as the Lady of the Red Hood had once used this cape to hide herself from detection, defying even Snow's magic mirror. Talia hoped it would do the same now, but the wolfskin sewn into the cape had other effects on the wearer, shortening her temper and making her yearn for something—anything—to hunt and chase.

Talia hopped from the rail and crossed the deck to listen as Danielle questioned the dolphins. Her communication with the animals went in only one direction, so she spent much of her time trying to understand the dolphins' reports. One of the dolphins darted away a short distance, then returned. The wind swallowed Danielle's question, but the dolphin jumped from the water, chittering loudly before diving beneath the waves.

Danielle's gaze followed them east. "We're gaining on them."

Talia swallowed her next question. If Danielle knew how far they were behind Snow, she would have said.

Had Bea been on board, the *Phillipa* would have already caught up with Snow's stolen ship. When the fairy queen gave this vessel to Beatrice years ago, much of its magic had been bound to her. But even without her, the *Phillipa* was one of the fastest vessels in the water. It was simply a matter of waiting.

Talia hated waiting. The cape added the wolf's impatience to her own, making her even more aware of every interminable moment.

Danielle was silent, lost in her own thoughts, so Talia strode toward Hephyra at the wheel. Stub, the ship's cat, perched on her shoulders. Stub was a scraggly-looking thing with only three legs, but he was as comfortable on the *Phillipa* as his mistress.

Hephyra reached up to scratch Stub's chin with one hand. "The last time I sailed for your princess, she nearly sank my ship," she said by way of greeting.

"Since when do dryads worry about 'nearly'?" Talia waited a beat, then added, "Since when do dryads worry about anything, for that matter?"

"True enough." Hephyra's sharp laugh carried over the noise of the crew. She turned to survey the ship, and her gaze lingered on Gerta. Gerta had scampered up the foremast with one of the crew. She sat on the yard, one hand clinging to a line, laughing as the ship bobbed and swayed.

Talia winced as Gerta pulled herself to her feet, but she acted as steady as any sailor. Her red hair streamed behind her like a banner. The wind flapped her jacket and pressed her shirt to her skin.

"Your friend has sailed before, I take it?" asked Hephyra.

"Gerta never even saw the ocean until two days ago."

Though who could say what skills Snow might have given her. Gerta could speak and read, knew magic, and in most ways behaved like a woman of twenty years instead of a creation less than a week old.

"She takes to it well. Much as you did." Keeping one hand on the wheel, Hephyra stepped close enough for Talia to feel the heat of the dryad's body. "And what of you, Talia? I could use a woman of your skills to help keep the crew in line. With Beatrice gone . . ."

It wasn't the first time Hephyra had made such an offer. Talia had never been able to figure out whether she was serious. "I've seen you fight. You don't need me."

"There are other kinds of needs." Hephyra looked past her to Danielle. "What holds you to Lorindar, now that your queen is gone?"

Talia pulled the red cape tighter against the wind. "Lorindar is my home. The only one I have."

"And I'm sure your feelings for Snow have nothing to do with it."

Talia's face warmed, drawing a chuckle from Hephyra.

"She's quite smitten with you, you know."

"What?" The word emerged louder than Talia had intended. "Snow never—"

"Not Snow. I felt it the moment she stepped on board. Almost magical, her hunger for you."

Gerta. Talia shook her head. "That's impossible. She's not—" She caught herself. They hadn't told Hephyra the full details about Gerta's origins. "She doesn't even know me."

"Sometimes that's a good thing. Adds mystery."

Talia said nothing.

"Ah, Talia. Men have killed for the chance to share my bed, but you turn me down. Young Gerta pines for you, and you hardly give her a second glance." Hephyra sighed. "You're like a beggar who shows up at a banquet hoping for jellied swan. You ignore the feast laid out around you, starving to death while you wait for that swan to arrive."

"I'm not starving," Talia said, too sharply.

"Of course not. You spent a month dining on your friend Faziya, didn't you?"

Talia's face grew hot, and Hephyra laughed.

"I know everything that happens on my ship, remember? Including how you and your friend spent your time on the voyage back from Arathea."

"Faziya stayed for six weeks, not a month," Talia said softly. They had both known it wouldn't last. Faziya's home was in Arathea, the one place Talia couldn't go.

"And you took advantage of the time you had." Hephyra clapped her shoulder. "Nothing shameful there. You were happy. You both were. Why not allow yourself to be happy again?"

"It's not that simple." Gerta wasn't even *human* . . . not that she expected such minor details to bother Hephyra. "Gerta . . . she's younger than she appears."

"Looks ripe enough to me."

Talia punched her on the shoulder, then winced. Even with the added strength and power of the wolfskin, it was like punching a tree.

Hephyra's expression turned uncharacteristically gentle. "How long do you plan to wait for her?"

"Talia!" Danielle hurried over, saving her from having to respond. "We're ready."

Hephyra clucked her tongue. "I still say you're crazy."

Talia wasn't sure whether the dryad was referring to their plan to rescue Jakob or Talia's feelings toward Snow. Either way, she was hard-pressed to argue.

"It's about time." Talia unlaced her boots, tugged them free, and tossed them aside. Her weapons she handed over to Danielle, all save a pair of daggers and her zaraq whip.

"That cape is going to weigh you down," said Gerta. Talia hadn't even noticed her climbing down to join them.

Talia jerked a thumb at Danielle. "That's why her friends will be doing the actual swimming."

Hephyra ordered the lanterns extinguished, all save one which hung from the mainmast. Talia could see no sign of Snow's ship on the horizon, but if Danielle's dolphins said they were close . . . "I hope your overgrown fish know what they're doing."

"They'll get you to Snow's ship, and they'll follow behind until you emerge with Jakob."

Talia tied her hair back. "They know I have to breathe, right?"

"I'll remind them," Danielle promised.

"That water is freezing," Gerta said.

Talia ran a hand over her cape. "The wolfskin should help."

"It's not enough." Gerta hurried toward the mainmast. She climbed just high enough to reach the lantern. Stretching out with one hand, she traced several symbols onto the glass with her finger. Talia winced, but the heat didn't appear to burn her.

Gerta ran back, her cheeks flushed. "Push back your cape."

Talia raised an eyebrow, but complied. Gerta put her hand on Talia's shoulder and traced the same symbols, whispering a spell in Allesandrian. Heat spread through Talia's shirt, almost uncomfortable.

"I took the warmth from the lantern's light," Gerta explained, her hand lingering on Talia's arm. She glanced at Talia, flushed, and jerked her hand away. "The heat is diffused, so your shirt won't catch fire. Hopefully."

"That *would* make it harder to sneak onto Snow's ship," Talia said dryly. Seeing the worry on Gerta's face, she added, "Thank you."

Gerta brightened. "It's not much, but it should help. Be careful."

"Why start now?" Talia made her way to the foredeck. Danielle's two dolphins swam alongside the *Phillipa*. She climbed onto the rail and swung her legs around to the outside. Waves broke against the ship, the spray chilling her bare feet. Holding her breath, she braced her legs and kicked off.

It was like diving into a wall of ice. Air burst from her lungs. Her cape yanked at her neck as she kicked for the surface.

She found herself staring into the glassy black eye of a dolphin. "I don't suppose you come with a saddle?"

The dolphin tilted backward until it was swimming upright with only the head protruding through the waves, almost as if it were standing.

"Could be worse," Talia muttered. "Last time, she called sharks."

The dolphin's skin was smooth, almost silken, yet it wasn't slippery. It reminded her of fine, well-oiled leather. She grabbed the dorsal fin with one hand and reached for a flipper with the other.

She barely had time to hold her breath as the dolphin's body curved and flexed, and then they were shooting through the water like they had been launched from a cannon. The dolphin surfaced a short time later, just before Talia ran out of air. She glanced behind to see the *Phillipa* already shrunken to the size of a toy. The dolphin's power was equal to any horse, and Talia stopped worrying about anything save breathing and holding on.

The heat of Gerta's magic enveloped Talia, pushing back the water's chill. Her hands and feet were numb, but her core was warm. Spray washed over her as the dolphin surfaced again. She could hear it sucking air through the blowhole on the top of its head. The second dolphin swam a short distance to her left, their movements almost perfectly synchronized.

Her hands were starting to cramp by the time she spied Snow's ship in the distance. The moonlight showed only a black outline sailing east. As they neared, Talia began to make out the details of the stolen ship. Snow had taken the *Lynn's Luck*, a square-rigged, three-masted vessel. She sailed in darkness, her lamps cold.

Anticipation warmed Talia's blood as they swam closer. She studied the *Lynn's Luck*, gauging the best way to sneak on board. A small boat hung from the stern, offering one option. She could also try to reach the anchors near the bow.

"The stern," she decided, giving the dolphin's dorsal fin a gentle tug. The boat shouldn't make much noise, and hopefully most of the crew would be looking ahead, not behind. She brought one bare foot up onto the dolphin's back, behind the dorsal fin. She braced herself there, legs taut and ready to spring as the dolphin swam closer.

Talia's breath hissed. The boat was still too high, and she had no way to climb the hull. Nothing that wouldn't draw attention, at any rate.

The dolphin ducked beneath the waves. Talia bit back a yelp as the water swallowed her. She clung to the fin as they swam deeper, then somersaulted underwater. The movement nearly flung Talia loose. The dolphin's body flexed hard, shooting them upward. Talia realized what was happening an instant before they broke the surface and launched into the air.

Any closer and she would have smashed her head against the boat. She reached out, catching the edge of the boat as the dolphin dropped back into the sea. The boat swayed, knocking once against the *Lynn's Luck*'s hull before Talia could steady herself. She waited, but nobody came to investigate.

Talia pulled herself up and grabbed the closest of the ropes securing the boat to the ship. She never could have done it without the added strength of the wolfskin. She climbed higher, doing her best to avoid the windows built into the ship's stern. She listened again, then pulled herself up to the rail and onto the *Lynn's Luck*.

She crouched low and slid a dagger from its sheath. A single crewman stood on the yard overhead, working with no light save the moon. Talia crept toward the pin-rail at the base of the mizzenmast.

Other shadows crawled through the sheets or worked the main deck. The *Lynn's Luck* could have been a ghost ship for all the noise they made. Not a single man spoke.

Talia sniffed the air, hoping to pick up Jakob's scent. Wrapping herself in the wolfskin would strengthen the wolf's senses further, but the transformation was far from subtle. Better to remain human for now. She sniffed again, but smelled only wet canvas, oiled wood, and the salt of the sea.

Talia moved to the edge of the deck and peered down. A stocky man stood at the wheel. But where was Snow? Did demons need to sleep?

Knowing Snow, she would have retreated from the cold, choosing the most luxurious cabin for herself. That meant one of the cabins at the back of the ship, almost directly below where Talia now stood. There was a good chance Jakob would be with her.

She counted at least twenty crewmen. A snarl began to build, deep within her chest. She could move through the ship, killing them one by one before they even realized she was on board.

Talia gritted her teeth. Those were the wolf's urges, not her own. These were victims, not villains, no more responsible for their actions than Prince Armand had been when he insulted Danielle.

Talia had wanted to pummel him, too.

She needed a distraction, something to lure Snow from her cabin long enough for Talia to sneak in and find the prince. Talia switched her knife to her left hand and slid a belaying pin from the rail. She hefted it once, testing the balance, then sat back to watch the man working the foreyard. He moved out from the mast, adjusting the sails.

Talia gauged the wind, then threw. The wooden pin flew the length of the ship, striking the man on the shoulder. He toppled forward, dropping soundlessly into the ocean.

Talia crouched behind the mast. Had this been a normal ship, the man would have cried out, and half the crew would now be working to rescue him. Instead, the crew carried on, oblivious. But if he had been poisoned with a sliver of Snow's mirror, she should have sensed his fall.

The cabin door below opened, and Snow hurried across the deck. *Now* the crew moved to save their companion, responding to unspoken orders as they trimmed the sails and tossed a line over the port rail.

Talia lowered herself to the main deck and slipped into the cabin. A single lamp burned on the small desk bolted to the floor. The cot was made, blankets folded neatly at the base. Either Snow had made up her bed, or else she hadn't slept recently. Knowing Snow, Talia guessed the latter.

It took little time to search the cabin. There was no sign of Jakob. Talia returned to the door and peeked through the crack. Even with the cape enhancing her senses, it took a moment to pick Snow out in the darkness. She and the other crewmen stood with their backs to Talia, peering into the water.

Talia snuck out and strode toward the nearest hatch. She barely touched the ladder as she jumped down into the main hold. A ship like this was unlikely to have a proper brig. Where else would Snow have put Jakob? Assuming the prince was still alive.

No, Talia refused to believe that. Demon or not, Snow wouldn't kill Jakob.

Two covered lanterns cast weak light through this deck, illuminating heavy beams and wooden walls to partition off the cargo. Barrels and crates were lashed to the walls, but the hold was mostly empty.

She sniffed the air. Down here, away from the waves, she could just make out the sweaty, frightened scent of Prince Jakob.

Movement in the shadows froze her in place. Shadows she had mistaken for cargo rose and stepped toward her. Talia counted six men. They appeared to have been sleeping on the bare decks, without blankets or hammocks. She glanced around and spied two more coming up behind her.

"Jakob?" She kept her voice low, in a likely futile attempt to avoid alerting the men above deck. She pulled a knife with her left hand and readied her whip with her right. The zaraq whip was an assassin's weapon, a thin line with a lead weight at the end. She twitched the whip, readying the weight and a short length of line.

"Aunt Tala?"

Talia spun, snapping the whip out at one of the men behind her. The weight struck the center of his forehead. He staggered, and Talia leaped close, looping the whip around his neck. She pulled hard, sending him headfirst into one of his companion. "Can you get to me?"

The rattle of chains answered her question. Talia kicked both of her downed foes, making sure they stayed down, then yanked her whip free. She stepped sideways, putting one of the support pillars at her back.

There were tricks to fighting a group. Normally Talia would have singled out the most dangerous of her opponents, hoping to demoralize the rest. But as they approached, the lantern illuminated identical expressions of hate and anger, as though she were a plague to be eradicated from this world. And Jakob was chained somewhere beyond them.

Talia pushed off from the pillar, reversing her grip on her knife and slamming the butt into the exposed elbow of the man on the left. She heard bone crack, but the man didn't even cry out. He swung his other fist. Talia twisted, taking the punch as a glancing blow to the cheek. She continued to spin, trying to keep him between herself and the others.

He grabbed her arm, and she growled, letting the wolf surge through her. She stabbed her knife into his shoulder and flung him back. Her whip lashed out, catching the leg of another man and pulling him to the ground.

"So you've turned against me as well." The inflection was Snow's, though the words were low and gruff, coming from a bearded man to her right. "So much for love. Tell me, do you plan to help Danielle lock me away, or will you simply try to kill me?"

"Not you." Talia punched the man in the nose, but Snow simply continued talking from another body. "The demon who's taken you."

"You Aratheans once called my people demons," the man said. "Whatever my mother enslaved in the mirror, it's helping me. You don't understand what they did, Talia. None of you know."

"So come back to Lorindar and tell us all about it." Talia's words came in tight gasps between blows. She dropped low, kicking her heel back and up into someone's groin. It was getting harder and harder to keep them away.

A hand grabbed her hair. Talia seized the wrist in both hands and spun. She had to dislocate the man's thumb to get him to release her.

"It's not too late, Talia. I can help you to see."

No matter how hard she struck, how many bones she broke, they kept coming. They had spread out, backing her toward the wall. And there were more above deck.

"Aunt Tala!"

She tried one last time to reach him, striking the next man in the throat so hard he dropped to the deck and didn't move. She could break through this group, but it would take time to free Jakob from his chains. They would never get past the rest of the crew on deck.

Tears blurred her eyes. "I'm sorry, Jakobena."

Jakob's voice rose. "Aunt Tala, please!"

Talia snarled, letting the spirit of the wolfskin take her. Her knife was a fang, ripping flesh wherever it touched. Hot blood splashed over her, but it wasn't enough. She couldn't fight the entire crew. She kicked a man in front of her hard enough to crack his ribs, and then she was running toward the ladder. "I'm sorry! Be strong. I promise I'll save you."

Another man was already climbing down, with more waiting above. With a shout, Talia ripped him from the rungs and slammed him to the deck. She snapped her whip upward, clearing space at the top. An ax descended toward her head as she climbed. She swung to one side, and the blade thudded into the ladder. She grabbed her attacker and pulled him off-balance, using his weight to open a path through the circle.

Something slammed her hip, and a blade slashed her arm, but she made it to the rail. She turned to see Snow watching from the bow, her arms folded. The moonlight exaggerated both the sorrow on her face and the red scars from her mirror.

"I'll save you both," Talia whispered, and leaped overboard.

* * *

Danielle sang softly as she stood at the rail, waiting for Talia to return. The song was an old one, a lullaby Jakob demanded most every night before bed. The familiar words loosened the knots in her stomach, even as her eyes watered at the thought of her son.

"You'll get him back," Gerta said, coming up beside her. "You'll be singing him to sleep soon."

Danielle nodded, but continued her song to the end, just as she had the prior night. Some part of her believed Jakob could hear her, that her voice might help him to feel less afraid.

Talia should have reached Snow's ship by now. If anyone could sneak on board and find Jakob, it was her.

Gerta stared out at the water. She had left the deck only once since Talia's departure, and that was to try to scry on Snow and the *Lynn's Luck*. Her efforts had failed, leaving her with pain she described as icicles stabbing the base of her skull.

A speck of cold landed on the back of Danielle's hand. A tiny snowflake melted on her skin. Clouds had drifted to block the moon. Scattered flakes of snow shone in the lamplight as they fell.

Hephyra climbed onto the forecastle, Stub curled in the crook of her arm. She scratched absently at the cat's chin. "The snow could be a problem if it gets worse. Even light snowfall will slick the rigging and the yards."

The *Phillipa* was already at half sail to make sure they didn't overtake Snow White before Talia could complete her mission. If luck were with them, Talia would return with Jakob before Snow even realized he was gone. Danielle had ordered blankets brought to the deck, and the small oven in the galley had been lit. The galley wasn't as comfortable as a cabin, but it would help to warm them both.

"Princess?" Gerta leaned out over the rail.

Danielle's heart pounded. "You see something?"

"Not Talia. Something magic."

Hephyra dropped Stub, who scampered away. "The

girl's right." She pointed to a swirl of snow blowing toward the *Phillipa*. "It's coming against the wind, from the direction of your friend."

"A storm?" Danielle asked.

Gerta shook her head. "Captain, I think you should order your men down from the yards."

Hephyra scowled and spun, barking orders to the crew.

Danielle took Gerta's hand and pulled her to the ladder, sending her down to the main deck. Over the noise of the crew and the waves, Danielle began to hear a low humming. She leaned out, peering at the swirling snow to see a swarm of insectlike creatures flying purposefully toward them.

The first streak of white buzzed over the deck. An older sailor named Pemberton swore and slapped his neck. "Whatever they are, the buggers sting like wasps from hell."

The insects were no bigger than bumblebees, and they blended into the snowfall. Danielle saw one man swinging wildly, only to curse when another of the creatures darted in to sting his hand. She drew her sword, but that wouldn't be much use against such tiny foes.

"Get to the cabin," Hephyra shouted.

The buzzing grew louder, and one of the creatures flew at Danielle's face. She ducked, then ran to grab one of the blankets. When the thing returned, she flung the blanket into the air to intercept it. The creature thumped against the blanket, and a tiny needle of ice jabbed through the heavy wool. Danielle folded another layer of blanket over it, then smashed the flat of her blade onto the squirming lump. She was rewarded by a crunch like breaking glass. When she opened the blanket, bits of ice clung to the material.

"Don't touch it," Gerta warned. She pointed to the center of the ice. "That's powdered glass from Snow's mirror."

"What are they?" Danielle yelled.

"Magical constructs of ice and glass." Gerta ducked. "Like wasps or bees."

Hephyra grabbed one of the oars from the boats, holding it like a quarterstaff. The oar's blade would give her a better chance of hitting such small targets. Most of the crew were doing the same with whatever weapons they could find, but the wasps were too quick. Danielle grabbed Gerta and began pulling her back toward the cabins.

"How many?" Hephyra asked.

"Thirty? Maybe more." Gerta twisted away and crawled over to study another of the wasps that had fallen to Hephyra's oar.

"It's still moving," Danielle warned. One wing was gone, but the other flapped furiously against the deck. The body was made of ice, dusted with mirrored glass that tapered to a sliver at the end. "Can you stop them?"

Gerta shook her head. "If they'd hold still, I could probably melt them."

Hephyra stepped closer, using her oar to knock another wasp away. "And maybe if you ask nicely, they'll stop buzzing about and line up to be smashed."

"Get me that lantern," Gerta shouted, pointing to the mast.

Hephyra crossed the deck, ducking another wasp. The lantern hung from a wooden hook that grew from the mast like a thick branch. It turned supple as Hephyra approached, bending to drop the lantern into Hephyra's hand.

Gerta stretched both hands around the lantern. Her fingers brushed the metal. "I cast a spell to give the lamp's heat to Talia. I can use that heat against the wasps, but it means removing the spell from Talia. If she's in the water—"

"Do it," said Danielle. The wasps meant Snow knew about them. If Talia had been captured, she had no need of heat. If not . . . Gerta's spell would do Talia little good if the *Phillipa*'s crew fell under Snow's control.

Gerta's brow furrowed as she mumbled her spell. Heat poured from her hands. She stepped back, and the heat went with her. The lantern itself was cold, despite the flame flickering within. She lowered her hands toward the injured wasp on the deck, which soon dissolved into a tiny sparkling puddle.

The next time one of the wasps swooped near, Gerta stretched out her hands as though trying to throw that heat. The wasp veered away, but didn't melt. "They're too fast. I can keep them back, but I can't destroy them."

Another man tumbled out of the yards, crashing to the deck with a scream.

"Can you protect another living thing from that heat?" Danielle asked.

"I think so," said Gerta.

Danielle flung her blanket at a pair of wasps, which darted to the side to avoid it. She sent out a silent call as she gripped her sword with both hands, watching the wasps to see whether they would attack or seek another target.

Another swing of Hephyra's oar sent them away, toward the helmsman. The wasps had adopted a new tactic, joining together to attack in groups. Seven of them swarmed over the poor helmsman, stinging his hands and face. Other crewmen tried to help him, and the wasps flew up out of reach, gathering in a small cloud as they searched for another victim.

A blur of black fur streaked up from belowdecks. Claws scratched the deck as Stub raced toward Danielle. His fur was raised, making him appear twice his usual size. He hissed at one of the wasps that came too close.

"Cast your spell on him," said Danielle, urging Stub to wait.

Stub's tail lashed from side to side, but he sat patiently while Gerta worked another spell. He even began to purr.

"I think he likes the heat." Gerta smiled as Stub rubbed his face against her hands. "It's done."

"Go," said Danielle.

Stub tore away. His missing leg slowed him hardly at all as he crossed the deck and clawed his way onto one of the tarp-covered boats. From there, he jumped onto a crewman's head. The man stumbled forward, hair smoking from the heat. Stub pounced. His distance was limited, but he managed to catch a wasp in his front paws. By the time he hit the ground, the wasp's wings were gone, and he was already scrambling after another.

Gerta winced. "Be careful!"

"That cat is mad," Hephyra said.

Danielle wasn't sure which definition she meant, but she agreed regardless. Even from here she could hear Stub hissing and growling as he chased the next of these flying creatures who had dared invade *his* ship. His pounce missed, but the heat was enough to start to melt the wings. The wasp's flight wobbled, and another sailor smashed it with an iron pan.

Down on the main deck, several of the men had gathered sailcloth to trap and crush the creatures. Stub continued his crazed hunt, bringing down the rest. He also set one of the sails on fire, but the crew managed to extinguish the flames before they spread too far.

Danielle caught Gerta's arm. "Are you hurt? Did they cut you?"

"I don't think so."

Danielle searched the exposed skin of Gerta's neck and face, then inspected her own. Neither of them appeared to have been cut. She hurried toward Hephyra. "Make sure none of your men touch the remains with their bare hands. A single cut from the broken glass is enough to enchant them."

Hephyra nodded and called out, "Anyone bloodied by those damn things, fall in on the main deck. You're relieved of duty until further notice. If you're cut and try to hide it, I'll feed you to the sharks myself."

"You'll have to confine them." The warning came from Talia, who was shaking as she pulled herself over the rail to collapse on the deck. Gerta grabbed one of the blankets and wrapped it around her.

Danielle swallowed. "Jakob?"

"I tried." Talia slammed a fist into the rail, hard enough to crack the wood. "He's alive and safe for the moment. He was chained below deck. I dealt with the guards, but Snow . . . she can see through their eyes. She was controlling them, like puppets."

Danielle sheathed her sword, forcing herself to accept the news. "Are you hurt?"

"Frozen and mad as hell, but nothing worse than some cuts and bruises."

"Oh, damn." Hephyra was staring at Stub. The cat favored his front left paw as he crossed the quarterdeck. Each step left a bloody print on the wood. "What will that curse do to him?"

"It depends." Gerta was sitting cross-legged on the deck, studying the crushed remains of a wasp. "The magic in these creatures is beyond anything I could do. Even beyond what Snow should be able to do."

"She's sent her mirrors away before, animating them like insects of glass and wire," Danielle protested.

"Not like this. Not so many." Gerta leaned down until her nose nearly touched the deck, and Danielle worried she would cut herself. "I touched the splinter she left in Armand. This latest attack is different."

Danielle's stomach knotted. "Different how?"

"She's getting stronger."

Chapter 9

THREE MORE DAYS AT SEA BROUGHT SNOW to the border between Hilad and the nation of Allesandria. From there, it was another half a day's ride on horseback to reach the city of Melavin, capital of the Allesandrian province of Yador and home of Ollear Curtana, Lord Mage Protector of the city.

One by one, she stripped away the outer protections of the antiquated tower where Ollear made his home. "The man is clever enough," she said to the white songbird on her shoulder. "But he lacks depth. He layers his magic instead of interweaving the spells to strengthen them."

The bird gave a frightened chirp, but it was preferable to the whining. She had transformed Prince Jakob before leaving the ship. With his wing feathers trimmed, he had no means to escape. If he did run away, he would be quickly devoured by a wild animal, or simply crushed underfoot.

Snow thought briefly of Talia and Danielle as she climbed the steps, absently sending her wasps ahead to deal with any servants or human guards. She closed her eyes, peering through those men on the *Phillipa* who had been touched by the demon's magic. They were confined in darkness, but their presence told Snow the ship was still under sail, far from shore.

So strange to be home once more, to hear the tongues of Allesandria instead of the grating cacophony of sounds that passed for language in Lorindar. Before the mirror's destruction, Snow never would have dared return. Nor would she have taken Jakob, or attacked Talia and Danielle. She held no illusions about the way the power of the mirror had changed her. There was a presence within her, helping to strip away the lies of the world, as well as the lies she once told herself.

Snow had been selfish, hiding away in Lorindar, squandering her magic on minor errands for the queen. She might as well have donned blinders, hiding from past and future, from those obligations that called to her from Allesandria.

Obligations like Ollear Curtana.

At the top of the stairs stood a construct of red stone, a magical guard carved in the likeness of the Lord Protector. It moved as smoothly as a living creature, drawing a stone sword as it advanced toward Snow.

She smiled. The sliver lodged in her eye had already shown her the key to the statue's false life. It had been born of mud blended with a rather complex potion, one brewed from the blood of the caster mixed with that of a loyal servant. She wondered idly if the servant had known the potion would require every last drop of his blood.

Snow pulled her own knife. The steel was razor sharp; she barely felt the cut as she slid the edge over her left palm. She clenched her hand in a fist, then flicked the blood at the approaching statue.

Given time, she could have wrested control of the statue, turning it against its creator. But there was too much to do. Instead, she simply willed the statue to return to its component elements.

The statue swung its sword at Snow's head. Snow raised an arm, and the blade splattered red mud over her arm and jacket. Its face contorted in a melted parody of confusion. Depending on how much of the caster's own blood flowed through the mud, it should have just enough awareness to realize something was wrong.

Fingers slid free of dripping hands. Snow sheathed her knife and smiled as any last resemblance to Ollear Curtana sloughed away. It gathered itself and lunged in one final attempt to smother her. Jakob squeaked and flapped his wings in alarm as Snow jumped back. The statue fell, splattering itself over the stairs.

Even as she trod through the mud, it clung to her boots. Its loyalty was impressive. Ollear must have improved his formula.

The wooden door atop the stairs was locked, but a quick spell swelled the wood until the planks split and fell away to reveal the grotesquely lavish bedroom of Lord Curtana.

The walls within were enchanted to be clear as glass, giving him a full view of the surrounding land. Dark clouds blotted the stars overhead, haloing the moon in silver. The same illusion blanketed the furnishings, turning them translucent. The wardrobe, the desk by the far wall, even the bed, where Ollear Curtana was busy with a woman far too young and attractive to be his wife. His scalp and face were clean-shaven, glistening with sweat. Like most nobles, he doubtless shaved each day, burning the hair to prevent it from being used against him by a practitioner of sympathetic magic.

"Hello, Uncle."

Both Ollear and his mistress bolted upright. They each wore a light robe of slavesilk. The thin material was naturally gray, but anyone with a hint of magical talent could change it at will, turning it clear. Snow kept a gown of the stuff for special occasions. The trick was to maintain your concentration as things grew more . . . distracting.

"Who are you?" Ollear looked past her. Searching for his guards, no doubt. His lips pressed together. "You look familiar."

Snow frowned, and both robes turned black. "I was hoping to talk to you about my father."

"Your . . ." He paled. "Princess Ermillina?"

Snow gave a slight bow. "Uncle Ollear. I go by Snow now." The years had worn away all but the faintest resemblance to the strong, handsome statue who had guarded Ollear's door. He appeared shrunken, with wattles of skin at his neck. Only his hands were as Snow remembered, thin and permanently stained from his potion work.

"You've aged so much." Old he might be, but he had never been stupid. "What magics have you been toying with, Princess?"

"I've done what was necessary." Snow glanced at the young woman beside him. "A student?"

"A member of my household."

A servant, then. Had she been magically skilled, politeness would have required Ollear to introduce her by name.

With one shaking hand, Ollear took a stiff black wig from the bedside table and positioned it on his head. He had to know he was outmatched. Snow had penetrated his tower and destroyed his guards. "Laurence told us you were dead."

"Not *King* Laurence? Such disrespect for your sovereign, Ollear. Where are your manners?" Snow strode around the room, looking out at the city below. Her feet sank into the white-furred rug. "I remember when my mother elevated you to your chancellorship at the university. Strange . . . to fall from such a position to this small border province."

"I serve as the king wishes, Your Highness," Ollear said carefully.

"The king is a fool to waste someone of your talents. I remember your visits to the palace. The potions you brewed for my mother."

"What do you want?" His gaze was openly calculating now. Snow was alone, but she was the daughter of the most powerful queen Allesandria had known in centuries. His fear was fading, replaced by hunger for the opportunities she might present.

"You're not the only one to be wronged by our new king. I mean to see justice done for those crimes."

"You *do* have a legal claim to the throne," he said

cautiously. "Yador is merely a border province, as you said, but I retain my seat in the Nobles' Circle. I could—"

"What would you ask from me in return?" Snow interrupted. "What cost to betray your king?"

"Nothing, Your Highness." Ollear stood, his hands spread. In other lands, it would be a gesture of peace, but in Allesandria, where every noble learned magic even before they mastered their letters, the lack of a weapon meant nothing. He stopped at a polite distance. "I ask only to help you correct an injustice."

And to place Snow in his debt. His lies wormed into her stomach, leaving her nauseated. "Do you remember my father, Ollear?"

"I do." The wariness had returned to his voice, though he kept his eyes averted. In Allesandria, to stare too long was to invite a magical confrontation. "He was strong in heart and mind, but his body failed beneath the demands of the throne. Your mother summoned me often to try to ease his pain."

"I was so young when he fell ill." Snow paced the circumference of the room, watching the lamplights below, the mountains in the distance. From this height, she could just make out the guard towers on both sides of the border. "I've spent years studying the healing arts, Ollear. I've yet to find a single malady that strikes with the same symptoms that took my father. Stealing his voice, withering his body, but also robbing him of his magic. A strange ailment, wouldn't you agree?"

"Your parents were powerful practitioners," Ollear said carefully. "They did much to expand the boundaries of magic, but as you know, all power carries a price."

"What was the price of your chancellorship?" Snow asked. "To prepare a draught which could slip past my father's charms against poison? One which would weaken him over time without attracting suspicion to my mother? Your skills are unmatched. You're the only one she would turn to for such help."

Ollear's companion edged toward the door. Snow waved, and the bedsheet leaped out to entangle her feet.

The other end of the sheet knotted itself to the bed. Snow stepped into the doorway, blocking their escape. Jakob chirped softly, burrowing into her hair as if trying to hide.

"Your mother had many allies," Ollear said. "If you mean to rule Allesandria, you would be wise to follow her example. You will need friends."

"I loved my father," Snow said softly.

Ollear lunged for his desk. He snatched what appeared to be an inkwell and flung the contents toward Snow.

Snow might not have had Talia's fairy-blessed reflexes, but her missions for Queen Bea had honed her reactions both physical and magical. By the time the sickly green liquid reached Snow, her magic had frozen it into a series of rippled icicles and droplets. She caught the largest icicle in her free hand, maintaining her own magic to prevent the heat of her flesh from melting it.

Ollear watched as though entranced as the ice in Snow's hand changed, growing paper-thin wings. The other pieces had broken when they hit the floor, but they too responded to Snow's will, forming insects the size of flies and gnats.

Sweat beaded Ollear's brow. "I can help you."

Snow pursed her lips and blew. A wasp the size of her hand shivered and flexed its wings. "I already have help."

Ollear fought well, destroying more than half of her insects before one slipped past his guard to sting his ear. Skin sizzled, and he screamed. The pain cost him his concentration, and soon the battle was over.

It wasn't a quick death, but as he had intended the same for her, she felt no remorse. Nor did she take any joy from his end. Death wouldn't undo his crimes, wouldn't restore her father to life. This was but the beginning.

"Look." She wrapped her fingers around Jakob's fragile body, tugging him free. She held him toward Ollear's twitching body. "No matter what lies we tell the world, death reveals the truth. Ollear Curtana was a traitor and a coward. The ugliness of his end matches the ugliness of his soul."

She turned to his friend, who was cowering behind the bed. "And how did you serve the Lord Protector, aside from the obvious?"

The girl's voice shook. "I'm his scribe, Your . . . Your Highness."

Snow returned the trembling bird to her shoulder and reached into the pouch at her belt. A scribe was a lowly enough position to go unnoticed, particularly in the chaos which would follow upon the discovery of Ollear's death. "Give me your hand."

She bit her lip and shook her head.

With a sigh, Snow slid a needle-long sliver of glass from the pouch. "This will hurt."

The sheets tightened, holding her in place long enough for Snow to jab the glass into the girl's neck. She screamed once, and then her struggles slowed as the tip snapped off within her flesh. Snow removed the rest of the sliver and wiped the blood onto the sheet.

"You will be questioned about Ollear's death. Either by the local mageguard, or perhaps by the king's Stormcrows." Snow pressed a larger shard of glass into the girl's hand. "Begin with them."

Danielle reread the note. This was the second message she had received from King Theodore. The queen's funeral had been held three days ago, under heightened guard. And Danielle hadn't been present.

She closed her eyes. Grief could come later. For now, better to maintain the dam, to focus on what needed to be done.

Tymalous and Father Isaac had made no progress at freeing Armand and the others from Snow's curse. They had managed to find the few remaining shards of Snow's mirror around the palace, and were spending every moment studying them for answers, but with no significant progress.

A soft quack made her jump. She smiled at the duck that had delivered the message. He was small for his breed, a black-and-gray-dappled bird with a smoke-colored bill. He ruffled his wings but settled down, waiting.

Danielle sipped her tea, grimacing at the medicinal taste, and returned to the letter she had begun writing to the king. She had described their failure to save the prince, and the futile search that followed. Danielle's dolphins hadn't returned, and Snow had evaded their pursuit since that night. Gerta suspected she was using the infected prisoners to track and avoid the *Phillipa*.

Seven men had been cut, along with Stub the cat. Stub was now confined to a small cage in the chartroom, and the infected crewmen were locked in the hold. Even if Snow looked through their eyes, she should see nothing to reveal their plans.

Gerta was probably right, but what more could they do, short of throwing the prisoners overboard? They were victims, innocents who had fallen to Snow's magic under Danielle's command.

Bells clanged from the deck. The duck squawked and beat his wings in alarm. Danielle hastily signed the note and rolled it tight, sliding it into a leather tube. She smeared wax over the seams to protect it from the elements, then bound it to the duck's leg. "Thank you. Please take this to the king as quickly as you can."

She tossed her cloak on over her nightgown and grabbed her sword belt. The bell continued to ring out as she opened the cabin door and stepped into the cold night air. Captain Hephyra was shouting orders, which the crew scrambled to obey. She waited for the duck to leave, then hurried over to join Talia.

"We've an escort," Talia said. Gerta was close behind, smothering a yawn. Talia pointed to the two ships which had emerged from a thick fog in the distance.

Gerta squinted. "They fly the royal banner. Inspectors, I'd guess."

"Do inspectors normally greet visitors with gunports open?" Danielle asked.

Gerta gave a half-shrug. "Not usually, but we don't

know what's happened in Allesandria these past few days . . ."

They had passed the northern coast of Hilad two days before, and were now in Allesandrian waters. By Hephyra's estimate, they should reach their destination tomorrow morning.

But Snow could be almost anywhere by now. What had she done to Jakob? Was he still locked away in the hull of her stolen ship? How long would her patience last as she tried to unravel the mysteries of his power? Or had she already—

No. Jakob was alive. He had to be.

"Stop that," Talia said.

Danielle blinked. "Excuse me?"

"Your eyes give you away. Jakob is alive, and we will find him. We'll save them both. If you want to worry, worry about what those inspectors will say about us arriving in a fairy vessel."

Danielle pursed her lips. She had studied the histories of Lorindar and its neighbors, including Allesandria, where the fairy folk had been ill-treated for centuries. Most had fled to friendlier kingdoms. Many of those who remained were destroyed or enslaved. Rose Curtana, Snow's mother, had paid a bounty for every fairy head, believing their magic to be a threat to her rule. King Laurence had reversed some of those policies, but after so many years of hatred, Hephyra would not be welcome.

"She will remain with the *Phillipa*," Danielle said. "She should be safe enough here. Anyone who comes aboard to harass her deserves whatever they receive."

Talia smiled slightly at that, but said nothing.

"They know we're coming." Danielle rested a hand on one of the lines running to the foremast. "Theodore has been in contact with King Laurence, and warned him about what happened."

The approaching ships spread out to flank the *Phillipa*.

"You're certain you can find this witch who helped Rose Curtana create her mirror?" Danielle asked.

"I . . . I think so." Gerta stared into the distance. "I was young and, well, not real."

"Assuming the witch is still alive," said Talia. "Assuming she exists at all, and this isn't some game Snow planted in your mind."

Gerta's face went blank, and she turned away. "Talia's right. It *feels* like a true memory, but how would I know?"

"It doesn't matter," said Danielle. "If not Noita, we find someone else. Allesandria claims to be the birthplace of human magic. There must be others who can help us free Snow from this demon and rescue my son."

Unbidden, the memory of the Duchess' offer pushed to the forefront of her mind. She could call right now. Perhaps fairy magic might succeed where Talia's rescue attempt had failed. Had the Duchess asked for anything else . . .

"What is it?" Talia asked. "You tensed."

"I was thinking of the men possessed by Snow's wasps," Danielle lied. The effects of Snow's magic were obvious. Stub hissed and clawed at anyone who came near. As for the men, when they deigned to speak at all, their words were venom. The hatred and disgust on their faces was even worse than Armand's had been, back in Lorindar.

From the Allesandrian ship on the port side came a shout. "This is the *Farrion*, sailing under King Laurence of Allesandria. Identify yourself." The words were heavily accented, a thickening of the words that reminded Danielle of Snow.

Hephyra jumped onto the rail at the bow. She stood as if rooted, unaffected by the wind or the sway of the ship. Cupping her hands to her mouth, she shouted, "This is Captain Hephyra of the *Phillipa*, out of Lorindar."

The wind and fog made it harder to hear the response from the *Farrion*. "Reduce your speed and prepare to receive inspectors. We'll be escorting you into the harbor. If you resist, we've orders to sink your ship."

Hephyra's response was short, obscene, and hopefully not loud enough to carry to the other ships.

"We have no proof they are who they claim to be," Talia pointed out.

Hephyra jumped down from the rail. "If they were pirates, they'd have struck farther out."

And if they had been infected by Snow's magic, it was too late to escape. "Do as they say," said Danielle.

Hephyra flung up her hands in disgust. "We wouldn't have to reduce speed if they weren't so damned slow." But she turned to shout at the crew, who began taking in some of the sails.

Already the two Allesandrian ships were lowering boats into the water. Danielle watched as they rowed toward the *Phillipa*. She counted ten men apiece.

"The man with the gold chain belt is the royal inspector," said Gerta. "He'll have studied magic for at least three years at the university. Don't try to lie to him."

The boats pulled alongside the *Phillipa*. The inspector lifted a rolled rope ladder in both hands and shouted a word Danielle didn't recognize. The ladder uncoiled as if alive, appearing to climb up the *Phillipa*'s hull. The end of the ladder twined tightly around the rail.

Hephyra stood with arms folded as the first man climbed up. "If I'm to be boarded, I like to be asked nicely, first." She was close enough to the rail that he had to move sideways to pass her by.

More followed, all armed with knives and small, polished hand axes tucked through their belts. Each wore a thick doublet, dark blue and heavily embroidered in white patterns that reminded Danielle of fancy carpeting. The inspector had added a white leather sash, decorated in gold, with pouches worked into the leather. He was the last to board. He laced his fingers together and surveyed the *Phillipa*, looking past Hephyra as though she were invisible.

"I am Relmar, Royal Inspector for His Majesty King Laurence of Allesandria." He was middle-aged, heavyset but still fit, judging by the ease with which he had climbed aboard. Stubble shadowed his face and scalp. His skin was darker than Talia's, and his accent marked him as a native of Najarin. Close to a third of his men appeared to be from other lands. Allesandria was known for taking in magically gifted children, training them in exchange for service to the crown. Most returned home when their service was complete, but others chose to stay in Allesandria.

"Princess Danielle Whiteshore, of Lorindar." Danielle clasped her own hands in greeting; an old Allesandrian formality to suggest no magic would be used upon your enemy. "King Laurence is aware of our mission. We were promised free passage in Allesandria."

"Your king said nothing about sailing a fairy ship into our waters, milady." The toe of Relmar's boot rapped the deck. Behind him, his crew was spreading out to examine the ship. "My men will need to look below as well."

"That's what they all say," Hephyra muttered.

Danielle smothered a smile. "Are you accusing us of smuggling?"

"Not at all," Relmar answered. "But with all due respect, have you inspected the hold? Have you searched every corner of this vessel? I've no doubt your mission is genuine, but fairies are masters of trickery and illusion."

Hephyra snorted. "Just as humans are masters of—"

"How long will your inspection take?" Danielle asked quickly.

Relmar scowled at Captain Hephyra, then went back to ignoring her. "An hour, perhaps two. The nature of this . . . vessel . . . makes it difficult to search for other magic." He frowned as he studied Danielle. Reaching into his sash, he produced an amber monocle which he held to his right eye. Tiny engravings marked the edge of the lens. "That sword you wear. Is it enchanted?"

"It is."

"There are protocols for bringing enchanted items into Allesandria. Duties to be paid, permits to be procured." He clucked his tongue and turned. "Your friend will need to do the same for her red cape, not to mention—" He frowned and paced a slow circle around Gerta, removing the monocle then replacing it again on his eye as if to confirm what he was seeing. "I am Relmar Yohannes Duban, Free Master of the Sorcerer's Guild."

Gerta raised her chin. "Gerta."

He scowled. "Perhaps you've been long enough from Allesandria to forget your manners. With whom did you study?"

"My sister."

"And that shape you wear. It's natural?"

"I've known Gerta since the day she was born," Talia said.

Hephyra chimed in, "Perhaps you should stop worrying about the girl's shape and get on with things."

Relmar started to respond, then frowned as two of his men climbed up from below deck and hurried toward him. Danielle could only pick out a few words of their conversation, but she saw Talia tense.

"You've prisoners locked below," Relmar said. "Men who have been struck by a particular curse. One of the men whispered again, and Relmar rolled his eyes. "Very well. Men and one cat."

"They were part of our crew," said Danielle. "We were attacked two days out of Lorindar."

Relmar appeared calm, but his people were another story. They kept their hands near their hips, ready to draw weapons. "Yet you survive." He scowled. "Allesandria has been attacked twice in as many days. Reports describe a single ship, protected by magic, leaving chaos and riots in her wake. The Lord Mage Protector of Melavin was murdered in his tower."

Danielle glanced at Talia, whose face was stone. "We've shared what we know with your king," she said, keeping her voice calm.

"Yes, I've heard the rumors. Snow White has returned to destroy us all." He didn't bother to hide his disdain.

"My orders are to quarantine anyone touched by Snow White's curse."

"You can't seriously believe us to be a threat," Danielle said. "You know the rest of us are untouched by any curse, and those men can harm no one."

"My first duty is to protect my nation," Relmar answered. "What if those men escape, or your fairy captain looses them upon our shores?"

"Inspector Relmar, I assure you they will not leave this vessel." Danielle reached into the pocket of her jacket and removed a sheathed knife. The hilt was gold, the pommel rimmed in tiny rubies. "However, I do understand your need to keep Allesandria safe. The magic in this blade is old and potentially dangerous. Perhaps it's best that it be turned over to you."

Relmar pulled the dagger free and studied it through his monocle. "Thank you, Your Highness. We will see that it's safely disposed of." He stepped back, studying the crew. "I'm assigning two of my men to this ship to strengthen and supervise the quarantine of your prisoners. The king may also send his Stormcrows to examine them. However, once we've examined each of you to guarantee you've not been touched by the curse, I will permit you and your friends—your *human* friends—to enter Allesandria."

"Thank you, Inspector," said Danielle.

As Relmar turned his attention to his men, Talia sidled toward Danielle. "There's no magic in that blade. I'd have smelled it."

Danielle shrugged.

"You brought that knife on purpose. You planned this. I never thought the day would come when Danielle Whiteshore bribed a lawful government official."

"Can you think of a faster way to reach the harbor? One that *doesn't* involve bloodshed," she added hastily.

Talia pretended to think about it. "How do you feel about severe bruising?"

Relmar returned a short time later. "I can't permit the fairy or the infected men to set foot on our land, but

I'll let you dock at the harbor. You'll be safe enough there."

"Not if Snow finds us," Gerta said.

Relmar gave her a patronizing smile. "Begging your pardon, but it's one thing to take on an old and unprepared border lord like Ollear. This is the King's own province of Tollavon. If Snow White is wise, she'll keep her distance. Should she sail too close, we'll take care of her."

"My son, Prince Jakob of Lorindar, is on that ship," Danielle said firmly. "He's not yet three."

"Rest your mind," said Relmar. "Our weather mages have dealt with hostile visitors before. The winds will drive her against the rocks to the east, ripping the hull and leaving her stranded upon the rocks. Once we've taken care of the witch, we'll board the ship and find your son, don't you worry."

Gerta was shaking her head. "You should evacuate the harbor."

Relmar studied the ship again before answering. "I know you're shaken. I recognize what you've been through, and the state of your crewmen below. But she's one witch. One ship. If she dares to press her attack against Allesandria—"

"She will," said Gerta.

"Then we'll face her when she does. If she's truly possessed, as you say, we've the means to deal with that as well."

Danielle wanted to accept his words. She wanted to believe Snow would be stopped, that Jakob would be rescued. Allesandria *was* known for its magic. They were far better prepared than Lorindar to face a threat like Snow. They might even be able to save her. Snow's mother had trapped the demon once, after all.

If Relmar was right, then Jakob would be safe. If he was wrong. . . . "Should she attack as you say and you do rescue our son, please tell him we'll be back as soon as we can. You've my word I'll reward you for your efforts."

"I'll look after him personally, my lady. I've three

children of my own." There was genuine sympathy in his words. "Your son will be with you again soon."

"Thank you." She looked to Talia and Gerta.

From the expressions on their faces, neither of them believed him either.

Chapter 10

TALIA HAD VISITED ALLESANDRIA ONLY once before. She hadn't liked it then, either.

Mountains rose like a wall of shattered iron to the east, the tops dusted in snow. Lines of smoke decorated the sky to the west as they passed another village, the third since entering Tollavon the day before.

The wolfskin fanned her frustration. A part of her had wanted to remain with the *Phillipa*, to stay and fight. If Snow wanted to reclaim her throne, she had to come to Tollavon eventually. This demon had beaten them twicc now. It wouldn't do so a third time.

She quelled the wolf's anger the best she could. She had been riding since she was five years old, and knew all too well how easily the animals sensed the tension of their riders. Her horse was jumpy enough about Talia's cape, and wouldn't have let her ride at all if not for Danielle's urging.

Danielle was right. They weren't ready to fight the demon. The cape might protect Talia from magic targeted at her, but it wouldn't stop the demon from opening up the earth to swallow her whole, or shattering trees to crush her. Nor would the cape help her if the demon chose to use Jakob as a hostage.

Talia wasn't the only one whose thoughts lingered behind. Danielle kept looking over her shoulder, her worry obvious even from a distance. She had barely spoken since leaving the harbor.

If Snow were here, she would have found a way to break the tension. An inappropriate joke or a ribald song. Even just prattling on about the white-barked trees along the road, the blue-tinged mushrooms growing on a fallen tree, or the techniques used to carve a path through the rock when the hills grew too steep. Talia saw no tool marks on the shoulder-high wall of dark, rippled stone which walled the road up ahead. No doubt it had been done with magic.

"I've finally come home." Gerta's expression was distant. She slowed her horse, allowing Talia to draw alongside. "I've returned to a land I've never actually seen. I could paint you every detail of our summer palace in the mountains, of the woods where my sister and I used to play, but I've never actually been there. None of it is real. All I have are memories."

Talia shrugged. "That's all any of us have."

Gerta stuck out her tongue, her expression identical to Snow's. "But yours actually happened." Her smile faded. "What do you think Snow intended for me as she cast that final spell, splitting me from herself?"

"Snow doesn't always plan things through," Talia said. "She acts. Her instincts are usually good."

"When she's not releasing demons from their prisons, you mean?"

"I said usually."

Gerta sighed. "How is this good? The demon took her, and I'm not strong enough to do anything about it. I'm not even sure I'm *real*."

Talia nudged her horse to the edge of the road. She reached out and broke off a small branch, which she bounced off of Gerta's shoulder. "You look real enough to me."

"I'm part of her. She gave me so many of her thoughts and memories. But I'm not her." Gerta lowered her eyes. Talia wasn't sure who she was trying to convince. "We're different. Different thoughts, different desires."

Talia stiffened. She had almost convinced herself Hephyra had been wrong about Gerta's feelings. "How long until we reach this witch?"

"Another day at most." Gerta guided her horse closer. "I don't know what Snow intended for me. But one way or another, she's going to want me back. If I'm to have such a short time on this world, why shouldn't I pursue the things I want?"

"You'll have time," Talia said uncomfortably. "Whatever happens, I'm sure Father Isaac can find a way to help you both."

Gerta stiffened. "Please don't lie to me. I know how you feel about her."

So much for pretending not to understand. Talia looked straight ahead. "Snow never wanted—"

"I'm not Snow."

Talia squeezed her knees, urging her horse forward. "You were a part of her."

"Maybe I'm the part of her that wanted you, that wanted to be able to return your feelings," Gerta said. "Did you know she considered taking a love potion for you?"

"What?" She spoke so sharply that Danielle turned around. Talia waved her on. Fighting to keep the anger and confusion from her voice, she asked, "When did— Why would she do that?"

"Because she trusted you."

"She never said anything." But of course, Snow wouldn't have discussed it. She would have just disappeared into her library and done whatever she wanted.

"She chose not to go through with it. Maybe because she knew how you'd react. Maybe because she was scared."

More than once Talia had daydreamed about herself and Snow, but she had known such imaginings would never be more than idle fantasies. Snow's preferences were obvious to anyone who knew her. What would Talia have done had Snow come to her, her emotions changed by magic? "It wouldn't have been real."

"You're an idiot."

Talia blinked. "What?"

"*I* was created by Snow's magic. Am I real?" Gerta was speaking louder now, earning a concerned look from Danielle. "Snow loved you. So much that she thought about changing who she was, just to be with you."

"Shut up." Talia's mind was already tormenting her with what could have been.

"Snow was afraid. I'm not."

"You're not her."

"Neither was Faziya." Gerta's voice dropped, taking on a new edge. "Snow gave me those memories, too, how you brought Faziya back with you from Arathea. How the two of you spent the weeks together like husband and wife newly wedded. How you moped for days after she left."

"I wasn't moping," Talia muttered. Had Snow actually been bothered by all of the time Talia spent with Faziya? If so, she had never let it show . . . but again, Snow wouldn't.

"Your time with Faziya showed her the kind of love she could have," Gerta said.

"And she chose not to," Talia said, trying to regain her balance. "Instead, she created you. Made you fall in love with me. Why?"

Gerta shrugged. "Maybe to make sure I stayed close to you, the one person she trusted to protect me. Or maybe she simply wanted us both to be happy."

Her voice was different than Snow's. Deeper, with a stronger Allesandrian accent, but the intonation of certain words was the same as her sister's. Her hair was flame, but with the impossible softness of Snow's locks. "So you would have me take advantage of a child little more than a week old?"

"Do I look like a child?" Gerta's lips quirked into a crooked smile. "I know you, Talia. Regret has been your bedmate for too many years, and I love you too much to see you alone and in pain."

"I'm not alone."

Gerta looked ahead. "Danielle has her prince. Beatrice is gone. Snow White has been taken from us all." She reached out, brushing Talia's arm with her fingertips. "Choose soon, Sleeping Beauty."

Desperation tinged her final words. Talia didn't answer, but her skin tingled with the memory of Gerta's touch.

Snow stood at the bow of the newly renamed *Snow Queen*, watching fog roll toward her from the two approaching ships. The winds had changed as she approached Tollavon, until even the most experienced sailor would be hard-pressed to tack into the harbor.

It was no matter. Their weather mages were mere gnats compared to the man who stood at Snow's side. Age had stolen much of Eminio Perin's stature. His head was hunched forward, and his hands were swollen at the knuckles, but he retained the presence of one used to dominating the stage. Snow had first heard him perform when she was six years old. He had stood before the queen and her court, a wig of soft auburn curls spilling down to his chest, as he sang a song of his own composition, glorifying Queen Curtana.

There were whispers about his private meetings with the queen, but few guessed his true profession. Perin was also a skilled wizard, and his fame as a singer gave him access to noble audiences throughout Allesandria. During the political slaughter known as the Purge, Rose Curtana's Deathcrows had executed dozens of nobles in their own homes. Perin had murdered eight that Snow knew of.

To most, the Deathcrows were but rumors, phantoms that fueled the nightmares of a generation of children. Some people refused to believe they had ever existed, but Snow knew better. Her mother had handpicked the deadliest of the Stormcrows to serve as her personal spies and assassins.

Only two of the queen's secret killers had ever been brought to justice for their actions. The rest had gone into hiding after Rose's death. But through the mirror,

Snow knew them all, including the man called The Butcher. Snow had no doubt she could have defeated him, but it had been easier to infect the young servant girl who answered the door of his mansion.

It was that girl who slipped a tiny shard of glass into the venison sausage Perin enjoyed for breakfast the following morning. Wrapped in illusion, the sliver had bypassed his protective charms. He had suspected nothing until the glass pierced the inside of his throat, and then he belonged to Snow.

Fog poured forth from the harbor, boiling up around the hull and spilling onto the deck. Magical, of course, seeking out other magic. It clung to the crew, tasting the splinters of enchanted glass within their flesh. It surged toward Snow, but a whispered spell chilled the air around her. The fog drifted lower, forming swirls of white frost on the deck.

It didn't interfere with her control. The crew worked in silence, struggling merely to maintain their position. Her men responded to her will without the crass disruption of shouted commands. It was both peaceful and efficient, and no mortal magic could tear her crew away from the beauty of their new queen. They were loyal unto death.

All save Jakob. Snow frowned as she glanced at her shoulder, where the prince shivered and fluffed his feathers for warmth. The boy knew no magic. His resistance came not from spellcraft, but from his very nature. Not for the first time, she considered killing him and taking what power she could, as her mother had once tried to do with her.

She shrugged and turned away. She would unravel Jakob's mystery soon enough. Through the fog, she could see the shadows of two ships moving closer. Cannons thundered, warning her to hold her position.

Snow glanced at the Deathcrow. "Master Perin, if you would?"

Perin spread his arms. His skin rippled and flexed as black feathers sprouted from his body. His clothes tore away, and he jumped onto the rail, talons of black steel digging into the wood. Lightning crackled from his wings. He launched himself into the air, a crow painted of ink and shadow, larger than the grandest eagle.

The approaching ships would likely kill him, but he would distract them long enough for Snow's magic to work. She reached into the pouch at her side, pulling out a mirrored triangle of glass no bigger than her palm. She had spent perhaps a third of the mirror's fragments to get this far, but there should be more than enough glass to reach King Laurence and deal with whatever opposition he offered. She held one corner of the shard between her finger and thumb and rapped it against the rail.

The glass broke, spilling fragments into the water below. Snow brushed her hands together, dusting the last of the shattered glass into the water. Blood welled from tiny cuts on her palms, but her skin healed even as she whispered a new spell.

As screams broke out from the other ships, courtesy of Perin, Snow's fragments rose from the water on wings of ice. This swarm was larger than the others Snow had created. With a wave of her hand, Snow sent her creations forth. They skimmed the waves toward the approaching ships.

Halfway there, the fog coalesced around her wasps. One by one, the magic holding them together began to unravel.

"Not bad," Snow said. Behind her, men raced to load the cannons. She concentrated, and the rest of her wasps plunged into the water where the fog couldn't reach them. They emerged again beyond the fog, and the shouts grew louder.

Most of her wasps were destroyed. She felt each death as fire magic melted her creatures, or gusts of wind smashed them to the deck, but it took only one, its wings shriveled away but its body intact, to crawl up a man's boot and lodge its stinger in his leg. Only one crewman to truly see the world's ugliness, and to turn against his fellows.

She pulled a second shard from her pouch and released another swarm. This time there was less resistance. She sensed Perin's sudden agony as he fell, wrapped in magical fire, but he had served his purpose. By the time the *Snow Queen* drifted into cannon range, there was little need for guns. She fired a broadside anyway, and holes exploded in the hull of the nearest ship.

Answering fire came not from the two Allesandrian ships, but from a third vessel sailing from the harbor. She approached quickly, wind filling her sails as she leaped forward to meet the *Snow Queen*. Even through the fading fog, Snow recognized the *Phillipa*.

The *Phillipa* approached at an angle, all of her port guns firing. The *Snow Queen* trembled as cannonballs tore through the hull. Captain Hephyra had never been one to turn from a fight.

The *Snow Queen* turned to port, but she was too slow to catch the *Phillipa*. Snow pulled the last of her wasps from the Allesandrian ships, sending them toward the *Phillipa*. They swarmed over Hephyra, who stood unflinching at the wheel. Hephyra's cudgel smashed several from the air, but others landed on her bare face and arms.

Snow blinked in surprise. The stingers wouldn't penetrate Hephyra's skin. She watched through the splinters of glass as Hephyra crushed another wasp with her bare hand.

Her wasps couldn't take Hephyra, and Snow wasn't entirely certain how well they would be able to turn the *Phillipa*'s crew against its captain. The dryad's fairy allure was almost as potent as Snow's own magic.

"Very well." Snow's wasps had taken the weather mages on the Allesandrian ships. In response to Snow's thoughts, the wind picked up, turning the *Snow Queen* about and launching her after the *Phillipa*.

As they closed, Snow climbed onto the rail and stepped out, summoning a cushion of air to lower her to the water. The sea froze beneath her feet. Waves broke against the ice, splashing her boots and legs as she walked. She smiled, casting yet another spell. The water hardened, forming armor of gleaming ice that encased her legs and moved higher.

So much power at her command. A week ago, simply fighting the fog sent by the Allesandrian weather wizard would have left her head throbbing from pain. Today, there were no limits to what she might do.

She allowed the *Snow Queen* to veer away. Shouts broke out on the *Phillipa* as someone spied her in the water.

Ice spread to cover her face. She concentrated, keeping the front of her helm as pure and clear as possible. Only the slightest ripple distorted her vision. Her heart slowed, each beat pounding harder, as if her blood itself were turning to ice. She turned her head, testing the armor. Ice scraped against ice, cracking and refreezing to allow her to move.

A crossbow bolt splashed into the water beside her. A second struck her stomach, gouging a chip from the armor. She brushed a gauntleted hand over the chip, and an instant later no sign of damage remained. A magical attack followed, but her armor deflected that as well.

Her wasps had stung only a few men on the *Phillipa*, but it was enough. She reached out to adjust the vision of the closest. She peered through his eyes until she spotted two men in Allesandrian uniforms, working to prepare another spell. Her slave killed them both before they knew what was happening.

As the crew reacted to this betrayal, Snow moved on to another crewman, showing him not a maiden of ice striding toward his ship, but a drowning girl. He threw down a line to help her even as one of his companions rushed to stop him.

By the time Snow's feet touched the main deck, her slave had fallen, but it no longer mattered. He had protected the line long enough for her to board. A sailor rushed her from the right, cutlass raised. The blade bounced from Snow's forearm. A single punch from her gauntleted fist sent him sprawling into the boats lashed to the deck.

She touched her hip, allowing her fingers to reach through the ice to the pouch at her waist. Most of her mirror shards were locked away on the *Snow Queen*, but she needed only a few. When she pulled her hand away, a knife of ice and broken glass followed. The blade was long as her forearm and frosted white. The edges were jagged glass, like silver teeth.

Another sailor grabbed her arm and tried to wrest the knife away, but the hilt was bonded to her grip. She clubbed him on the side of the head, then sliced her knife along his forearm, allowing a single sliver of glass to break away.

"Keep back." Captain Hephyra stood with a wooden cudgel in one hand. To Snow's eyes, she was all but glowing with rage and magic that flowed through her and the ship both.

"Tell me about the girl." The ice helm muffled Snow's words, but Hephyra appeared to understand.

"Funny. I never thought you were interested in girls."

Snow jabbed her knife. "Your crew belongs to me, body and mind. I can see their memories. Who is this girl Danielle and Talia brought along? She feels familiar. I want her."

"And I want the fairy queen's body fertilizing my roots, but we can't have everything we want, can we?"

Snow circled, studying Hephyra. Red scratches showed where the wasps had tried to sting her, but not one had penetrated to the blood. Or sap. Whatever it was that flowed through the dryad's veins. "Tell me where they've gone, and I'll—"

"Rot it all, just shut up and fight." The cudgel slammed Snow's knife out of the way, then struck her forehead, sending white cracks through Snow's vision. But the ice healed itself as fast as Hephyra could attack.

Snow's weapon should be strong enough to pierce even a dryad's skin, but every time she tried, Hephyra knocked her arm aside. Chips of ice flew from Snow's armor with every blow. Snow stepped sideways, trying to regain her balance, but Hephyra stayed with her. Had Snow been unprotected, her bones would have been shattered a dozen times over by now.

The spray of the waves gave her more than enough water to repair and maintain her armor. "What did they do to earn such loyalty?"

Hephyra smashed Snow's arm hard enough to spin her around. The next attack landed between Snow's shoulder blades, driving her to her knees. "I like the prince. I met him last fall." Heavy blows punctuated each sentence. "He said I was pretty, and he liked my ship. Also, you hurt my cat."

Snow swung at Hephyra's legs, but the dryad jumped back, avoiding the knife with ease. Snow yanked a second knife from her armor, keeping Hephyra away long enough to regain her feet.

"So what is this all about?" Hephyra asked. She wasn't breathing hard, but she pressed a hand to the capstan as though drawing strength from the wooden wheel. "What are you after in Allesandria?"

"Allesandria has always been corrupt. A place of chaos and bloodshed and ugliness." She thought back to the nobles who always fawned over her mother, scheming and squabbling like beasts to gain her favor. She had fled that ugliness for so brief a time, hiding in Roland's cabin in the woods, but there was no escape.

"So you mean to fix that by killing everyone?"

Snow glanced at the crew, who had gathered in a ring on the main deck. Hephyra remained free, but the crew were no longer hers. "Allesandria banished your kind. Lorindar enslaved you. Why do you care?"

"I don't, particularly." Hephyra's next blow struck the side of Snow's helm and made her vision sparkle, but it wasn't enough.

Snow dropped one knife and grabbed the end of the cudgel. Hephyra ripped it away, but not before frost began to spread over the wood. Snow smiled as the cold seeped into the weapon. The next time Hephyra attacked, the end of her cudgel broke away.

Hephyra cried out. "Damn, but that stung."

Snow raised her own weapon to attack, but the dryad lunged again, stabbing the pointed end of her broken cudgel into Snow's chest.

The wood gouged Snow's armor, driving her back until she hit the rail. Hephyra bore down, trying to force the point through Snow's chest. Cracks spread through the armor, but it held. "You never should have come after me on my own ship."

"My ship now." Snow thrust her remaining knife up, using both hands to sink the blade into Hephyra's stomach. The broken cudgel clattered to the deck. Snow pushed harder, until the hilt of her knife pressed against the dryad's skin.

She stepped back, yanking the knife free. Dark blood dripped more slowly than Snow would have expected, almost like syrup as it froze to her blade and gauntlet.

Hephyra staggered to the mainmast. One hand gripped her stomach. The other clung to the mast, smearing blood on the wood. Her lips pulled back in a smile. "Not yet it's not."

With a crack like thunder, the foremast toppled toward Snow. Lines snapped, and the yardarms broke away as it fell. Snow dove to one side, barely avoiding the mast as it crashed to the deck. The entire ship shuddered from the impact, and a mass of rope slammed Snow face-first to the deck. Crewmen screamed in pain, bones crushed by the impact. The mast had snapped one of the yards on the mainmast and torn through much of the rigging on the port side.

Snow pushed herself around, clawing her way through the ropes. The *Phillipa*'s lines were thin, but the sheer volume held her trapped. She slashed out with her knife, cutting everything within reach. She pulled herself up and began to crawl toward Hephyra. The dryad was still smiling, clinging to the mainmast. The ship was her tree, responding to her will. She could sink them all if she chose.

If she had time.

Snow flung her knife, pouring her magic into the mirrored shards in the blade. Moments later, Hephyra lay unmoving on the deck.

Snow's breath clouded the ice of her visor as she studied the damage. The *Phillipa* was useless as a sailing ship, the weight of the broken mast tilting her to port. Most of the crew were digging their way out from the mess, or doing their best to free the injured.

She glanced toward the harbor, where four more vessels were approaching through the fog. "Very well." She retrieved her knife from Hephyra's throat and turned it in her hand. The ice began to melt, forming into wings. One by one, the wasps took flight, their wings tinged pink by Hephyra's blood. Her knife hadn't held as many fragments as she might like, but it was enough to take the remainder of the *Phillipa*'s crew.

Snow climbed over the ruins of the fallen mast. Let them send as many ships as they liked. She had four ships now. The *Phillipa* was dying, but she could still serve Snow's purpose. At least one of the approaching ships would approach to investigate the damage and help the survivors.

"You banished me," she whispered as she left the ship, returning to the *Snow Queen* and her mirror shards. Her own cousin had signed the order that she be executed should she ever again set foot in her homeland. She remembered the false sympathy in Laurence's voice as he told her what he had done.

"I can't change their minds," he had said. His pale face was soft, his eyes shadowed. *"You murdered the queen. Burned her to death with your magic."*

"She killed Roland." Tears had choked Snow's words. She had expected to die, had prepared herself for that. Instead, she would live . . . but she would never again be permitted to set foot upon Allesandrian soil. *"She tried to kill me."*

"I know. But it's not enough. She had too many allies."

Allies like Ollear Curtana and Eminio Perin. Laurence had been too weak to fight them. In truth, it made no difference who sat on the throne. Allesandria had always been a land ruled by greed and cowardice.

Behind her, the crew of the *Phillipa* worked to reload the guns.

Chapter 11

TALIA STOOD IN ANKLE-DEEP SNOW AT the edge of the river, examining the skeletal birches on the opposite bank. "You said you'd be able to find the witch's cabin once we reached the river."

"I only came here once." Gerta paced along the shore. "Rather, Snow came here, but she imagined I was with her. To give her courage. She was nine years old, and was finally starting to believe some of the rumors about our mother. Snow followed her, hoping to learn the truth. Mother left the capital and headed east, following the river. I remember Noita's cabin being near the shore . . ."

"Near the shore of *which* river?" Talia scowled at the second, smaller stream, which veered away at an angle from the first. The wolf's senses were no help, since she didn't know what exactly she should be tracking.

Gerta cupped her eyes and peered at the sun. "I only saw the outside, but it was a small cabin, probably one room. The windows were colored glass, square panes of blue and red. I remember the smell of flowers, and two oak trees that grew to either side of the door. They reminded me of soldiers guarding the entrance."

"We could split up," Danielle suggested. "If we each follow one fork—"

Talia brushed the black fur of her cape. "This cape is the only thing stopping Snow from finding us. We stay together."

"Maybe someone else should take a turn wearing

that," Gerta suggested. "You've been fighting the wolf's influence for a long time without rest."

"I'm fine," Talia snapped. "Or I will be as soon as you find the damned witch."

Gerta smiled. "You see what I mean? That was testy, even for you."

Talia started to respond, but caught herself. Gerta was right. The magic of the cape gave her strength and speed, but at a cost. She wanted to hunt, to fight. "So how do we find it?"

"I was created from magic and memories." Gerta kicked a chunk of snow into the water. "I need to relive that memory."

"How?" asked Danielle.

Gerta unfastened the clasp of her cloak and handed it to Talia. "We were cold. Snow hadn't thought to bring extra clothes, and she was afraid to try magic, for fear that our mother would notice."

The back of Talia's neck tingled, and a burning smell indicated the presence of magic as Gerta paced a wide circle. Gerta traced her footsteps a second time, then a third, until a shadow began to form in the center.

Each pass solidified the illusion, painting a young girl with long black hair and cheeks red from cold. Talia's chest tightened as she recognized a much younger Snow White. She wore a thick blue dress, but her hands were bare, and she clutched her arms over her chest for warmth.

"Stay down," hissed the young Snow. "Do you want her to see us?"

Gerta crouched low, peering upstream at something Talia couldn't see. "Where do you think she's going?"

Snow flashed a gap-toothed grin up at Gerta. "Why? Are you scared?"

"I'm not!"

"You're afraid she'll throw you into a pot and boil the flesh from your bones, aren't you?" Snow poked Gerta's shoulder. "Then she'll raise you from the dead and make you dance every night, nothing but a skeleton with your bones clattering against the floor."

Danielle stepped closer. "She was a morbid child, wasn't she?"

"Look who raised her," said Talia.

Gerta appeared not to notice them as she huddled beside Snow, shivering. "I don't want her to lock us away again."

"She can't punish us if we don't get caught!" Snow cupped her hands to her mouth and blew, then jammed them back beneath her armpits. "She's probably just collecting ingredients for a potion, or something like that."

"Alone in the woods?" Gerta asked. "In the middle of winter?"

"Maybe she's discovered a fairy plot," Snow said eagerly. "She could be disguising herself as one of them to learn their secrets."

"There are no fairies in Allesandria," Gerta said primly.

Snow stuck out her tongue. "Shows what you know. I saw a pixie in the sky just last month."

"Did not."

"I did so!" Snow punched Gerta in the arm. "Come on, before we lose her."

They hurried upstream, following the larger branch of the river until they reached a stone bridge. Snow raced across, stopping only to toss a rock into the water. She and Gerta laughed and shushed each other as they ran through the woods.

The horses followed behind them, staying close to Danielle. Talia searched the trees, but the woods were quiet, save for the occasional crow.

"Maybe she's not even human," Snow said. "Maybe she's a monster who plans to eat us both!" Her laughter gave the lie to her fears, though Gerta appeared worried.

Snow and Gerta led them to a small clearing at a bend in the stream. The air was warmer here, and the snow was little more than a thin crust over the branches. The cabin was built back from the water, hidden by a thick grove of pines. The smell of magic made Talia's nose wrinkle. It smelled like old perfume, cloying and stale.

Snow dragged her sister down to crouch behind a fallen tree. Following their gazes, Talia could just make out a shadowy figure approaching the cabin door. Gerta's memory of Rose Curtana was tall and imposing, her body held straight as steel, her chin tilted upward.

Snow waited until her mother went inside, then tugged Gerta's hand. "Come on, let's go around back. Maybe there's a window."

Gerta began to tremble. "We should leave."

"Don't be such a polatto."

"Polatto?" Danielle whispered.

"Morovan slang for a coward," said Talia. "It means tail-flasher, after the deer who run away at the slightest sound."

Gerta yanked her hand away. "I don't want to see what's back there."

"I'm going." Snow stood and stepped out from the trees.

Gerta's voice rose. "Snow, please!"

Talia grabbed Gerta by the shoulder. "It's just a memory." Gerta stared through her, her eyes round. "Gerta, you've found it. You can end the spell."

Gerta shrieked. Talia slapped a palm over her mouth. The illusory Snow White had already vanished behind the cabin.

Danielle caught Gerta's arms. "Gerta, it's us."

"Wrap the edge of my cape around her," Talia snapped.

Danielle did so, and the worst of Gerta's trembling started to die as the cape's magic shielded her from her own illusions. Gerta spun, burying her face in Talia's shoulder.

"I'm sorry," Gerta said.

Talia watched the cabin, but the door hadn't opened. If Noita was still here, hopefully she hadn't heard Gerta's aborted scream.

"What happened?" asked Danielle, her voice gentle.

"We snuck around to the back, making our way to

Noita's garden." The worst of the panic had faded, but Gerta clung to Talia like a child woken from a nightmare. "There were three bodies, laid out in shallow graves. I thought Mother was helping Noita to bury them, but—" Another shudder cut off the rest of her words.

"You're safe," Danielle said. "You found the cabin."

Gerta pulled away. "I'm sorry." She turned toward the cabin. "I wanted to run away, but Snow stayed. She watched . . . we both did."

A growl built in Talia's chest. She yanked her sword from her belt and strode into the clearing. There was no light through the windows, nor smoke from the chimney. The steeply angled roof came almost to the ground. Dirt and frost obscured most of the color.

Brown ivy strangled the knee-high stumps that dotted the small yard. A pair of skeletal oaks, each an arm's length in diameter, stood to either side of the door.

"Are you certain this witch is still alive?" Talia asked.

"Even if she's not, there might be something inside that can help us," Danielle said. "She was a friend of Rose Curtana, after all."

The door creaked open. Talia stepped closer, sword ready.

The woman who emerged appeared to be in worse shape than her home. Layers of clothes and quilted blankets made her look like a shambling pile of mismatched laundry. Dirty laundry. Tangled white hair hung past her shoulders. Her face sagged loosely on her skull. Red-stained fingers clutched a thick wooden crutch as she limped into the yard. Talia could smell her magic from here, like moldy leaves in late autumn.

"Ermillina Curtana," she breathed, studying Gerta as though she were a painter's masterpiece. "Never imagined I'd see you again. What have you done to your hair, child?"

Gerta glanced at Talia as if for reassurance before answering. "Ermillina is my sister."

"You'd trespass on my land and lie to my face?" Noita clucked her tongue as she examined Gerta, who flinched. "For a princess, you've no manners whatsoever.

I pulled you from your mother's loins, girl. These hands cut the cord and wiped you down. I know you."

"Gerta's telling the truth," said Talia.

Gerta stepped closer to Talia. "My name is Rose Gertrude Curtana. I *am* Snow's sister. Sort of."

"The old queen had only the one child. Someone lied to you about your parentage, girl. Go home. There's nothing for you here."

"Did my mother bring you the bodies for your garden?" Gerta was hiding her fear the best she could, though Talia could hear the faint quaver in her voice. "Did she kill them for you, or did you cut their throats before laying them out in the earth?"

"What bodies?" Noita demanded, too quickly. "What stories have you been listening to?"

"I saw you." Gerta's courage seemed to grow as Noita shrank back. "Snow brought me. We watched as you planted your seeds in their bodies, pushing them deep into the flesh. Snow . . . she knew one of the boys, from the palace"

Noita sighed, sagging inward to lean more heavily on her crutch. "That was a long time ago. A different time." She shoved tangled hair from her face. "You do share her features . . ."

"I am Snow's sister."

Noita hobbled closer and reached out with one hand. "May I?"

Talia raised her sword in warning. Danielle drew her own weapon.

"I'll not hurt the girl. I only want to understand who she is."

Gerta nodded, but stayed close to Talia. Talia's nose wrinkled at the sharp scent of spellcasting.

Noita grunted in surprise. "Well that's impressive."

"What is?" demanded Talia.

Noita stepped back. "There are spells to split the soul, to send a part of yourself away. Dangerous, but useful for sending messages, digging out secrets, and so on. I've never heard of anyone casting such spells in quite this fashion, though."

"Snow liked to bend the rules," Talia said.

"Little Snow White," Noita whispered. "Not so little anymore, I imagine. I've not seen her in a lifetime. I've often wondered what became of her after she murdered her mother."

"Murdered?" Talia's hand tightened around the worn leather grip of her sword. "Rose Curtana ordered her killed. She hunted Snow down, murdered the man Snow loved, and would have done the same to her."

"Yet when they faced one another, Snow White was the one to walk away. How did she manage that? The girl had talent, but lacked discipline. Even with the best of luck, to defeat a witch like Rose . . ." Noita clucked her tongue.

"Snow beat her twice," Talia said. "The first time, she killed Rose's body. The second, Snow banished her spirit. Luck was not a factor."

"Luck is always a factor." Noita hunched her shoulders, her head poking forward like a turtle's as she turned her attention to Talia. She poked her crutch at Talia's cape. "What do you want from me?"

Talia swatted the crutch away.

"Please," said Danielle. "We need your help." Her words were slow, her tongue stumbling over the foreign words. She was far from fluent, but knew enough of the language to make herself understood.

"What do you know of Rose Curtana's magic mirror?" asked Gerta.

"Ah." Noita rested both hands on her crutch. Her body slumped, making her appear even older. "I should have known. You'd best come inside."

Talia went in first. If this was a trap, she had the best chance of overpowering it.

Noita stopped to stomp her feet on a woven mat in the doorway. Her home was small and sparsely furnished, but had a cozy feel. Thick blue curtains covered the windows. The fire in the hearth crackled merrily, but without smoke. Split firewood lined the wall beside the hearth, making Talia wonder where it had come from.

Noita certainly didn't look strong enough to gather it herself. Dried flowers hung from the ceiling. A few of the withered, papery petals fell to the floor as Noita shut the door behind them.

With four people, there was barely room to stand. Noita made her way to a rocking chair beside the fireplace, the only chair in the cabin. A square wooden table sat against the wall, a bowl of ripe cherries near the edge. A scattering of pits and stems explained the dark red stains on Noita's fingertips. "Please, help yourself."

Gerta started toward the table, but Talia caught her arm. "Ripe fruit in the middle of winter?"

Noita smiled. "You thought witchcraft was only good for cursing beautiful maidens?" She popped a cherry into her mouth and spat the seed onto the table. "So Snow White took her mother's mirror when she fled Allesandria. And now it's turned on her, yes?"

"She's taken my son," said Danielle.

"Never trusted that mirror." Noita pursed her lips. "Rose believed she could control it. She was arrogant. Convinced she was smarter and stronger than everyone else. Usually she was, but not this time. That mirror killed her, you know."

"What do you mean?" asked Gerta.

"'Who's the fairest of them all?' A simple enough question, right?" Noita bit another cherry, and a rivulet of dark juice ran down her chin. She blotted it on her sleeve. "It's a matter of opinion though, isn't it? A farm boy looks at his first love and proclaims her the most beautiful woman in the world. An educated city man looks at her and sees a bumpkin, plain and dirty. Was young Snow White truly the fairest in all the land? Some might say so, but what does a mirror know of beauty? Why did it choose her, unless it knew what would come of that choice?"

Talia rested her hands on the edge of the table, which creaked from her weight. "We know about the demon."

Noita's voice was distant. "I warned Rose against it, but she wanted the power. We never should have brought that damned creature into this world. It's broken free, hasn't it?"

"It took Snow," said Danielle.

"Then Snow White is gone." Noita's words, spoken so matter-of-factly, burrowed into Talia's chest.

"You helped my mother imprison the demon," Gerta said.

"Yes, though the price was a blot on both our souls." She rolled another cherry between her fingers. "I've no doubt it remembers what I did." She sighed and sank back in her chair. The creak of her rocking was the only sound, until Talia thought she might have fallen asleep.

"Noita?" Gerta asked.

"I warned her," Noita said. "This was no lesser creature, but a true demon, all but immortal. Her mirror was a thing of genius, but it couldn't endure forever. I looked to the future, and I saw what would happen when that mirror failed."

"What did you see?" asked Talia.

"My death." Noita licked her lips, and her gaze flicked to the back door of the cabin. "Fire and chaos. Death and madness, spreading throughout Allesandria. Even working together, Rose and I barely had the strength to trap the demon. Now that it's free, with Ermillina's power added to its own, I can't—"

"She took my son," Danielle interrupted. "You helped bring this creature into our world. You *will* help us to stop it."

Noita started to answer, then sighed. "You're right. I was part of the ritual. I share the responsibility." She rose and moved to the rear of the cabin. Wood scraped against wood as she pulled open the back door, revealing a view so different Talia thought she might be looking through a magical portal.

A thin layer of snow crusted a grass path through a flower garden in full bloom. Delicate violets circled a stand of cherry trees. Lilies and snapdragons swayed together in the wind. Sunflowers as tall as Talia bordered the doorway like guardsmen. The smell of magic made her eyes water.

The plants seemed unaffected by the cold. Not a single leaf or petal marred the ground. The snow crunched beneath Talia's feet as she followed Noita into the garden. Talia paused after a few steps, remembering what Gerta had said. How many bodies had fertilized these seeds?

"It's too still." Danielle was looking about. "There are no animals. No insects. It's like a painting or a sculpture, an imitation of the real thing."

"Imitation? Pah." Noita limped to the center of the garden. "Flowers wither and die at the first touch of frost. Trees shed their leaves, sleeping through winter. This is better. My magic flows through this garden, giving it the strength to survive. This garden is as well-protected as the king's palace."

"They're magical." Gerta pressed thumb and forefinger to a sunflower's stalk. "Each flower is enchanted, fed by the flesh and blood of the dead."

"All plants feed on the dead, absorbing their strength. It's the natural course of things." Noita leaned against an apple tree and rubbed her leg. "You've seen the mirror, the vines worked into the platinum frame? That was my magic, strengthening the mirror's hold. But the spells were Rose's. Even then, I wasn't strong enough to imprison this demon on my own."

Talia's eyes were still blurry, and her nose had begun to drip. The floral smell of magic was thick as smoke. It was as bad as being in Snow's library when she was experimenting with new perfumes.

"You helped Rose," Gerta protested, covering a yawn with one hand. "You have to know the spells she used. I could work with you to—"

"Your mother was always possessive of her secrets. You think she would share this kind of power, even with me?" Noita hobbled to a small stone bench, all but hidden by green, teacup-shaped flowers Talia didn't recognize. "The fruits of this garden have shown me the future. I foresaw your visit weeks ago, all save your wolf-clad friend. And I've seen what happens if we try to fight this demon."

Talia started forward, but something tugged her leg. Thorns tore her trousers as rose vines spiraled up her calf. She pulled harder, trying to wrench the vine from the earth.

Gerta had already collapsed, asleep. Danielle managed a single step, but the vines clung to her leg. She swung her glass blade through one of the vines, and then the sword slipped from her grasp and she fell.

Talia ripped her leg loose, even as more roses reached up to grab her other foot. A swing of her sword sent rose blossoms tumbling to the ground.

The hell with this. Talia stabbed the sword into the dirt, pulled a dagger, and flipped it in her hand to throw.

"Kill me, and they'll never awaken," Noita warned. "The spell that holds them in sleep can drag them down into death just as easily."

White flowers tinged with pink covered the branches of the apple tree. Those flowers hadn't been in bloom when they first entered the garden. That tree was the source of Noita's spell.

A growl built in Talia's chest. Those were apple blossoms. "Snow's mother paralyzed her with a poisoned apple. She got that apple from you, didn't she."

Noita shrugged. "There are many poisons—"

"Poisons that work with the first bite? That could overcome Snow before she cast a single spell? I know poisons, witch. None work so quickly." Another vine caught her wrist. Talia jerked free, barely feeling the thorns that bloodied her skin. Had Noita been close enough, Talia would have snapped her neck with her bare hands.

"Snow is gone." Noita stood, jabbing her crutch at Talia. "You should be more concerned about the friends you have left. Surrender that cape, or they die."

That cape was the only thing protecting her from Noita's magic. Talia bared her teeth, but hesitated. The others' breathing had grown shallower. Noita wasn't bluffing.

Talia dropped the knife and reached up to unfasten the red cape. The vines now trapped her legs up to her thighs. She yanked the cape free of the thorns. In a single motion, she reversed the cape and pulled it tight around her body, so the wolf's fur was on the outside.

Pain crushed her body, forcing her to her hands and knees. Thorns stabbed her skin as her limbs reshaped themselves into those of the wolf. She snarled, tugging and jerking as the vines tried to close around her. New strength pumped through her legs. She ripped one of her rear legs free, then twisted to bite the vines holding the other. With a snarl, she lunged forward, tearing the last few vines from the earth.

She crossed the garden in an eyeblink, knocking Noita backward over the bench. Before Noita could do more than open her mouth, Talia's fangs were upon her neck.

The wolf was fully roused now, urging Talia to clamp down and rip out the witch's throat, to kill her for her betrayal and for what she had done to Snow all those years ago. Instead, Talia simply snarled.

Noita's eyes were huge. Withered fingers grabbed Talia's muzzle, trying without success to force the jaws open. Rose vines punched through the earth, twining their way up Talia's legs. Talia bit harder, tasting blood.

Noita made a squeaking sound and raised her hands in surrender. She gestured toward the apple tree, and Talia saw the blossoms begin to close.

The others woke as swiftly as they had fallen. Danielle grabbed her sword and walked over to place the tip at Noita's throat. *"We need her alive, Talia."*

Danielle's words, spoken without sound, pierced the wolf's rage. Grudgingly, Talia backed away, licking blood from her chops. She sat back on her haunches and used her teeth to dig at the seams of the wolfskin, peeling it from her body. The process was a painful one, but it was the sound that bothered her the most. Joints popped and bones ground together, until Talia was herself again, curled on her side and panting for breath. She used one hand to switch the cape back around, wrinkling her nose at the smell of wolf sweat.

"My visions have shown me what's to come," Noita said despondently. "What the demon will do to this land. What it will do to me if it discovers I've helped you."

"So you'd do nothing?" Danielle asked. "You'd watch as this thing you helped bring into our world now seeks to conquer it? You saw Rose Curtana's cruelty. Imagine Allesandria under the rule of a demon queen."

Noita's hands shook. "I told Rose what could happen if this thing were to escape. With Snow's power added to its own . . ."

Talia retrieved her weapons. "What does the demon want?"

"Fear. Chaos. Death." Noita started to rise, but Danielle's sword remained at her neck, keeping her in place. "This is a creature of hell, a torment meant for the damned. I saw Rose after she bound the demon. It touched her only briefly, but that one touch haunted her. She was never a kind woman, but the demon sapped any remaining joy from her soul."

Talia thought back to the last time she had seen Snow, at Whiteshore Palace. The demon had crushed the merriment from her eyes, carving away her happiness and leaving her hollow. How long would it take her to rebuild herself, once this demon was destroyed?

Anger surged through her, and this time she didn't fight. She gave herself to the wolf, shoving past Danielle to seize Noita by the throat. She hauled the witch to her feet. "These visions of the future. Did they show what I'll do to you if you don't help us?"

Noita swallowed. "They didn't show *you* at all. Only your friends. That cape of yours shields you from my visions."

The terror in Noita's eyes almost made Talia pity her. Then she looked to the apple tree and thought of Snow. "If I can change what happened here, I can change the rest of it." Her fingers tightened. The wolfskin gave her strength, and Noita was an old woman. It wouldn't take much effort to snap her bones.

"Talia." Danielle caught her arm. "*Talia.*"

Noita's fingers dug at Talia's hands. She was wheezing, trying to force air past the slowly constricting grip on her neck.

Talia took a deep, shuddering breath, and released

her. The witch fell, gasping and holding her neck. "The spirit in this cape may not be as powerful as this demon, but there's a very important difference. The wolf is here, right now. And it doesn't like you very much."

"I know Rose cast her spell at the winter palace." Noita's face was pale. "I merely helped with the preparations. I never saw the summoning circle, but a circle that powerful would leave traces. It might still be there. A hidden room, maybe? Rose had many secrets, but your witch might be able to find it."

Gerta broke a rosebud from a vine and twirled it in her fingers. "I have a better idea. If your magic can show you visions of other times and places, perhaps it can show us what we need to see."

"Rose warded her secrets against scrying," Noita protested.

"But Rose is dead," said Gerta. "With my magic added to yours, maybe we can finally get ahead of this demon."

Chapter 12

IN ANOTHER LIFETIME, SNOW MIGHT have found this fun.

The stolen sleigh all but flew up the pass, steel runners scraping over ice and stone alike. Prince Jakob clung to her side. Frightened as he was of her, the prospect of skidding from the trail and tumbling down the mountain terrified him even more.

Snow mentally lashed her ghost mounts to greater speed. She had killed the four reindeer at the height of their fear, fear which they carried into death. The reindeer's spirits would never tire, but their fear gave them speed.

"They'll kill us both, you know." Snow used magic to make her words carry over the sound of the sleigh. "If Lord Duino could, he'd rip us from the pass or pull the snow from above to crush us. His fear is such that he would happily murder an innocent child if it meant he would be safe from me."

Allesandria's army was second to none in its magical capabilities, but an army was little use against a small, mobile enemy. Snow had once described her homeland as a relatively small nation. While Allesandria was many times the size of Lorindar, much of that land was sparsely populated, particularly the mountain ranges . . . meaning there were so many places to hide.

How many hunters had Laurence deployed after Snow fought her way through his forces at the harbor?

She could feel them searching for her, some scrying through crystals or pools, others watching through the eyes of the birds and other animals. But they had an entire nation to search, and mirror magic was particularly good for deflecting attention.

"What do you say, Jakob? Should we let Duino's hunters catch us? Let them kill us both with their magic? Or do we destroy them before they can strike?"

"I want to go home."

Snow made a *tsk* sound. "You think home is any safer? This was my home, Jakob. There are those in Lorindar who have plotted your death since the day you were born. Just as the Nobles' Circle did with me. Some will act from greed, others from simple fear of what you are. You can allow them to threaten you and drive you into hiding, but you'll never truly escape. Or you can act to protect yourself."

Far below, smoke rose from the town built into the mountainside at the edge of the lake. They had ridden for much of the morning, but it was a slow climb. The homes were built close together, reminding her of animals crammed into a pen. Their bright colors were a futile attempt to counter the whiteness of winter.

The ground thrummed like the string of a lute. Small rocks and chunks of ice tumbled down, clattering against the sleigh. One struck Snow's shoulder. Another hit her arm hard enough to bruise even through her cape. Duino was getting closer.

"Choose, Princeling. Shall we fight those who would kill us? If we do nothing, I promise we will both be dead before nightfall. Are you ready to die, Jakob?"

Jakob shook his head.

"Then you choose to fight. Very good." The ghosts of the reindeer leaped forward, straining against their invisible bonds.

Duino was old, even for Allesandria. Some said he had lived more than a century, and had spent most of that time studying magic. Though his body was frail as ash, he could project his spirit forth with all the strength and vigor of a young man. In such form, he was immune to the sting of Snow's wasps, as were those who marched beside him. Snow had counted more than twenty astral warriors running after her as swiftly as any horse.

She could circle back to the town to attack his physical form, but he would have prepared for that. She had no way of knowing which house hid his body, and by the time she found him and broke through his defenses, they would be upon her.

She glanced upward. From the strength of the tremors, Duino had recruited help, perhaps even the king's own Stormcrows. She toyed with the idea of turning those tremors against them, trying to pull down the mountainside to bury Duino and the rest of the town. But it would take time, and Duino was too close.

The sleigh slowed again. Snow put a hand on Jakob's shoulder. He was trembling like a frightened kitten. "Do you know what a soul jar is?"

He shook his head.

"I learned of them from a mermaid." Yet another betrayal, one that had almost cost Snow her life. She searched the sleigh for anything that would work as a jar, but found nothing.

She climbed out of the sleigh and closed her right eye. The sliver of glass embedded within the left enhanced her vision as she watched for Duino's approach.

The spell at the heart of a soul jar was the mystical equivalent of spider silk, stretching out to entangle rogue spirits and draw them into a cocoon of magical energy. The physical jar merely anchored the web. Lacking such a jar, Snow would have to use an alternate anchor.

She could see them now, their spiritual forms like animals spun from fog. Animal spirits were an eastern innovation, one Duino had apparently mastered. Duino himself was a stallion charging up the trail. An eagle flew above. Snow spied a wolf, a hunting dog, a pair of apes, even one of the great maned cats from farther south.

Snow opened her mouth, and a thread of magic snapped out from her throat to intercept Duino. He reared as the thread lashed round his neck. His companions drew back in alarm. A snake tried to bite the thread, but merely entangled itself in the trap.

Duino's struggles tickled deep inside Snow's chest, where she had anchored her spell. It felt as though she had swallowed something alive, something which struggled to crawl free. But Duino was spirit, whereas Snow was flesh. Bracing herself, she pulled the thread back.

Duino changed tactics. Magic rippled along their connection, trying to tear Snow's own spirit free of her body. It might have worked, had there been only a single spirit within her.

More threads flew from her mouth, trapping the other souls as they tried to free their leader. They sent what spells they could, and Snow used the mirror's power to reflect them back. Through the magic of the soul jar, she shared their pain as the spells crackled through those who had cast them.

The snake was close enough now for Snow to see the spirit's true form within, that of a young woman missing her left hand. Snow opened her mouth wider, and the spirit disappeared down her throat.

It was a curious sensation, like swallowing air on the coldest day of winter. She felt . . . bloated.

Duino was next. He tried one final spell, seeking to split his spirit like a lizard shedding its tail, but Snow's magic was too strong.

She could hear their screams, taste their thoughts.

"You spoke with Laurence," she whispered, seeing that exchange through Duino's eyes, hearing the king's promises to send reinforcements. But Duino refused to wait. He had to protect his people, to put an end to the chaos Snow's minions spread through his land.

Duino was believed to be a good man who had devoted his life to serving his people, but Snow was privy to his innermost desires, the secrets he hid even from himself. In his heart, Duino was as rotted and maggot-ridden as the rest, no matter how pure he appeared from without.

"You can't!" Duino's voice, strained and desperate as he glimpsed her plans from within. *"Allesandria—"*

"Has earned its fate," Snow said firmly. She closed her eyes, allowing him to see more.

"So alone . . ." Duino's struggle faded. Was that *pity* in his words?

Snow reached out, feeling those touched by her mirrors. Hundreds now, and soon they would be thousands. "Not anymore."

With a thought, she tightened the threads and crushed the two captive spirits to nothingness. Her body belched in response, and then she was drawing the rest into herself.

Ever since an unexpected journey to Arathea months before, Danielle had been spending more time with her tutors, trying to learn the languages of her neighboring kingdoms. She was nowhere near as fluent as Talia or Gerta, but she was making progress. Not enough to follow all of Noita's conversation, but she recognized the word "flowers" when Noita gestured toward a cluster of tall, flame-colored tiger lilies.

"She's telling Gerta to pick a flower and inhale its scent," whispered Talia. Like Danielle, she kept her weapon ready. "They show the future, and might help us to see what we must do."

"Have her go first," said Danielle. "To prove it's not another trap."

Talia barked another order. Noita sagged and walked over to pick one of the flowers. She brought it to her nose and breathed deeply.

"My garden." Tears filled Noita's eyes. "My beautiful garden."

Danielle couldn't follow the rest. Noita wept, repeating the same phrase over and over.

"'She destroyed it all,'" said Gerta. "I think she's talking about Snow. Noita meant to hide here, but Snow finds her. Because of us." Gerta used a small knife to cut another flower. She pressed her nose to the petals and inhaled. She frowned, then tried again. "I think I have a bad flower."

"What do you see?" asked Talia.

"Nothing." Gerta dropped the flower and cut a new one from the ground. "Maybe Snow's magic is blocking the vision. There's nothing but blackness."

Talia snarled something at Noita, whose face softened.

"You poor girl." Even though Danielle didn't understand most of the words, she could hear the sadness in Noita's voice as Talia continued to translate. "Snow might be able to hide herself, but there's only one reason the flowers would fail to show anything at all. The flowers show your future. Continue upon this road, and you have none."

Gerta paled. She stared at the flower, then inhaled again, more deeply this time.

"Death clouds everything around it," Noita said. "Not even your mother was strong enough to foresee her own end."

Gerta flung the flower away. "Talia—"

"Those flowers also told Noita she'd be able to capture us, remember?" Talia said. "Magic is unreliable at its best, and she doesn't strike me as the most trustworthy witch."

"Let me try," said Danielle.

"You're sure?" Noita clucked her tongue. "Like your friend, you might not want to see the truth."

Danielle used her sword to cut another tiger lily. Without a word, she lifted it to her face until the petals stroked her nose.

"Concentrate on the one you want to see," Talia said, continuing to relay Noita's words. "Your will and focus guide the visions."

Danielle sniffed the flower. The garden melted away, revealing walls of ice. Fog carpeted the floor. Jakob sat playing with flat shards of ice, so clear they looked like glass. His skin was pale, his lips and fingernails blue from the cold, but he wasn't shivering.

"What is it?" Talia's voice, though Danielle barely heard her. Talia sounded as though she were shouting from a great distance.

"Jakob. He's alive." Tears dripped down her cheeks. The fog shifted enough for her to glimpse the floor, made of broken tiles of ice so smooth she could see her son's reflection.

Jakob's fingers were cut and bleeding, but he continued to rearrange the pieces of ice, his round face wrinkled in concentration. His breathing was far too slow.

"Jakob, it's me!" In the past, Jakob had sometimes been able to sense when Danielle looked in on him through one of Snow's mirrors, but not today.

"Where are they?" Talia's voice, hard and emotionless.

Danielle's vision shifted. She spotted Snow sitting on a throne of ice, watching Jakob. Snow had always been pale, but now the red had faded from her lips and cheeks. Even her eyes had lost much of their luster. Her hair was swept back, and she wore a crown of crystal or ice. Animated flakes of snow and glass flew about, haloing their mistress.

"It's a palace of ice," Danielle whispered. Green light shimmered and danced beyond windows of clear ice.

Snow rose from her throne. Her lips moved, but Danielle couldn't make out what she was saying. Snow's crown brightened like the sun, filling Danielle's sight until she turned away.

A scream shattered the fading vision. Danielle spun, flinging the flower away and grabbing her sword.

"What is it?" Talia asked.

Danielle wiped her eyes, trying to will her surroundings into focus. The flower on the ground had wilted, the petals wrinkled and brown. "I heard . . . I saw Jakob. He's alive."

"What else did you see?" Noita asked.

"There was a scream. I don't know whose." She could still hear the sound, sharp with fear and pain. "I glimpsed Snow. She was so pale."

"So Noita wasn't lying about the flowers." Gerta stared at the tiger lily in her hands.

"I'm sorry, Gerta." Was it Snow who killed her? For all she knew, that could have been Gerta's scream.

"The flowers show what *might* come," Talia said firmly.

"If I'm to die—"

"Shut up," snapped Talia. "You're not dying."

Danielle said nothing. Could they really change Gerta's fate? What if she refused to accompany them, trying to save herself by avoiding Snow White? Danielle could order her to return to the *Phillipa*, send her back to Lorindar, but who was to say Snow wouldn't intercept her before she reached the harbor? And could they find Jakob without Gerta's help?

Danielle spun around. Despite the garden's impressive size, she suddenly felt closed in. She needed out, to be somewhere the birds sang and the wind blew.

"That doesn't give us enough." Talia grabbed one of the last tiger lilies. "We have to know how to stop her."

"Wait," said Danielle, but Talia was already inhaling the flower's scent. Her pupils grew large, and her features went slack.

Relief surged through Danielle, followed immediately by guilt. She had been afraid Talia would see nothing, as Gerta had. Danielle waited, her attention split between Noita and Talia. For Noita's part, the strength seemed to have left her. She rested on her bench, body folded over her cane as she watched.

"What do you see, Talia?" asked Danielle.

"King Laurence. He's bleeding. Snow cut him with her mirror." Talia shook herself, then swore in Arathean. "If she controls the king of Allesandria, she'll have one of the largest armies in the world at her disposal."

"We'll send word to Laurence," said Danielle. "How far to the palace?"

"Less than a day's ride." Gerta sounded distant. Her obvious fear jabbed Danielle's heart. If they continued upon this path, Gerta would die.

No . . . Noita had foreseen their arrival, but she hadn't seen Talia. She hadn't predicted this. That future had already been changed. So could Gerta's.

"What do we do about her?" Talia asked, waving her blade at Noita.

"Leave her." Danielle pushed open the door. She called out with her mind, summoning their horses to the front of the cabin. She called to the birds as well, to carry a message to King Laurence.

Talia hadn't moved. "There's kindness, and there's stupidity. She meant to kill us all. She helped Rose to poison Snow. She—"

"She failed," Danielle said. "And she's seen what will happen to her if we don't stop Snow." She gestured to Noita, who remained slumped on the bench. "She needs us to succeed."

"Is that how you mean to rule Lorindar?" Talia asked. "Oh, sure, she tried to assassinate the queen, but that's all right so long as she doesn't do it again."

"Which is more important, punishing her for what she tried to do, or saving Jakob and Snow?" *And Gerta, if they could.*

Danielle stomped through the cabin without waiting for an answer.

Talia could feel the pounding of her horse's blood, fear making it pulse faster than usual. Even a day after leaving Noita's cabin, with Danielle doing her best to calm the beast and allow Talia to ride, its eyes were wide, and it twitched and shook its head as if wanting to toss her free. Talia had switched horses twice, simply to make sure they didn't exhaust themselves through terror.

"I could wear the cape for a time," Gerta said, riding alongside.

Talia grabbed the front of the cape, instinctively pulling it tighter. "I'm all right."

"Liar. I saw you scowling at Danielle when we left. The cape makes you tense. You're always hunting."

"Better the hunter than the prey," Talia said. "Danielle was right. Noita's no threat anymore." Though it wouldn't have taken much time at all to snap the witch's neck and fling her broken body to the ground.

"Will the cape shield us if you take it off?" Gerta

asked. "Tuck it away in your pack until we reach Kanustius."

Talia tried to keep her annoyance in check. Did Gerta really think she hadn't thought of that? "The cape has no life of its own."

"So let me take a turn." Gerta tossed her hair back, exaggerating the movement. "It doesn't really match your complexion anyway."

Talia laughed. "All of your magic combined with the wolf's temper? That's a bad idea if ever I've heard one."

"You're right, of course. Far better to let it continue fanning *your* temper until you lash out and kill one of us." Gerta cocked her head. "Though you're rather sexy when you smolder. It's the eyes."

Talia flushed. "Stop that."

"Make me." Gerta's brows wagged, but then she sighed and looked away. "I'm sorry. I only thought, since the cape hid you from Noita's visions . . . maybe if I were wearing it, that would explain why I saw nothing of my own future."

Her matter-of-fact tone made Talia flinch. "Noita couldn't see me, but she saw the rest of us. The cape might hide you, but from what Noita said, you still should have seen *something*."

"So now you take Noita's word?" Gerta snapped. "When did you become so trusting?"

"Gerta—"

"Or is it just me you don't trust?"

Talia stared heavenward. "Can you blame me? You showed up in the most secure room of the palace—"

"Naked," Gerta added, her anger vanishing as quickly as it had come.

"Yes, naked." Talia scowled. "You were conjured by Snow White, who then kidnapped the prince and set off to conquer a nation. We don't know how you were made, or to what end. Would you trust you?"

"I think so," Gerta said slowly. "I have a very trustworthy face."

Gerta's expression was so serious Talia couldn't help but laugh again. She nudged her horse sideways, grabbed a handful of snow from a low-hanging pine branch, and flung it at Gerta. Gerta ducked, grinning.

Unbidden, Talia found herself thinking back to those first weeks in Lorindar, and her growing awkwardness and confusion around Snow White. Talia had been young, lost, and furious with the world, but when Snow smiled at her, all of that had melted away.

"What do you think will happen to me if Snow dies?" Gerta asked softly.

Talia's shoulders tightened. "She's not going to—"

"You don't know that." Gerta nudged her horse ahead, squeezing through a narrow spot on the path where the trees crowded together. "We're connected. Does that mean whatever happens to her will happen to me as well? Or can I survive alone, independent of my sister?"

"I've never understood magic," Talia said, troubled by the direction of Gerta's thoughts. How far would she go to protect herself? "What do you know of King Laurence?"

Gerta gave her an amused look, as if she knew exactly what Talia was doing. But she played along with the change of topic. "He was young when we met him. Cute, but a little too skinny for Snow's taste. He grew up east of the mountains. The politics weren't quite as nasty in eastern Allesandria, away from the capital. He's a skilled wizard. Not as powerful as Snow, but trained since the time he could walk, like all nobles."

"I hate magic," Talia muttered.

Gerta laughed. "Says the woman blessed by fairies, wearing an enchanted cloak while riding horses charmed by her friend."

Talia grabbed another handful of snow.

"Allesandria was founded by magic," Gerta continued, smiling. "It's in our blood. People from throughout the world come here to study spellcasting."

"Talia!" Danielle had crested the hill. She was staring at a cloud of smoke in the distance, black against the gray sky.

Talia squeezed her knees, urging her horse forward. When she reached the top of the hill, she swore.

Kanustius, capital city of Allesandria, was on fire.

The flames spread in a perfect circle around the city, burning as tall as the palace walls back home. The flames were purple at the base, turning blue higher up. Violet sparks popped and flew from the ground.

"It's all right," Gerta said. "It's supposed to do that."

Danielle stared. "They set the city on fire on purpose?"

"Not the city. Only the wall." Gerta pointed to the flames. "When we get closer, you should be able to make out the fence within the flames."

"A fence?" Talia squinted. "Why?"

"Stone walls can be scaled," Gerta said cheerfully. "It's much harder to climb a wall that's on fire."

"It wouldn't do much against cannons or catapults," Talia said.

"Kanustius has other defenses." Gerta gestured. "Two fences of flame circle the city. Each fencepost generates its own flame, adding to the wall. The Stormcrows can also manipulate the individual flames, sending them out like weapons to defend the city. In wartime, the entire outer ring can be used to repel attackers while the inner ring protects the people. Cannons and black powder don't last long here. Nor catapults, for that matter."

"Stormcrows?" asked Danielle.

"The magical branch of the king's army," said Talia. "Nasty fighters, but they rely too much on their spells."

"How do you know that?" Danielle shook her head and held up a hand. "Never mind. I don't want to know."

"So what triggered the defenses?" asked Talia. There was no sign of any army. What she could see of the clearing around the city appeared calm. Judging from the size of the smoke cloud, the gates had been burning for at least an hour.

Gerta's smile faded. "Snow. They know she's coming, if she's not already here. Allesandria doesn't take chances when it comes to magical attacks."

"Will the wall stop her?" asked Danielle.

"I doubt it. She's of royal blood." Gerta sucked her lip as she stared down at the city. "The flame will burn anyone she brings with her, though. She'll be able to enter the city, but there are other guardians protecting the palace. She won't have an easy time reaching the king."

Talia nudged her horse down the path. "Whatever secrets your mother left in the palace, we need to find them soon."

Chapter 13

DANIELLE HAD GROWN UP WITHIN SIGHT of Whiteshore Palace. She had visited most of Lorindar, as well as four other nations, since her marriage to Armand. But Kanustius was easily twice the size of any city she had seen.

From the hills she could just make out the palace at the center. The architecture was similar to the palaces of Hilad, a design that always reminded Danielle of oversized toadstools pressed together. Every domed roof shone like gold. Given Allesandria's wealth, it wouldn't have surprised her to learn it really was gold.

The burning city wall blocked her view as they approached. Back home, small homes and businesses had sprung up outside of the city, crowded most closely at the gates, but here the clearing was empty. The snow had melted, turning the ground to mud. Steam rose from the earth nearest the wall. She could see stone towers positioned beyond the flames, little more than dark shadows. There would be lookouts watching the roads from within, no doubt. "How do we get inside? There's no gate."

"There is, but we can't reach it unless the Stormcrows decide to let us through." Gerta pointed to where the road met the fire. "You can see it behind the flames."

Danielle pushed back her hood and wiped sweat from her brow. She squinted until she spied the rectangular framework in the flames. "You said the fire could be used as a weapon against intruders?"

"They say the wizard who founded Kanustius slew a hundred dragons by magic. He buried their skulls in a ring around the city, binding them to protect all who lived within." Gerta watched the flames as if entranced. "I remember Mother ordering the fires raised once, when we were young. We were returning from the mountains, and she had heard rumors of a Morovan assassin. I remember thinking how pretty the sparks were. Snow used her magic to call one to our carriage, thinking to keep it as a pet. She burned a hole in her cushion."

"What will it take to persuade them to admit us?" asked Talia. Her gaze flicked from one tower to the next as they left the protection of the trees. "They'll have been watching us ever since we crested that last hill."

Talia's horse whinnied and stepped sideways. Eyes wide, tail compressed against her hindquarters, the mare backed away from the wall, ignoring Talia's commands.

"Easy," Danielle whispered. She stroked her own horse's neck. She didn't blame them for being afraid. If the heat was this intense, how much worse would it become when they tried to pass into the city? Only Gerta appeared unaffected, her hands tucked into her sleeves for warmth as she stared at the wall.

"We can walk from here." Gerta dismounted and stepped away from her horse.

"Wait here, please," Danielle said to the horses as she and Talia followed suit.

They started toward the gate, but made it only a short distance further before the heat grew too intense. Talia grimaced and said, "Subtle they're not."

"You thought we'd simply waltz into the city to request an audience with the king?" asked Danielle.

"You did tell him we were coming, didn't you?" Talia cupped her hands to her mouth, then froze.

"What's wrong?" asked Danielle.

Talia tilted her head to one side and sniffed the air. "Magic."

Gerta laughed. "The three-story wall of blue fire gave it away, did it?"

Talia didn't smile. She turned around, squinting at the trees behind them. She reached under her cape.

Gerta's smile vanished as she grabbed Talia's wrist. "Are you mad? Draw weapons here, in full view of the towers, and you're dead. Not even you can dodge the Stormcrows' magic."

Talia scowled, but withdrew her hand. "So what would you suggest we do about them?" She pointed to the woods.

These wasps were bigger than the ones Danielle remembered, their buzz lower in pitch. She counted seven streaking from the trees. "Get as close to the wall as you can. They won't like the heat."

The horses ignored her. Between Talia, the wall, and the wasps, it was all too much. They nickered and galloped away, fleeing toward the woods. Danielle did nothing to stop them. The wasps didn't appear to care about the animals. The horses were probably safer in the woods than they would be if they stayed here.

Talia snarled and jerked her sword free of its sheath. "The Stormcrows can't kill us for defending ourselves."

"They can, actually," said Gerta, but she drew a dagger of her own.

Sweat stung Danielle's eyes as she backed toward the flames. The wasps flew at chest height, fast as sling stones. They split into two groups to attack from both sides. Danielle ducked as they buzzed over her head and circled back away from the fire.

Gerta jumped back, yanking her cloak away from her body. A wasp clung to the material, its mirrored stinger tearing one hole after another.

"Don't move," said Talia. Her sword smashed the wasp to the ground.

Gerta yelped. One hand went to her ear, as if checking to make sure Talia hadn't severed it. Talia simply grinned and swung at another wasp.

"You said the wall would allow Snow to pass, because she was of royal blood?" Danielle asked. "You're her sister. Will the wall recognize you?"

Gerta bit her lip, her face pale. "I . . . I don't know. If I'm truly Snow's sister—"

"Do it." Danielle shoved her away. "They can't follow you into the flames. Stay within it as long as you can, until they're gone."

Gerta hadn't quite reached the wall when the wasps regrouped for a second attack. Danielle braced herself.

Blue fire crackled through the air like the breath of a dragon. Smoke and steam exploded from the earth. Four of the wasps vanished in an eyeblink, blasted to vapor. The rest tumbled to the ground, their wings dripping to nothing.

Talia swore. Fire flickered on the edge of her cape. She threw herself into the mud, rolling back and forth until the flame was completely smothered.

The column of fire continued to burn a few moments longer, roaring almost as loudly as a living dragon. It originated from the top of the wall, arcing outward like water from a fountain. It died in much the same fashion, thinning to a trickle that fell back into the wall. Danielle jumped to the side to avoid small bits of flame that splashed down.

"Are you all right?" Talia asked.

Danielle nodded. Talia appeared unhurt, as did Gerta, who stood frozen at the wall as if uncertain what to do next.

"Snow knows we're here." Talia brushed mud from her cape, a futile gesture that only spread the dirt. "If she didn't before, she does now."

"You think her wasps were following us?" Danielle asked.

"More likely she sent them here as scouts. If she'd known where we were, she would have attacked already." Talia peered up at the wall. "I want to know why Snow never built us something like this back in Lorindar."

"She couldn't," said Gerta. "The raw materials alone

would cost more than your kingdom is worth. The fence is made of—" She jumped back as a man stepped through the wall beside her. The fire splattered from his body like rain, hissing where the individual flames touched the earth.

He was clearly one of the city's wizards, but he didn't look like any wizard Danielle had seen before. For one thing, he was wearing armor. The mail appeared to be made of gold and steel, the individual rings little thicker than wire. The gold links wove a swirling pattern like snakes converging toward his heart. His only weapon was an ebony-handled athame at his hip. He wore a black half-cape and matching trousers tucked into fur-lined boots.

He doffed a metal helm and gave a slight bow of greeting. He was slender and bald, his brown scalp shining in the firelight. Even his eyebrows had been shaved. He studied them each in turn, but kept most of his attention on Gerta. When he spoke, his words were calm, but firm.

"He's warning us, ever so politely, that we'll be killed should we attempt to fight or flee," Talia said, never taking her eyes from the wizard. "His fellow Stormcrows listen from the towers. He wants to know who Gerta is and how she approached so close to the wall."

"Be careful what you say." Danielle glanced at the puddle where one of the wasps had fallen. A sliver of glass lay half-buried in the mud. "They may not be the only ones listening."

Talia continued to translate as Gerta said, "My friends and I need to enter the city."

"I'm sorry," said the Stormcrow. "Those things that attacked you, this isn't the first time we've fought them. They possess their victims. At least four Stormcrows have been turned, along with gods know how many civilians. We're working to track them down, but we can't risk letting more inside."

"So you're saying your magic can't even show whether or not we're infected?" Talia asked.

He almost smiled. "I sense no evil in you, but it's the

height of arrogance to assume none are powerful enough to conceal their spells from me. We prefer not to take the risk."

"So instead you'll wait for the next swarm to fly over the wall and attack your people?"

This time, his smile broke free. "They've tried three times. The flames stretch up as well as out."

Gerta folded her arms. "Unless things have changed since my last visit, that cape marks you as an officer. You can communicate directly with the king, and he with you?"

"If the need arises, yes."

"Good." Gerta kicked mud over the exposed slivers of glass, then stepped past him and plunged her hands into the flame before he could stop her. In a low voice that barely carried over the sound of the fire, she said, "Please let Laurence know that his cousin, Princess Rose Gertrude Curtana, wishes to speak with him."

The Stormcrows moved with impressive speed. Gerta barely had time to remove her hands from the wall before two more armored Stormcrows stepped through to seize her arms.

Talia dropped into a low stance. One hand went to her sword. The remaining Stormcrow, the officer, raised his hands and spread his fingers in response. Talia's lips pulled back, and her heart beat faster. She should have no problem taking him out before he could cast a spell, but his companions were another matter.

"Don't," Danielle said softly. "It's not like we can fight our way through this wall."

"How will you know unless you try?" But Talia forced herself to relax.

The Stormcrow lowered his hands, though he kept a wary eye on Talia. "The king says to bring them in." To Danielle, he said, "My name is Forssel, Captain of the northern wing of the King's Stormcrows. These are Colville and Vachel. We'll be escorting you to the palace."

Talia relayed the man's introduction, as well as Danielle's thanks. The Stormcrows didn't bother to take their weapons. Given the way Colville and Vachel were eyeing them, Talia didn't believe for a moment the Stormcrows trusted their guests, which meant they didn't think weapons would matter. She glanced at the scorched starburst on the ground where blue fire had incinerated Snow's wasps. They were probably right.

"Take my hand as we pass through the wall," said Forssel. "Keep your heads low, and let me go first. Otherwise, your bodies will be little more than charcoal when you tumble out the other side. There's no air, so don't try to breathe. Colville will remain here to retrieve the remains of those creatures."

One by one, the Stormcrows led them into the city. Talia was the last to grip Forssel's hand and approach the blue flames. The heat was almost unbearable, emanating as much from Forssel's armor as the fire itself. When he neared the wall, fire leaped to meet him, dancing over his helm and through his armor. Sparks followed the gold patterns in his mail, jumping to the ground when they reached the bottom.

Talia had prepared herself for the light and the heat, but not the wind. Her hair rose, and her cape flapped as the air rushed upward past her body. Sparks burst from the edges of the cape as the wolf's enchantments interacted with the dragon fire. The wall was thicker than she had realized. It was four paces before she emerged on the other side.

She stepped away from the flames, blinking the dryness from her eyes. The others were waiting, and appeared unharmed.

"Welcome to Kanustius," said Forssel, backing to what was considered a polite distance in Allesandria. Still close enough for Talia to reach him with her sword, if necessary.

The streets were paved in red-tinged stone, cutting tight paths between low, blocky buildings. Smoke rose from most of the chimneys. Painted knot work, mostly in blues and whites, trimmed the doors and the narrow windows.

The air was far too quiet for a city of this size. Talia could see people watching through cracked shutters. Those on the streets moved quickly, looking straight ahead.

"This is how things felt when my mother ruled," Gerta said softly. She stared like a newcomer, her forehead wrinkled as she took in her surroundings. "Smothered by fear. No one was allowed in the streets after dark without a permit."

"The curfew was overturned years ago," said Forssel. "The blue wall serves as a warning to the people as well as a defense. They keep to their homes, trusting the king to deal with the threat. But the wall has been raised for several days now, and tensions are growing."

"How did it begin?" asked Danielle.

"Every city is under heightened alert," he said. "We've been hunting Snow White ever since the murder of Lord Ollear."

"Yet she remains free," Talia observed.

Forssel didn't appear to take offense. "Allesandria is well protected against invasion. Whole armies have entered our woods, never to emerge. Lyskar once attempted to expand their borders. The king of Allesandria turned the very mountains against them. But Snow knows the land, and she travels alone.

"Alone?" Danielle repeated sharply.

"She's scattered her followers. They move singly, or in small groups." His face tightened. "Yesterday, a seer from the university dreamed a silver cloud raced inland from the harbor. King Lawrence sent a full unit of Stormcrows to intercept the cloud."

"What happened?" asked Gerta.

"It wasn't a cloud, but a swarm. Hundreds of those damned things racing toward the capital. The Stormcrows' spells were reflected back upon those who cast them. Six were killed instantly by their own magic."

"The mirrors."

His face tightened. "Exactly. Much like the protective charms Queen Curtana would wear to guard herself from attack." He glanced at the other Stormcrows. "The rest were stung. We've been forced to kill three of our own people today." He touched his hand to his heart and whispered three names, presumably those of the fallen Stormcrows.

"I'm sorry." Gerta repeated the names. "The palace is north of here. Where are you taking us?"

"There's a quicker way, and safer, if any of Snow White's slaves have infiltrated the city and are watching." He pointed to a stone building at the end of a street lined with inns and bars.

"An icehouse?" Gerta asked. The building was squat, not even a full story high. "I don't understand."

"Could this be a trick?" Danielle asked softly. Talia wasn't sure whether the Stormcrows spoke the tongue of Lorindar, but neither of them reacted.

"A little late for that question." Talia shook her head. "Nothing's certain, but if they wanted us dead or captured, there are easier ways to go about it."

Vachel unlocked the icehouse door. It was twice as thick as a normal door. Fog spilled into the street, and Talia glimpsed large blocks of ice stacked against the walls inside. Straw lined the stone walls and carpeted the floor, save for a wooden trapdoor in the center of the room.

"Watch the steps," Forssel said as he led them inside and hauled open the trapdoor, revealing a narrow staircase.

"You're not worried about people discovering your secret way into the palace?" asked Talia.

Forssel grinned. "Anyone watching saw a group of workers coming in for ice. A charm of suggestion, not true illusion. It dampens curiosity, and as they wander away, their minds will convince them they saw us emerge hauling a block back to a nearby tavern."

Candlelight flickered to life from Forssel's fingertips. Vachel hauled the door shut. There were no windows, and the single flame didn't provide much light. Talia stepped carefully, testing each step as she descended after Forssel. Inside, the air stank of magic.

Downstairs was even colder. She pulled her cape tight, but couldn't block the icy air that snuck through the layers to chill her skin. The floor was crushed gravel. Larger blocks of ice lined three walls. A variety of hammers and chisels hung from the fourth.

"In summer, this room is filled and sealed off," said Forssel. "But for winter, the people move smaller blocks upstairs for easier access. Runoff from the streets, magically purified, feeds into this room through the pipes in the corners."

"I see no passageway or tunnel." Talia kept her hands in her sleeves.

"It's here." Gerta squinted at the ice. "The enchantment isn't in the ice, but in the pipes."

Forssel frowned. "That's right." He stepped past Gerta and pressed his hands to the ice, which began to melt at an unnatural rate. Water poured down, splashing and disappearing into the gravel. When he stepped back, the outline of a doorway remained, perfectly carved in the ice. "If you're truly who you say, this will take you to the palace."

"What if we're not?" Talia asked.

Vachel chuckled. "In that case, it will take you . . . somewhere else." He and Forssel backed toward the stairs, not so subtly blocking the only other way out.

Danielle straightened. "Thank you." She touched a hand to the ice. Cold water dripped down her palm and trickled along her wrist.

Talia caught her shoulder. "I'm going first."

"I thought you said this wasn't a trap," Danielle said.

"I did." Talia touched the doorway. The door opened inward, revealing a dark tunnel through the ice. "I've been wrong before."

Talia stepped into the darkness. She had taken only two steps when a voice spoke from behind.

"You know, you're much prettier when you smile."

Talia spun. The ice room had vanished, replaced by

old ruins and desert sand. Her friends were gone, as were the Stormcrows. In Forssel's place stood Snow White, dressed in a yellow Kha'iida robe, her headscarf hanging loose from her neck.

"Don't get me wrong," Snow continued. "The smoldering look works for you, but I've always preferred your laughter."

Talia's sword shook in her hand. Snow's face showed no sign of scars or cuts. Her hair was pure black, as it had been when they first met. Her eyes were wide, full of amusement, but it was the untainted joy in her laughter that convinced Talia to lower her weapon. "This is Arathea."

Snow shrugged. "We had to leave in such a hurry the last time. We didn't even have time for a proper tour of your homeland. This is the palace where you grew up, isn't it?"

Talia turned about. The last time she was here, she had fought a fairy army. As if conjured by the thought, the sound of hoofbeats chilled her skin. Her sword snapped into a guard position. Howling filled the air, followed by screams. "The Wild Hunt?"

"They're dreams, nothing more."

Talia tried to calm her breathing, fighting memories of the destruction the Hunt had left in its wake. They were victims of an ancient fairy curse, twisted into the very embodiment of chaos and death. "So they can't hurt us."

"I never said that." Snow's lips quirked. "Dreams have power. You should know this."

Talia snorted. "And you should know it's been a while since I've dreamed."

Snow acknowledged the point with a tilt of her head. "It's a shame, really." She stepped closer, sliding a hand up Talia's arm. "Dreams can be quite . . . invigorating."

Talia shivered. She was dressed similarly to Snow, in a jade robe and matching head scarf. Her red cape was gone, and with it her best hope of fighting the Wild Hunt.

"Don't worry," Snow said, tugging Talia's scarf free. Real head scarves were thick, woven to protect the wearer from the desert sun. This one floated away like silk. "They're not coming for you this time."

Talia forced herself to pull away. "Are you real? Or is this some trick, an illusion cast by the demon?"

"If so, then you're already lost," Snow said matter-of-factly. "You might as well enjoy it."

The Hunt was closer now. Talia could see the growing dust storm that marked their approach. "You said they weren't coming for me. Who—?"

Snow gestured past Talia, to where Danielle and Gerta sat upon a crumbled wall, sharing some kind of green melon. Talia tried to shout a warning, but no words emerged. She started to run. Her feet sank into the sand, deeper with each step.

"You can't protect us all," said Snow.

"Watch me." Talia snarled and turned to face the Wild Hunt. Dream or no, she still owed the Hunt for the things they had done in Arathea.

Lips brushed her cheek, but when she spun around, Snow was gone. The thunder of the Wild Hunt fell silent. Light faded, and cold air embraced her. She took a step, and the sand beneath her feet changed to wood.

Magic jolted her body, so sharp she felt as though her heart momentarily stopped beating. She found herself in a small, finely furnished sitting room. The floor was patterned wood tiles, alternating triangles of light- and dark-stained oak that made the shapes appear to rise from the floor. Gerta was already here, sitting in one of the blue high-backed chairs spread around a low table. There were no windows, though the painted vines and trees on the wall gave the illusion of being in the woods.

"Danielle should arrive shortly," Gerta said.

"Thank you." Talia was unsurprised to see only unbroken wall behind her. There was only a single door on the opposite side of the room. She tried the handle and found it locked. She heard nothing beyond. "That dream. What was it?"

"You think the king would allow strangers into his

home without first examining their minds and motives?"

"He saw that, did he?" Talia retained both her weapons and the red cape. She pulled the latter tight, feeling exposed. "What happens if he doesn't like what he sees?"

"In my mother's day, they said you would emerge . . . elsewhere. Some say she had hundreds of rooms built into the foundation of the palace, coffin-sized chambers with no light and no way out. Nothing but darkness, too cramped even to move as you slowly starved to death." She cocked her head. "Though I don't know if my mother would trap you somewhere she couldn't question you. Somewhere she couldn't listen to your screams."

Talia studied the portraits on the walls while she tried to squelch the need to tear out the throat of the king of Allesandria. A central painting in an arched, gold frame showed King Laurence and Queen Odelia. Smaller paintings to either side depicted their two children. The girl looked about five years old. The boy was closer to Jakob's age. Both children were painted in the stiff, full-body pose that was popular these days.

She wondered how the king and queen had kept their children still long enough for the artist to paint them. She still remembered the trouble Danielle and Armand had gone to. In the end, Danielle had simply dressed a tailor's dummy in Jakob's clothes. The artist had added Jakob's face and hands later.

Danielle emerged then, stumbling through an opening in the wall that vanished as quickly as it had appeared. She clutched her sword in both hands, swinging downward at an unreal foe. The tip gouged the floor.

Talia darted forward and caught Danielle's wrist, tugging the sword from her hand.

"I'm sorry," said Danielle. She crouched to run a finger over the damage to the wooden tile. "Glasspaper should smooth out the damage, but it will need to be restained." Her hands shook, giving the lie to her calm words.

Slowly and deliberately, Talia rested the tip of Danielle's sword on the floor and leaned on the hilt.

"We're guests here," Danielle reminded her.

"You don't greet 'guests' with visions of—" Talia swallowed, then handed the sword back to Danielle. "Are you all right?"

"We were back at the palace," Danielle said. "Jakob was playing another of his hiding games. Armand and Snow were both there. Beatrice too, I think. But we couldn't find him."

"The king will be here soon," said Gerta. "I can feel him studying me." She pointed to the stained wood trim along the walls, like an intricately carved chair rail, only at chest height. "That runs unbroken through the entire palace, allowing the king and queen magical access to every room. My mother ordered it made, to better spy on her guests and servants."

She seemed calm, almost bored, making Talia wonder what she had seen as she entered the room.

"I was running," Gerta said, answering Talia's unspoken question. "I couldn't see whether it was Snow chasing me or something else, but then I recognized the dream magic."

"What did you do?" asked Talia.

Gerta smiled, but it didn't reach her eyes. "I stopped playing."

The door opened, and a man in his late twenties entered. "She tried to pull me into the dream with her."

"King Laurence." Danielle's nod was rather less than the formal greeting of one noble to another, but the king didn't appear to notice.

He was a heavyset man with pale skin and jet-black hair too perfect to be natural. A gold sash crossed his formal, thigh-length white jacket. Gleaming black boots came to the middle of his shins. He carried a scepter, a gold rod slightly shorter than a cane, topped with a simple circle of gold. He spoke the language of Lorindar with only the slightest accent. "Welcome to Allesandria, Princess Whiteshore. I hope you'll forgive my intrusion into your minds."

"You can hope," Talia muttered.

Danielle shot a warning glare at Talia. "I trust you saw enough to confirm our identities, Your Majesty?"

"I saw that, and more." He turned his attention to Gerta. "Forssel relayed your actions at the wall. Combined with your attempt to disrupt my dreamspell—"

"Attempt?" Gerta repeated.

The king seemed tired, but his wry smile reminded Talia a little of Snow. "It's not every day a cousin I've never met enters the palace, accompanied by the Princess of Lorindar and the Lady of the Red Hood."

"Talia's not—" Danielle began.

"Here to kill anyone," Talia finished. If he wanted to believe she was a legendary assassin, who was she to argue with a king? Laurence had certainly prepared as if she were the Lady of the Red Hood. Talia could smell the protective spells that encased him like dwarf-forged mail.

"You're not the one I was worried about, Talia." Laurence watched Gerta closely. "Everything I saw in your dreams suggests you're who you claim, but I find it difficult to believe even Rose Curtana could have hidden you so thoroughly."

"Long-lost heirs show up all the time," Talia said.

"Not in Allesandria." He gestured to the chairs. Both Danielle and Gerta sat, but Talia refused. It was another violation of Allesandrian manners, one which forced even a king to remain standing. "I saw your fears as well, Gerta. Like your friends, you fear for Ermillina. But there's something more. You're afraid of being reclaimed."

"I was formed from her essence," Gerta said.

"Meaning I've welcomed a part of Ermillina Curtana into my palace." Laurence massaged his brow.

"I would never—" Gerta started.

"I know." He raised a hand. "Had I seen anything in

your dream to suggest you were a threat, you never would have emerged. But the fact that you wouldn't knowingly act against Allesandria means little. Should Ermillina find a way to act through you—"

"She doesn't know who . . . *what* I am," Gerta said softly. "She burned my memory from her mind, and Talia's cape shields us from her vision."

"For now." Laurence began to pace. "Years ago, Queen Beatrice promised me Ermillina would never return to this land. I'm familiar with Beatrice's gifts, crude and untrained though they were. She gave me her word. Yet my cousin has murdered at least two members of the Nobles' Circle. Her spells have enslaved hundreds."

"Beatrice told the truth," Gerta said. "Sight such as hers was often unreliable, even more so when one tries to see beyond one's death." She bit her lip at that, looking suddenly vulnerable.

"I trusted her." Laurence's knuckles were white around his scepter. "How many of my people are dead today because I allowed your queen to talk me into helping Ermillina escape?"

The beat of Talia's blood threatened to drown out the king's words. "Her mother tried to murder her," she snapped. "You 'helped' her by stealing her throne for yourself."

The room fell still. Danielle cleared her throat. "Talia, you're not helping."

Laurence no longer bothered to hide his anger. "Allesandria never would have allowed Rose's daughter to—"

"How many people are dead today because you were too weak or afraid to stand up for a young girl whose only crime was to protect herself from a murderer?" Talia finished.

"I could have argued on her behalf," Laurence admitted. "I could have defied the Circle, lent my voice to Ermillina Curtana . . . and I would have been shouted down, sent back to the eastern provinces while another claimed the throne. One less willing to allow the daughter of Rose Curtana to live, even in exile."

"You should tell her that when she arrives," said Talia. "I'm sure she'll be very interested in your excuses."

Danielle stood. "I must have misunderstood the plan." She matched Talia's stare. "I thought we had come to search for the means Rose Curtana used to imprison this demon. Not to provoke an incident between Lorindar and Allesandria."

Talia's blood pounded hot in her veins. She opened her mouth to respond.

"Which is more important?" Danielle asked mildly. "Venting your anger, or helping Snow?"

Talia clamped her jaw and slowly lowered herself into her chair.

"What is right is not always what is possible or practical," said Laurence. "I wish every story ended as neatly as that of Cinderella—"

Danielle raised an eyebrow.

"—but we live in a world where fear and greed overrule justice. A world where a mother tries to murder her own daughter out of jealousy. I received the birds with their warning, thank you. We've taken precautions, but . . . that mirror never should have left Allesandria. If it had been destroyed—"

"Then the demon would have escaped even sooner," said Gerta.

"This is where Rose Curtana captured it." Danielle gestured at the walls. "Did she have a study or a laboratory, a place she might have used for such summonings?"

"My people searched every room when I took power. Four were killed by traps my aunt had left behind. Seven others were injured or driven mad. Believe me, we've examined this palace quite thoroughly. There is no such summoning chamber."

"There has to be," said Talia.

Laurence rubbed his eyes, and for a moment, the royal mask fell away to reveal worry and fatigue. "Who told you of this chamber?"

"Her name is Noita." Gerta raised her chin. "She's the one who helped my mother prepare it."

"The flower witch?" Laurence gave a bitter laugh. "We hunted down most of Rose Curtana's companions. Noita appeared harmless."

"She's not. I was there." Gerta hesitated. "Snow was, I mean. We saw— She saw Noita helping our mother."

"I will have the Stormcrows search again," said Laurence. "But there is another possibility we must pursue. Your connection to Ermillina could give us the means to act against her."

"We've tried to find Snow through Gerta," said Danielle. "Our people—"

"Are not Allesandrian." Laurence twisted his scepter in his hands. "When it comes to magic, Allesandria is second to none. If Gerta is who and what she appears to be, we can use her against my cousin."

"Without harming her?" Danielle demanded.

Laurence hesitated ever so slightly. "We will do everything in our power to preserve her."

Talia stepped between Gerta and the king.

"That's why you allowed me to enter," Gerta said.

"The Stormcrows advised against it," Laurence admitted. "They feared you could be a trap. But Ermillina has avoided capture for too long. If we can strike at her through you, then I felt it worth the risk."

"She's a person," said Talia, struggling to keep the wolf under control. "Not a weapon."

Laurence started to answer, then stiffened. "Forgive me," he said, stepping toward the wall. He pressed his fingertips to the wood trim circling the room. He rapped the end of his scepter against the wood, and a low hum filled the room. "In Allesandria, the distinction is often slim. As it turns out, the argument may be moot."

"What do you mean?" asked Talia.

Footsteps pounded down the hallway. The door opened inward to reveal a woman in the silver mail of a Stormcrow. She bowed, speaking too softly for even

Talia to overhear. Laurence clasped her arm and said, "Double the guards, and order the halls cleared."

"What is it?" Danielle asked.

"My Stormcrows have captured Snow White. They're bringing her to the palace now."

Chapter 14

CAPTURED, NOT KILLED. RELIEF FLOWED through Danielle, but confusion was quick to follow. What of Noita's visions, and her own? Allesandrian magic might be powerful, but could it really be so simple to change the future? "Was Jakob with her?"

Laurence shook his head. "They took Ermillina, but there was no sign of the prince."

"Let me speak with her," said Danielle. "We can—"

"Whatever creature has taken her, it may try to escape to another host," said Laurence. "The Stormcrows have done what they can to secure her, but you are defenseless as a babe, magically speaking. I cannot risk you being taken."

"So let me go." Talia bared her teeth. "Or do you think me defenseless as well?"

"I understand she was your . . . friend . . . and I appreciate your willingness to help." The king took a step backward. His scepter rang once more against the wall, the sound stretching out an unnaturally long time. "Ermillina Curtana is a daughter of Allesandria. She attacked my nation, and was captured by my Stormcrows. You are welcome here, but if you accept my hospitality, it will be as guests only."

"Can you free Snow from this demon?" Danielle asked.

"They're not going to try." Talia was like a statue, arms hidden beneath her cape. The Stormcrow stepped into the room, taking a protective position to Laurence's left. "Are you?"

Laurence said nothing.

"What of my son?" demanded Danielle. "Snow is the only one who knows where he is. Kill her, and we might never find him. Would you sentence the Prince of Lorindar to death as well?"

"I'm sorry. You should prepare yourself for the worst. Ermillina was alone when she was taken, which means your son may already be—"

"Jakob. Is. Alive." Danielle advanced upon the king, catching herself only when the Stormcrow moved to intercept her. "I *saw* him. Snow and Jakob both, in a palace of ice. He was cold and afraid and lost, but he was alive!"

"Magical visions from an old witch, one known to have been a friend to Rose Curtana." Laurence put a hand on the Stormcrow's shoulder, gently moving her aside. "One possible future, glimpsed by an untrained mind. My seers have looked to see what will happen if Ermillina Curtana is allowed to live. Each time, they foretell the destruction of the palace. Fire and chaos spreading through the city and beyond. I cannot risk—"

"If you do this," Danielle said, nails digging into sweat-slick palms, "you make an enemy of Lorindar."

"What would you do?" Laurence lowered his scepter. "Would you sacrifice Lorindar for the sake of a single child, for the *possibility* that he might yet live?"

"You sacrifice nothing by letting us speak to her."

"Rose Curtana could kill with a single word. I am sorry, Danielle. I would save her if I could. I knew Ermillina as a child. I tried to protect her after the death of her mother. Perhaps I should have done more, but I can't protect her anymore. Once she is dealt with, we will do everything in our power to find your son. But ultimately it is Ermillina and the demon who are responsible for her fate.

Talia spat on the floor, close to the king's polished boots. "The magic of Allesandria is known throughout the world. Surely your mighty Stormcrows can handle a single demon.

Another Stormcrow entered, taking a position to the right of the king and whispering something too low to hear. Gerta swallowed and moved closer to Danielle.

"Give us time," Danielle pressed. "The key to binding this demon is somewhere in the palace. Give us a week to search. A day, even, to—"

Laurence clutched the scepter in both hands. "The order has already been given. Your friend is dead."

Danielle stared, not comprehending. Snow couldn't be dead. The king's words echoed in her mind.

"The scepter," whispered Gerta. "When you struck the wall that last time. That's when you gave the order."

Talia lunged at the king. The closer Stormcrow raised her hands, but Talia was faster. Her fist twisted into the Stormcrow's mail, and she tossed the other woman as though she were a toy. Gerta jumped back as the Stormcrow crashed through the table. The second Stormcrow waved his hands, and the chairs shot at Talia, shattering against her back. It stunned her for a moment, but she shook off the debris and leaped.

"Talia, stop!" Danielle rushed toward her, knowing she wasn't fast enough. Talia was impossibly swift even without the red cape. With the cape's magic, she could kill the king before anyone else had time to draw weapons.

Laurence raised his scepter. Talia caught it in one hand and drew back her fist.

Lightning crackled along the scepter's length. Laurence shifted his grip, twisting it free, then slamming the butt into the side of Talia's head. Blue sparks popped from the scepter as he twirled it about, aiming it at Talia.

Talia's hand was red and blistered. She touched her temple as she rose. With her other hand, she pulled the cape around her body.

Danielle stepped between them, facing Talia. "My son is out there. *Jakob is still alive.*" He had to be. "That skin lets you track like a wolf. Between that and Laurence's magic, we might yet be able to find him. Would you let Jakob die, too?"

At first, Talia didn't move. Only the rapid flare of her nostrils showed she was still breathing. Her pupils were tiny black beads, looking past Danielle to the king. A group of Stormcrows had gathered behind him in the hallway, but he raised a hand, keeping them back.

"I need you," Danielle said.

Talia shuddered once, violently. Blood and tears dripped down her cheek, and her hands trembled.

Danielle grabbed her shoulder. Talia's other arm jerked up to strike Danielle's hand away. She hesitated, then brought her hand down on Danielle's. Her grip threatened to break bones.

"Are you sure, Cousin?" Gerta asked softly.

Laurence frowned. "Sure of what?"

"That Snow White is truly dead?"

Talia's shoulders jerked at Gerta's words. Danielle held tight, though she wasn't strong enough to stop Talia should she choose to do something impulsive. But for the moment, the fight appeared to have drained from her.

"We're connected, yet I felt nothing," Gerta continued.

"You believe we executed an imposter." He pursed his lips. "Others have tried to infiltrate the palace, sending spies under cover of illusion or shapeshifting into innocuous forms. One of the early kings of Allesandria was killed when his brother secretly replaced six grapes at dinner with tiny elementals, transformed by magic."

"Why send an imposter?" asked one of the Stormcrows. "Knowing she would be bound, unable to perform magic or act against us."

"Perhaps so we would call off our hunt," said Laurence. "But our protections are built for such trickery. I'm familiar with the shapeshifting magic her mother used. Such spells would not fool us. The Stormcrows can peer beneath the flesh of their prisoner to see the very core of the person."

"A core tainted by Snow's mirrors," Danielle said. Hope and despair threatened to rip her in two. "Mirrors which carry a fragment of Snow herself into everyone she infects."

"My mother underestimated her, too," said Gerta. "Snow and I are magically bound. I doubt I could even survive with her dead."

Laurence's eyes narrowed. "Does that mean—"

"No," Gerta said quickly. "I'm but a small part of the whole. Killing me would destroy whatever remains of Snow's humanity, but the demon would survive."

Danielle kissed Talia's brow, then turned her full attention to Laurence. "Your Majesty, whoever you killed, it was not our friend. If you hope to prevent those visions, I suggest you let us see the body."

Laurence was already whispering to his Stormcrows. Two left at a run, presumably heading toward the body. "Come with me. If Gerta is right about her bond, she should be able to tell us for certain whether it was my cousin we brought into the palace."

Talia followed the others through the curving hallways. There were few corners, only passages that wove to and fro like knot work. The wolf's anger surged through her with each step, but every time it ebbed, it left only emptiness. Every step eroded away a little more of her soul.

No, Gerta was right. She had to be. Snow was alive.

Talia wiped her cheek with her shoulder. Her face throbbed where King Laurence's scepter had struck, and the skin of her hand was blistered, pain flaring with every movement.

"This place reminds me of Mother," said Gerta. "Caked in plaster and whitewash, decorated in too much gold leaf. Give me the naked stone of the summer palace, the exposed beams and the honest strength of the walls."

The king brought them to a wide marble staircase. "This leads into the Stormcrows' tower," he said, hurrying up to the heavy oak doors at the top of the stairs. A rap of his scepter opened the doors, and lanterns flared to life inside.

Snow White lay in the center of the room, her skin even paler than normal. Her throat had been cut. Blood stained her cloak and shirt bright red. Candles burned at the corners of a chalk rectangle around her body. Her hands and feet were bound with chains of blue metal.

"The chains inhibit her magic," Laurence said softly. "From the moment she was captured, she was unable to use spellcraft. Her ice wasps were destroyed. Any that tried to follow would have been stopped by the magic of the palace walls."

The sound that wrenched from Talia's throat was somewhere between a whimper and a shout. Nobody tried to stop her from approaching the body, but as she reached the chalk marks, she found herself unable to move closer. Nothing pushed her away, but when she tried to take another step, her foot slipped to the side. She stretched out, and her arm was deflected to the left.

She dropped to one knee. She could smell the wards, like dust and honey. The smell grew stronger as she pressed one hand toward Snow, but the more she forced her hand forward, the more that force was turned against her.

"Even the magic of your cape isn't strong enough to break through this barrier," Laurence said.

"Why?" Talia gestured at the rectangle.

"If this is truly who it appears, then the demon was banished with her death, but we don't know what other protections she might have carried. It will take days to cleanse her body. Until we do, nothing can pass in or out of the wards."

Gerta sighed. "Only this isn't her body."

"Where was she captured?" Danielle asked. Her body was taut, and she blinked back tears as she looked at Snow.

"In the mountains to the north."

The mountains. If Jakob was alive, that was where they should start hunting for him. For him and for Snow.

Talia closed her eyes, choosing Gerta's truth over the evidence before her. What did the demon gain? This was more than simply an attempt to throw the Stormcrows off of her trail. Could the body be diseased? Plague was a mundane threat . . . but it was too slow and uncertain a weapon. Anything carried by the imposter was trapped with her.

She spun toward Laurence. "Who captured her?"

"Selerin led a force of six Stormcrows." He bowed his head. "Two were killed in the fighting. A third was badly injured, though he will survive."

Meaning four had returned with the body. Snow could have infected them— Or would Laurence's magic have detected that? Inspector Relmar had recognized the demon's touch, back on the *Phillipa*. Better to sneak her mirror shards into the palace, but how would she hide their magic?

"Those chains," she whispered. "Do all of your Stormcrows carry them?"

"Yes," said Laurence.

And Snow had fought and killed any number of Stormcrows. "What would happen if a splinter of glass were set within one of the links?"

"The metal would render it inert." Laurence's expression turned grim. "Until something jostled them free."

"The injured Stormcrow." Snow could have planted the chain on him during the fight. All it would take was for a single splinter to fall free, at which point its magic would return. It would pull the cold and moisture from the air, using its ice body to climb up and infect the Stormcrow, who could then shake the rest loose.

"Where are Selerin and the others?" Laurence demanded.

"They left after the execution," said one of the Stormcrows, an older woman with a collection of silver-and-gold rings squeezed onto the fingers of her left hand. A minor enchantment decorated her fingernails, which shone and changed color like the sunrise. An intricate tattoo of interlinked symbols circled her bald pate like a crown.

Laurence's scepter rang against the wall.

"Spiderweb," Gerta said. "A spider's silk is strong

enough to hold a shard of glass. Even I could command spiders to weave their webs into the links of the chain."

The older Stormcrow took the king's arm. "Your Majesty, if there's a chance this demon has infiltrated the palace, we must get you to safety."

The king's response was far too coarse and common for royalty. He kept his scepter pressed to the wall. "There are reports of a commotion at the library."

"You underestimated her," said Talia.

He didn't try to deny it. "Ermillina was never formally schooled."

"She taught herself," corrected Gerta.

To the Stormcrows, he said, "Half of you find Queen Odelia and our children. Once they're safe, search the palace for Selerin and the rest. We may yet have time to stop this. Summon as many guards, magical and mundane, as you need. Princess Whiteshore, you and your friends will come with me."

Lightning struck outside as they were leaving, close enough to illuminate the staircase through the shuttered window. The thunder sounded like someone had fired a cannon inside the palace. As the sound faded, Talia heard a low humming in the distance. "Her wasps are here."

"Fire magic works well against them," said Gerta.

Laurence didn't break stride. He spun his scepter, and a ball of blue fire appeared in the ring at the end. When the first wasp appeared at the base of the stairs, he jabbed his scepter, and the flame shot out like a smaller version of the dragon fire from the city walls. Both wasp and flame vanished in a hiss, and a tiny spark of glass dropped to the floor. One of the Stormcrows conjured a small ball of clay, which he used to retrieve and encase the glass.

Danielle raised her voice as another lightning bolt struck outside. "Whatever Rose Curtana used to summon the demon is here. Are you *sure* there's nothing that might have been overlooked?"

"Most of her artifacts were destroyed. The rest were locked away, and have been thoroughly studied by myself and others." Laurence grimaced. "With one significant exception, of course."

Talia pushed open the shutters of the closest window, trying to see what was happening outside. Across an open, circular courtyard, a tower of black smoke rose from the opposite side of the palace. "How good are your Stormcrows at summoning rain?"

"Easier to steal the life of the fire itself." Laurence gestured to one of his wizards, who stepped to the window and began working a spell.

A young boy stumbled into the hall ahead of them. He wore what appeared to be a page's uniform, dark blue and yellow, and slightly too short for his gangly limbs. His cheek bled from a single small cut.

Talia moved to the side, one hand palming a dagger. "So much for getting the king to safety."

"Hello, Talia." The page smiled. "Before you act, please keep in mind that I'm merely borrowing this body. Go ahead and destroy it, if you like. I've found plenty more."

The Stormcrows stepped forward to protect their king. The hair on Talia's neck rose as they prepared their magic, but the boy didn't seem to care.

"What do you want, Ermillina?" asked Laurence.

"To begin with, I'd like you to stop calling me that. Ermillina is the name my mother gave me. I prefer Snow." The page strode toward them. "I trusted you. You knew what she was like, Cousin. You knew what she did to me. What she did to Roland. Yet you signed the order for my death all those years ago."

"I protected you as much as I could," Laurence protested. "But when you killed the queen—"

"Yes, yes." He waved a hand, sounding bored. "So tell me, Laurence. Who will protect you now that you've done the same?"

Laurence frowned. "What are you talking about?"

The page sighed. "I thought about using one of your Stormcrows, but this was more poetic. I wonder what thoughts ran through your wife's mind at the end. Did she know it was your order that put the knife to her throat, believing she was me?"

"Odelia." Laurence paled. The scepter dropped to the floor.

The page used that moment to fling two ice wasps. One of the Stormcrows gestured, and the first wasp slammed into the wall. Talia jumped high, bringing her cape around to intercept the second. She crushed it through the cape, then ripped her zaraq whip from her belt. The thin, weighted line snapped out, catching the boy's wrist. She tugged hard, dragging him to the floor. Before he could rise, Talia was on top of him, lashing his wrists together.

"He's lying." Danielle grabbed Laurence by the arm. "Queen Odelia is safe. Whoever was executed, they were escorted into the palace as a prisoner. It was someone Snow found before her wasps ever entered these walls."

Laurence straightened and pulled away. "Of course. Forgive me." He picked up his scepter and touched it to the wall. His visage tightened. "They still haven't found her, or my children."

"*They* haven't . . ." The boy's laugh was so much like Snow's own it raised bumps on Talia's skin. "Think of your family as your guards fight their way through the palace, never knowing if the enemy they cut down is a nameless servant or your own flesh and blood."

"Where are you, Snow?" Danielle asked.

He ignored the question. "The same holds for you, Danielle. I could be Jakob for all you know. Think well before you use that glass blade."

"You're not Jakob." Talia hauled the boy upright.

"Are you willing to wager the prince's life?" he asked.

Talia hesitated. The wolf's senses could pierce most illusions with ease, but this was no illusion. King Laurence's own Stormcrows hadn't seen through Snow's magic.

Danielle stepped closer, and her glass sword flicked out to cut the boy's arm. "This blade would never harm my son."

It was all the confirmation Talia needed. She tossed him to the ground at the Stormcrows' feet. "Your Majesty, I can take us to the queen and your children, no matter where they've gone. But only if you promise to spare Snow's life. She must be given to Danielle and Lorindar."

Laurence started to shake his head.

"She's our friend," said Danielle. "Would you be so quick to order Odelia's death? We've no time to negotiate, Laurence."

"If there is a way to spare her life, I will."

Talia's teeth ground together. It was the best they were going to get. "I'll need something of theirs. Preferably something which carries their scents."

They had made it halfway to the library when one of Laurence's guards arrived carrying items from the king's wife and children: an old wig, a pair of shoes, and a frayed blanket. The Stormcrows continued to pressure Laurence to leave, but he refused to abandon his family.

Talia set each of the items on the floor and unfastened her cape. He had a point. If he fled, the possessed queen would be in an excellent position to seize power.

"You're sure this will work?" asked Danielle.

"I should be able to track them to wherever they were taken. If the demon transformed them, the trail will lead me to the place it happens. I'll be able to smell the magic and pick up the scent of their new forms." She flipped the cape about and pulled it tight. "Probably."

The skin rippled to life, clinging to her body as it twisted and crushed her into a new shape. She dropped to the floor, holding her breath as the wolf swallowed her.

"Be careful." Danielle's lips hadn't moved.

With the wolf's senses, Talia could hear the sounds of fighting throughout the palace. Thunder cracked in the air, far too close for her liking. Yells and screams surrounded her, and the burning tang of dueling magic suffused her nose.

Her blood pulsed faster as the wolf urged her to sprint toward the closest battle and throw herself upon her enemies. Instead, she forced herself to take a single step forward, sniffing each item in turn. The blanket's scent was the strongest, smelling of sweat and saliva. The shoes were the daughter's, sour and musty. The wig was the queen's, and carried the scent of clover, most likely from her perfume.

Talia bounded down the hall. The palace was obscenely oversized, with too many places to hide, too many fights spread over too much space. The courtyard at the center could have held all of Whiteshore Palace, with room to expand.

She picked up the queen's trail first. Her perfume lingered in the air, leading Talia around the western side of the palace. She was so intent upon the trail that she nearly collided with a group of Stormcrows in the midst of battle. Ice wasps buzzed angrily overhead as one of the king's wizards spun to face Talia. His hand went to the athame at his waist, and he barked out a spell.

Talia sneezed as the magic washed over her. The cape had been created to deflect spellcraft as effectively as the armor the Stormcrows wore. That armor was little use against an angry wolf. Talia's paws struck his chest, and her weight knocked them both to the floor, sending several others sprawling. A quick nip to the wrist took care of the athame. She clamped her jaws into the metal rings of his armor and tossed him against the wall.

Fire streaked overhead, destroying the wasps. Without a sound, half of the Stormcrows turned and fled. The others started to pursue, but King Laurence ordered them to wait. He pulled two injured men aside. "See to the prisoners, and make sure every fragment of glass on the floor is found and destroyed."

Talia was already running ahead toward double doors which had been battered open. The library beyond was two stories high, a round room with shelves that lined the walls and extended inward like the spokes of a wheel. Tall, narrow windows were spaced so that sunlight fell between the shelves, protecting their contents. Snow would have been in Heaven.

"Are they here?" Danielle asked.

Talia pressed her nose to the floor. The scent was stronger here. She padded into the library, then out again. Clover and sweat. Both of the children had been with the queen when she left the library.

She raced away, following the trail to a staircase where a small mob was holding off a group of Stormcrows and soldiers. The mob fought in silence, armed mostly with knives and shovels, though she spied a few swords and spears. The guards were doing their best to avoid harming them.

"She's there? Beyond those steps?"

Talia gave Danielle an exaggerated nod, and she relayed the message to the others.

As Laurence and his Stormcrows advanced, Talia heard shouts from atop the stairs. The language was Morovan. She didn't recognize the words. Something magical, judging from the burning scent and the way her hackles rose. Stone cracked, and the stairs began to crumble. Two of Laurence's guards yanked him away.

Most of Snow's slaves jumped clear as the staircase collapsed, but others fell into the wreckage. There were no screams, no protests. Dust obscured the worst of the damage, but the smell of blood was strong.

Talia growled, stepping onto the rubble of the bottom steps. The queen was close. She could climb this.

"Don't." Laurence was already turning away. Pain clipped his words. "The magic that shattered the staircase is strong enough to pull the ceiling down upon anyone who tries to climb the wreckage."

"There's a balcony outside," Gerta said. "We can reach the queen through the courtyard."

Outside, the burnt-metal smell of lightning saturated the air. Across the courtyard, flame and smoke devoured the middle of the three-story wall. The roar of the fire drowned out all but the loudest shouts.

Talia's vision flashed white as lightning stabbed the middle of the flames. Thunder buffeted her body. She squeezed her eyes shut, seeing the imprint of the bolt on the inside of her lids.

She scooted into the cover of the doorway and dug at the edge of the fur with her teeth. She ripped the pelt back, tugging and pulling until its magic released her and her body returned to its natural form.

"Queen Odelia is a weather mage," said Laurence. "I recognize her spellcraft. This is her doing."

Dust and smoke billowed through the courtyard as a section of the wall collapsed in flames. "A single weather mage couldn't do this," said Gerta."

Laurence flinched as another bolt struck the wall. "She leads them in their work."

Talia peeked out of the doorway. She could see the balcony to her left, guarded by a waist-high stone rail, but she saw no sign of Queen Odelia.

The fighting wasn't limited to magic. Talia spied one figure running along the rooftop, only to fall when an arrow took him in the thigh. She heard the clang of metal from somewhere behind her.

"Can you make it up to that balcony?" Danielle asked.

"Without knowing what's inside?" Talia studied the wall. The bricks were smooth, with only the thinnest lines of mortar between them. She could probably climb it, but not quickly. "Maybe."

The lightning had finally stopped, though thunder still rang in Talia's ears. Either the other Stormcrows had wrested control of the storm away from the queen, or else she had accomplished whatever destruction she intended. Given how things had gone thus far, Talia's money was on the latter.

She spat on her hands and wiped them on her trousers before approaching the wall. As she stepped out of the doorway, a swarm of ice wasps burst from the balcony overhead. They spread throughout the courtyard, seeking every window and open door.

Talia shoved Laurence back and yanked the door shut. "New plan. We get the king out of here before we lose him, too."

Laurence started to argue. "The queen. My children—"

"Are gone," said Danielle. "Along with whatever Rose Curtana left behind for controlling this demon. Did you see how the fire and lightning were concentrated upon one particular part of the palace? The secret is probably nothing but ashes now."

Talia knew how the king must be feeling. She had retreated from Snow twice before. As a result, Snow had taken Prince Jakob. Now she had Queen Odelia and the power to conquer Allesandria. "You can't protect your nation if this demon enslaves you."

Laurence turned toward the rubble. Talia could see the thoughts going through his head. The stairway wasn't completely impassible. The noise of the fighting would cover the sounds of their approach. If they could take the queen by surprise, they might have a chance. "Ermillina has my wife," he said. "My children—"

"Are with her," said Talia. "I smelled them. It's too late."

Laurence straightened. He tapped his scepter against the wall and closed his eyes, his lips moving silently. "I've ordered all who can to abandon the palace."

"What then?" Gerta stared at the door. "With my mother's secrets destroyed . . ."

They had no way of stopping the demon. No way to save Snow. "First we worry about getting out of here," said Talia.

"And then?" asked Gerta.

Nobody answered.

Chapter 15

KING LAURENCE LED THEM TO A HIDDEN passage that emerged into a small, circular garden filled with marble obelisks. Danielle guessed there were close to a hundred. The walls here had no windows, no doors save the one they had taken. The sounds of battle were muffled here.

Talia scowled. "Unless I got turned around, we should be in the northern part of the palace."

"We are." Laurence stabbed his scepter into ash-dusted earth. The top of the scepter flared to light like a lantern with too much wick. He pointed to the new-formed shadows of the obelisks against the wall. "This garden is hidden, partly by magic and partly by architecture. The shadows will form a doorway. The spell was designed to allow the king and his family to escape the palace."

Danielle approached one of the obelisks. Each was slightly different from the next. This one was black as ink, its six sides polished smooth as glass. Specks of green sparkled within the stone. "What are they?"

"Monuments to the dead." Gerta was standing before a smaller obelisk, round and trimmed with gold. She pressed a hand against its surface. "This is my mother's. Her ashes are worked into the stone. Why was she given a memorial here?"

"She was Queen of Allesandria," said Laurence.

"She was evil."

He tilted his head in acknowledgment. "So we should pretend she never existed?"

"Argue later," Talia snapped. "Finish the spell."

"The portal is almost ready." Sweat beaded Laurence's forehead. The light was brighter now. Two of the shadows were sharper than the rest, forming the sides of a doorway. He adjusted the scepter until the tips of the shadows touched the next row of bricks. The mortar darkened, forming the doorway's upper edge. The stones within began to fade.

Behind them, the door swung inward. Danielle pulled her sword free and ducked behind one of the obelisks for cover. Talia stepped in front of Gerta.

The guards who had accompanied the king moved to block the door. Fire streaked over their heads, spattering against the base of the wall and ruining the shadows of Laurence's magic. Danielle didn't understand Laurence's angry words, but she could guess the meaning from the tone. He yanked up his scepter and turned to face their attackers.

Queen Odelia stood in the doorway, flanked by Stormcrows. Danielle spied others crowded behind her, easily outnumbering those who stood with the king.

The queen was unarmed, dressed in a dark red cloak with wide, black-cuffed sleeves. The backs of her hands were marked in the intricate brown patterns of Morovan tattoos. "Hello, Danielle. Talia."

The buzzing from the hallway meant some of Snow's ice wasps had survived. Danielle could hear others gathering on the gutters overhead. "Where is Jakob?"

"He's safe enough, for now."

Laurence kept his scepter leveled at Odelia and her guards. "Release my wife and children."

Odelia waved a finger, scolding him. "Be careful, Your Majesty. Your marriage might have led to peace with Morova, but what happens to that peace if you kill me? The king of Morova was quite fond of his cousin Odelia. As I recall, he never approved of her marriage to an Allesandrian sorcerer."

Danielle lowered her sword. She gave a silent plea

for help, praying the fire and lightning hadn't driven all of the animals away.

"You know I can't give you the throne," said Laurence. "Even if I wanted to, the law is clear. Ermillina Curtana was sentenced to death. The Nobles' Circle would never accept your claim."

"The throne?" Odelia made a face. "Why would I want that old chair? It's dusty and uncomfortable, the cushion fouled to the core by generations of royal farts."

"Then what?" asked Danielle.

"I want my cousin to answer a question." She pointed to Gerta. "What did you see in her mind when she entered the palace? Answer truthfully, and I'll return your son. If you lie, I'll change him into a butterfly and rip his wings off."

"I saw fear," said Laurence. "Uncertainty. She fears her future."

"Useless prattle," Odelia snapped. "I could learn as much from any false street witch. *What* is she?" For an instant, she appeared confused. "I recognize her, and yet I don't remember . . ."

Danielle could see the conflict on Laurence's face. He knew Snow had no intention of letting them go free, but what choice did he have? "She . . . is you. Her body was born of magic. Her soul is yours, as are her memories."

"Impressive." Odelia entered the garden, staying close to the wall as she circled. All of her attention was on Gerta now. "So Snow gave you her memories in order to lead you here, hoping to find a way to rob me of my power."

"Give me my son," said Laurence.

Odelia reached into her cloak and retrieved a large toad. "Toads are traditional for princes, aren't they?" She planted a quick kiss on the toad, then tossed it lightly to the ground, where it grew into a small boy. His round face and awkward movements reminded Danielle of Jakob. He wore a bulky jacket that went all the way to his fur-trimmed boots.

Laurence dropped to one knee and held out his hand. "Come to me, Henri."

"Be careful," said Danielle. A red line marked the boy's cheek. "You said you'd return him. Remove the glass splinter from his body."

"He's happier this way," said Odelia.

Danielle shook her head. "He's forgotten happiness."

"He's seen beyond it." Odelia trailed her fingers over one of the obelisks. "Beyond false hopes and dreams. Beyond lies and deception. Much like your own son, Danielle." Odelia's blue eyes were dead, despite the amusement in her voice. "I know what he is, what the darklings awakened in you back in the Duchess' caverns. I realized the truth when I fought Hephyra. My mirrors pierced her body, but even as she died, her blood resisted my magic. Fairy blood draws its power from another realm, a world long forgotten by mortals."

Danielle's stomach knotted. This was another trick ... but there was no lie in Odelia's eyes. "You killed Hephyra?"

Odelia shrugged. "I would have preferred to keep that one, but her death served me just as well. She gave me the key." She watched Danielle closely, and her smile grew. "You knew, didn't you? I can see the truth in your face. You knew your son wasn't fully human."

"Please, Snow. Give him back to me."

"Oh, no," said Odelia. "I have plans for him."

Danielle looked to the rooftop. The buzzing had died down. Snow's wasps were in position, ready to swarm into the garden. Danielle concentrated, calling to any birds which might have been close enough to hear her earlier plea. As Odelia waved a hand, Danielle ordered them to strike.

Wasps flew through the doorway and swooped down from above. Laurence's Stormcrows stopped many, but Danielle saw two Stormcrows fall. Fire from Laurence's scepter raced upward, intercepting the second wave of wasps. The caw of blackbirds announced the arrival of Danielle's reinforcements. There weren't as many as she had hoped, but they attacked the wasps without mercy.

It wasn't going to be enough. Talia struck with her sword in one hand, the hem of her cape in the other.

Gerta joined the king, working to try to reopen their escape route, but the shadows danced and flickered despite their best efforts.

Danielle backed toward Talia, staying close to one of the larger obelisks for shelter. More of Snow's Stormcrows slipped into the room, keeping to the walls.

"Henri!" Danielle jabbed her sword into the dirt and lunged for the prince, who was running toward his father. She caught his wrist and twisted him back. He punched with his free hand, but she ignored the blows, tightening her grip until he dropped the icicle-thin shard of glass he had been holding.

Gerta dropped to the ground, scooping the shard with the hem of her shirt. She closed her eyes. "Mirror shattered, power spread. Magic twisted, demon fled. Sister broken, trapped and bound. Let that sister now be found."

One of the wasps slipped past the blackbirds, flying straight for Gerta. Talia jumped over Henri and swung her sword two handed, obliterating the wasp with the flat of the blade.

Odelia stumbled. Her wasps slowed their attack, even as Laurence and the birds continued to destroy those that remained. Odelia squinted at Gerta. "I . . . I *do* remember you."

Stormcrows spread out to surround them, but held back. For the first time since leaving Lorindar, Danielle felt hope. Could Gerta's spell have worked? Was this the reason Snow had created her, to serve as an anchor to help Snow find her way back to herself?

"Do you remember sitting together in our room, the night our mother cursed Baron Estralla?" Gerta asked. "We were so young. As you listened to him beg for mercy, we whispered about what we would do when you ruled Allesandria. The changes you would bring. The lives we would save. Come back to me, Sister."

Talia was crushing the last of the wasps. King Laurence whispered a spell and touched his scepter to his son's forehead. Henri collapsed, asleep.

"Let us take you home," Danielle said.

"I am home." Odelia shivered. "I used to believe I could change this nation. That I could undo the damage my mother had done. Allesandria . . . this world . . . the rot runs too deep. I see what will happen, and what I must do."

"Allesandria will never accept the daughter of Rose Curtana," Laurence warned.

"I've no interest in ruling." Odelia shuddered and stepped back. "You're as naive as I once was, Cousin."

"Snow, please." Gerta flung the glass sliver away. Tears dripped down her cheeks. "You don't have to do this."

Odelia stooped to pick up the half-melted body of one of her wasps. She flicked her fingers, and the stinger flew through the air to bury itself in the king's neck. Just as Talia had described in her vision. Danielle raised her sword and braced herself for the same.

Odelia hesitated. "Take them," she said softly. "Danielle has fairy blood of her own, and Talia burns with fairy magic. I'll need to examine them both to see how that magic responds to my own."

"What of Gerta?" asked Danielle.

"I intend to study her as well, before I reclaim her," said Odelia. Gerta flinched at the word *reclaim*. "Hold them until I arrive."

The guards blocked the only escape from the garden. Talia could do nothing as her weapons were stripped away. They took her cape first, then her sword, knives, and zaraq whip. They also took the rods she used to keep her hair back. Snow would know how effectively Talia could use those rods to kill. Finally, they took the lockpicks from her boots, the fang-shaped punching dagger from the small of her back, and the iron fighting spikes tucked up her sleeves.

One of the Stormcrows secured a blue metal chain around Gerta's neck. It rippled like water as he pressed the end links together until they merged into one.

"This isn't you, Snow," said Talia. "When your mirror broke, a demon—"

"I know what happened." So strange to hear Snow's earnestness from the mouth of a Morovan witch. "It's a partnership. Look at me, Talia. I can cast spells without pain for the first time in years. I can see the world as it truly is."

"How do you know? How many times have you cast illusions to fool those around you? How do you know the demon isn't doing the same thing?"

"Oh, Talia." The exasperation on her face was so typical of Snow it made Talia's breath catch in her chest. "It would be like trying to explain music to a deaf child."

Talia took a small step closer. "What about the demon? What does it take from you?"

"Freedom. I've given it freedom, and it has given me the same."

Even unarmed, Talia could have killed Odelia. A kick to the knee, turning her body and bending her low enough to grab the head. One hand to the chin, while the other grabbed the back of the head. Twist and haul downward to snap the neck. Odelia would be dead before she could speak . . . and it would accomplish nothing. Snow and the demon would survive, with hundreds of slaves at their command.

Odelia's lips quirked as though she knew what Talia was thinking. Knowing Snow, she probably did.

"You saw what they intend to do to me," Odelia said. "How quickly Laurence ordered my double's murder."

Talia clenched her fists. When she closed her eyes, she could still see Snow's body lying dead on the floor.

Odelia took the scepter from Laurence's hand and turned away. The king followed her from the small garden, leaving eight Stormcrows to escort Talia and her companions back through the palace. Servants and guards moved in silence through the halls, an eerie contrast to the chaos of battle such a short time before. Talia could hear screams elsewhere, but within this part of the palace, all was quiet.

The guards brought them down a narrow staircase near the Stormcrows' tower to a small room without windows. A woven rug covered most of the wall, and a trio of fat candles burned in one corner. Two cots were shoved against the walls. Though narrow, the mattresses appeared clean and uninfested. Thick quilts were folded at the foot of each cot. The moment Talia and her friends were inside, the Stormcrows slammed the door behind them.

Gerta slumped against the wall, the candles illuminating the despair on her face. "I thought I could reach her."

"You did," said Danielle. "I could hear it in her voice."

"It wasn't enough."

"Maybe it was." Talia was already searching the room. The cots were framed with wood. Pine, from the smell. It should be easy enough to break them apart for weapons. "She could have killed us or infected us with her mirrors, but she didn't."

"She will." Gerta hugged herself. "When I cast my spell, just for a moment, we were one. When she said she doesn't intend to rule Allesandria, she meant it."

The deadness of her words made Talia stop what she was doing. "What do you mean?"

"She wants to destroy it."

"How?" breathed Danielle.

"I'm not sure."

"Whatever the demon plans, I doubt it will be content to stop at Allesandria's borders." Talia checked the door next. There was no lock, no handle of any sort. The hinges were on the outside, and the crack beneath was too narrow for her fingers. She scraped skin from her knuckles trying to reach through.

"It won't work," said Gerta. "None of it's real. I always hated this room."

"You've been here before?" asked Danielle.

"It responds to the will of the king or queen." Gerta flicked her fingers through the candle flames. "Our mother used to put us—used to put Snow in here, rather. Sometimes for days, until one of her servants reminded her to let us out." She licked her fingers and pinched one of the wicks. When she removed her fingers, the flame sprang back to life.

Wood trim ran along the middle of the walls. Talia tried to dig her fingernails beneath the wood to pry it away, but the trim was seamless. "Can she watch us through this?"

"Probably not anymore." Gerta touched the wood. "This conduit ran unbroken through the palace. When Snow burned down part of the building, she broke that circle . . ." Her eyes widened. "Talia, it was an *unbroken circle.*"

Talia stared, not understanding.

"My mother added this trim when she first became queen. I thought it was so she could communicate with her servants, and to spy on them. But a ring this size could also be used for summoning."

"That's how she trapped the demon," Danielle said.

Gerta nodded excitedly as she picked at the trim. "I bet Noita's enchanted trees provided the wood. She never came to the palace, as far as I know, so she might not even have realized how our mother used her trees."

"Can the circle be repaired?" asked Talia.

Gerta's smile faded. "I wouldn't know how. Even if we knew what kind of tree she used, and we could get more wood from Noita . . . I'd need years to figure out how she did it."

"Snow knew," said Danielle. "That's why she attacked the palace. She destroyed the one thing that could stop her."

"Not Snow. The demon. It would remember how it was first trapped." Talia paced the room. She felt naked without the cape. She had come to rely on the wolf's anger. Without it, it was all she could do to keep her grief at bay. "It's Snow's words. Her thoughts. The demon twisted her, but she's still in there."

"She created me to save her, and I couldn't," said Gerta. "I couldn't reach her."

"You'll get another chance," Talia said. "We know the demon plans to destroy Allesandria. What's its next step, now that they've taken Laurence?"

"I saw a palace of ice," Danielle said. "On a lake."

Talia snorted. "There are hundreds of lakes in Allesandria."

"She may intend to punish the king personally, first." Gerta sighed. "Snow was grateful for everything Laurence did, but deep down she also resented him for receiving everything that should have been hers."

"She never spoke of it," said Talia. Snow rarely talked of Allesandria at all. When she did, it was about the beauty of the mountains, the crisp winter air, the colorful fashions . . . not once had she shown any hint of anger or bitterness.

How much else had she kept to herself?

"They have to return for us eventually," said Danielle. "Sooner or later, the door will open. That will be our only chance to escape. If I summon the rats—"

"Magic keeps all such vermin from entering the palace." Gerta tugged at the chain around her neck. "So long as I wear this, I can't cast the simplest spell. Your weapons are gone. A single Stormcrow could overpower us all, and Snow controls most of the palace."

"Stop calling her that," Talia whispered.

They both turned to look at her.

"That thing. It's not Snow." Talia hammered a fist against the door, which swallowed the impact with hardly a sound. "Snow *fought* this thing. She ripped herself in half so we would have the key to stopping it. It's not her fault we're too dense to figure out how to use that key."

She spun away from the door, rubbing her arms against the chill and fanning her anger until it was almost a match for the wolf's. "Every time you call her Snow, you're giving up on her. You're saying she's gone, that we can't save her. You're wrong."

"Nobody has given up," Danielle said, her words gentle.

"*Don't* try to calm me down." Talia clenched her fingers together.

"You truly love her, don't you?" Gerta's eyes shone.

Her pain broke through Talia's anger. A part of her wanted to apologize. Another part simply wanted to get away. She hadn't asked Gerta to fall in love with her. It wasn't her fault.

No, it was Snow's. She had chosen to give Gerta these feelings. But why?

"I have an idea." Danielle stared at the floor, not meeting anyone's eyes.

"I'm not going to like it, am I?" asked Talia.

"No." Danielle took a deep breath. "This room is enchanted to keep us from escaping. Does that enchantment also prevent others from entering?"

"Absolutely not." Talia's face was red, her expression taut.

Danielle couldn't blame her. If there were any other way . . . "Snow told us the demon's magic was less effective against fairies. The Duchess—"

"You spoke to her?" Talia asked. "You bargained with a fairy criminal? In your own bedchamber! Did you ever think what might have happened? You invited her into your home, risking—"

"When we came to Fairytown to rescue Armand, the Duchess warned that I would need her help again." Danielle heard her own voice rising to match Talia's, and fought to regain her calm. "If you have another idea for escaping this cell, this would be a good time to share it."

"What price did she ask?" Talia knew better than anyone that all fairy bargains came at a cost.

"I had hoped we would be able to save Jakob and Snow both, without her help." Had she accepted the Duchess' bargain before, could they have saved Snow sooner? How many people would still be alive? Danielle took a deep breath, then told them what the Duchess had demanded.

Talia stared. "You're mad."

"The Duchess is powerful," said Danielle. "She could help—"

"Some help isn't worth the price." Talia spun. "Why do we need her aid? We have you. Jakob resisted Snow's power. Couldn't you do the same?"

"Danielle might have fairy blood, but the human is

stronger," said Gerta. "Her mother must have been of mixed-blood. The child of a fairy and a human will be more human than not, and only pureblooded fairies maintain their connections to the fairy hills. After several generations, you'd be indistinguishable from humans, save for the occasional magical quirk."

Talia frowned. "By that logic, Jakob should be even more human, and more vulnerable, than his mother."

Gerta was playing with the candle flames again, cupping her hands around them and studying the red glow of her skin. "The Duchess' darklings awakened Jakob's magic when he was in the womb. Their spells blended the fairy and human magic in him."

"What will Armand say if you give Jakob to the fairy who kidnapped him?" Talia asked softly.

Danielle met her anger without flinching. Anger was preferable to the anguish and loss knotting her chest. "You don't know what I would give to be able to talk to him, to not have to make this choice alone. But Armand is gone, and I don't know how else to get him back."

"The Duchess—" Talia began.

"Had I accepted her offer before, Captain Hephyra might yet be alive." Danielle's voice broke. She had no doubt Snow had been telling the truth about Hephyra's death. "We tried to stop her, and we failed."

"You know what she's done," Talia said. "To you. To Armand. To your stepsister Charlotte. Each time, she evaded the justice of fairy and man alike. You would forgive all that? You would hand your son into her keeping?"

"She also honored her bargain with my stepsisters. Gave them the power they needed to—"

"To try to kill you?" Talia folded her arms. "Your stepsisters are both dead as a result of their dealings with the Duchess!"

"I saw him, Talia." Danielle closed her eyes, remembering her vision from Noita's garden. "I saw Jakob shivering in the cold, so thin he was little more than a creature of sticks and skin."

"We'll find another way," Talia insisted. "One that

doesn't hand the Prince of Lorindar to a fairy. You saw how far the fairies have come in taking control of Arathea. Would you give them the key to your homeland as well?"

"Jakob is my son. Nothing the Duchess does will ever change that. He would only be with them for six months at a time." Fairy bargains were unbreakable. So long as she was careful about the terms of the bargain, she would get Jakob back.

"Do you believe your people will accept a king known to have lived among the fairy folk?"

"Do you have a better suggestion?" Danielle asked.

Talia's lips parted, but she said nothing. Eventually, her shoulders sagged. "No."

Chapter 16

DANIELLE KNELT IN PRAYER. "I NEED YOU, mother. If you've some magic to share, some guidance . . ."

There was no response. She closed her eyes. All of Danielle's life, she had believed her mother's spirit watched over her. The animals that helped with her chores and provided companionship. The gown and glass slippers that led her to the ball and Armand. The glass sword that had saved her life more than once.

Her mother had given her so much, but how much had truly been a gift of her mother's spirit, and how much was simply an artifact of her fairy blood? For so long Danielle had taken comfort from the knowledge that her mother was still with her, but now . . . "If you can hear me, please help us to save your grandson."

"Will the Duchess even be able to respond to you here in this room?" asked Talia.

Gerta shrugged. "It depends on how badly Snow damaged the palace and its protections." Through unspoken consensus, they had backed toward the walls, clearing the center of the room.

Danielle's lips parted, but the words wouldn't come. What would King Theodore say of a princess who bargained his grandson away to fairies? How would she explain to Jakob, when the time came to send him away?

She blinked back tears. Who knew how long it would be before Snow returned. She couldn't afford to stall any longer. She took a deep breath and called the Duchess three times.

The answer came as quickly as before. The rug *thinned*, like oiled paper, until Danielle could see the Duchess beneath, her features silhouetted in blue light. Long fingers stretched out to claw through the rug, as though she were attempting to clear cobwebs from her path, but nothing happened.

"Can you hear me?" Danielle asked.

"So nice to see you again, Princess." The Duchess gave up trying to remove the illusory rug. "How fares your son?"

Danielle held her tongue, refusing to be baited. To her left, Gerta had dropped to her hands and knees. She jabbed a finger at the rug, directly into the middle of the Duchess' face.

"Stop that." The Duchess waved a hand. Gerta yelped and pulled her finger back.

"I wanted to ask whether you've reconsidered your terms," said Danielle. "Think of your future, Duchess. You are a fugitive, hunted by the rulers of Fairytown. You would do well to have the future queen of Lorindar in your debt. I could—"

"You know my price, Danielle." Her profile shifted as she examined their surroundings. "Just as I know you wouldn't pay that price if you had any other choice. I take it you and your friends have failed in your efforts."

King Laurence lost to Snow's magic, Hephyra slain, Jakob still a prisoner . . . there was no point in denying the truth. "If you take my son, it shall be by my rules. No magic to sway his heart or mind. No charms to deceive his senses."

"No magic at all," the Duchess agreed, "save that which is necessary to ensure his safety while in my keeping. He will be well-treated in every way. You have my word."

"Six months only." Danielle reviewed the Duchess' words in her mind again and again, searching for loopholes. "As determined by our calendar. Six months after entering your care, you will return him safely to us."

"Six months of each year, yes." Blue light danced on her features. "In return, I will send one of my darklings to help you find your son."

"A darkling?" Danielle clamped down on her nervousness, remembering the last time she had faced one of the Duchess' darklings. She didn't know how powerful they were, but Snow had destroyed several of them before. "Will one darkling be enough to rescue Jakob?"

The Duchess waved a hand, dismissing her fears. "He will be older than the ones you encountered. Not as powerful as the Dark Man, but strong enough to help you. Remember, I gain nothing without Jakob. It's in my interest to help you rescue the boy."

"We must all be safely returned to Lorindar." Danielle wouldn't put it past the Duchess to order her darkling to kill them all and steal Jakob.

The Duchess laughed, a much deeper sound than Danielle would have expected from a woman of her size. "I can't promise your safety, or that of your friends. I'll not harm you myself, but if one of you should come to harm, that doesn't absolve you of your obligations. Once Jakob is safely returned to Lorindar, I will count my side of the bargain fulfilled. Six months from today, you will summon me again, and I will open a fairy ring to bring Jakob to me."

Danielle glanced at Talia. From her expression, her thoughts were following the same path as Danielle's. They didn't *have* to return home. So long as they kept Jakob away from Lorindar, the terms of the bargain weren't met.

Which meant she could either give up her son for six months of every year, or abandon her home forever, leaving Lorindar without an heir. It would mean stealing Jakob away from his home, away from his family.

"We must be allowed to talk to him while he's in your care, to make sure you're keeping your word," Danielle stalled.

"You may speak together once per week, for no longer than half of one of your hours." The Duchess pressed pale, slender fingers together. "Do we have a bargain, Princess?"

Talia stepped closer. "Your darkling will obey us until we are safely returned home."

"Yes, yes." She waved a hand, clearly growing bored.

Danielle didn't speak. She reviewed the terms in her mind, searching for omissions the Duchess could exploit. What was she missing? "When he comes of age, this bargain ends."

The Duchess pressed her fingers together. "When he is a man, he may choose for himself where he wishes to reside."

"A man by my culture's rules," said Danielle.

"And which culture might that be, my dear? Human or fairy?"

Her jaw clenched. "Human."

Gerta cleared her throat. "The longer we delay, the more likely Laurence or his Stormcrows will return."

Danielle nodded. "We're prisoners in the winter palace in Kanustius. Can your darkling help us escape?"

The Duchess' smile was visible even through the rug. "Once you are free, he will bring you to those who can help you save your son."

"Who?" demanded Danielle.

"Bellum and Veleris, fairy queens of the underworld in Allesandria. They can protect you and help you rescue little Jakob. I imagine they may even be able to help you save Snow."

Fairy queens in Allesandria. Danielle stared into the illusory pit. "I don't understand. Allesandria drove the fairies from their land."

The Duchess laughed again. "My people are not so easily banished. We can be defeated. We can be pushed into hiding. But we existed long before your kind claimed dominion over this world, and we shall exist long after your age ends." She leaned closer. "If you agree to my terms, spill three drops of blood into the portal."

Danielle looked to Talia and Gerta. Gerta sat against the wall, staring into the pit. Talia's jaw was tight, but she nodded ever so slightly.

They had no weapons. Danielle searched for a way to provide the blood to seal the bargain, but nothing in the room appeared sharp enough to cut skin.

"Your nails," Talia said softly.

After a week of travel, Danielle's nails were a ragged mess. She bit one, tugging the corner until the skin tore and blood seeped from the skin.

As she held her finger over the carpet and squeezed blood from the tear, she wondered if Armand would be able to forgive her . . . or if she would ever forgive herself.

Talia inhaled sharply, then slowly forced the air from her lungs. It was a sik h'adan breathing exercise designed to control fear and anger before a fight. It had never worked very well for her. Her jaw was tight. Her fists clenched as she waited.

The darkling didn't climb from the hole so much as he *flowed*. His limbs were shadow, the edges of his form a blur. Long fingers yanked the illusory rug aside.

"What is he?" whispered Gerta. Snow must not have shared those particular memories when she created Gerta.

"A darkling, a child of the Dark Man." A single drop of sweat trickled down Talia's back. The Dark Man was both bodyguard and assassin. His touch could wither a limb or turn a man's eye to dust in the socket. He served none but the queen of Fairytown, and nobody knew how the Duchess had come to control his children.

The darklings they had faced in Fairytown had been little more than children. This one was older, a slender adult with overly long limbs. His movements reminded Talia of a sea creature, sinuous and boneless.

"The king may have sensed the darkling's arrival," said Gerta. "The palace's wards may be damaged, but if he holds his scepter, he'll know magic was used to transport something into these walls."

"Can you get us out of here?" Danielle asked the darkling.

It stepped to one wall. Illusion melted away like ice

shying from a fire as he reached out, revealing bare stone walls. He touched the wall, then drew back.

"The prison was built to contain magic," Gerta said. "Even fairy magic. Entering is easier than leaving."

"So we fight our way out." Talia slipped out of her jacket, wrapping it tightly around her left forearm as a makeshift shield. "The walking ink stain should help. If the king sensed this thing's arrival, he'll be sending his people to investigate."

Talia kept most of her attention on the darkling as she stepped toward Gerta. "You were able to pass through the city walls. Could you also control this room enough to create an exit?"

Gerta tugged the chain around her neck. "I might be able to, if not for this."

"Good." To the darkling, she said, "Your touch ages flesh. Does it work on metal?"

Without a word, the darkling reached out. Gerta shuddered as black fingers curled around the necklace. Talia stepped closer.

"It's all right," said Gerta. "He's not hurting me."

The darkling backed away a short time later. The necklace remained around Gerta's neck, but the metal had lost its luster where the darkling had held it. The links were pitted, and rust flaked away as Gerta grabbed the chain and tugged. The necklace snapped. She flung it against the wall where the door had been a moment before.

"Did you do that?" Danielle asked, indicating the vanished door.

Gerta shook her head. "They know about the darkling. The first thing they'll do is try to use the room against us."

"How—?" Talia bit off her question as the cot behind Gerta disappeared. The candles vanished next, though the light remained. Gerta had captured the candle flames, which now flickered upon the tips of her fingers. The light illuminated water seeping through the naked stone floor.

"Is it real?" asked Danielle.

"Real enough to drown you." Gerta moved to the wall, splashing through ankle-deep water.

"I thought they intended to keep us alive," said Talia.

"Laurence could remove the water before we drown. He might just want to make sure we're helpless when they come in to deal with the darkling." Gerta dropped to her knees, squinting at the wall. "Or Snow might have changed her mind about letting us live."

The water was almost to Talia's knees. Ice cold, it swirled around her legs, real enough to make her shiver. "Can you send it away?"

"I can't fight Laurence. The palace obeys him, and he's too strong." Gerta was tracing lines onto the wall with her finger, over and over. She reached into the water to retrieve the chain. Using one of the broken links, she sliced her fingertip and painted blood onto the stone. The blood washed away, swirling through the water, but she didn't stop. "But I *think* I can do something even better."

Gerta pushed with both hands, and a section of wall slid outward. She held her breath, ducked beneath the water, and crawled through.

"Go," said Talia, pushing Danielle through. She glanced around thc room one last time. To the darkling, she said, "Follow after me. If anyone else tries to come through, stop them."

The cold shocked much of the air from her lungs. The entire opening was submerged, though the water didn't seem to be flowing out through the hole. She squeezed after Danielle, her shoulders brushing the stones to either side. Only a few paces beyond, she found herself on the floor of the icehouse. She was dry, though the frigid air was little improvement over the water. "How did you manage that?"

"The passage works both ways." Gerta grinned, her teeth chattering. "I remember the enchantments used to connect the palace to the icehouse. I reshaped our prison to mimic that enchantment, but there was no way to do it without Laurence knowing. He'll be sending his Stormcrows to find us."

"Nice." Talia turned to the darkling. Without the red cape, they had lost their magical protection. "Can you conceal us from magical eyes?"

The darkling nodded silently, and the room seemed to dim for an instant.

Talia pushed past them, hurrying up the stairs to snatch one of the chisels from the wall. The handle was too thick and the blade was triple the weight of any dagger, but it was better than nothing. Gerta followed suit, grabbing a small hammer. She handed a second chisel to Danielle. "Your sword . . ."

"It's gone." Danielle's words were flat.

"We could sneak back inside," Talia began. "Find Laurence and try to—"

"No." Danielle stepped to the door and cracked it open. "There's no time. Snow controls the palace. We have to escape Kanustius."

Footsteps from below signaled the arrival of Snow's slaves. Talia pushed the door wide and shoved Gerta outside. The darkling slipped past her, all but disappearing into the shadows. Talia and Danielle hurried out and slammed the door behind them.

Talia wedged her chisel beneath the door to jam it, but it wouldn't delay their pursuers for long.

The sun had set, but the streets were as crowded as a market at midday. Families pressed together, lugging packs and wagons toward the blue glow in the distance where the city wall yet burned. Talia took Danielle and Gerta by the hands and dragged them past a horse-drawn cart. A tarp was tied over the cart, and two small children rode with their mother on the very back.

"They must have seen the battle at the palace," Gerta said. "It's been more than a hundred years since anyone breached the walls of Kanustius."

Behind them, black smoke continued to rise from the heart of the city. "And now the palace burns." Talia scowled at a boy who had approached too closely. "Keep an eye out for pickpockets."

"Where will they go?" Danielle asked.

"Most will head south, assuming the guards allow

anyone to leave the city," said Gerta. "Some will try to cross the mountains. Most of the roads are snowed in, but the king keeps two passes cleared throughout the winter."

"Does it matter?" Talia kept close to the edge, avoiding the worst of the pressing crowd. "Snow took the capital of Allesandria in less than a day. At this rate, she'll destroy the entire country before the month is out."

"Allesandria has been at war before," Gerta argued. "Against fairies and humans both. The Circle will know the king has fallen. They will already be sending their forces to Kanustius to try to retake the palace."

"Maybe that's her plan," said Danielle. "To drag Allesandria into civil war and let it consume itself."

A loud crack elicited screams from those closest to the icehouse. Talia glanced behind to see four Stormcrows emerging from the shattered door. They looked around, but so far the darkling's protection seemed to be working.

Talia lowered her head and walked faster, trying to keep the cart between them and the Stormcrows. Just ahead, a girl carried a little boy on her shoulders. He was bundled in a fur blanket with only his face exposed, and he kept twisting around and pointing behind him. He was crying, and kept wiping his nose on the blanket, but it was the girl's expression that most disturbed Talia. Her lack of expression, rather. She simply stared as she trudged ahead. Not a slave to the demon's magic, but another victim, lost and in shock after seeing her palace burn.

Talia's tension grew with each step. There were too many people packed too tightly together, bumping and brushing against each other. It would be far too easy to slip a knife into your neighbor's ribs. The press of bodies would keep the victim upright, and you'd be gone before anyone noticed.

She did her best to watch Danielle and Gerta, guiding anyone remotely threatening away with none-too-gentle jabs of her elbows and fists. She couldn't see their pursuers anymore, but given the Stormcrows' powers, that meant little. Magically disguised, they could walk right alongside Talia and without her cape she would never know.

The darkling had changed form, melting into something that resembled a blackbird if you didn't stare too closely. It flew along the rooftops beside them.

From the murmurs around her, the people knew Allesandria had been attacked, but not by whom. Some stated confidently that King Laurence was dead, and Hiladi soldiers were even now marching upon the city. Others claimed the attack had come from Morova, and that Laurence should never have married Odelia. One man argued it was a rebellion from within, that the king's Stormcrows were attempting to seize control.

"Mark my words," he said. "It's the Deathcrows, Queen Rose's personal killers. They've been waiting for the right time to rise up and destroy her usurper. It's the second Purge."

Talia could see the wall now, burning taller than the trees. Armored Stormcrows peered through the windows of the towers to either side of the gate.

Angry shouts broke out from those closest to the gate. From the left tower, one of the Stormcrows shouted, "By order of King Laurence, the city is sealed. Return to your homes." His voice carried clearly through the protests of the crowd, far too loud to be natural.

Talia glanced at the darkling, perched lazily upon a chimney. The darkling didn't seem to notice the smoke passing through its body. "We could try to fight our way out."

"Storm the tower?" Danielle asked. "With a chisel?"

"I have a hammer, too!" Gerta offered.

"Do you have a better suggestion?" Talia asked, mimicking Danielle's intonation from before.

Danielle scowled. "Gerta, can you open the gate?"

Gerta shook her head. "I can't control it. I might be able to get through the flames, but there's nothing to stop the Stormcrows from killing me as I emerge on the other side."

A change in the tenor of the crowd warned her. Talia had grown accustomed to the subdued murmurs, the muttered complaints, the weeping of children and the forced comfort of their parents and caretakers. The voices grew louder, more fearful behind her. Talia turned and swore.

The four Stormcrows had spread out. Each wielded a wooden rod that glittered blue in the firelight. As Talia watched, one Stormcrow absently clubbed a man on the face. He staggered back, and blood began to well from the cuts the Stormcrow's weapon had left.

"The clubs are coated in glass dust from Snow's mirror," Gerta said. "Back in Lorindar, it took time for the demon to control its victims. Now it's strong enough to do it almost instantly."

People were screaming now, pushing one another to try to get away. The Stormcrows moved without haste, striking everyone in their path. Already the first man infected had succumbed to the demon's power. He seized a woman by the arm and dragged her toward the Stormcrows.

The crowd surged past, trying to escape. Some pounded the doors of the tower. Others fled through the streets.

"Fine," snapped Talia. "You storm the tower. Find a way to open that gate and get out of here." She plucked the chisel from Danielle's hand. "I'll need this."

"What about you?" asked Gerta.

Talia squeezed past a man bent double under the weight of the belongings strapped to his back. "I'm going to try to slow them down. Go!"

The four Stormcrows spied her at once, and began pushing through the crowd toward her. A man with a bloody hand grabbed her shoulder. She punched him in the nose, but the pain didn't seem to affect him. With a curse, she seized his finger and twisted, snapping bone to make him release her.

She shoved her way into an alley between a tavern

and some sort of clothing shop. Chunks of ice dropped onto the street, her only warning before a body leaped from the roof to land on top of her. She rolled with the impact, coming up on top of her attacker, a heavyset, gray-haired woman who looked like she should be bouncing grandchildren on her knee.

Once again, pain was no deterrent. Talia had to dislocate the woman's shoulder to free herself, and by then more of the demon's slaves were following her into the alley. She could almost hear Snow teasing her over yet another ill-thought-out plan.

A cold shadow swooped past her head. The darkling dropped to the ground and strode toward her pursuers. Talia glanced back to see hands seize the darkling's arms. Moments later, those hands began to wither, fingers drying and crumbling to dust. "Don't kill them if you can help it!"

She tried the servant's entrance to the tavern, but it was locked and barred. Behind her, there was a flash of light. Squinting through her fingers, Talia could just make out one of the Stormcrows driving the darkling back. Where were the other three? Hopefully, they had spread out to trap her instead of chasing Gerta and Danielle.

She hurried into the next street, where she deliberately crashed into a man wearing a heavy cloak of bear fur. This was no demon slave. He shouted and fought as Talia yanked his cloak free.

From the corner of her eye, Talia spotted the darkling coming up behind her. She bared her teeth. "You can give me the cloak, or you can take it up with my fairy friend."

The man paled.

"Sorry," Talia said as she flung the cloak over her shoulders. She joined the fleeing crowd, adjusting her posture to try to make herself appear shorter and broader of shoulder. To the darkling, she said, "Get to Danielle and Gerta. Keep them safe."

And then she waited, allowing herself only furtive glances over her shoulder as the Stormcrow and his slaves spread into the street, searching for her. She spied a second Stormcrow a block down.

The screaming was worse now. People pressed together with no regard for safety. Few even knew what they were running from. Their panic was infectious. Talia's heart pounded faster, and her stomach tightened. Sweat dripped into her eyes. She fought the need to push through the crowd and escape.

Instead, she stayed at the back, feigning weakness. A hand closed around her arm, spinning her roughly around. She allowed herself to fall to her knees, keeping her hood over her face as she watched the feet around her until she spied black polished boots approaching and heard the rippling jingle of Stormcrow armor. Two men hauled her to her feet.

She slammed the butt of her chisel into the center of one man's forehead. The other she elbowed in the throat. The Stormcrow raised his weapon high, blood dripping from the glass dusting the wood.

Talia dropped her chisel and stepped close, one hand catching the Stormcrow's wrist, the other clamping around his elbow. She kept moving, taking him off-balance and twisting the weapon from his hand. A sharp blow to the back of his neck dropped him to the street. She crouched long enough to seize the athame from his belt with her other hand.

Two more Stormcrows ran toward her. A look back showed the third coming from behind. They weren't alone.

"Fine," Talia muttered to Snow's imagined teasing. "You're right. This was a stupid plan."

She ran back through the alley, lashing out with knife and club to clear her way through the demon's slaves. Possessed or not, the crowd's reflexes were still human, and there weren't enough to simply overpower and smother her. Not yet, at least. She sacrificed the cloak and lost a bit of hair when someone grabbed it, but she made it through.

The instant she emerged onto the street, she felt the

change. The people here were free, and surged *toward* the gates. The walls still burned, but the gate itself was open. "Thank you, Danielle!"

She jumped onto a cart, ignoring the protests of its owners. She glanced behind. The Stormcrows weren't close enough to catch her.

The closest pulled a gold-tipped rod and pointed it at her. There was a heavy impact on her shoulder, but she saw nothing. Instead, the spell seemed to splatter over her body. It felt . . . *sticky*, like someone had bathed Talia's skin in molasses.

Talia grabbed her knife. Every movement tugged her skin, slowing her movements. With the wolfskin, she could have easily torn through the enchantment. Without it . . . she clenched her jaw, pulling back to throw even as the Stormcrow's spell threatened to tear the skin from her bones.

A dog snarled and seized the Stormcrow's leg in his teeth. A rat scurried through the crowd to join him.

"I told you to get to the tower," she yelled.

"Is that what you said?" Danielle asked innocently. "I'm sorry, I must have misheard." She looked skyward, and a pair of blackbirds swooped down to harass another Stormcrow.

"Don't move," ordered Gerta as she scrambled onto the cart. "The more you struggle, the faster you'll be torn apart."

A donkey brayed and dragged its wagon across the road, barreling toward the Stormcrows.

"Hurry," said Danielle.

Gerta squinted, then jabbed her thumb into Talia's shoulder deep enough to bruise. She repeated a hasty chant, then spun and pressed her thumb to the side of the wagon.

The pain vanished. Talia flung her club, catching the first Stormcrow in the stomach. She grabbed Gerta by the arm and jumped down.

They had gone only a short distance when the wagon creaked and splintered behind them.

"I couldn't break the spell, so I had to transfer it. That's what would have happened to you." Gerta looked over her shoulder at the wreckage of the wagon. It had been reduced to kindling. "It's not a nice spell."

Talia swallowed and grabbed Danielle and Gerta by the hands. She had already begun to sweat from the heat of the walls. "How did you get the gates open?"

"The people in the towers haven't been infected yet," Danielle said. "So we told them the truth. It took some persuasion, but their spells confirmed our words."

"What truth?" Talia asked.

Gerta's voice hardened. "That Kanustius has fallen."

Chapter 17

THE LAKE WAS THE CLOSEST THING TO beauty Snow had seen since the demon showed her the world as it truly was. With her followers waiting silently at the shore, the lake was lifeless and frozen and perfect. "What do you think of your new home, Jakob?"

Beside her, Prince Jakob shivered and plopped down to sit on the ice. He had spoken less and less of late, but for the first time in more than a day, a spark of interest lit his eyes. He brushed off a spot on the ice and examined his reflection. "It's a mirror."

"Very good." She conjured a gust of wind to clear a larger patch. "From the outside, Allesandria appears strong. These people have warred with humans and fairies alike, defeating all who challenged their borders. When Allesandria falls, the fatal blow will be struck not from the outside, but from within."

With Laurence fallen, the Nobles' Circle would pool their forces both physical and mystical to retake the palace. Nobody wanted to risk another ruler like Rose Curtana. But Snow's mirrors had already reached the Circle.

She watched the ice, peering from one mind to the next to eavesdrop on the Circle's debates. The Lord Protector of Voma worked to raise a stone army to defend his city. The ruler of Caronia called for an exception to the laws governing the summoning of demons, claiming it was the only way to meet this threat. One young noble even proposed raising Queen Curtana. "Better an undead queen who can be controlled than a demon-possessed king."

Snow reached through the mirror, nudging her servants. Unlike the king, these slaves would not fight openly; they would bicker and argue, delaying consensus and sabotaging the Circle's efforts as the chaos spread.

A thought opened a new window in the ice, allowing her to see through King Laurence's eyes. She extended herself through the mirror shard in his flesh, donning his body like an ill-fitting dress. She stayed only long enough to plant her next command before turning her attention back to Jakob. "Your mother bargained with fairies to escape Kanustius. You're going to help me find them."

Several of Snow's Stormcrows had seen the darkling. Danielle must have dealt with the Duchess. So much for those high ideals she lorded over everyone else. She was no different. When her life was at stake, she had no compunctions about dealing with criminals.

Jakob was on his hands and knees, tracing one finger over the ice. It was the most attention he had paid to anything since leaving Lorindar.

"Would you like to learn mirror magic, Jakob?"

He nodded.

The ice cracked at Snow's touch, offering up a frozen shard the size of her palm. She handed it to Jakob. "Why don't you try searching for your mother? Be careful. The edges are sharp."

Sharp enough to draw blood. The more he tried to use the frozen mirror, the more his blood and magic would seep into the ice.

"I'm hungry," said Jakob.

Snow blinked. When had she last eaten? She no longer paid any mind to the complaints of her body, but it had been at least a day . . . She gestured to those gathered on the shore, sending a small group away to hunt.

The wind blew harder, swirling snow into the air. Instead of dispersing, the snow began to solidify. Strands of ice grew like a crystalline web stretching up around her.

She glanced down at Laurence, who clutched his scepter in both hands as he spoke to the surviving members of the Nobles' Circle, passing along Snow's offer. Many would refuse, but some would seek her out, hoping to bargain for power as they had with her mother.

It was poetic. Almost beautiful, in its own way. Their corruption would lead them to her, and that same corruption would damn Allesandria for its crimes.

Talia used shoulders, elbows, and the occasional low kick to clear a path. The road beyond the gate was wide enough to spread out, and Talia dragged her companions ahead, all but running. Only when the road reached the outer edge of the woods and the trees began to block the flaming wall from view did she slow.

"Our supplies are gone," Danielle commented.

"You want to go back and get them?" Talia asked. She searched the trees until she found the darkling. It had returned to what she assumed was its natural shape, crouching like a monkey in a snow-dusted pine.

When the road neared the top of the hill, Talia turned back to look at Kanustius. Smoke still rose from the palace, and she could make out smaller plumes where other fires had spread through the city. Were those started by the demon's slaves as well, or were they merely a symptom of the spreading chaos?

"Snow would have taken the city regardless," said Danielle.

"It happened so quickly." Less than a day to infiltrate the palace, seize the royal family, and destroy their one hope of trapping the demon. "She has an army now."

"Her power has limits," said Gerta. "The Stormcrows fought hard, and many of her fragments have been destroyed." Her voice caught, and her gaze went to the city.

"What is it?" asked Danielle.

"She created me to stop this, but I wasn't strong enough. I didn't find the circle in the palace until it was too late. I couldn't stop her from taking Laurence and Odelia."

"You got us out of that prison," Talia said firmly. "We're alive, and we're free."

"For now." Gerta shook herself. "I'm sorry. You're right. We should keep moving. We know the demon is vulnerable to fairy magic. The Duchess said her darkling would lead us to Bellum and Veleris. That they could help us to save Jakob and Snow."

They stopped at a crossroads a short distance ahead. Most of the crowd trudged south, though a smaller number turned north toward the harbor. Talia watched the darkling, which had reverted back to its blackbird shape. It flew straight ahead, toward the mountains.

Talia waited until they had left the other refugees behind to call the darkling. "Where exactly are you taking us?"

The darkling swooped to the ground, landing in the snow without a sound. *"To Speas Elan."*

Talia's teeth grated at its voice. She had never heard a darkling speak before. The words were like steel scraping over bone. The voice was high-pitched, somewhere between male and female.

"How long a journey will this be?" asked Danielle.

"I will carry you."

Talia raised an eyebrow at the darkling.

"Even if you could carry us all, your touch would destroy us," Danielle said.

"Only if I wish it."

Talia snorted. "How comforting."

The darkling's body was already shifting, expanding into the form of a large reindeer. As Talia watched, he split apart, until a second reindeer stood beside the first. They appeared . . . *thinner*. She could see the shapes of the trees through their bodies.

"They're identical," said Gerta. "You can see the thread of darkness connecting them."

Talia squinted until she spotted the shadow stretching from the back of one reindeer to the horns of the second. What would happen if that line were cut? Would it hurt this creature, or would they simply end up with two smaller darklings?

Nobody moved toward the reindeer. The darkling said nothing, simply waiting.

"It was your idea to call this thing," Talia muttered to Danielle.

Danielle made a face, but stepped closer, stretching out one hand as carefully as if she were reaching over an open flame. Both reindeer turned to watch her, the heads moving in unison. Her fingers brushed the first on the neck. When nothing happened, she put a hand on the reindeer's back. With her other hand, she grasped the base of an antler and pulled herself up.

Talia grimaced and followed suit. The reindeer was cool to the touch, but felt as solid as any horse. Her skin tingled at the contact. Gerta climbed up with her, settling herself in front of Talia. The darkling didn't appear to mind the extra weight.

"So who exactly are these fairy ladies that are supposed to help us?" Talia asked, trying to relax into the rhythm of the darkling's odd, bouncing gait.

"I've never heard of them," said Gerta. Her back rested ever so lightly against Talia, reminding her of the last time she had ridden with Snow. Snow had leaned against her in just that way.

"That's good," said Danielle. "Hopefully, Snow doesn't know them either."

Talia glanced to the side of the road, searching the trees. The reindeer made good speed, but it was hardly subtle.

"Few people brave these roads in winter," Gerta said, as if reading her thoughts. "Officially, most of the mountain passes are closed from first snowfall through the spring thaw."

"Someone's been through here," Talia said, pointing to the road. The earth was frozen hard as rock, but she could make out other tracks in the snow.

"Unofficially, the mountains are home to those who prefer to live outside of the cities and the king's law. Criminals and others who don't wish to be found, like Noita."

"Or Roland," Talia said, remembering the name of Snow's first lover.

Gerta nodded. "Or the fairies."

"What do you think they'll ask in return for their help?" Talia asked.

Even from here, she could see Danielle tense. "We'll face that once we find them."

"I just hope they can help us at all," said Gerta. "The fairies of Allesandria aren't what you're used to in places like Lorindar or Arathea. The strongest of their race were hunted down more than a century ago. The survivors fled."

"Obviously not all of them." Talia grabbed the reindeer's antlers and tugged, trying to slow the creature.

"What's wrong?" asked Gerta.

Talia twisted to search the woods behind them. "Hoofbeats, but they've stopped."

Danielle turned to look. "You're sure?"

"Sure enough." Without her cape, her senses were merely human.

"Snow's people?" Danielle asked.

"I don't think so," said Gerta. "We're still alive, aren't we?"

Branches rustled in the woods to the left, and a startled pheasant burst from the bushes. It might have been nothing. Or it might have been one of their pursuers running ahead to warn his friends to prepare an ambush.

"If I were planning to rob a group of unarmed travelers, I'd choose a place where I could surprise them," said Talia. "Beyond that hilltop, or hidden among the trees where the forest is thicker."

Danielle was whispering to the air. A short time later, the pheasant returned to land on the road beside her. She bent down, still speaking in that same soft voice. The pheasant shook its feathers, spread its wings, and flew off. It landed in the trees at the crest of the hill and cried out with a rusty, "kor, korr."

"A shame he can't tell me how many are waiting," Danielle said. "Do you think they'll have archers?"

Talia shook her head. "Not likely in this cold, unless they want their bows to crack. Slings, possibly. Or simple stones."

"We could go back," suggested Danielle. "Try to find another way."

"I'm tired of running. And like you said, we need supplies." Talia jumped down from the reindeer, jogging ahead toward where the pheasant continued to shout an alarm. She tugged the knife from her belt, as all of the anger and helplessness of the past days surged to the surface. She raised her voice. "Hail the bandits!"

Behind her, she heard Gerta sigh. "Did she just—"

"Yes." Danielle raised her voice. "Talia, please try to remember that not all of us share your gifts."

"So stay out of my way." Talia stopped in the middle of the road to wait. She had already spotted one bandit perched in the trees. The pheasant had landed almost within arm's reach, and he was trying unsuccessfully to shoo it away.

Others stepped out from hiding. Talia counted seven, including the one in the tree. Add a few more coming up behind, and there could be as many as a dozen. They looked more cold and miserable than dangerous. Most were bundled in jackets and furs, making it all but impossible to tell male from female. The apparent leader brandished a gleaming hunting knife twice the size of Talia's blade.

"Put that toy away, girl." A woman, middle-aged from the sound of it.

Talia gave a quick peek over her shoulder, making sure Danielle and Gerta were staying back. They had dismounted, and were standing behind the reindeer. Good thinking.

"Nobody's going to hurt you," the bandit woman went on. "Not unless we have to."

"I want that one, Mother," said a girl wearing a goatskin wrap. "The red-haired one with the pretty boots and the fancy jacket."

Talia smiled and pulled out a small purse. The two closest bandits raised weapons. One carried a small spear, the other a leather sling. From the way it hung, he had already loaded a stone or metal shot. Talia simply twirled the purse, then tossed it to the ground with a clink. "You're welcome to all the gold we have. All you have to do is take it."

She glanced at Gerta, who nodded and turned to face the other way. Gerta's magic should make sure nobody came up from behind. Talia turned her attention back to the man with the sling.

She didn't have long to wait. He looked to his leader, and the sling drooped slightly.

Talia whipped the knife through the air. It lodged in his forearm, and he fell back with a cry. Talia was already twisting to the side by the time the spearman threw. She slapped the spear away and grimaced. She would have a bruise on her forearm from that one.

For days she had faced demons and wizards. She had lost her best friend and stood helpless to protect the prince. She had watched the capital of Allesandria fall, and throughout it all she had wanted nothing more than an opponent with whom she could stand and fight. Now the bandits had given her that opportunity.

The battle was disappointingly short. Most of the bandits had fallen or fled by the time Talia squared off against their leader. Of the five that remained, three were unconscious or choosing to pretend. The other two were crawling away. Talia grinned and twirled a single-edged short sword she had taken from one man. "That's a nice knife you've got there . . ."

Soon Talia, Danielle, and Gerta were bundling their newfound supplies together. The bandits hadn't been carrying much, but they had extra cloaks and blankets, not to mention better weapons.

"You enjoyed that." Danielle sounded like she hadn't decided whether she should be annoyed or amused. She strapped the short sword to her belt. "And where did you get that purse?"

"You don't want to know." Talia tucked the bandit woman's knife through her belt and hid a second, smaller dagger in her boot. "Besides, better I deal with them than our darkling friend." She rubbed her arm.

"Let me see that," said Gerta.

"I'm fine."

"Flesh and bone against spear?" Gerta scooped a handful of snow. "Sure you are. Hold this against the arm for the swelling."

Talia hissed as Gerta pressed the snow to her arm, but she didn't pull away. "It's just a bruise."

"You're lucky."

"Luck had nothing to do with it." Though her timing was off. She had grown too used to the added strength and speed of the cape.

"Come on," said Danielle. "If you're through playing, we have fairies to find."

The next day and a half passed without incident, as the darkling carried them higher into the mountains. The air was colder here, freezing the inside of Talia's nostrils each time she inhaled. With fewer trees to block the wind, she had taken to riding with her head down, the hood of her stolen cloak pulled low.

The darkling stopped without warning, twin reindeer shaking their heads in unison. When he refused to move, Talia slid to the ground and stretched. The snow was ankle-deep, swirling in the wind like the desert sands of home. "What is this place?"

"We're on an old mining road," said Gerta. "The mountains are riddled with them."

The reindeer stepped together, melting into the darkling's humanoid form.

"This is where we'll find help?" Talia searched the landscape, finding nothing but snow-covered outcroppings, gnarled trees, and the overgrown hint of the old road.

"They're watching us." Gerta turned in a slow circle. "I can't tell you where it's coming from. There could be a glamour of some sort. If I had my mirrors—" She flinched. "Snow's mirrors, I mean."

Danielle blew on her hands for warmth before tucking them back beneath her arms. She straightened and called out, "I am Danielle of Lorindar. The Duchess of Fairytown said you would help us."

"The Duchess is far too free with other people's secrets." The voice came from an orange-hued rise of rock to their left, which appeared to have been carved away to clear a path for the road. Knife in hand, Talia moved cautiously toward the rock.

Green-tarnished metal poked through the drifted snow at its base. Talia knelt, brushing away the snow to reveal a copper cone that appeared to have been hammered point-first into a crack in the rock. The rim was pitted, and flakes of metal fell away at her touch. Warm air wafted from a small hole in the back of the cone.

Danielle crouched beside Talia. "We wish to speak to Bellum and Veleris."

"And so you have." This was a new voice, deeper than the first. "We've granted your wish. Now go away."

"Please," said Danielle. "We need your help."

"Ask for her still-beating heart," said the second voice, chuckling. "See if she's serious."

"Hush." That was the original speaker again. "All are welcome here, Princess. To the right, you should see a small doorway."

Talia and Gerta dug away more snow until they found a square doorway built into the earth, edged by stacked stones. A rusted ring hung from the center. "That door wasn't there a moment ago," said Talia.

"It was." Gerta was frowning at the door. "We just couldn't see it."

Danielle reached for the ring, but Talia moved to stop her. "Let me. We don't know what's on the other side."

Talia yanked, and the door scraped open, revealing a tunnel that sloped down into the darkness. Fog puffed out like the breath of the mountain. Wooden beams were pressed into the earth, forming crude stairs.

"Don't stand there all day," said the second voice. "You're letting the heat out."

"And what's waiting for us at the end of this tunnel?" Talia asked. There was room to enter, but she would have to crawl. Meaning anyone on the far side would have an easy time dispatching intruders.

"Only one way to find out." Laugher followed her from the metal cone. "We meant what we said. Everyone is welcome to enter. Whether you'll be allowed to leave is another matter entirely."

Chapter 18

THE STAIRS WERE WORN, BUT DRY. Roots poked through the walls and ceiling of the tunnel like white threads. Danielle crawled on hands and knees, her shoulders brushing the dirt and boards to either side.

"You think they'll help us?" Gerta asked from up ahead. She had conjured a small light from the setting sun, capturing a soft orange flame which scurried ahead like a flickering mouse.

"The Duchess wants Jakob." Speaking the words gave strength to the despair Danielle had worked to hold at bay. She clenched her throat, swallowing the fear until she regained her self-control. "Until we save him, she gets nothing."

Sweat trickled past one eyebrow, down the side of her cheek. She paused to loosen her jacket. Only a short distance into the tunnel, and already it felt like summer. The dry air smelled faintly of smoke and oil.

The darkling pulled the door shut behind them. For the moment, Danielle was more worried about the darkling than the Duchess. This one was older than the ones she had fought before, and seemed less . . . *wild*. So far it had obeyed the Duchess' commands to protect Danielle and her companions, but that didn't make her any less uncomfortable with it creeping silently along behind her.

The tunnel opened into a small, square room, reinforced by thick square-cut beams and wooden boards. On the opposite wall, an open doorway led into darkness. Gerta clucked her tongue, and her light scurried closer to one of the beams. She examined a series of simple pictures carved into the wood. "This was used as a supply room. Food, water, new tools."

"And now it's the entryway into a damned fairy lair," said Talia.

A handful of gravel flew out of the darkness. Most struck Talia, though some caught Danielle in the face and shoulder. Talia jumped to the side of the doorway, knife in hand.

"Mind your tongue, human. There's no cursing here." A pulsing orange glow approached from beyond the doorway. "Or have humans given up any pretense of civility when entering another's home?"

"Our apologies," said Danielle, cutting off Talia's response. "You understand our language?"

"Aye. Veleris feels it's important for us to learn the surface tongues." The glow was getting closer. It reminded Danielle a little of a blacksmith's forge. "I'll be taking you to our queens myself. But first, cease that magical light. Are you trying to draw the fairy hunters upon our heads?"

Gerta ended her spell. "I didn't know—"

"No magic! Nothing that could be detected by the surface."

"What about your glamour on the doorway?" Gerta demanded.

"Fairy magic is natural. Subtle. Easier to hide. Even so, we use only what's necessary to survive."

Danielle's eyes had adjusted enough for her to make out the outline of their guide and his mount. She stepped back as they emerged into the already cramped room. She reached for her missing sword without thinking. "Is that a dragon?"

"They're the best thing for riding about the mines." The dragon was as long as a horse from head to tail, but its body was much lower to the ground. The scales were a dirty red, almost brown. The orange glow Danielle had seen came from the dragon's mouth, brightening with each breath. The wings were little more than stubs growing behind the forelegs, which made Danielle suspect this was a young dragon.

The rider was a dingy man, no higher than Danielle's knee. He wore a round helmet and heavy, oft-mended clothes so filthy she couldn't begin to guess the original color.

"He's beautiful." Gerta crouched in front of the dragon, holding out one hand. "What's his name?"

"Careful." The man tugged a silver rope which was looped around the dragon's neck. "I've raised Koren here from an egg, but he'll still take your fingers if you startle him."

"And who are you?" asked Talia.

He raised a small shovel and rang the blade against his helmet in salute. "You can call me Tommy."

Danielle tilted her head. "Your name is Tommy?"

"No. I said you can call me Tommy." He tucked his shovel into an oversized leather sheath he wore over one shoulder. "Even if I trusted you with my name, you humans can never tell us apart anyway. Easier to share a name among ourselves when dealing with the likes of you."

"He's a knocker," said Gerta, rubbing the scales along Koren's snout. "A mountain fairy, kin to the kobolds."

"Only handsomer and better behaved," said Tommy.

Gerta continued to fawn over the dragon. "What does he eat? How often does he shed his skin? Where will he go when he's full grown?"

"They'll eat just about anything, though Koren here has a fondness for fish. When he gets too big, he'll run off into the deeper tunnels to join the rest of his kind." Tommy leaned down to pound the side of Koren's neck. The dragon curved his head around, and a tongue the length of an eel slapped Tommy's face. He laughed and shoved Koren's face away. "Their breath will curl your beard."

"You'll take us to Bellum and Veleris?" Danielle asked.

"Right this way, my lady." He drew his shovel and knocked it against the ground. The dragon swiveled about, away from the sound. A few more raps guided the dragon back into the tunnel. Thankfully, this tunnel was large enough for Danielle and the others to walk upright.

"Most of the main entrances to the mine are long buried," he said. "We keep a few of the old vents cleared out, but given the way your people feel about our kind, we don't encourage visitors down here. Not even those who've been vouched for by fairy nobles."

"The Duchess is no noble," said Talia. "She's—"

"She rules over her kingdom, small as it may be," Tommy interrupted. "That makes her noble to us. Over in Fairytown, they might cling to their old ideas about the noble caste, but when you've been driven into the dark, you worry less about blood and more about survival.

"The laws against fairykind were overturned years ago," said Danielle. "Why do you continue to hide?"

Tommy snorted. "Show me the law that can soften the hate and the fear in people's hearts, and then we'll talk."

It didn't take long for Danielle to become disoriented as they made their way deeper into the mountain. Tunnels veered off at seemingly random angles. She thought they were sloping downward, but her senses weren't sharp enough to know for certain.

The fairies kept their home in good repair. Bright planks showed where aging wood had been replaced in the walls and ceiling. She would have expected an abandoned mine to be quiet, but the air moving through the tunnels created a low background hum. She heard the occasional clank of metal against stone in the distance, though she couldn't have said which direction the sounds came from.

"Here we go," said Tommy, steering his dragon into a small room with a square-framed pit in the floor. "Mind your step." He rapped his shovel against the dragon's flank, and they disappeared into the pit. The dragon didn't bother with the wooden ladder built into the side; his claws gripped the rock with ease.

When Danielle reached the bottom, she found herself in a larger cavern. Stalactites hung from the ceiling, about thirty feet up at the highest point. The floor had been smoothed flat. Barrels lined the wall to the right. A crude, waist-high barrier of stacked stone blocked a drop-off on the far side.

Four knockers were currently working to shore up that barrier. One tamped a stone into place with his shovel. Another was tapping the blade of his shovel against the wall, listening intently to the sounds.

They turned away from their work and greeted Tommy in a language Danielle didn't recognize. He laughed and jumped down from Koren. Without warning, he grabbed his shovel in both hands and swung it at the nearest knocker.

The knocker did the same. The clang of the shovels nearly deafened her, but the knockers were all laughing.

"They greet each other by swinging shovels at each other's heads," Gerta said.

Danielle smiled wryly. "Sounds like Talia's kind of people."

Tommy beckoned them forward. "Welcome to Speas Elan. Gold Haven, in your tongue. Though most of the gold was hauled out long ago."

"How many of you whackers live down here?" Talia asked.

"*Knockers*, thank you very much. It's well over two hundred at last count."

The air was even warmer here. Danielle could feel the heat wafting up from the drop-off behind the barrier. She wiped sweat from her face, tucking her hair back behind her ears.

When she had first entered Fairytown in Lorindar, back before Jakob was born, she had been struck by the grandeur of the place. The vivid colors, the larger-than-life flowers and trees, the glow of magic. Speas Elan was the opposite, as if something had leached the color from this underground world. Dirt and dust painted everything in shades of red and brown. Even the flames of the knockers' lanterns appeared subdued.

Through stairs cut into the left side of the cavern, Tommy brought them down into a second chamber. Here, a group of pixies, goblins, and a troll of some sort sat at a table with what looked like a normal human man.

"Oh, yes," Tommy said to her unanswered question. "We have a few humans living down here. Fugitives, for the most part. Veleris has a soft heart. So long as they mind their place and earn their keep, they're allowed to stay."

"And if they don't?" asked Talia.

Tommy winked. "The dragons can't eat fish all the time, eh?" He dismounted and tied his dragon to a stone rail carved into the wall. After a short exchange with the troll, he turned back and said, "The Ladies are in the next room. Try not to make them angry."

"What will they do?" Danielle asked.

"Oh, they probably won't hurt you, not with the Duchess vouching for you," Tommy said. "But most people prefer talking to Veleris. Make them angry or upset, and Bellum takes over. Mind your manners, and you'll do all right. Leave your weapons with Oklok there, and come along."

The troll held out a hand large enough to crush a human's skull. Danielle handed over the short sword she had taken from the bandits, and waited while the others did the same. Gerta gave over a sling and dagger, and Talia did the same with her hunting knife.

Danielle cleared her throat. "Talia?"

Talia's answering look was half innocence, half challenge.

"We're guests here, asking for help."

Talia rolled her eyes, but slipped the black-hilted athame from her sleeve and gave it to the troll.

The next room was larger, dominated by a low oblong table carved from the stone. For seating, the floor had been dug out around the table like a moat. At the table, midway through a meal of mushrooms and fish, were a handful of goblins, a greenish wart-skinned creature of a race Danielle didn't recognize, and—

"The Fairy Ladies of Allesandria." Tommy rapped his shovel to his helm twice as he bowed to the two-headed giant sitting at the head of the table. "Veleris and Bellum." He leaned toward Danielle and whispered, "Veleris is the head on your right."

The giant stood. Bellum continued chewing, seemingly absorbed in her meal as Veleris wiped her mouth on her wrist and studied them. They—or was it she?—stood twice as tall as a man, and three time as broad. Her arms were thicker than Danielle's thighs. She wore a thick knee-length skirt dyed orange, with matching boots. Her skin was as pale as Snow's.

Veleris smiled, displaying yellowed teeth the size of a horse's. Her black hair was pulled to her left in a braided rope that brushed her shoulder, and she wore a leather headband studded with crudely hammered nuggets of gold.

"Thank you, Tommy," said Veleris. Danielle recognized the voice. She searched the ceiling until she spotted a small metal cone in the rock, currently blocked by a wooden plug. They must have somehow run pipes through the entire mine to carry the sound to the door on the surface.

Tommy saluted again and backed away. To Danielle and the others, he whispered, "Good luck."

"So the Duchess sent you to us," said Veleris, studying them each in turn. When she came to the darkling, she grimaced. "And you've brought one of her spies."

Danielle bowed. "The darkling helped us escape Kanustius, Your Grace." She wasn't certain of the Ladies' proper title, but "Grace" was an accepted default among fairy nobles.

Veleris and Bellum glanced at one another. Bellum's hair was shorter, slicked to her right with some sort of oil or grease. Her face was a mirror of Veleris', broad and blocky, with a heavy brow, but where Veleris seemed genuinely pleased to meet them, Bellum looked like she wanted nothing more than to step across the table and start crunching bones.

"We are aware of the attack on Kanustius," said Veleris. "What help would you ask of us?"

Danielle stepped closer to the edge of the table. "I was told you could help me to find my son, and that you would know how to stop the demon which has attacked Allesandria. The demon which has now taken King Laurence." As quickly as she could, she summarized what they knew of the demon.

"Find your son *and* stop a demon," Bellum muttered. "That's *two* favors. Large favors. Humans are fools. Conjuring demons, then running around like children when their plans sour. A true demon, from the sound of things. You might as well burn your kingdom now and save yourselves the time."

"I'm afraid I must agree," said Veleris. "Your people are impulsive and quick to act. It can be a strength, but you neglect to think beyond your short lives to the consequences of your actions."

"We didn't crawl through miles of dirt and rock for a lecture," Talia said. "This demon has already burned the palace."

"Let them burn!" Bellum snatched the headband from Veleris and placed it on her own brow. "Let them know what it feels like to be hunted down, to be driven from their homes and destroyed. The more of you the demon kills, the safer this world becomes for our people."

The other fairies at the table slunk away, escaping Bellum's anger.

"Safer?" Talia repeated. "This thing has already murdered the dryad who brought us to Allesandria."

Bellum slammed her hand on the table. "That's what happens to our kind when we help humans."

Danielle tried again, speaking as calmly as she could. "The Duchess—"

"The Duchess does not speak for Speas Elan," snapped Bellum. "What goes on in your world is of no concern to us. Your people summoned this thing. You deal with it."

"So you'll do nothing?" demanded Talia.

Veleris whispered to Bellum, who rolled her eyes. "No," Bellum said, not bothering to conceal her disgust. "We will help you. You may stay here. This place is safer than any in Allesandria. Whatever hell this demon creates, it won't last forever. One day both you and we shall return to the surface. If not you, then your children, or theirs."

"My child is a prisoner," said Danielle. "I *will* get him back."

"Then go," said Bellum. "None here will stop you."

Danielle glanced at her companions. Talia appeared ready to attack the giant barehanded. The darkling waited silently in the shadows, as did Gerta.

Danielle studied the giant more closely. Bellum glared right back, her yellow eyes daring Danielle to argue. Veleris, on the other hand, simply stared into the distance, her expression one of weary sadness.

"You've lived down here a long time," said Danielle.

"More than a century."

Well before the laws of Allesandria were changed. Rose Curtana had been but one in a long line of ambitious rulers who feared or hated fairykind. "I'm sorry."

"Sorry?" yelled Bellum. Veleris' eyes fixed on Danielle.

"And how long have you ruled Speas Elan?" asked Danielle.

"Ever since the day we fled underground," Bellum said. "By then we were hiding in small bands. Always moving. Always hiding. Your people hunted us for sport, did you know that?"

Danielle thought back to what Tommy had said about castes. Giants were servant caste, not royal. "You weren't expecting to rule when you fled underground, were you? You weren't trained for this. I know what it's like to be thrust into leadership."

"The royal caste ordered us to fight," said Bellum, her tone wary. "They tried to rally a fairy army against your witches and wizards. Most of my kin joined them. They fell."

"The demon will hunt humans and fairies both." Danielle beckoned Gerta forward. "This woman is kin to King Laurence. If you choose to help us, both Lorindar and Allesandria would be in your debt."

Veleris smiled. Without a word, she reached over to take the headband from Bellum. The headband marked which head was in charge at any given moment, Danielle realized, though she wasn't entirely sure how they decided when it should be passed. She thought back to Tommy's warning. *Try not to make them angry.* Perhaps Bellum dominated in matters of anger and conflict, while Veleris ruled for more peaceful topics.

Both of the giant's heads turned toward Gerta. "What *are* you?" asked Veleris. "There's an aura to you that reminds me of a fairy changeling, but your magic is human."

"She's like a changeling, only fresher," said Bellum. "She stinks like a newborn."

"A conjuration, to be certain," Veleris said. "Hastily constructed, a painting not yet dried."

Gerta sniffed. "I beg your pardon?"

"Typical human sloppiness," Bellum concluded.

"I'm not—"

Danielle grabbed Gerta's arm and squeezed. "Don't upset them." To Veleris, she said, "She is our friend. And there must be some way you could help us. I give you my word we'll do whatever we can to aid you and your people in return."

"The help of a dead woman's little use to us," Bellum muttered.

"Come with us," Veleris said. "We will give you what aid we can, within limits. We won't risk our people's safety."

"I understand," said Danielle. "Thank you."

"That's it?" Talia asked warily. "No price, no bargain? What kind of fairy are you?"

Veleris smiled. "The kind who recognizes that the things I want are beyond your power."

"Or the kind that doesn't expect you to survive long

enough to fulfill your side of any bargain," Bellum added with a chuckle. "Come along, O short-lived ones."

The giant led them through another tunnel to a large, rectangular doorway. A dragon guarded the door, this one larger and darker in color than Koren. A thick chain ran from his leather collar to a bolt in the floor. He lay curled on his side against the wall, eyeing them warily as they approached. He must have decided they were safe, because he stretched, then curled his neck down and began to spit tiny gouts of flame against his own backside.

"What is he doing?" asked Gerta.

"Cleaning himself." Veleris pounded the dragon's neck as she stepped past. The dragon climbed to his feet and rubbed the top of his head against Veleris' palm, like a dog begging to be petted. Veleris chuckled as she opened the door. "If I wasn't with you, he'd already have barbequed you and your friends."

Danielle wished they had been allowed to reclaim their weapons. Tame or not, the creature was still large enough to rip off an arm or leg with a single bite. Though she doubted the dragon would even notice an attack by anything less than an enchanted blade.

The giant's room was modest, little more than an oversized storeroom with wood-planked walls and old support beams. At some point in the past, the wooden wall on the back had been torn down and crude shelves carved into the rock. Oversized parchments, each tightly rolled and tied, were stuffed onto the shelves. A dirty curtain partially concealed a smaller cave, where rumpled blankets were tossed over a woven mat. A small oil lantern hung on the wall to the right of the doorway.

"Make sure you shut the door," said Veleris. "The beast likes to sneak in and steal a snack." She patted a barrel that smelled of old fish.

"What's his name?" asked Gerta as she pulled the door closed.

"What gives me the right to impose a name upon another creature?" Veleris began digging through the parchments, scanning small symbols jotted on the ends of each. With a satisfied grunt, she yanked one out and unrolled it across the floor. "Hold that, will you?"

The parchment was the size of a small carpet, covering more than half the floor. Line after line of tiny brown characters were broken only by meticulously precise drawings. Danielle had spent enough time with Snow to recognize various summoning circles.

"What kind of skin is this?" asked Gerta.

"Dragon," said Bellum. "It lasts much longer than ordinary parchment."

"My mother trapped the demon within a mirror," said Gerta. "Bound by a platinum frame. The summoning ring was built into the palace, but it was the mirror that held the demon."

"Mm." Veleris scowled. "Your mother summoned the creature in spirit only. Clever. But even so, no simple circle would have held this demon."

"What would?" asked Talia.

"Power." Bellum bared her teeth. "There are techniques to trap magic within the metal. Build a forge fueled by the bones of a hundred wizards, quench the white-hot metal in their blood . . . you might be able to contain even a major demon for a while. But that frame lost its hold when the demon escaped, and it has a body now"

"What does that mean?" asked Talia. "Do we need the bones of two hundred wizards? Give me a week in Kanustius, and—"

"Snow gives the demon physical form." Veleris grabbed another scroll and unrolled it over the first. "That can be a weakness as well as a strength. Snow White's power is added to its own, but the demon's magic is now channeled through her human body."

Bellum grunted. "Fairy magic would likely resist her power, at least for a time."

"It does," said Danielle. "My son . . . he has fairy blood. The demon's magic didn't work on him."

Veleris stared at her a long time, her face furrowed. "I'm not going to ask."

Gerta was crouched on the floor, squinting as though she could figure out the language on the giant's parchment through sheer willpower. "I've touched the demon's power, seen what it can do. How can a young child resist that, even with fairy blood?"

"It's not what he does," said Veleris. "It's what he is." She pointed to a small illustration of intersecting circles. "Your kind believe demons are creatures of Hell, yes? Made to torment the damned for all eternity?"

"There are some who believe that," Danielle said.

Veleris smiled. "What hold would such a being have over a fairy, destined for neither Heaven nor Hell?"

Bellum snorted. "Mystic claptrap. Fairies are magic, that's all. Fairy magic and human magic overlap, as do human and demon, but fairy and demon magic are like oil and water."

Gerta paled. "That's why she—why the demon needs Jakob."

Everyone turned to face her.

"Danielle, when you saw Jakob in your vision, you said he sat upon a frozen lake polished smooth as glass. A mirror of ice. He was playing with shards of ice, and his hands were bleeding. Jakob was born of darkling magic. He has fairy power in his blood, as well as human. What would happen if that blood were mixed into a mirror formed of ice?"

"She's already used a great many shards from her mother's mirror," Danielle said. "She has to be running low. But if that lake serves as a new mirror, every splinter of ice carrying her magic . . ." The demon would have a never-ending supply of power. One infused with her son's blood and magic as well as her own.

Veleris whistled softly. Bellum scowled. "Possible," she said. "I don't understand human magic that well, but—"

"Snow could do it," Gerta said. "I couldn't, but she could figure it out."

"How much—" Danielle swallowed and forced herself to finish. "How much of his blood would she need?"

"It's hard to say." Bellum shrugged her shoulder. "How many drops of poison does it take to kill a man?"

"Depends on the poison and the weight of the man," Talia shot back.

"She could keep him alive," said Veleris. "Bleed him each day, taking only what she needs. With care, he could survive for years."

"Don't give them false hope," Bellum said. "More likely, once the demon figures out how to use the boy's blood, it will kill him and spill it all. Demons aren't known for their patience."

"Enough." Danielle's voice, trembling from her effort to retain control, cut through their discussion like steel. She jabbed a finger at the parchments. "Tell me how to stop it."

Gerta sucked her lower lip as she thought. "There has to be a way to summon it out of Snow. Build a new circle, call it here, and kill it."

Veleris shook her head. "Even if you found someone strong enough to summon the demon, it would drain the strength from your friend when it felt itself being pulled away. She would be left an empty husk, and the demon would only find a new host."

Talia grabbed the parchments and flung them aside. "The Duchess said you could help us to save Snow White. Either tell us how, or put us in touch with the Duchess so we can tell her you've made a liar out of her."

"We *can* save your friend," Veleris said softly.

"How?" asked Danielle.

"With me." Gerta stood against the wall, staring at the floor. "I'm right, aren't I?"

"Snow crafted her, didn't she?" asked Veleris. The giant rose, both heads studying Gerta. "She's the key."

"Gerta can destroy the demon?" asked Danielle. She had to strain to hear Gerta's response.

"No. I tried to fight her . . . but that's *not* why she created me."

Veleris reached out to cup Gerta's face. "How long have you known?"

Gerta pulled away. "I started to suspect back in Noita's garden. I wasn't certain until after I tried to fight her, back in Kanustius. I thought you might have another way."

Veleris said nothing, allowing Bellum to explain. "The girl is incomplete. I can feel the darkling shielding her, hiding the thread that ties her back to her creator. Use that connection to strike at Snow through Gerta. The demon will try to escape. Every infected soul is a potential host. But if you can trap it, block off those paths, then it will share Snow's fate."

"Snow's fate?" Talia repeated.

"Use that bond," Gerta whispered. "By killing me, you could kill her as well."

"No." Danielle shook her head. "The Duchess sent us here so you could help us save our friend. Not kill her."

Bellum scowled, her eyes going to the headband on Veleris' brow, but apparently the giant wasn't yet angry enough for Bellum to take control. She looked at Danielle and asked, "Your friend is possessed. Enslaved to a power you still don't understand. This is the only way to save her from her torment. How long will you waste in pointless protest? How much time do you think your son has?"

Danielle didn't answer. Save her son by murdering Snow?

"You can't be considering this." Talia grabbed Danielle's arm. "I won't let you kill them."

Danielle's eyes blurred. "Talia—"

Talia's fingers tightened. "Don't try to justify this."

"Snow knew," said Gerta. "This is why she made me, so we'd have a weapon to use against her."

"Then we find another weapon!" Talia was shouting now. "When Danielle's stepsisters took Armand, we saved him. When the mermaids attacked Lorindar, we beat them. Danielle faced down the Wild Hunt. We can—"

"I'm sorry," said Veleris. "The longer you wait, the longer your friend suffers, and the more powerful the demon becomes."

"Snow White was dead the moment the demon took

her," added Bellum. "Stop dragging things out because you're too selfish to let her go."

Talia's hand moved toward her boot.

"Talia," Danielle said sharply. When Talia looked over, Danielle shook her head. Did Talia think she hadn't noticed one dagger was missing from the weapons they had turned over to the troll?

Slowly, Talia straightened. "We find another way, and we do it now."

"How?" asked Bellum. "You think you can just sit down and rewrite the laws of magic?"

"You're safe from the demon's magic," Talia yelled. "You can help us."

"We might resist enslavement," Veleris said. "But we can still die, like your dryad friend. We're not soldiers, and we will not send our people to their deaths for you."

"It's all right, Talia." Gerta swallowed. "I've known what was coming. I've seen my future, and I've been preparing myself."

Something in her tone raised the hair on Danielle's arms and neck. She took a step back, her chest tight. "Gerta . . ."

"Noita said those futures could be changed," Talia said.

"And she was right." Gerta lifted her head. "I'm sorry."

Gerta gestured at the lantern, and Danielle dropped to the ground as fire exploded through the room.

Chapter 19

TALIA JUMPED TO THE SIDE, putting the giant between herself and the blast. She braced herself against the flames as she searched the room. Where was the giant's water barrel?

She heard the door open. Through the smoke and fire, she saw Gerta disappear into the tunnel.

Veleris patted out her hair while Bellum stomped the worst of the fire on the floor. Danielle had swept off her cloak, using it to smother the rest of the parchments.

The curtain was beginning to smoke as well, orange embers spreading over the edges. The darkling moved toward it, thinning to cover the entire curtain. The glow died with a hiss.

Bellum snatched the headband from Veleris. A growl reverberated in her chest. "You came into our home to beg for our help, and instead your friend *attacks* us?"

Talia swatted out an ember on her sleeve. The fire had been more flash than substance. The lantern burned merrily, blackened but otherwise undamaged, though Gerta's stunt appeared to have consumed most of its fuel. She glanced at Danielle. "Fix this, would you? I'm going after Gerta."

Danielle stared. "You expect me to—"

"Thanks!" Talia ducked out of the room and slammed the door.

Outside, the dragon was on his feet, straining to get

into the room to see what had happened. A knocker yanked futilely at the chain, trying to calm him down.

"What happened in there?" the knocker demanded. "Don't you people know magic is prohibited?"

Talia jumped past the dragon and scanned the tunnel. She spotted a faint light retreating to her left, heading deeper into the mine.

The tunnel was worn smooth, and she gained ground before Gerta ducked around a corner. Talia should have swiped the giant's lantern, bulky as it was. Gerta's magical light was enough to see the outlines of the tunnel, but if she extinguished that light or if Talia fell behind, she would be left in total darkness.

"Leave me alone!" Gerta shouted.

Talia ran faster. She heard raucous singing from one corridor that smelled of tobacco. The scent of fresh fish wafted from another. She passed through a small room, barely dodging around a wooden winch set into the floor beside a square pit. Something snarled at her as she passed, but she didn't stop long enough to determine if it was animal or fairy.

The tunnel opened into a larger cavern, with stairs curving down along the side. Gerta was already halfway to the floor. The air was warmer here, more humid. Talia stopped to gauge the distance, then grabbed the railing and jumped.

Gerta spun, fingers flared as she shouted a spell.

Talia's feet hit the rock and shot from beneath her. The ground was slick with ice. She twisted the best she could to cushion the fall, but the impact jarred the air from her chest. She lay stunned, trying to force her body to breathe.

"I'm sorry," yelled Gerta as she ran. "Please don't make me hurt you again."

Talia rolled onto her side, grimacing at the pain in her elbow. Her palms were scraped bloody, and a lump the size of a marble had already begun to swell where her elbow had struck the rock. She flexed the arm to make sure the bone wasn't broken.

"Are you all right?" A group of goblins had been working in here, shoring up the broken beams of another tunnel.

One of the goblins spat. "Magic. Is your friend *trying* to expose us?"

Had Snow been here, she would have made an indecent quip about exposing herself. Talia swallowed, pushing the thought aside. Gerta's light was already fading down another tunnel, going deeper into the earth. Talia carefully stepped out of the frost-edged area which had been frozen by Gerta's magic. "Where does that passage lead?"

"To one of the older areas of the mine. It flooded years ago. Great fishing, but it can be a dangerous place if you're not careful. Even for your witch friend."

"Sorceress," Talia muttered, limping after Gerta. This was another square-cut passage, with log beams supporting the planked walls and ceiling. Dust and mold obscured old carvings in the wood. Warnings, or simply the accumulated scrawls of old miners and fairies?

Thankfully, Gerta had slowed as well. Snow had never trained as hard physically as she did mentally. It looked as though that was another thing she and Gerta shared.

"We'll find another way," Talia shouted. "I'm not going to let either one of you die."

"Please don't lie to me, Talia." Gerta's voice echoed strangely, and the sound of her footsteps had changed. Moments later, Talia discovered why.

The tunnel emerged at the top of an enormous cave, easily as large as the palace courtyard back home. The air smelled of steam and sulfur, and a lake filled the lower portion of the cave. A wooden walkway was built into the side of the rock, descending back and forth toward a stone bridge on the far side where the lake narrowed, connecting to another cavern through a ragged gap in the wall. The lake's surface was perfectly still, like black glass.

Talia tugged off her boots. Not even Snow White was strong enough to freeze the entire lake. This was a higher drop than the last, but the water should break her fall. Assuming it was deep enough.

Gerta was halfway to the bridge. Talia gripped the railing in both hands and took deep breaths, filling her lungs. Her elbow was throbbing, and hip and thigh complained as well. As Gerta's light bobbed lower, Talia climbed onto the rail and leaped.

She hit toes-first, keeping her knees bent and arms spread to absorb the impact as she plunged into the water, but she needn't have worried. She couldn't see how deep the lake was, but her feet never touched bottom.

It was hotter than she expected, uncomfortably so, and tasted of salt. She kicked to the surface and wiped her face, slicking back her hair. Gerta had hesitated on the stairs. "You can't keep running," Talia shouted.

Talia wasn't the strongest swimmer, but Queen Beatrice had insisted she learn. She kicked toward the bridge, swimming on one side to favor her injured arm and leg. Gerta was close, but Talia should reach the bridge first. Gerta could try to flee back up the tunnels, but it would mean running uphill. Even from here, Talia could see that she was sweating and out of breath.

If she was truly a part of Snow, she wouldn't give up easily. Talia watched Gerta the best she could, ready to duck beneath the water at the first hint of spellcasting.

Something splattered against the back of her head, hard enough to knock her face into the water. Talia stopped, kicking to keep herself afloat while she touched her head with one hand. Whatever it was, it had the consistency of hot syrup. It had sprayed the lake around her as well, judging from the rings spreading through the water. "I don't know what kind of spell that was, but it's disgusting!"

Gerta hurried toward the bridge. "Talia, get down!"

Talia dove, trusting the terror in Gerta's shout. Moments later, the water over her head exploded in orange flames.

Talia kicked deeper to escape the searing heat. The surface was already boiling from the fire. She swam as far as she could, waiting until the fire stopped and her lungs forced her to the surface. Steam rose from the water, and each breath hurt her throat and chest. She took one more quick gulp of air, then ducked beneath the water again.

This time, she managed to make it to the bridge. She pulled herself past one of the stone support pillars, keeping her eyes and nose above the surface and doing the best she could to control her breathing.

Another burst of flame illuminated the dragon on the far shore. This one was far larger than either of the "tame" dragons she had seen higher up. The dragon slipped into the water with hardly a ripple. The faint glow from its mouth vanished with a hissing sound.

"Where's a knight when you need one?" Historically, knights had never done well against dragons, no matter what the bards said. But at least Talia could have gotten away while the dragon was busy baking the knight in his armor. She grabbed the pillar and lunged higher, reaching for the edge of the bridge.

"Look out!"

Talia twisted to see the dragon swimming closer, head raised from the water, orange glow clearly visible. With a curse, she dropped beneath the water and pulled herself between the pillars. She yanked her knife from her sleeve. When the flames died, she surfaced and flung the knife at the dragon's mouth. It bounced off the scaly snout.

"Brilliant," snapped Gerta as she reached the bridge. "Are you *trying* to make the dragon angry? Maybe next we can go find a griffon so you can pull its tail."

"Shut up, unless you want it to go after you." Talia bobbed beneath the surface, dodging another gout of flame. The pillars supporting the bridge were built too close together for the dragon to follow. The water was clear enough to see the dragon swimming from side to side, moving as easily as a fish. The small legs kicked in a way that reminded her of a dog, but the dragon also used its wings and tail for speed. There was no way she could outswim this creature.

She pulled herself through to the far side of the

bridge, then swore. In the second cavern, she could see another orange glow moving through the water toward her, no doubt attracted by the commotion.

The first dragon's head snaked between the pillars. Talia twisted, and sharp teeth caught her sleeve. She braced herself as the dragon yanked back, slamming her against the stone hard enough to make her vision flash. The collar of her shirt cut off her breath like a garrote, and then the sleeve ripped away.

"If I help you, you have to let me go," Gerta said.

"If you help me, you'll get yourself killed." Her face and neck stung as if singed by the desert sun. She used the beams to pull herself toward the far shore. The dragons kept pace with ease. "I'll lead them away from you. Wait until they follow, then get out of here."

Slow footsteps stopped directly over Talia's head. "Promise me."

Talia reversed direction, dodging another lunge. She ducked beneath the water to avoid a rush of flame. When she surfaced, steam hid the dragons from view. She squinted, trying to protect her eyes from the heat. "Fine, I promise."

She pulled herself to one side as both dragons snapped at the sound of her voice.

"You're lying."

"Of course I'm lying!" The second dragon slipped its head between the columns. Talia punched it on the eyelid, bloodying her knuckles. She needed a plan, but the dragons wouldn't ease up long enough for her to think. All she could do was react. "You know what the demon has done. I can't—"

She swore and ducked again. When she surfaced, she spied another fire approaching from the shore, and her chest tightened. If the fire was any indication, this dragon was bigger than any Talia had seen so far, and it was approaching quickly. "Get out of here, Gerta."

"Shut up." Gerta's voice was resonant.

The first dragon raised its head, spouting a halfhearted tower of fire that quickly sputtered out. The one on shore answered in kind.

Talia bobbed in the water. Sweat stung her eyes. She was certain her rapid breathing would soon pull the dragons' attention back to her, but she couldn't control it any more than she could stop the drumbeat of her heart.

The dragon on the shore breathed again. As if this were a signal, the other two dove away, disappearing into the water.

"Get up here."

Talia didn't question. She braced her back against one pillar and her feet against the next, pushing herself higher. Her muscles screamed, but she kept climbing until she reached the bridge itself. Gerta grabbed her wrist, helping her over the railing.

Talia's legs gave out. She clung to the rail, trying to stand. Her limbs felt like warm dough. "The third dragon—"

Gerta extended a hand toward the shore and closed her fist. The flame vanished. "The other two were both male. They weren't hungry enough to take on a mother dragon."

"A mother? All I saw was the fire." Talia collapsed onto her back, staring at the stalactites overhead.

Gerta rolled her eyes. "The males' flame is narrower and hotter. You really need to read more, Talia." She spread her fingers, gesturing at Talia's body. Water crackled as Talia's clothes and hair froze to the bridge.

"What are you doing?" Talia grimaced as the ice reached her arm where the dragon had torn her sleeve. She flexed, testing Gerta's magic. Her hand peeled away from the stone. She might lose some skin, but she should be able to wrench herself free. "I suppose freezing to death is less painful than dragon fire, and the ice will help the swelling on my elbow, but—"

"Shut up." Gerta knelt beside Talia. One hand reached out, fingertips tracing Talia's cheekbones, then moving down the side of her neck. "I couldn't let you die. I should have, but I couldn't."

"I'll be just as dead from the cold."

Gerta rapped Talia's nose. "Why would she do this to me? I understand splitting off her soul, protecting a part of herself so I could be used to stop the demon. But why make me love you?"

"Maybe to stop you from running away once you realized what we had to do?"

Gerta wrinkled her nose. "You smell like dragon spit."

"Dragon spit?" Talia sniffed. There was a rather foul smell, now that Gerta pointed it out. A combination of mucus and fetid meat.

"It's one of the ways they hunt," said Gerta. "By spraying spit over the water. The ripples bring fish to the surface to investigate, and then *whoosh*." She pantomimed breathing fire.

If Gerta hadn't told her to duck . . . Talia stopped struggling. "Thank you."

Gerta turned away, searching the water. "Snow was jealous of you, you know."

Talia stared. "I don't understand."

"When you returned from Arathea with your friend Faziya. She watched the two of you, saw how happy you were together."

Talia's breathing and heartbeat had gradually slowed as her body realized she was safe, at least for the moment. Now both increased again. "Why? Snow had—"

"Companionship, yes. Not love. When Faziya returned to Arathea and you retreated to your room to pout, that's when Snow prepared her love potion, one which would allow her to love you the way Faziya did."

"I wasn't pouting."

Gerta rolled her eyes.

Talia relaxed, concentrating on the feel of the frozen spikes of her hair that jabbed her scalp. "So why didn't she?"

"You know why." Gerta sounded distant. "She's always enjoyed the company of men, but have you ever known her to fall in love?"

"Only once. Before she came to Lorindar."

"Roland," Gerta agreed. The hunter Snow's mother had sent into the woods to find her, to cut out Snow's heart and return it to the queen. Instead, he had fallen in love with Snow, and they had lived together for a time . . . until the queen found them. Snow had never shared the details of that encounter, only that her mother had tortured Roland to death while Snow lay helpless to stop her. "She was scared, Talia. Scared to lose you the way she lost him. Scared to feel that pain again."

"I'm not that easy to lose."

"So I've noticed." Gerta placed her hand over Talia's, weaving their fingers together. "Look at me, Talia. What do you see?"

Talia looked up. The light Gerta had conjured still glowed faintly from her right hand. Her red hair hung in tangled waves, thicker than Snow's, but falling in the same way. Dirt smeared her pale skin. Her brown eyes never left Talia. Eyes that held much of the same sadness as her sister's, though Snow rarely allowed anyone to see it. "I don't understand."

"You look at me, and you see *her*. Like I'm nothing but illusion, and eventually the spell will break and Snow will emerge, safe and whole once more." She traced her fingertips over Talia's arm. "She created me from the memories of a sister who never existed. Am I just a repository of her dreams? Am I a weapon to use against her? I don't know anymore, Talia. But the way I feel when I think about you, when I hear your voice . . . when I touch you . . . that's real."

"You'd be better off asking Father Isaac those questions," Talia said. "Even our two-headed friend knows more about magic than—"

"I don't care about magic. I want to know what—*who* you see when you look at me." Tears dripped onto Talia's chest. "I want you to see me."

Had Snow ever cried in front of her? Talia instinctively tried to reach for Gerta's face, but the ice held her fast. "I do see her. The way you lecture me. The excitement and fear in your eyes when you do magic, your forehead wrinkled in concentration, your teeth nibbling your lip."

Gerta looked away, but not quickly enough to hide

her pain at Talia's words. "It's intoxicating, rewriting the laws of the universe."

"Not for you," said Talia. "You don't love it the way she does."

"It frightens me," Gerta admitted. "If I was created by magic, I can be destroyed the same way. I keep wondering when the universe will realize I was never supposed to exist and take steps to correct that mistake."

"You're not her," Talia said softly. "Snow would have joked about the universe being full of mistakes, like manticores."

"You have to admit, they're bizarre-looking creatures," Gerta said with the hint of a smile.

"I always envied her ability to joke in the midst of danger. Anger, fear, she never let them control her."

"Snow wouldn't have run away." Gerta stared into the darkness.

"She wouldn't have told me how she felt about me, either." Talia shivered. The cold felt like it was penetrating to her bones. "Courage comes in different shapes."

"Maybe I'm just not as smart as her."

"Go easy on yourself. You're only two weeks old."

That earned a laugh, so similar to Snow's, only somehow . . . lighter. More free. Gerta pulled away. "Do I *look* like an infant?"

"No," Talia said softly.

Gerta reached out again, this time touching her fingertips to Talia's lips. Her fingers carried the taste of saltwater. She brushed Talia's chin, sliding down to the hollow in her throat.

Talia's hand clenched reflexively into a fist, breaking free of the ice.

Gerta jerked back. "I'm sorry. I wouldn't—"

"I know." Talia's voice shook. "I don't like being helpless."

Gerta folded her hands in her lap. "And I don't like being told my only purpose is to die."

Talia closed her eyes, tempted to lie, but Gerta would never believe her. "I can't leave Snow like this. Even if it means—"

Gerta rubbed her eyes. "I know. I can't either. She's my sister."

The cold was seeping deeper into Talia's body, making her shiver. "So what do you plan to do with me?"

"What will you do if I free you?"

"I can talk to Bellum and Veleris. Well, to Veleris, anyway. Assuming they don't kill us on sight. There has to be another way to—"

Gerta put a hand on her lips. "If there were, don't you think we'd have found it already? Noita, Laurence, Father Isaac . . . Veleris is right. I'm the key."

Talia sighed. "I have to save her. But if there's any way to do so without hurting you, I promise I'll do it."

"Thank you." Gerta stretched out beside her on the bridge, the warmth of her body pressing against Talia's side. She moved her hand over Talia's arm. The ice cracked and broke. Talia started to sit up.

"I'll go back with you," said Gerta. "But please let me have this."

Talia bent her arm, causing bits of ice to flake away from her sleeve. Pain shot through her elbow. She did her best to shut it out as she gently wrapped her arm around Gerta's shoulders and lay back, closing her eyes. Gerta rested beside her, using her free hand to remove the remaining ice.

"What if one of those dragons comes back?" Talia asked.

She could feel Gerta's smile. "Let the dragon find its own woman."

Chapter 20

THE SNOW-AND-ICE WALLS OF THE PALACE swallowed the sounds of Snow's footsteps as she prepared to greet her visitors. Tiny frozen servants scurried about, buffing every imperfection from the surface of the frozen lake. They swarmed behind her feet, a tiny cloud erasing all evidence of her passing. The room was empty of furnishings, save for a throne of ice in the very center. Simple, uncluttered . . . this was the closest she had felt to comfort since leaving Lorindar.

Prince Jakob sat beside the throne, manipulating the ice shards Snow had given him. He had managed to fit three pieces together, forming an irregular shape roughly the size of a hand mirror. The longer he worked with the shards, the more the edges scratched his palms, and the more his blood and power seeped into the ice.

The polished floor let her see everything that took place within the palace. She watched impatiently as white-furred mounts that had once been human stepped out of the woods, carrying the six nobles who had accepted Snow's offer.

They had left their weapons behind, but none were truly unprotected. Two had taken potions to strengthen their magic. Another had swallowed a pearl to help him resist mental control. Nor were their magics purely defensive. Snow could see the charms on one man's fingers, the nails sharp and hard as talons, and coated in some sort of magical toxin.

She gathered her cloak around herself as her creatures escorted the men into her throne room. One of the men stepped forward and knelt. "Queen Ermillina. I am Stevan Tirill, Lord of Kettunen." His companions followed suit. "I was there when your cousin claimed your throne. I spoke against him, but the Nobles' Circle chose to grant the crown to Laurence."

Snow didn't bother to conceal her revulsion. Tirill was a yellowed husk of a man, a minor noble whose ambition had always exceeded his ability. He dressed in the gaudiest of fashions, silk and silver clashing with his foxskin jacket. Greed and fear spilled from his words, soiling all who heard them.

Like the others, he wore powerful magic. His protective spells had been tattooed onto the bone of his skull. It was a painful and archaic process, once performed upon noble children when they were first born. He was well guarded against outside influence or attack, but the skull shifted as it grew, introducing imperfections into the spell. Snow studied his magic through the mirror until she found those flaws.

"Your Majesty, Allesandria will soon fall into civil war." He paused for effect, then shook his head. "No, war is too neat a term for the chaos spreading through this land. Laurence means to disband the Circle and give the crown to you. Half the provinces have already spoken out against him."

"Only half?" Snow asked.

Tirill stumbled. "Your Majesty, Allesandria has seen your power. Word has spread that Queen Ermillina is returned to her homeland to take the crown from her cousin the usurper. I would offer my allegiance."

"The rest of you would do the same?" Snow approached, her eyes lidded as she continued to examine their magic through the mirror of her lake. "You would swear to me. Yet you each swore an oath to King Laurence when he took the throne."

"King Laurence now serves you," said Tirill. "By doing the same, I fulfill my oath to obey him."

Snow smiled. The man knew full well Laurence was

not himself, but this deception served his greed and ambition. "Tell me, Stevan. What will you do if I refuse this . . . offer?"

He spread his hands, the picture of false modesty. "Without the Lords, I'm afraid you'll never consolidate your hold over Allesandria. Even your mother knew this nation was too large for any one person to control alone."

Snow watched his wrinkled face as she strode closer, enjoying his battle between arrogance and fear. "My mother believed in control." She flexed her hand, feeling the stiffness of healing cuts on her palm. "Answer me one question, and I'll accept your oath."

He rose and took an eager step closer. "What question is that, Your Majesty?"

"After my mother died, when the Circle called for my execution, to whom did you lend your voice and support?" When he didn't respond, Snow began to pace around him. "Those loyal to my mother sought to punish me for her death. Others saw it as a chance to free Allesandria from the rule of Curtana, to put a new family on the throne. Not even Beatrice would fight for my birthright."

He blinked. "Beatrice, Your Majesty?"

"How did you vote, Stevan?"

He bowed low. "I had seen Queen Curtana's cruelty, both to her people and to her daughter. You acted to protect yourself. I said you were innocent of wrongdoing. Alas, the Circle would not listen to my arguments."

The lies were foul as spoiled milk. The man wore his greed like a crown. His fat tongue flicked hungrily over cracked lips. Even as he lowered his head, he stared lustfully through his lashes. His gaze crawled over her skin, and the raw desire made her shudder. Desire both for her body and for her power.

"Thank you for coming." Snow offered her hand. He took it eagerly, his sweaty fingers tight as he kissed her knuckles. Snow concentrated, casting a minor variation of a familiar spell that slipped through the cracks in his defenses. "I remember you well, and had hoped you would accept my invitation."

Stevan risked a smile, even as he flexed his hand. "Thank *you*, Your Majesty." He frowned and shook his fingers. "I'm glad to see you returned home at last. Under your wise rule . . ."

Snow backed away. "I am not my mother, Stevan. Flattery is but another lie, and I've no tolerance for such. Nor for groveling cowards who care for nothing but their own fortunes."

Stevan cried out and clutched his arm. The other nobles backed away. Several whispered warding spells, but none yet dared to act against Snow.

"You say you knew her cruelty, yet you did nothing to stop her?" Snow returned to her throne, settling herself on the ice. "You stood by as she tortured those who displeased her? Burned their bodies to ash while their loved ones looked on?"

He fell, whimpering. By now the blood in his arm had frozen solid. Chunks of ice would be breaking away, flowing through his veins toward his heart. He would be dead long before the rest of his body froze.

Snow turned her attention to the other nobles. "And what of you? How many of you watched and did nothing?"

One man stepped forward. "Your Majesty, I know not what my father did, but he died only two years past. I never knew your mother. Nor did we know you yet lived."

"Are you hoping to convince me of your loyalty?" Snow asked. "Your honesty? Yet you also took an oath to serve King Laurence, and now you've come to me. Or did you accept my invitation in order to discover my location and destroy me? You think I've not noticed your failed telepathic attempts to summon help?"

He attacked without warning, but the others were quick to follow. There was little artistry to their magic. A simple spell of flame, a curse to destroy her senses, another to make her sleep . . . one woman did attempt a rather unusual form of teleportation, trying to transport parts of Snow's body to different locations. Snow wondered briefly where she had learned that particular trick.

Their spells never touched her. Snow stood upon the largest magical mirror ever created. It absorbed their attacks, reflecting them back not at the casters, who would presumably know how to counter their own spells, but at their companions.

Within seconds, three more nobles had fallen. Snow's guardians, men twisted into creatures of fur and fang and claw, closed in to deal with the remaining two.

"Take the bodies to the edge of the palace. Spill their blood in an unbroken ring." Noble blood, full of magic. "I will not be alone, my dear Stevan."

A flicker of magic tugged her attention to the child. Jakob had finally managed to conjure an image within his makeshift mirror. He sat with his back to the carnage, his shoulders shaking. Snow walked over and tugged the bloody ice from his hands.

When she saw what he had done, she nearly dropped it. Within the ice was Snow herself. Not as she was, but as she had been: her face unscarred, her smile one of genuine merriment. The reflection wore a green jacket, and was sucking frosting from her fingers. This was a memory, from Jakob's birthday celebration earlier this year. "I'd expected you to summon up your mother or father."

"Aunt Snow will fight you."

"She tried." A flick of her finger should have banished the image. Instead, the reflection turned to stick out her tongue.

Snow yanked the image from the small mirror and transferred it into the ice at her feet. For a moment, that tug echoed within her, giving her the key. Jakob might have instinctively summoned a comforting memory from the mirror, but even with his fairy blood, he couldn't have given that memory life.

"Much better." The reflection stretched, then turned to look at Jakob. "He's smarter than you realize."

"He's a child. He might even appreciate being a part of my mirror. Instead of a too-brief mortal life, he'll live on for all eternity."

"Eternity?" Snow grinned from the ice. "I'll wager a hundred crowns you don't survive the month."

By now, the last of the nobles had been dragged away, leaving only the sheen of blood to mark their fall. "I know what you've done. Cutting out a part of your soul, blotting her from your memories to hide her from me. Using her to protect a fragment of your own soul. Clever, but I'll have Gerta back soon enough."

"Just like you had her in Kanustius?"

"That was you." She thought back to Kanustius, to her confusion. Her weakness. She had intended to order Danielle and Talia killed, and Gerta placed into magical hibernation until she could be studied. "Gerta's magic drew you out, gave you strength enough to save your friends' life. You realize those same friends mean to kill us?"

"They mean to kill *you*." The reflection folded her arms. "But I hate waiting."

The ice cracked beneath Snow's feet. She jumped back with a curse. Magic pulled at her legs, trying to drag her through, but it was human magic, weak and easily turned away. A wave of her hand sealed the surface of the ice, trapping the reflection within. The next spell it cast was turned back, and the reflection screamed in pain.

Jakob had done her a favor. Whatever remained of Snow's humanity was now trapped and powerless within the ice. Better to keep it there, where it couldn't influence her the way it had back in Kanustius.

Satisfied, she turned to study the boy again. Perhaps there was a way to hurry Gerta's destruction along. "It's time to find your mother, child."

Jakob deliberately avoided looking at the puddles and smears of blood on the far side of the room.

"She's in danger, but fairy magic hides her from me. You have the power to find her. She needs your help."

"No, she doesn't." Jakob spoke so meekly she barely heard, but there was no uncertainty in his words.

The reflection gave a weary chuckle. "Told you he was smart."

"It doesn't matter." To Jakob, she said, "She's in danger nonetheless. This might be your last chance to see her alive."

She turned her attention to the ice, showing him the chaos spreading through Allesandria. A hurricane battered one city, courtesy of a possessed weather mage. Another was a blackened ruin, with flickers of green flame still dancing over the wreckage left by her rogue Stormcrows. Hundreds of her servants had been killed, but more than a thousand fought on. With Laurence fallen under her control—

"First Allesandria, then the world?" her reflection asked, sounding bored. "How unoriginal."

She scowled. "Find me one ruler worthy of their throne. Show me a single nation not founded on lies and bloodshed." She turned toward Jakob. He was watching the destruction as well, his eyes round. "Your mother is trapped in this madness, Jakob. I could save her. Find her for me, and I give you my word she will be spared this."

"The word of a demon," Snow repeated from the ice. "I've got a word for you. How about—"

A wave of her hand silenced the reflection. She approached Jakob. "You are clever. Clever enough to know what I'll do to your mother, and to you, if you refuse me, right?"

Jakob bit his lip and nodded.

"Very good." She bent down, planting a cold kiss on the top of the boy's head. "Find her."

Deep in the ice, the reflection raised one hand in an obscene gesture.

Don't show fear. It was the first rule of fairy diplomacy, but as Bellum roared her fury, Danielle was less worried about diplomacy and more concerned with avoiding those ham-sized fists. Bellum had already smashed one barrel, spilling paper-wrapped blocks of cheese across the floor. *Stand proudly. In a society where a creature who resembles a child's doll can command ogres, size means nothing.*

"We invited you into our home," Bellum shouted. "Offered you shelter. In return, your pet witch unleashed yet another spell. She tried to—"

Danielle straightened. *Confidence is everything.* As if she were correcting her son, she said in a mild voice, "Will you please stop whining?"

Two sets of eyes blinked in shock.

"Were you or anyone else injured by Gerta's spell?"

"Every spell makes it more likely someone from the surface will find us," Bellum argued. "She might have killed us all!"

"She was frightened." Danielle pointed to the shelves. "She could have filled this room with fire, but your scrolls are untouched. She singed your curtain, blackened a few parts of the floor."

"My hair—"

"Will grow back." Half of Speas Elan had to be able to hear Bellum's rage. She lowered her voice, forcing Bellum to do the same in order to hear. "You have my word there will be no further magic, nor attacks against you or anyone else in Speas Elan."

"The word of a human isn't worth the breath it takes to speak it," Bellum scoffed. "If Allesandria discovers us as a result of her carelessness—"

"The humans of Allesandria are a little busy right now. Anyone with magical ability is more worried about fighting this demon than they are about finding you." She sat and grabbed one of the blocks of cheese. "Besides, if you punish Gerta, you risk all of Speas Elan learning how a human girl and her magic got the best of you."

The giant had quieted somewhat, which was a good sign. Bellum scowled and looked to the door. "Your friends are likely dead anyway, depending on where they ran off to. There's a nest of feral kobolds in the deeper tunnels, not to mention the dragons, a few poisonous snakes, and a one-armed centaur. Poor bastard lost his arm to fairy hunters sixty years ago, but even left-handed, he can throw a spear hard enough to crack rock."

"Talia has faced worse. I trust them to take care of themselves." Danielle unwrapped the cheese and took a bite. Her eyes widened, and she coughed. The cheese had a hard, crusty rind, and that single bite filled her head with an overpowering taste that reminded her of dandelions and onions, with a strange nutty aftertaste. "What—" She hurried to the water barrel in the corner and snatched the copper dipper, drinking deeply. "What *is* that?"

"You're happier not knowing." Bellum took a large bite and grinned. "Humans. So delicate. Try this." She tossed Danielle a strip of smoked meat.

Danielle nibbled warily. The meat had a peppery taste, but was positively mild compared to the cheese. "Thank you."

Bellum and Veleris sighed in unison as they surveyed their home before sitting down across from Danielle. "The least you could do is tell the Duchess' coldhearted slave there to clean up the mess."

Danielle glanced at the darkling, who moved to obey. She and the giant ate in silence for a time. Food appeared to calm Bellum's temper. Danielle slipped into the role of servant girl, fetching food and drink for them both until the giant sat back and belched from both mouths.

Danielle folded her arms, studying Bellum closely. "So what did the Duchess promise you?"

Both faces stilled. "What do you mean?"

"She sent us here, expecting you to help us," said Danielle. "The Duchess is the most calculating person, human or fairy, I've ever met. Her darkling knew the way to Speas Elan. She knew you wouldn't attack us or turn us away. Which means she had already arranged things with you."

"Fairy politics is a maze of bargains, oaths, and obligations." Bellum's face wrinkled with distaste.

"And the wise ruler seeks not to escape the maze, but to rule it from its heart," Danielle said, recognizing the quote.

Veleris' eyes brightened. "You've studied the Eightfold Path?"

"I've read it," Danielle said. Part of it, at any rate. She had flung the book away after only a few incomprehensible chapters. "What bargain did you and the Duchess reach?"

Bellum looked past Danielle to the darkling, and there was no hiding the hatred in her face. Veleris simply appeared sad. "We were unprepared to lead," Veleris said softly. "As the war turned against us, Bellum and I, along with a few others, sought aid from the kings and queens of the other fairy hills. They refused. The Duchess was the only one willing to help such low-caste fairies as ourselves. She sent dwarves and goblins, the same fairies who built her own kingdom, to help us hide. She demanded only two things. The first was loyalty."

Which would explain why the Duchess knew they would help Danielle. "And the second?"

"That not a single fairy of noble blood accompany us," said Bellum.

Danielle exhaled, thinking back to what the giant had described of their battles with humans. "To save yourselves, you had to leave them behind to die."

"As if they'd have listened to a giant. They refused to give up their homeland. They would have led us all to our deaths."

Instead, with the nobles dead, Bellum and Veleris had been forced into leadership of the fairy refugees . . . and by their bargain, the Duchess commanded Bellum and Veleris.

"It's how she operates," Veleris said. "Conquering not through warfare, but through favors and obligations, entangling all who bargain with her."

Including Danielle, and through her, Jakob.

Chains rattled outside the door, which swung open a moment later. Gerta was on one knee, scratching the dragon's chin. Talia was damp and bedraggled, but both she and Gerta appeared unhurt. Danielle raised her eyebrows, indicating Gerta with a tilt of her head.

"She'll help us," Talia said flatly.

Bellum stared. Even Veleris appeared surprised, asking, "What did you threaten her with to accomplish that?"

"Leaving her here with you," Talia shot back.

Veleris chuckled. Bellum simply scowled.

Danielle stepped between Talia and the giant before things could progress any further. "Bellum, what help can you give us?"

"We've told you what you have to do," Bellum grumbled. "It's up to you to figure out how to get close enough to Snow to stop her."

"You can offer me in trade," Gerta said quietly. She appeared almost calm, making Danielle wonder anew what had happened between her and Talia. "Tell Snow you're willing to give me up in exchange for Jakob. If it gets us close enough—"

"Close enough for her mirror wasps to enslave you all, you mean?" asked Bellum. "She'll own you before you ever reach her palace."

Danielle frowned. "You know of her palace?"

"We've hidden ourselves away from your world." Veleris glanced at the metal cone in the wall. "That doesn't mean we've stopped listening. A few sprites still wander the surface. We listen, and we wait."

"She's built her fortress to the north," said Bellum. "Where the mountains split, there is a lake shaped like a curving teardrop. She's hidden herself well from human magic, but not from fairy eyes. If your darkling carries you, you could make the journey within two days."

Two days to plan. Two days to find another way, one which didn't involve sacrificing Snow and Gerta.

"The longer we wait, the more people will die," said Gerta softly. "I think I know the lake she means. West of the summer palace. We ran away once and spent the night on the shore. Our mother sent one of her Deathcrows to retrieve us." Her voice trailed off, her lips set in a grim line.

"You'll need supplies," said Bellum. She grabbed an oversized pair of fur-lined mittens and stuffed them into a sack. Next she opened a barrel of dried fish and began piling them onto an old sheet of parchment.

"Thank you," Danielle said, trying to hide her surprise.

"She's just trying to hurry you on your way." Veleris

winked. "And she's giving you the oldest, toughest meat. Here, let me do that." She slapped Bellum's hand away and took over the preparations. "You'll leave in the morning. You're far too exhausted to set out now."

Danielle glanced at her companions. She wanted to argue, but the fatigue on Gerta's face matched her own. "Weapons would also speed us along. And perhaps a change of clothes that didn't smell like bandit sweat?"

Talia snatched one of the fish and took a bite.

"Gerta . . ." Danielle swallowed. Gerta's red hair was damp, her face weary, but the panic was gone from her eyes and her movements. Danielle searched for something to say, anything that might bring comfort.

"It's all right," said Gerta. "She's my sister. This is what I was made for."

"There has to be a way to send the demon back to wherever it came from," Danielle protested.

Gerta shook her head. "Even if I could duplicate the magic my mother used to summon the demon . . . even if I were willing to try that kind of magic . . . the demon is stronger now. It has Snow's power as well as its own. We might be able to kill it—"

"Doubtful," Bellum scoffed.

"—but control it? No." Gerta's hand moved, almost as if she were reaching for Talia, but she stopped herself.

Danielle swallowed. "How do we trap the demon long enough to kill it? Won't it try to escape to another host?"

"Gerta and I talked about that on our way back." Talia reached into her pocket and pulled out the broken blue chain Laurence had used to suppress Gerta's powers, back at the palace.

"It won't hold for very long," said Gerta. "It wasn't designed to contain a demon, but the chain follows the principles of a binding circle. If you can secure it around Snow, I think it will last long enough to . . . to do what you must."

"Save these until you're on the road," said Veleris as she finished wrapping the rest of the fish.

"Thank you." Danielle bowed. "We're in your debt, and I give you my word as Princess of Lorindar that none of us will reveal your secret."

Veleris smiled. "Princess Whiteshore, you never would have found us without your darkling friend. You couldn't lead another soul here if you tried."

"Not that I expect you to live long enough to come looking," added Bellum.

Chapter 21

DANIELLE SPENT THE NIGHT HAUNTED BY dreams of Jakob, trapped in an icy prison, searching and calling for her but unable to find her. When she tried to answer, her throat refused to obey, and her limbs were like stone. She awoke feeling even more exhausted than before.

Tommy guided them through the twisting tunnels to the surface. Danielle ate as she walked, forcing herself to finish a hard smoked roll that tasted of mushrooms and smoke and old meat.

The sun was low in the sky when they emerged, and Danielle shivered even within the bundled jacket and oversized mittens the giant had provided. Their weapons had also been returned, along with blankets, rope, and other supplies crammed into musty, dirt-stained packs.

Tommy jabbed his shovel to the northeast. "Head that way until you reach an old mining trail. It should take you the way you want to go."

"Thank you," said Danielle.

The knocker was already retreating through the small hole from which they had emerged. He raised his shovel in salute, then rapped it against the wooden frame of the entrance. The impact collapsed the drifted snow overhead, burying the way in.

Gerta used her boot to clear away the worst of the snow. She frowned, then dug deeper. Her efforts revealed nothing but snow and rock. "That's a nice trick."

The darkling shifted its form, becoming a pair of shadow-thin reindeer once more. Climbing onto the creature's back was no less disturbing than the last time, but the darkling was the fastest way to reach the lake.

Danielle watched Gerta and Talia as they mounted the other reindeer, wondering what had happened in the mine. Gerta's fear was still very much present, but the edge was gone. As for Talia, she was hurting, though she tried to hide it. The clipped tone of her words, the tension in her body . . . she meant to save Snow, no matter the cost. Danielle could see it in the way she moved, deliberate and purposeful.

Danielle prayed for the same, but if Bellum and Veleris were right and there was only one way to stop this demon . . . She prayed that it wouldn't come to that, for all their sakes.

Talia scowled when she saw Danielle watching her. "Come on. The sooner we leave these damned fairies behind, the happier I'll be."

"Damned fairies?" Danielle repeated. "Does that include me as well?" The words sounded strange. In her mind, she was as human as Talia . . . though perhaps that wasn't the best comparison, given the magic flowing through Talia's blood.

"Don't be stupid," Talia snapped.

Danielle knew Talia well enough to know her barbs weren't personal, her anger not directed at Danielle. "It changes things," she said. "The people were wary enough when their prince married an ash-covered servant girl. What will they say to the revelation that their future ruler is less than fully human?"

Talia scowled. "Your lives—Jakob's life—might be easier if certain things were kept secret."

As they rode, Danielle found herself thinking of the bargain the Duchess had reached with the fairies of Speas Elan. The fairies of Allesandria had been hunted down, nearly driven into extinction, but was Lorindar any better? Their own war with fairykind had ended with Malindar's Treaty, which confined fairykind to a single walled city. Was that treaty so different from the Duchess' terms?

Every history she had read described conflict between human and fairy. In Arathea, the fairies had used Talia's curse to wipe out the ruling line, plunging the nobles into chaos. In Allesandria and Lorindar, the humans had triumphed. But they were all variations of the same basic war, played out again and again. "Do you know of any land where humans and fairies live in peace, as equals?"

Talia raised an eyebrow. Gerta shook her head and said, "Not for very long."

"Fairy magic could have fought this demon," Danielle said, "but Allesandria slaughtered its fairies." The most powerful fairies would have been the first to be destroyed. Had the demon recognized its vulnerabilities? Was that another reason it had fled to Allesandria?

Jakob was both human and fairy. Danielle would have sooner died than give her son into the Duchess' hands, and yet . . . he would be king of Lorindar when he was older. What could he accomplish, with connections to both worlds?

She closed her eyes, imagining Jakob as a man. A leader, trained to navigate human politics as well as fairy. He could change things. Humans and fairies, no longer enemies bound by a treaty, but true allies.

Noble families had been known to send their children to serve in foreign courts. The King and Queen of Fairytown rarely spoke to one another, but it would make sense for Jakob to visit both . . . when he was old enough.

Instead, the Duchess had claimed him. Her bargain with Bellum and Veleris was proof of her hunger for power, a hunger which would doubtless twist Jakob as well, poisoning that future. Instead of bringing human and fairy together, the Duchess would use Jakob against her enemies on all sides.

Danielle refused to consider the possibility that they might be unable to save her son, that both he and Armand would be lost to her forever.

"You're still thinking about Jakob," Talia guessed. "We *will* find a way to destroy this demon. As for the Duchess—"

Danielle raised a hand, cutting her off. The darkling served them by the Duchess' order, but Danielle had no doubt the creature was listening to their every word, and would report back to its master.

"I made a bargain." To rescue Jakob from the demon, only to lose him again. She closed her eyes, waiting for the pain to recede enough for her to reclaim those images of her son grown to adulthood. Taking his place as King of Lorindar. Reaching out to Fairytown and rewriting the treaty. Taking a wife. Having children of his own.

"We'll get him back," said Talia. "We'll get them all back."

Danielle managed a smile, but said nothing. Talia sounded much like Danielle had several years ago, always insisting everything would work out. Danielle remembered well what Talia had said to her at the time.

"Just because your story had a happy ending doesn't mean everyone else's will."

They discovered Veleris' message on the second day, printed upon one of the dried fish. Tiny black marks, slightly smeared, covered the yellowed meat like an old tattoo.

"It's a spell," Gerta said.

Danielle peered closer. The letters appeared to have been written in haste. "On a fish?"

"To hide it from Bellum," Talia guessed.

"She writes that it's an old charm used by giants before battle, to toughen the skin," Gerta read. "She says it should protect us from Snow's ice wasps. It's fairy magic, but she believes the spell can be adjusted for human use."

"Can it?" Danielle asked. Snow had been able to cast fairy spells before, but she wasn't certain about Gerta.

"I think so. I'll need time . . ."

"You can read while we ride," Talia said, snatching another fish from their supplies.

Gerta didn't appear to hear. She muttered to herself as she studied the spell, brows furrowed in a way that made her look like her sister.

"Those wasps won't be the demon's only protection," Talia said.

"I know." Danielle finished packing snow into a small pot and handed it to Gerta, who barely even looked up as she used her magic to melt it into drinking water. "I've been thinking about that."

"And?" Talia asked.

Danielle rubbed her shoulders, where the straps of her pack had dug into the muscle. "I'm still thinking," she admitted.

"Think harder."

She did, testing one plan after another in her mind and discarding them all. By the time they reached Snow's palace toward evening of the second day, Danielle could see only one way to get them inside. But the cost made her ill.

The woods ended at the shore of a vast, frozen lake, covered in ankle-deep snow. Toward the center of the lake stood the palace Danielle had seen in her vision, like a miniature mountain range of ice. Crystalline towers stretched skyward, illuminated from within by green and blue lights. Drifts of snow buried much of the lower part of the palace.

They waited while Gerta read the protective spell Veleris had prepared. Gerta clutched the dried fish in her hands, mumbling to herself and touching her forehead. She repeated the gesture with the others, chanting in a language Danielle didn't recognize.

"If you turn me into a troll, I swear to the gods I'll eat you," said Talia.

Gerta's lips quirked as she continued her spell, reaching for Danielle. Danielle's face tightened at Gerta's touch. Her skin felt warm and dry, as if she had spent too much time in the sun. When she flexed her arms, there was a stiffness in her skin that reminded her of the heavily starched gowns that had been so popular last season.

Talia pulled out her knife and dragged the edge over her thumb. The blade failed to break the skin. "Not bad."

"It's no substitute for armor," Gerta warned. "A strong sword thrust will kill you, but we should be protected from glancing blows and smaller stings." She rubbed a thumb over the writing on the dried fish, then shrugged and took a bite. "Tastes like magic."

The lake offered no cover. Danielle saw neither guards nor windows, but she had no doubt Snow was watching. "Night should help—"

"Not against Snow. The entire lake serves as her mirror. The moment we step out . . ." Gerta pointed toward the palace. "There are creatures in the drifts. So cold they're barely alive."

"Prisoners?" asked Talia.

"I don't think so." Gerta squinted through the trees.

Danielle fought to control her breathing. Jakob was there, beyond those drifted walls. Close enough he might hear her voice if she shouted. "It doesn't matter."

Gerta's magic wasn't strong enough to overpower Snow. The darkling wouldn't be able to conceal them either, not here. Snow had made this place her new home. The moment they stepped onto the ice, she would know.

"How do we get inside?" asked Talia. "There are no doors."

"She doesn't need them," said Gerta. "The ice responds to her will. We'll have to scale the outer wall or break through."

Danielle stepped down to the shore. The lake's edge had frozen into a lacy ribbon of frost that crunched beneath her feet.

The drifts at the base of the palace wall shivered. Large shapes stepped free. Most were humanoid, clothed in fur and frost and ice. Others walked on all fours, though they were unlike any beasts Danielle had ever seen. At this distance, it was difficult to make out the details. She spotted a white winged serpent twice as high as a man. An animal that appeared a cross between dog and bull shook snow from its spine-covered hide. Every one of the creatures was white, as though all color had been bleached from their bodies.

"I estimate close to a hundred," said Talia, her tone calm and calculating.

"That's just from the front section of the palace," Gerta pointed out. "She could have five times their number waiting in the rest of the drifts."

"Welcome, Danielle." Snow's voice boomed over the lake. "Have you no words of greeting for your loyal crew, the men who fought so briefly but valiantly to protect the *Phillipa*?"

Danielle swallowed. "Gerta?"

"She's telling the truth." Gerta was paler than usual. "They're human. Or they used to be."

These were men Danielle had sailed with. Men she had joked with and even fought beside, more than a year ago. "Are you strong enough to undo—"

"I'm sorry." Gerta stared out at the bestial army before them. "I might be able to change one or two, given enough time, but not like this."

Ever since leaving Lorindar, Danielle had imagined what she would say when she found Snow White. She had searched for the words that would break through the demon's power and help her friend to throw off its hold long enough for them to destroy it. Long enough for them to save her.

"Your son told me you'd arrive today," said Snow. "A marvelous child, who sees far more than most. I daresay he'll soon forget you and Armand. He'll forget everything, save me."

"Forgive me." Danielle closed her eyes. Many times throughout the years she had prayed to her mother's spirit. It was her mother who had helped her escape her stepmother's home, leading her to the ball and Armand. Her mother had given her the glass sword, which had saved Danielle's life on more than one occasion. Her hand went to her hip, imagining the comforting weight of the glass blade, now lost.

"Watch over your grandson," she whispered. "Keep him safe." No matter what happened to her.

Talia cleared her throat. "You realize if we fail, we're handing the Princess of Lorindar over to this demon?"

"So don't fail," said Danielle.

Snow's voice came again. "Have you come to bargain? To trade the girl for your son? Surrender to me, and I might be willing to listen to your offer."

Danielle glanced at Gerta. She was formed from Snow White. It was no surprise Snow would guess at the very plan Gerta had suggested back in Speas Elan.

Talia's face was stone. "Even possessed, she's a lousy liar."

"I didn't come to bargain," Danielle called out. "I came to ask you to return my son. And my friend."

"Oh, Danielle. You should have let them go." Snow's creatures moved in unison, marching toward the shore.

Danielle had always believed her ability to summon animals to be another of her mother's gifts, but perhaps the Duchess was right. Perhaps it was merely the result of her own fairy blood. Whatever its origins, Danielle drew upon that gift now as never before.

Rats, doves, horses, and more had always answered her pleas for help. They had aided her in her chores. They had fought and died to protect her. Even the horses of the Wild Hunt had listened to her commands.

The darkling moved forward, putting itself between her and Snow's forces. Danielle had seen the damage darklings could do, but Snow had faced them before and won. The darkling wouldn't be enough.

She called again, forgoing words, projecting her summons as far as she could reach. Ignoring the monsters crossing the ice, the demon within those walls. Ignoring everything save her *need*.

"Are they coming?" asked Gerta.

Danielle made a face. "It's not like the animals talk back to me." She searched the woods for movement.

A pair of white egrets responded first, streaking overhead like angels and swooping down to stab dagger beaks into one of Snow's monsters. Crows followed, their harsh cries filling the air. Hawks and owls burst from the trees, and then the ground itself began to vibrate underfoot.

A herd of reindeer exploded from the woods, charging past so closely Danielle could have reached out and brushed their sides. One of the largest stopped and bowed his head to Danielle. He was slightly smaller than a horse, with antlers that curved like gnarled oak. She climbed onto the reindeer. "My friends, too, please."

Two more reindeer stopped. Gerta shook her head as she mounted the nearest. "Strangest army I've ever heard of."

"Things are about to get stranger." Talia turned to the darkling. "What are the limits of your shapechanging powers?"

The darkling spread his hands.

Talia sheathed her dagger. "I could use a better weapon."

The darkling grew taller and thinner. Talia leaned forward, tugging the reindeer's head to guide him, then snatching the darkling up in one mittened hand. Moments later, she held a lance of pure blackness.

"Reins would be helpful," Gerta commented, clinging to her reindeer's mane.

"Just keep your head down and hold on," said Danielle. "Don't try to fight. Stay close to Talia."

She had gained some measure of skill on horseback, but the reindeer was a smaller animal, and the back was built differently, with a bit of a hump near the neck. Not to mention the lack of a saddle. The darkling must have used magic to smooth its gait while in this form, because now that she rode a true reindeer, it was all she could do to keep from falling off.

More animals soon joined their battle. A pack of wolves charged across the lake to her right. A lone fox darted underfoot, weaving past the reindeer. A family of bears lumbered onto the ice on her left.

"Punch through their line and make for the palace," Talia shouted. "Danielle, try to get those wolves to guard our flanks. Once we pierce the line, have them follow us through and spread out to keep the demon's monsters from following."

Danielle did her best to relay the commands. Everything was happening so quickly. Snow's creatures roared as they fought back against the birds. Animals and monsters alike struggled for footing as they clashed. The winged snake snapped an owl from the air, crushing it in its jaws. Moments later, a wolf sank its teeth into one of the snake's wings.

"Stay low," Talia yelled. Wasps swarmed over the palace wall, glittering orange in the sunlight. Some struck the animals, but most flew directly at Danielle and her friends.

She pressed her face close to her reindeer's neck as the stingers ripped through her clothes to jab her skin, but they failed to pierce Veleris' magic. She grabbed one that had become tangled in her hair. Unlike the other wasps Danielle had seen, this one had a stinger made entirely of ice, which continued to stab futilely even as it melted from the warmth of her hand.

Wolves closed in around them, forming a spearpoint. Talia thrust her black spear to either side, every hit earning howls of pain. The darkling weapon soon dripped blood that was all too human.

Gerta shrieked as a white-spined ape swiped her leg. Talia turned, but Gerta was already gesturing at her attacker. The ape's feet slipped out from beneath it. When it fell, its head struck the ice hard enough to make Danielle wince in sympathy.

Between the wasps and the monsters, Danielle could barely even see the palace. She stayed low, wanting to urge her reindeer to greater speed, but unwilling to risk a fall. Blood and bodies made the footing more treacherous, and she could feel her reindeer struggling to maintain his balance on the ice.

So many animals lay dead or dying. Snow's monsters, too. Monsters who had once been human. More birds swooped down, and when she looked behind, she saw other animals continuing to charge forth from the woods. But Snow had also sent reinforcements. Danielle could hear their cries closing in from either side.

The animals forced their way forward, even as the creatures tried to surround them. If they slowed, Danielle doubted they would be able to fight their way free. Wolves threw themselves at Snow's guardians, snarling and snapping. A brown bear reared up and struck a six-legged lizard that looked vaguely like a dragon. Talia's spear knocked a giant porcupine aside, and then they were through.

The wolves followed, spreading out in a thin line behind Danielle and her friends. More animals joined them, a wall of claws and teeth against the frozen creatures who tried to reach them. Talia jumped from her reindeer, clutching her spear in one hand as she tossed her pack to the base of the wall. She stabbed the spear into the snow and grabbed a coil of rope. "Gerta, I need another knife. Danielle, give me a boost."

Gerta tossed her dagger to Talia. Danielle braced herself. Talia climbed Danielle's body as easily as a spider until she stood balanced upon Danielle's shoulders. Danielle grimaced and did her best not to move. Her legs were weak after two days' hard riding, but she held firm as Talia rammed the blade into the ice. She had to strike three times to get it to hold. She pulled herself up and stabbed her hunting knife into the ice with her other hand.

Danielle picked up the darkling spear and moved to join the animals. She stabbed past the line at the twisted creatures beyond, doing what she could to help and trying to ignore the cold, sickly feeling of the darkling in her hands.

"This isn't going to be fast enough," said Gerta. She whispered a quick spell. The next time Talia struck, her blade sank deeper into the ice, and Danielle saw steam emerge.

Danielle backed toward the wall, their defensive line shrinking into a tighter and tighter arc as one wolf after another fell to Snow's monsters.

"I'm ready!" Talia shouted from atop the wall. One end of the rope dropped to the ice.

Danielle didn't turn. "Gerta, get moving."

Gerta hurried up the wall, and then Talia was yelling for Danielle.

Danielle flung the spear straight into the air. Talia snatched it and set it down beside her. Danielle hesitated only long enough to thank the animals for their help. Then, tears blurring her eyes, she grabbed the rope and climbed. She was halfway up when she spotted a white shape streaking along the top of the wall toward Talia. "To your left!"

"I see it." Talia flung her darkling spear, catching the monster in the side. It howled and toppled away, out of sight. Talia reached down with her free hand.

Danielle climbed faster, ignoring the burning of her muscles and the cramps in her fingers until she was able to reach up and grasp Talia's hand.

There was a short clearing on the opposite side, about ten paces between the wall and the palace itself. Gerta stood at the base of the wall below, dagger in one hand as she searched the snowy courtyard, but Danielle didn't spot any of Snow's monsters here save the one Talia had struck with her spear. It lay dead in the snow, the darkling standing beside it.

The palace was relatively small, perhaps half the size of Whiteshore Palace. It was a thing of spires, like three narrow mountaintops pressed together in a tight triangle. Icicles as long as spears lined every visible edge.

"How do I get down?" Danielle asked.

Talia gave her a wicked grin and pushed. Danielle bit back a shriek as the air rushed past. She had just enough time to hope the drifted snow was enough to cushion her fall, and then cold arms caught her body. The darkling set her gently upon her feet.

"She did that to me, too," said Gerta. She had tied her scarf around the wound on her leg. "I say we feed her to the wolves."

Danielle backed away from the darkling. "Sounds good to me."

Talia landed on all fours in the snow. The impact looked solid enough to make Danielle wince, but Talia shook it off.

"I know this place," Gerta whispered. "She built it from our daydreams, back when we were children. It's been so long I'd forgotten. The palace of the Snow Queen, the true ruler of all Allesandria, who would use her magic to fix all that was wrong in the world. She'll be in the throne room at the center."

As would Jakob. Danielle stopped herself from calling out to her son. "Can you get us to Snow?"

Gerta limped toward the palace. Snowflakes swirled around her, and more of the ice wasps circled overhead. They merely watched, no longer trying to sting. Gerta stopped before a door of frosted ice. She held out one hand, and Talia slapped the hunting knife into it without a word. Gerta jammed the thick blade as deep as it would go.

Danielle shivered. The sun was setting, and the wind had picked up. "Whatever happens, I want you both to know how much—"

"Shut up," said Talia. "We know." She jabbed a finger at the darkling. "You. I need my spear back."

"Gerta . . ."

Gerta managed a one-shouldered shrug, but her fear was easy to see. "This is what I was made for."

"Thank you." The words were inadequate, but they were all she had. And then a blur of white leaped from atop the palace, and there was no time for words.

Chapter 22

TALIA JUMPED BACK AS THE MONSTER dropped into the snow. The darkling hadn't finished changing back into its spear form, so she grabbed it by one spindly arm and flung it directly into the monster's face. The darkling clung like an insect, and the monster roared from shock and pain. Talia slammed into it from the side, trying to force it away from Gerta.

She needn't have bothered. The darkling's touch had done its job, and the monster soon stopped moving. Talia grimaced and looked away, trying to shut out the image of mummified flesh and dry bone.

Snow's next attack was magical in nature. Three of the icicles overhead cracked and dropped like spears. Talia yanked Gerta back as the ice shattered on the ground, close enough that smaller shards jabbed her legs. "What other sort of protections did Snow daydream about?"

"Mostly traps that would protect us from our mother." Gerta ran the knife around the edge of the hole she had created, widening it with every touch. "Bottomless pits. Passages that seal behind you. Things like that."

"Is that all?" Talia grimaced.

"No." Gerta forced a smile. "But we don't have time to list all the ways we dreamed about stopping her."

Talia glanced at Danielle, who appeared unfazed by the traps. She looked ready to carve her way through every wall in the palace if that was what it took. Talia hoped her determination wouldn't get her killed.

"I'm ready." Gerta stepped back from a hole just wide enough to squeeze through. "It probably won't stay open for long."

Talia retrieved her knife and pushed past. To the darkling, she snapped, "Aren't you supposed to be a spear?"

Between one step and the next, a white-furred arm shot out and seized the darkling by the throat, dragging it inside. Talia swore and climbed after them.

The darkling was doing its best to hold off a troll-shaped creature with claws of ice. Darklings were quick and agile, but the troll held it fast. One white hand crushed the darkling's neck while the other slammed its head against the ice wall. The darkling tried to shift its form, but the troll wouldn't let go.

Talia flung her knife into the side of the troll's neck. When that did nothing, she reached back through the hole to take Gerta's knife, which she used to stab the back of the troll's leg. She ducked as it swiped at her with one hand.

That distraction was enough for the darkling to seize the troll's other arm. Ice and fur fell away, and the flesh beneath withered. The troll roared, but the darkling clung tight. Dust fell from its fingers, and the limb dropped away. There was no blood.

The darkling sprang, one arm wrapping around the troll's head, the other grabbing Talia's dagger, still lodged in the troll's neck. Talia grimaced as the darkling yanked the knife free and slashed the troll's throat.

"Are you all right?" Danielle asked.

Talia nodded, watching the darkling as it tossed the knife to the ground and backed away. It had fought as fiercely as a wild beast, but that final blow had been artistic in its precision.

Gerta had dropped to one knee, brushing snow from the floor to reveal the frozen surface of the lake. The ice was clear as glass, showing only blackness below, and reflecting the tall, curved hallway around them. Green and blue light flickered within the walls, like slow flames trapped in the ice.

Gerta wiped away more snow. White cracks were spread through the ice in a pattern too regular to be natural. Like tiles, if every tile were a plate-sized puzzle piece, no two identical. "Something's wrong."

"You don't say," Talia muttered.

"The mirror . . . it's tainted." She glanced back at the wall. "When we entered the palace, we passed into a magical circle."

That couldn't be good. "What kind of circle?" asked Talia.

"A line of blood, traced just below the surface of the ice. I think it's for a summoning."

"Remember what she said back in Kanustius," Danielle said, her voice tight. "She doesn't mean to rule Allesandria. She means to destroy it."

A summoning circle the size of a palace. Just like Snow's mother had used. "Can one demon summon others?"

"I'm not sure. With Snow's help . . ." Gerta trailed off.

"It's a mirror." Talia crouched beside her. "Snow could always shatter her mirrors at will. Can't you do the same to this? Crack the circle enough to disrupt its power?"

"But not enough to drop us all into the lake, please," Danielle added.

"Mirror, mirror, cold and bleak—" But even as Gerta spoke, frost spread over the ice. She swore and yanked her hand away. "It's Snow's mirror, not mine. The mirror, the traps, the entire palace is attuned to her." She gave a weak smile. "In a way, it's comforting. The fact that the palace rejects my control proves I was more than just a piece of my sister. That I was my own person."

Talia's jaw tensed at the word "was." She straightened. "Stay behind me. There will be other traps."

"We don't have the time." Gerta extended a hand to Talia. "I can get us through."

"How?" Talia asked.

"Snow and the demon have been trying to reclaim me ever since she learned what I was. It's time to let her."

"No." The word slipped out before Talia could stop it. Gerta had made her choice back in the fairy mines, but this was too soon. There had to be another way.

Gerta took her hand. "I'll hold on as long as I can." The tightness of Gerta's grip and the cold sweat of her palm belied her calm tone. "Hopefully, as she starts to pull me back into herself, it will be enough to make the palace accept me. I should be able to control it for a short time, before I lose myself to her."

Talia glanced down the hallway. "How long?"

"That's hard to say." Gerta managed a halfhearted smile. "I've never done this before."

It was the kind of thing Snow would have said, only Snow would have hidden her fear better. Talia blinked. "Fight it."

"Snow tried to fight the demon, too," Gerta said, her fingers squeezing Talia's palm. "She couldn't—"

"Snow was alone when this thing took her. You're not. Listen to my voice. Stay with us."

"She's always been stronger." Gerta smiled, her eyes momentarily lost in memories. "I'm ready."

You're all I have left of her. Talia held her tongue, knowing the words would only hurt.

Gerta began to whisper.

"What are you doing?" asked Danielle.

"Removing Veleris' spell on myself." She knelt and slid her fingers along one of the cracks in the ice. Blood welled from her fingertips. For an instant, Talia spotted a glint of ice in the cut, and then it was gone. Gerta's body tightened, and she squeezed Talia's hand hard enough to bruise. "She's so strong."

"So are you," said Talia.

Gerta clung to Talia's arm as though she would fall without support. "It's like balancing on the edge of a cliff, trying to lean out without falling."

"I've got you," said Talia.

"So does she." Gerta shuddered. "This way. Quickly."

Talia helped her down the hallway into a small, circular room. Coffins of ice were laid out in a circle. Danielle rubbed her hand on the closest, clearing the frost.

"Members of the Nobles' Circle," said Gerta, her voice strained. "Dead. She used their blood to form the circle."

Gerta started across the room, but bumped into one of the coffins. "You'll need to help me, Talia. One of the mirror shards is in her eye. It blinds me. I see what she sees. I can feel her. Them. Snow and the demon both tugging me toward them."

Danielle peered into the far hall. "It looks clear."

"It's not," said Gerta. "The floor thins here so she can drop unwanted visitors into the lake. But I can get us through. The palace recognizes me now."

Meaning Gerta was fading. Talia held her arm, helping her through the doorway. The air was colder here, making her shiver even through the heavy furs.

Gerta stumbled. "It feels like she's trying to drown me."

"Stay with us." Talia began to sing an old Arathean song about a queen's journey into the desert to rescue her lover from a deev. She kept her voice low, pitched for Gerta's ears alone.

"I thought . . . you hated to sing."

"I do." Talia gave a gentle pull, guiding Gerta onward. "Does it help?"

"It's beautiful."

One tortured step at a time, they made their way down the hallway. Three more times Gerta stopped, and each time Talia feared they had lost her. If the demon took Gerta now, it could attack them all through her, and everything they had done would be for nothing. But each time, Gerta pushed herself onward, leading them through one trap after another until they reached the door.

It opened at Gerta's touch, swinging inward to reveal a broad, domed room. Snowdrifts edged the floor, blending seamlessly with the walls and giving the illusion of an endless white plain.

"Welcome home, Sister." Snow White sat upon a white throne in the center of the room. Blocks of ice formed a dais, a miniature glacier atop the frozen lake. Jakob sat to Snow's left, shivering and playing with shards of ice. He didn't appear to notice them.

"Jakob!" Danielle started forward.

"*Wait.*" Only the sharpness of Talia's tone halted Danielle's rush toward her son.

"Thank you for returning her to me," said Snow. She wore a sleeveless white gown. Her skin was even paler than usual, and her lips had lost their color. Both of her eyes were open, but one was scarred and sallow. Even the strands of white in her hair blended almost invisibly into her surroundings, as if the palace were slowly consuming her. A crown of ice circled her brow, every spike gleaming like glass. She rose, and the edges of her gown clinked as she stepped down beside Jakob.

"Don't touch him," Danielle warned, short sword in hand. But it was twenty paces to Snow's throne. The demon would strike them all down before anyone could reach her.

"What was your plan?" Snow asked. "I know you won't kill me. Danielle clings to the hope that I might yet be saved, and Talia lacks the strength to murder the woman she loves. You're welcome to try, of course. You wouldn't be the first to betray me."

There was nothing of Snow White in her voice. Her body was taut, reminding Talia of a reptile poised to strike. She frowned, and sunlight shone from her crown, piercing the darkling and pinning it to the wall. It squealed and fought, but couldn't break free.

"What was yours?" Talia countered. "To murder the people who tried to save you? To burn your homeland and entomb its nobles the same way your mother once did to you? To loose demons upon the world and watch it fall into ruin?"

"Not to burn, but to cleanse. Oh, Talia, you don't understand what it's like to finally *see*. The spirits you call demons will purge the lies and the corruption from this world."

"What of joy?" Danielle asked. "Will you purge that, too?"

Snow tapped a foot to the floor. Her reflection shivered, and for a moment Talia saw not the demon but Snow White, unscarred and trapped within the icy mirror. "Your friend's spirit survives, you know," she said lightly. "It was Jakob who found that lingering shred of humanity, thinking it could save him. Kill me and you kill what remains of her as well."

Talia stepped forward. As if that were a signal, cold winds swirled to life. She tried to cling to Gerta's hand, but the wind ripped Talia away and flung her against the wall. Ice and snow all but blinded her, turning the others to mere shadows.

"Not that I mean to give you the chance," Snow added.

"Talia!" She could hear Gerta's cry, but couldn't see her. And then the wind weakened enough for Talia to push away.

Gerta clung to Danielle's arm for support. Her eyes were squeezed shut, fists knotted.

"You're trying to possess a demon?" There was no strain in Snow's voice. She sounded delighted, as though a pet had just learned an unexpected trick. "Not even Snow White was bold enough to try that."

Gerta crumpled to the ground. She turned toward Talia. "Please . . ."

"I won't let her take you," Talia promised. Tears froze on her cheeks.

Snow's voice hardened. "She was mine from the moment I created her."

Gerta's lips moved in unison with Snow's. Her face had gone slack. Whatever magic she had used to try to control the demon—to try to protect Talia—had merely opened her to the demon's power.

Talia lunged to the side, stepping between Snow and the darkling. The sunlight was warm, but didn't burn human flesh the way it did the fairy. The darkling dropped to all fours behind her. "Do it," Talia snapped.

The darkling scrambled forward, its body smoldering

from Snow's attack. Snow's crown flared with light, but Talia kept herself ahead of the darkling, protecting it as it crawled not toward Snow, but to Gerta. It tugged her onto her back, then pressed a single finger to Gerta's left eye.

A scream filled the palace, shared by Snow and Gerta alike. The winds died, and the sunlight blinked away. Talia raced to Gerta. "Are you—"

Gerta rolled onto her side, clutching her ruined eye. White dust trailed from her fingers. "I can feel her pain, and her fury."

Talia hesitated.

Gerta pushed her away. "Go, damn it!"

Danielle was already running toward Jakob. Talia tore herself from Gerta and ran after Snow. She reached into her jacket, pulling out the magic-inhibiting chain they had taken from the palace. She had braided rope handles through the end links the night before, while the others slept. She grabbed one handle in each hand, tugging the chain taut.

Snow held one hand to her eye. In her other, she had created a sword of ice. She blinked her good eye, as if trying to focus. Talia ran faster, nearly slipping on the ice. She had to strike while the demon was disoriented.

Ice swirled around Snow's body, forming armor that resembled clouded plates of quartz. She stabbed her blade into the floor and waved a hand at Talia. Danielle cried a warning as the shards Jakob had been playing with tore from his grasp and flew through the air. Two struck Talia, but the giant's magic protected her. The darkling was less fortunate. Three shards pierced its chest, and it fell, blackness seeping over the ice.

Snow snatched up her sword. Talia dropped into a slide, kicking Snow's legs and sending her face-first to the ice. Talia slammed into the edge of the dais and pushed herself to her feet. As Snow rose, Talia kicked the sword from her hand and swung the chain like a whip, looping it around Snow's neck. Talia grabbed the other end and pulled tight, crossing the links to form a circle that dug into the ice protecting Snow's throat.

Icy claws bloodied Talia's forearms. The demon was too strong, pushing herself up even as Talia tried to hold her. Talia kicked the back of Snow's knees, trying to keep her off-balance.

Snow lurched backward, slamming them both onto the dais. From the sharp pain in Talia's side, the impact had either bruised or broken a rib. She twisted the rope handles together, clutching them in one hand, and drew her knife.

"Go ahead," Snow said, her voice harsh. "Murder the woman you love. You'll be killing Gerta as well. How long will you survive with those deaths upon your heart?"

In the edge of her vision, Talia saw more of the white monsters enter the room. She couldn't feel her fingers anymore. Blood covered her arms, dripping toward her hands.

Snow's elbow cracked the back of Talia's hand, and the knife fell away. Snow bucked, and it was all Talia could do to hold on to the chain.

She could hear Danielle shouting to her son, telling him she was sorry. Sorry for what, Talia didn't know. Gerta lay unmoving on the ice, ignored by the creatures that spread to surround the throne. Talia pulled harder, but the armor kept the links from cutting off Snow's breath.

And then Danielle was there, clutching her sword in both hands. Blood trickled down the edge, though Talia hadn't seen her stab anyone with it. Perhaps Danielle had used it against one of the monsters.

No . . . it wasn't their blood. It was Jakob's blood. *Fairy* blood. Jakob was huddled behind the throne, and his left hand was bleeding.

Snow saw, too, and she stopped struggling. When she spoke next, she sounded almost like herself. "Danielle. You were my friend."

"I always will be." Danielle raised the sword.

Talia buried her face in Snow's hair. She could feel the impact as Danielle drove the sword into Snow's side. Snow grunted. Her armor cracked and began to fall away.

Gerta screamed. Talia could see her clutching her side.

"Gerta could still live," Snow wheezed. "Release the chain. I give you my word Gerta will survive."

"Don't let go," Gerta yelled.

Danielle had turned to face Snow's creatures. She held her sword in one hand, and picked up Snow's ice blade with her other. Danielle wasn't the best student, but her years of practice with Talia had paid off. Despite the odds, Danielle stood in a low, balanced stance, her body relaxed. It wouldn't be enough, but Talia had no doubt she would take several of the creatures with her.

They didn't attack. Over the pounding of her blood, Talia made out the sound of Gerta chanting a spell. Her voice was weak but determined.

"I know what you left behind, Talia," Snow whispered. "Your throne. Your lover. Your children. You could have them all back again."

"You wouldn't want them," said Danielle. "You'd look upon your home and see only ugliness. Your children would be repulsive to your sight."

"Shut up. Both of you." Talia closed her eyes. Snow's hair was damp with sweat and melted ice. Her body was so cold, making Talia want to pull her closer, to share her own warmth.

"Took you long enough to get here."

Talia's eyes snapped open. The voice was Snow's, but without the bitter edge of the demon. It had come from within the ice. In the blood-smeared reflection, she saw herself clutching the necklace around Snow White's throat, but in that reflection Snow had turned around to face her, a weary smile on her face.

"Snow?" Talia whispered.

"I tried, Talia. As soon as the mirror cracked, I felt it reaching for me. I realized what my mother had done. I tried to fight it—"

"It's not your fault." Talia's voice broke. A part of her wondered if this was the demon's doing, a trick to get her to release the chain. If so, she didn't care.

"It is." Snow's smile fell. "I tried to cheat death. I couldn't let go of Beatrice. I'm sorry, Talia."

"Beatrice? What does—" Talia frowned, remembering Snow's behavior after Bea's death. Snow had created Gerta, a fully formed woman, from nothingness. It would have taken months to prepare such a spell . . . a spell to create a new body, one which could receive the spirit of another. "Oh, Snow."

"I couldn't let the demon escape. I knew Gerta would figure it out. In my daydreams, she was almost as clever as me." Snow's smile was full of mischief, even as her words grew faint. "Tell Danielle to make sure Jakob gets a good teacher. He's a gifted one."

"I will." Talia almost let go, wanting only to touch the reflection in the ice. "The mirror wouldn't have held forever. If not you, someone else would have broken the glass. Someone less able to fight this thing."

"I know. Mother's demon would have . . . destroyed everything. I couldn't let her win."

"You didn't," Talia whispered. "You beat her."

"Damn right." Snow blinked and looked about, as though disoriented. "Gerta loves you, you know. We both do."

"I know." New tears welled. She turned to where Gerta lay dying on the ice.

"So why haven't you . . . kissed her yet?"

Talia smiled. She would have stayed here forever, just to listen to Snow tease her, but even as she watched, Snow's reflection was fading. When she spoke again, Talia had to press her ear to the ice to make out the words.

"Danielle . . . clever woman. Jakob's blood . . . weakens the demon . . . enough for me to do this." In the reflection, she slipped a hand around Talia's neck and kissed her cheek. The other Talia released the chain, which fell away to reveal the paleness of Snow's throat.

Snow looked through the ice and winked. "Promise me . . . you'll take care of her. She deserves to be happy. You both do."

Talia's vision blurred. She twisted her head, furiously wiping the tears on her shoulder.

"Happy ever after . . . is a choice." Snow glanced away. "I'm sorry, Talia."

"Please don't go," Talia whispered.

"I created her. I bound her. I can . . . free her." Snow touched the underside of the frozen lake. "Mirror formed of ice so cold . . . sever now my magic's hold."

And then both Snow and the demon were gone.

Chapter 23

DANIELLE FELT THE MOMENT THE MAGIC on Snow's sword failed. The ice blade grew heavy, and the hilt began to melt in her grip. She tossed it away, and it broke apart when it struck the ground.

She didn't fool herself into believing she stood a chance against Snow's beasts. Not that it would stop her from doing her best to slay them all if they came too close. But they didn't attack. They stumbled about as though drunk, snarling and swiping at one another if they collided, but mostly keeping to themselves.

"I'm cold, Mama."

Danielle stepped sideways, moving toward Jakob. He ran up and grabbed her jacket, pressing against her like an animal burrowing for warmth. His hands were bloody, the fingertips an unhealthy blue tinge, and he had lost so much weight. His cheeks were sunken, and there were shadows beneath his eyes. But he was alive.

"I've got you." She crouched to pick him up with one arm. He wrapped his arms and legs around her body, clinging with all his strength.

Talia and Snow lay on the ice at the base of the throne. Toward the door, Gerta had managed to stand. She was unsteady, and held one hand to her side, but there was no blood.

"Gerta?" Danielle kept her sword ready. Talia had never released the chain. The demon shouldn't have had anywhere to go. Yet how could Gerta live, with Snow—

Danielle forced back tears. It was like swallowing a stone.

"It's gone." Gerta's head was tilted, allowing her red hair to fall over the ruin of her eye.

"How?" Danielle glanced at Snow. "You said the two of you were bound. I thought—"

"I should be dead. Back in Noita's garden . . ." Tears fell from Gerta's good eye. She sounded dazed, though whether the shock came from the loss of her eye or the fact that she was still alive, Danielle couldn't have said. "This is the death I saw. I was part of her, our fates bound."

"Was?"

"She saved me," said Gerta. "She and the demon were both dying, but Snow was able to cast one final spell. She severed that bond between us."

With Danielle's help, Gerta made her way toward the dais. Talia's body was taut. The chain had fallen away. Pinched, bloody skin showed where it had dug into Snow's neck.

The sight brought new tears, and Danielle hugged her son tighter.

"Is he all right?" Gerta asked.

"He's cold." Danielle remembered the fear in his face when she asked him to hold out his hand. But he had obeyed, knowing what was needed. He had cried when she cut him—they both had—but he never flinched away. She unbuttoned her jacket, wrapping it around him. "What of you? Your eye, your side—"

"Hurt like hell, both of them," Gerta admitted. "But I'm not bleeding." She pointed to the weapon in Danielle's hand. "You shouldn't need that. With the demon gone, the mirror shards have no hold over them anymore. They're free, all of them."

Even Armand. Danielle sheathed her sword and sat, her muscles gone weak as though her limbs were melting. The creatures stumbled about, confused and frightened, but no longer hostile. Jakob climbed into her lap, and she held him with one arm. With her other, she gently reached over to touch Talia's back. Talia's muscles were like stone.

Years ago, Talia had awakened from a fairy curse to find her entire family dead. She had fled to Lorindar, where Beatrice and Snow found her and took her in. Now Bea and Snow were both gone.

"Snow chose this," Gerta said. "The moment our mother's mirror cracked and she sensed what hid within. She trusted her friends to help her destroy that evil."

"I know." Talia didn't move. Her hair hid her face. "This is Allesandria, home of magic. There must have been something more we could have—"

"There wasn't." The certainty in Gerta's voice was absolute. "You saw how many nobles fell to the demon, not to mention the king of Allesandria. Snow spent her life studying magic. She was gifted enough to rule, stronger even than our mother, though she never believed it. She knew there was but one way to undo what Rose Curtana had set in motion. She wouldn't want you to grieve. She'd want you to celebrate her victory."

A cracking sound echoed through the throne room. A thin curtain of snow drifted from the ceiling. Danielle rose. "What happens to this place now that the demon is gone?"

"Nothing good."

An animal like a dog with vestigial wings of edged ice charged toward them. Its snarls sounded more panicked then angry. Danielle tried to stand and draw her sword, but Gerta was faster, slapping a palm to the surface of the frozen lake. The dog yelped and limped away, favoring its front left leg. Blood dripped from its paw.

"We can't stay here," said Danielle.

Talia took a deep, shuddering breath. She rolled Snow's body to face her, then leaned down to kiss her lightly on the lips.

Danielle held her breath. Once before, deep within Fairytown, Talia had awakened Snow from a curse with just such a kiss . . . but Snow was gone. Talia seemed to shrink into herself.

"Talia, we have to go." Danielle wasn't letting go of her son, and Gerta was too badly hurt to physically drag

Talia from the palace, assuming Talia didn't knock her unconscious for trying.

"You promised her," Gerta said.

Talia didn't move. "You heard that?"

Gerta tugged Talia's shoulder. "Do you have the faintest idea what her spirit will do to yours if you stay here and let yourself die? It won't be pretty."

Slowly, Talia nodded. She lifted Snow's body, cradling her to her chest, and stepped away from the throne. "What about the traps?"

"I should be able to take care of them now," Gerta said.

Danielle did her best to call out to Snow's creatures, warning them to flee. She didn't know whether they could understand her, or if they simply sensed the danger as the magic holding the palace together began to unravel. By the time they reached the doorway, the throne room was empty.

Outside, a light snow was falling, but it couldn't hide the carnage of battle. Tears spilled down Danielle's cheeks at the sight of animals and monsters scattered over the ice, their blood staining the snow crimson. Trails of blood showed where the wounded had dragged themselves away into the woods. "I'm so sorry," Danielle whispered. "Thank you."

With the darkling dead, they had no way of traveling, yet Danielle couldn't bring herself to call upon the animals again. Not when they had given so much. "We'll need shelter."

"No, we won't." Once they reached the edge of the lake, Gerta dropped to her knees and cleared a patch on the ice. Unlike the floor within the palace, the ice here was rippled and flawed, but Danielle could see Gerta's reflection in the surface. "Frozen lake beneath my hand, show the ruler of this land."

Nothing happened at first. Danielle looked to the woods. "Should we—"

"He heard me," Gerta said firmly. "I imagine things are rather chaotic right now. Give him time."

It wasn't long before Laurence appeared in the ice.

His features were blurred, making it difficult to discern his expression. Or perhaps he obscured himself deliberately. "Gerta? You found Ermillina?"

"The demon is gone, Cousin." Her words were edged, particularly the last.

Danielle stepped to Gerta's side. "Snow gave her life to destroy it."

"Princess Danielle. I'm glad to see you well." Something in Laurence's manner broke, making him sound not like a king but a man, exhausted and lost. "What of your son?"

"Jakob is safe," Danielle assured him.

"I will send my people to escort you to the docks. Allesandria is in chaos, and I would not have you hurt as we work to bring things under control."

"No," said Danielle. "Tell your people to bring us to Kanustius."

Laurence stared. "Your Highness, Kanustius is in ruins. Half the palace is destroyed."

"Snow was Princess of Allesandria. She deserves to be remembered alongside her father."

Talia pursed her lips. "I think she'd like that."

"Princess Whiteshore, Snow White attacked this nation. The lords of eleven provinces are dead or missing. She slaughtered—"

"She accepted this fate in order to destroy the demon her mother summoned." All of Danielle's grief, her fury at Snow's death, threatened to pour forth. She tightened her grip on her son. "Rose Curtana was a monster. Snow destroyed that monster, an act which gave you your throne, and you banished her for it. Today, she protected you from Rose Curtana's power a second time. She gave her life to protect you. You will *not* turn your back on her again."

"I helped my cousin to escape before," Laurence said. "But the law—"

"Damn your law." Danielle glanced at the others. Gerta's lips were tight with her own anger. Talia simply nodded. "You will pardon Snow White and give her the honor she deserves. Lorindar gave you your throne, Your Majesty. You *will* give this to Snow."

Laurence didn't respond. A distant voice in the back of her mind warned she had pushed too far, but she couldn't bring herself to care. She took a breath to calm herself, then added, "Also, I would reclaim my sword from your keeping, along with our other belongings, which you took while we were imprisoned in your dungeon."

Even through the distortions in the ice, she saw him wince. "Very well, Princess Whiteshore. I will send one of my Stormcrows to retrieve you."

"Send as many as you can spare," said Danielle, looking back to the crumbling palace. "There are many victims here in need of their magic."

Aside from Danielle and her friends, only the king and one of his Stormcrows attended Snow's funeral. Her body had been cremated, her ashes mixed into the stone that formed her obelisk.

That obelisk was in place by the time Danielle arrived in the memorial garden. The garden had been better protected than much of the palace, and the walls had survived relatively unscathed, but the smell of smoke lingered in the air. Danielle identified Snow's memorial at once by the fresh-turned earth surrounding its base. Made of white stone, speckled with polished silver, her monument stood beside the obelisk of Snow's father.

Talia stepped forward, touching the letters carved into the side. The Stormcrow frowned at the breach in etiquette, and Laurence started to speak, but a glare from Danielle silenced him. She and Gerta joined Talia. Gerta wore a white bandage over her ruined eye. No healing magic could restore what the darkling had destroyed.

"What is it, Mama?" Jakob asked from Danielle's arms. He had refused to be separated from her, and Danielle was more than willing to keep him close.

"It says there lived a woman called Ermillina Curtana," said Gerta. "She was Princess of Allesandria, and she died protecting her nation."

The Stormcrow began to speak. A slight hunch stole his height, and his bald scalp was spotted by age, but his voice carried clearly through the garden.

"An old blessing," Gerta whispered. "It means 'Be at peace.'"

Laurence stepped forward next. He used his scepter to cut his palm, and paced a slow circle around the obelisk, dripping blood into the earth. Gerta translated his words as he vowed to protect both Snow's remains and her memory.

"Thank you, Your Majesty," Danielle said softly. She prayed he would keep his word.

There were no songs. No prayers. Nothing but cold stone to mark Snow's resting place. There had been no official proclamation, nor had Snow's body been presented to the people as would be done with most nobles, but she was here among her family. She was home.

Laurence stared at the monument, his expression impossible to read. "Tell me, Danielle. Was she happy?"

"Almost always." Danielle hesitated, tempted to leave it at that, to forget her other obligations and simply grieve for her friend. Instead, she turned to face him. "She searched for joy in everything she did, and if she couldn't find it, she created it. Yet . . . there was pain. Loss. She kept it locked away, but it was there. She missed Allesandria. Her family. It was that buried pain that helped the demon turn her against you."

Laurence's lips pursed. "You blame me."

"Blame changes nothing that has happened. But this was her home." She watched him closely, searching his face. "As it was home to the fairies."

"I see." Laurence was no fool. "You've not said how you were able to locate Snow's palace, nor how you reached her without succumbing to her wasps."

"No, I haven't."

"You believe fairykind will rebel against us, as my cousin did?"

Danielle sighed, thinking of Bellum and Veleris. "I believe some of them are content to hide, while others bridle against the loss of their homes. I believe they are dangerous enemies, but they can be valuable allies as well."

And what of those who are both? She stepped away, leaving him to his thoughts. Talia had warned her, years ago. Never bargain with fairies. They always got the better of the deal. The Duchess had risked nothing but a darkling servant, and in return, she won Danielle's son.

"You're welcome to remain here as long as you need," said Laurence, "but I would recommend you let my people escort you to the harbor. The palace is broken, with only the crudest protections. With so many dead, my Stormcrows are spread thin."

They had at least taken the time to restore the monsters from Snow's palace. The survivors of the *Phillipa* had already been returned to the ship, to repair the damage done in the demon's attack and prepare for the voyage back to Lorindar.

"Thank you," said Danielle. "We will leave today." She watched Gerta closely, uncertain whether she would want to remain in Allesandria. According to King Laurence, the law would not recognize a magical construct as a person, but if it was what Gerta wanted, Danielle intended to tell him exactly where he could put his laws. But Gerta simply nodded, keeping close to Talia.

"One more thing, please." The king spoke briefly to the Stormcrow, who bowed and left the garden. Danielle glanced at Gerta, who shrugged. Laurence waited until the door closed. "Ermillina came to Allesandria seeking vengeance. She murdered those who stood with her mother."

Danielle said nothing, uncertain where he was going.

"As king, it is my duty to appoint new members of the Nobles' Circle. Traditionally, those seats would go to the heirs, but that is tradition only, not law." He gave her a tight smile. "Every crisis is an opportunity, and I believe I can gain enough support in the Circle to appoint those more worthy of the word 'noble.'"

Meaning some good would come of Snow's actions. "Thank you, Laurence."

"If there's anything else you need, you have only to ask it."

Danielle looked at Talia, who hadn't moved. She stood like a statue, staring at Snow's memorial. "Nothing you can provide," she said sadly. She squeezed Jakob tight. "Only transportation to the harbor. It's time for us to return home."

Chapter 24

BY THE TIME THE *PHILLIPA* ARRIVED IN Lorindar, a crowd had gathered to meet them. Even before they docked, Talia could see Prince Armand fidgeting impatiently at the front of the crowd, cupping his eyes as he searched the ship for Danielle and Jakob. When the crew lowered the gangplank, Armand was the first to board, nearly knocking one of his guards into the water in his eagerness. When he found his wife and son, pulling them both into an embrace, those on the docks broke into cheers.

Talia used the celebration to slip away, hurrying down the gangplank and through the crowd. She didn't begrudge them their happiness. The gods knew it had been hard-earned. She simply couldn't be a part of it right now.

The noise made it easy enough to liberate the prince's horse from the post where he had left it. As she rode past the naval ships and into the commercial part of the harbor, she fought the urge to board the nearest ship, to sign on with anyone who could take her to a land where nobody had ever heard of Cinderella, Sleeping Beauty, or Snow White.

Instead, she rode to Whiteshore Palace. She gave the horse over to a stable hand, saying only, "Armand decided to take a carriage back with his family." From there, she went to the chapel.

The heavy door in the back of the chapel which led to the royal mausoleum was locked, but there were no magical protections. Talia retrieved a small packet of metal tools from her left boot. Moments later, the lock was open and she was descending the stone steps. Soft flame flickered to life in the hanging lanterns, enchanted by Father Isaac to recognize visitors.

Talia had always found northern burial traditions strange. Hiding the body, sealing it in earth and stone beneath the very ground where the living trod, felt disrespectful. Yet for more than two hundred years, the Whiteshore family had buried its dead here in this low-ceilinged room. The first Whiteshore king lay entombed with his wife in the center of the room, their coffins carved from the bleached stone that gave the family their name. Later kings and queens were laid to rest in the walls to either side.

Talia strode toward the back of the mausoleum, where the newest stone tablet gleamed white. Beatrice's marker was modest compared to some of the others, marked only with her name and a carved swan.

How long she stood there, staring at Beatrice's marker, she didn't know. Eventually, she heard the creak of the door, followed by light, careful footsteps.

"Hello, Danielle." Who else would it be?

Danielle didn't say a word. She simply joined Talia in front of Bea's grave.

"We should have been here for her burial," said Talia. It had been close to three weeks since Beatrice's death. There was no way King Theodore could have delayed the funeral for so long, and yet . . .

"I know."

Talia swallowed. "Hephyra invited me to leave Lorindar, to sail with her. She told me I would never have Snow, that Beatrice would soon be gone, that you had your own family to look after."

"You're a part of that family," Danielle said firmly. "No matter what you choose." Her unspoken question filled the mausoleum.

"I don't know if I can stay here. If Hephyra still lived . . ." Memories of Snow and Beatrice saturated every room, every hallway.

Danielle put a hand on Talia's shoulder. "Trittibar has asked that the *Phillipa*'s mainmast be brought to the palace, to be planted in the courtyard."

For the first time since reaching Lorindar, Talia looked Danielle in the eyes. "Planted?"

Danielle smiled. "She's a dryad. Hephyra's tree—the ship—survives. Trittibar says it could take years for her to recover, to heal the part of herself that was lost. But she will heal."

"That's good." Talia meant the words, even if she couldn't feel them. She turned back to Bea's marker. "And Armand?"

"He is himself. Isaac and Tymalous have removed the glass from all those who were infected. Armand spent the entire trip from the harbor apologizing for the things he said and did. There seem to be no lasting effects of the demon's touch."

"Good," she said again.

"If there's anything you need, anything you want, you know you have only to ask it."

Talia took a slow, even breath. "Right now . . . all I want is to be left in peace."

"I understand." Danielle took Talia's hand, squeezed almost hard enough to hurt. "You're not alone, Talia."

Talia nodded, but didn't answer.

For the next two weeks, Talia performed her duties as though in a trance. She moved through the palace from one task to the next, barely speaking to anyone. Danielle tried to engage her in conversation, but Talia had no heart for it. Even Jakob had done his childish best to make her smile, but their efforts only made Talia feel guilty when she was unable to respond. She spent more and more time away from the others.

Talia still expected to find Snow flirting with the blacksmith, or hear her teasing Danielle. Her chest clenched every time she passed a woman with black hair, every time she heard laughter ringing through the halls.

She was locked in her room, paging through a century-old book of Arathean poetry, when someone pounded on her door hard enough to rattle it in the frame. "It's Gerta. Open up."

Talia almost smiled at the impatience in her voice, so similar to Snow's. Since returning to Lorindar, Gerta had been doing her best to fit into palace life. Danielle had given her permission to go through Snow's library and try to make sense of Snow's rather eccentric notions of organization.

Gerta knocked again. "Last chance, Talia. I know you're in there."

Talia glanced over to make sure the door was latched. "Go away."

Silence. There were no footsteps, so Gerta hadn't left. Talia tucked the book beneath her pillow. As she stood, she smelled smoke rising from the door. Orange flames licked about the latch. The fire confined itself to a small ring, burning the wood to ash until the latch fell free and hit the floor with a clang. The door swung inward.

Gerta tossed a bottle. Talia snatched it from the air without thinking. Arathean wine from the cellars.

"Come with me," ordered Gerta.

Talia's attention went to the embroidered green patch that covered Gerta's lost eye. Another reminder of that day. Gerta said she was working on crafting a glass eye, one with a mirrored pupil, but perfecting the magic of that eye would take months. "What's going on?"

Gerta held two more bottles by the necks in her right hand. "Princess Whiteshore commands it."

"Did she command this, too?" Talia asked, lifting the wine.

Gerta spun away. Considering Gerta had burned through the door to find her, Talia figured it best to see what Danielle wanted. She grabbed her zaraq whip and followed Gerta out into the hallway.

Gerta led her to the northern drawing room, a smaller chamber often used for entertaining royal guests. The walls were a garish green, covered in a textured paper imported from Morova. A fire burned in the hearth, countering the chill from the windows. Danielle sat with Trittibar and Ambassador Febblekeck at the tile-topped table in the center of the room.

Danielle rose, but before she could speak, Gerta set both of her bottles on the table and jabbed a hand at the fairies. "Out. Both of you."

Trittibar's brows shot up. Febblekeck flew from his chair, shedding glowing dust onto the carpet. "You forget your place, human."

Danielle watched Gerta as though trying to read her intention. "Can this wait, Gerta?"

"No." Gerta folded her arms and waited.

"Very well," said Danielle. "Trittibar, Febblekeck, if you wouldn't mind?"

"Of course, Your Highness." Trittibar rose and bowed.

Febblekeck reached out to pluck a grape from the platter of bread and fruit at the center of the table. "*I* mind. This girl is—"

"She is a member of my household," Danielle said softly. "And a friend."

"She's not even real," Febblekeck protested. "Any fairy can smell the magic on her. She's but a changeling, cobbled together by human magic, her soul a torn and crudely-stitched quilt of clumsiness and haste."

Gerta flinched. Talia twirled the wine bottle in her hand. Given the pixie's size, the bottle should be heavy enough to smash him from the air.

Danielle stood, smiling a too-sweet smile. "You should leave now," she said softly.

"I am here as a representative of the king of Fairytown," Febblekeck countered.

Danielle's smile vanished. "And I would be most grieved to have to tell your king that his ambassador was snatched and devoured by a hungry owl."

"You wouldn't dare."

"I ask the animals to leave our guests alone, but I can't be blamed if one refuses to listen." Danielle stepped around the table. "Owls are so quiet in flight. The prey hears nothing, no warning at all before the talons pierce the body."

Febblekeck brightened. "You can't—"

"We can continue our conversation later, Princess Whiteshore." Trittibar snatched Febblekeck's arm, tugging him away before he could say anything further.

Danielle pursed her lips and sat back in her chair. "I sometimes suspect Febblekeck was appointed to this position because his king wanted an excuse to kick him out of Fairytown." She rubbed her temples with both hands. "He and Trittibar have been helping me to understand the Duchess' bargain. She agreed to raise him as her son, and to protect him from harm, but fairies view 'harm' differently than—"

"Your bargain called on you to give Jakob to the Duchess six months after your return to Lorindar," Gerta interrupted.

Danielle frowned, looking more confused than annoyed. "That's correct, and therein lies the problem."

"It's a problem that will still be waiting in the morning. You've more than five months to find a solution." Gerta wrapped a hand around one of the wine bottles and whispered a spell. The wax seal softened, and she plucked it neatly from the neck. The cork followed, jumping into her palm.

"You interrupted my meeting for wine?" Danielle asked. Talia could hear the warning in her words, similar to the tone she used with Jakob.

"Yes." Gerta glanced at Talia. "Sit down."

Talia shook her head. "You told me Danielle ordered me here."

"I lied." Gerta gestured at a chair, which swiveled on one leg as if to invite Talia to sit. Gerta nibbled her lower lip, her confidence vanishing. "I have the memories Snow gave me, but they're a puzzle with only half of the pieces. Mostly I remember a childhood that never happened. I . . . I was hoping you could tell me about her."

She took a drink, then offered the bottle to Talia. When Talia didn't move, Gerta sighed and slid it to Danielle.

"Snow giggled too much," Gerta said. "She always thought me too dour, and sought to cheer me up. When we studied magic, Snow would read the incantations in the voices of various Lords. It made our mother so angry . . . There was one noble, I forget her name, who spoke with a horrible lisp. Snow was mimicking her while casting a spell which was *supposed* to purify a goblet of poisoned wine. Snow slurred the words so badly the wine exploded from the cup. Everyone it splashed developed the most awful rash."

"I see." Danielle held up the bottle. "Should I be worried about this?"

Gerta grabbed the second bottle, using magic to open this one as well. "Not about poison or magic, no. The taste, on the other hand . . . Arathean wine is far too sour for my liking. Much like some Aratheans I know."

Talia ignored the barb. She set her own bottle on the table and backed away. "I have duties to attend to. If you need anything—"

"One of your duties is to guard the princess." Danielle took a drink from the bottle. "With this much wine, I'll likely need your protection by the time this night is done. Join us, Talia."

Talia didn't move. "Is that an order?"

"Does it have to be?"

Reluctantly, Talia took the chair beside Gerta. Gerta slid her a bottle hard enough to make it tip. Talia caught it instinctively.

"What would you like to know, Gerta?" asked Danielle.

"Everything." Gerta drank several swallows of wine, then made a face. "I have my memories, and the things I've learned going through her library, but I want to know her. Who she was in your eyes."

Danielle pursed her lips. "With the exception of Armand and his parents, Snow was the first person to make me feel truly welcome here." Danielle stared at one of the windows. "I first learned who she was in the library, shortly after Armand was kidnapped."

Talia forced herself to listen as Danielle described their first journey together into Fairytown, to rescue Armand from the Duchess and Danielle's stepsisters.

Gerta spoke next, describing a time she and Snow had snuck through the palace to visit their father. Snow had rarely spoken of him, save to describe him as crippled by her mother's magic, little more than a puppet of skin and bone. Gerta and Snow had brought him wildflowers, which they wove into his hair as he slept. "He looked so pale, almost colorless."

"Like Beatrice," Talia said, the words slipping out.

Gerta glanced up, then nodded. "Snow gave me very few memories of Beatrice, but yes."

Talia raised her bottle, drinking deeply and concentrating only on the smooth, smoky taste of the wine. She returned the bottle to the table and used her thumbnail to pick at a bit of wax that clung to the side of the mouth. She had spent far more time with Snow than either of them, but a part of her wanted to keep those memories, to protect them and lock them away.

Talia glanced at Gerta's eye patch. Talia had lost so much, but Gerta . . . she had never even known her sister. Not really.

Talia stared at her reflection in the glass. "Snow once made it rain urine in Prince Armand's bedroom."

Both Danielle and Gerta gaped. Gerta's eye was wide, and Danielle's mouth opened and shut several times before she finally asked, "How did this come about?"

Talia shrugged one shoulder. "It was two months after I arrived in Lorindar. I don't know what Armand said, but Snow took it personally. Beatrice realized something was wrong when Snow kept sneaking off to get more to drink."

"More to . . . ah," Gerta said, nodding. "Sympathetic magic. She would have needed to cast that spell from a privy. How long did she manage to keep it going?"

"More than an hour." Talia took another drink, remembering Beatrice's expression as she ordered Snow to clean up the mess, all the while fighting to keep from laughing. "The smell lingered for a month."

"I'll talk to Armand tonight," Danielle said, smiling. "I have to know what he said to earn such retribution."

"The best part came later." Talia pushed her chair back, staring at the window. "Beatrice demanded to know what good could come of such pranks. Snow looked her in the eye and said, 'I wanted the prince to know what it felt like to be a peon.'"

There was a pause, and then the groans came in unison. Danielle grabbed a piece of bread from the platter and threw it at Talia. "That's terrible!"

Talia caught the bread and took a bite. "I told Beatrice that whatever punishment she assigned, it should be doubled for that pun."

Her throat was tight. Even that single bite of bread hurt to swallow. She washed it down with more wine as Danielle started talking about a time Snow had flirted her way onto a ship suspected to be carrying smuggled silks. Talia had been along for that mission, and remembered Snow's unabashed enjoyment.

That was who Snow had been. That was who Talia wanted to remember. Even now, memories of Snow bleeding onto the ice threatened to suffocate her. She pushed them back, clinging to the laughter. The joy in Snow's eyes.

Danielle was watching her as she talked. Talia scowled. "This *was* your idea, wasn't it?"

Danielle shrugged. "Gerta suggested the wine. I merely gave her my blessing to drag you here by whatever means necessary. After two hours with Trittibar and Febblekeck, I needed the break."

Talia wadded a bit of bread into a ball and flicked it across the table, bouncing it off the center of Danielle's forehead. Danielle stuck out her tongue. Gerta simply laughed.

Danielle grabbed an apple from the platter. "Tell her how Snow and Beatrice found you."

Talia groaned. "It's embarrassing."

Danielle grinned. "I know."

Talia threw more bread, but she told Gerta how she had hidden away in a ship, hoping to slip unnoticed into Lorindar. How Beatrice and Snow had discovered her . . . and how Snow had used magic to knock her senseless.

At some point during the evening, servants quietly carried in a dinner of roast pork and mushrooms, and a pot of chilled strawberry soup. Talia hadn't had much of an appetite since returning to Lorindar, but tonight she found herself devouring the meal.

Many of the stories she shared made her smile, remembering arguments and antics she hadn't thought about for years. Others brought tears. It was hours after sunset when Danielle finally stood to excuse herself. Her face was red, her hair loose and disheveled. She hugged Talia from behind. "Make sure Gerta doesn't drink too much."

"I'll do my best," said Talia.

"Thank you." Danielle kissed her on the cheek, then moved to embrace Gerta as well.

Once she had gone, Talia turned to Gerta. "You owe me a door."

"Your door is fine. Mostly." Gerta stifled a yawn.

Talia stood. "I can clean up here, if you need to sleep."

"Sit down." Gerta smiled. "We've almost an entire bottle left, and I haven't even told you about the time Snow snuck out to hunt a unicorn."

"A unicorn?" Talia raised her eyebrows. "How did she plan to hold one?"

"I don't know that you could call it a 'plan,' really . . ."

Talia sank back into her chair to watch Gerta talk. In her mind, she heard Snow teasing her, asking again why she hadn't yet kissed Gerta.

Hush, Talia said silently. There would be time to sort such things out later. For now, this was what she needed. A friend who could help Talia to remember and celebrate Snow's life. It didn't change the pain in Talia's chest whenever she thought of her death, but it provided a buffer, something to help her through that pain.

The sun had risen when Talia finally escorted Gerta back to her room, one hand on her elbow to keep her steady. Gerta stopped in the doorway, scowling at Talia with mock anger. "Have you made your choice yet?"

Talia blinked. "My choice?"

"Whether or not you're going to leave." Gerta kept her voice steady, but Talia could see the way her face tightened as she braced herself.

Oh. Talia stepped back. "Someone has to keep an eye on you and Danielle. Snow would never forgive me if I let something happen to you."

Relief suffused Gerta's face. She jumped forward, throwing her arms around Talia's neck and kissing her cheek. "Good."

She slipped into her room and shut her door, leaving Talia alone in the hallway. Talia touched her cheek with her fingertips. With her other hand, she reached into her pocket and pulled a single sharpened steel snowflake from its flat leather sheath. She turned it until she could see her reflection.

"Yes," she said softly, remembering her final exchange with Snow. "I've made my choice."

Chapter 25

SIX MONTHS FROM THE DAY DANIELLE brought Jakob home, she strode through the courtyard toward the chapel. Talia and Gerta were already waiting outside the door. Talia was armed, a curved sword on one hip, her zaraq whip on the other. Heaven knew what else was tucked away beneath her red cape.

Danielle wore only her glass sword and the dagger Talia had given her years ago.

"You think those will be necessary?" Gerta asked.

"Always," Talia said before Danielle could respond.

The others waited inside. Father Isaac stood before the altar, looking troubled. Trittibar sat beside Armand, who rose to greet Danielle with a quick kiss.

"Jakob?" she asked.

"In his room. Isaac has warded it to the best of his ability. He's as safe there as he is anywhere in Lorindar."

"Thank you." Armand's words weren't as reassuring as she might have hoped. "I'm sorry."

He waved the apology away. He had been angry when he first heard of Danielle's bargain, and angrier still when he learned of the Duchess' warning from years before, which Danielle had kept from him. They had fought three times, each worse than the last. Looking back, Danielle realized now how much of that anger had come from grief and fear.

Today she fought to keep that fear under control. If

this didn't work— She kissed him, perhaps a bit harder than was considered proper, but Danielle didn't particularly care. She held him close, allowing herself another moment of comfort before turning to Father Isaac to ask, "The chapel is prepared?"

"I've opened the wards to allow you to speak with the Duchess," Isaac said. "If things go wrong, I'll do my best to protect you all, but I can make no promises."

"I understand." Danielle drew a deep breath. "I've already made my promise."

"Good luck," said Armand.

Danielle walked to the front of the church, rested a hand on her sword, and spoke the Duchess' name three times.

The wooden floor warped and split, boards appearing to fall into endless shadow. The Duchess appeared soon after. "Greetings, Your Majesty. My congratulations on your coronation."

Danielle gave a slight bow. Theodore had stepped down four months after the death of his wife. He remained in the palace, but now spent his time advising his son and spoiling his grandson. "Thank you, Your Grace."

"To King Armand as well," the Duchess added. "Given your new responsibilities, I'm flattered you remembered your obligation to a lowly fairy such as myself."

How could she forget, when she had thought about her oath every day since making it? "What was your plan for Jakob? To enchant him as you once did Armand? Or to force him to swear loyalty to you, to enslave him as you did the fairies of Speas Elan?"

"It was your stepsisters who attempted to steal your husband," the Duchess corrected. "As for my plans, I'm afraid they're none of your concern. Unless you'd care to bargain for that knowledge?" When Danielle said nothing, she laughed softly. "Once Jakob passes through this portal, he will be safe. Safer than he would be anywhere else in this world. You have my word. Six months from today he will return to you unharmed."

Six months . . . *that* was the loophole Trittibar had discovered. So long as only six months passed in the mortal world, the Duchess would have kept her part of the bargain. Danielle knew the stories of mortals who passed into a fairy hill and were lost in their realm. They could wander for years and return to find only a single day had passed. To manipulate time was difficult, but within the Duchess' power. Jakob would return in half a year's time, but he might have aged years. And after so long in the Duchess' care, he would have little or no memory of his human life.

"I remember our terms." Danielle folded her arms. "You've expressed so much interest in my son. I wanted you to be among the first to hear the news."

"What news?" Wariness sharpened her question.

"Yesterday evening, in this church, my son Jakob was wed to Princess Rose Gertrude Curtana of Allesandria."

Gerta stepped forward and raised her hand, flashing a gold wedding band where all could see.

"An . . . interesting match," said the Duchess. "Though his father was equally daring in his choice of bride. Had I known, I would have sent the boy a gift."

"Man, not boy." Danielle glanced at Armand, who nodded. "Under the laws of Lorindar, once married, my son is officially a man. As our bargain was only until Jakob came of age, that bargain is now ended. Lorindar thanks you for your aid."

The chill that followed was so palpable Danielle expected to see frost rising from the hole. She and Armand had spent many long hours discussing this move with Febblekeck and Trittibar. Both agreed with this interpretation of fairy and human law, but there was no way to guess how the Duchess would react. Danielle glanced at Talia, who slipped her hands into her sleeves. If things went badly, silver-bladed knives would be flying into the hole before anyone else could blink.

The Duchess simply reached out, fingers spread as if searching for something unseen. According to Trittibar, had they been within the bounds of Fairytown, the

Duchess would have sensed the instant the bargain was fulfilled. But Jakob had been wed in human lands, shielded by Father Isaac's magic.

The Duchess tilted her head in salute. "Well done, Queen Danielle. Perhaps your fairy blood is stronger than I realized."

"Perhaps," Danielle said evenly.

"Be wary. One day Jakob will leave the safety of your palace, and who knows what he might encounter. Your stories tell of those lured by the beauty of fairy magic, men who abandon the colorless mundanity of your world to join ours."

"Is that a threat?" Armand asked softly.

"Not at all, King Armand. Merely a warning. You yourself have known our hospitality. If you could not resist, what chance will he have?" She paused briefly before adding, "I could teach him to protect himself . . ."

Gerta stepped to the edge of the hole. "I'm more than capable of protecting my husband."

The Duchess laughed. "Child, you flatter yourself if you think you've the means to keep him from my reach. Your power is but a shadow of Snow White's."

Gerta matched her smile. She reached into the pocket of her gown and produced a silk-wrapped bundle. She carefully unwrapped the silk to reveal a rose of mirrored glass. The petals were thin as foil, just beginning to open. Every thorn was sharp enough to draw blood. Colored light from the windows of the chapel flashed over the rose's surface. "Not a shadow. A reflection."

"You sheltered my stepsisters when they kidnapped my husband," Danielle said. "Your darklings tried to help them steal my child. You aided Arathea against us, resulting in the death of my stepsister."

"My darkling saved your lives in Allesandria," the Duchess countered.

"And we are grateful for its help and sacrifice." She took the rose from Gerta and held it lightly in her hands. The glass was warm to the touch. "Just as we are grateful to Speas Elan for their aid. But you have never answered for your crimes against Lorindar, and I will not allow you to threaten my family again."

The Duchess had opened this portal expecting to receive Prince Jakob. When Danielle dropped the rose into the hole, it passed from the chapel into the Duchess' realm. She reacted at once, clapping her hands loudly enough to make Danielle flinch. The rose shattered.

"That was a mistake," Gerta whispered.

Light poured from the broken glass, bathing the Duchess in orange and red. "What is this?"

"A sunrise, Your Grace," said Danielle. "Captured within the mirror by Gerta's magic, and released by your own hand."

The Duchess froze.

"Six hundred twenty-four mortal years ago, the rulers of Fairytown sentenced you to death for your crimes." Trittibar spoke more formally than Danielle had ever heard. "That sentence has never been lifted, though the king promised to postpone your death until the day you witnessed one final sunrise as a free woman. That oath is now fulfilled and witnessed."

The Duchess' fury burned away any trace of humanity in her face. Her white hair swirled as though in a maelstrom. Smoke and flame danced over her skin. The floor shifted, as though the entire chapel would be sucked through. The Duchess reached up, fingers curled—

The hole in the floor vanished. Father Isaac kissed the crucifix on his necklace. "I take it your conversation was ended?"

Danielle stepped back and grabbed Armand's arm for support. He appeared almost as shaken as she felt. His face was pale, and she could feel his pulse pounding even through his sleeve.

"I've already sent orders to increase the guards," Talia said. "Gerta and Isaac should strengthen the wards around the palace as well."

"Prudent precautions," Trittibar agreed. "But I suspect the Duchess will have more pressing concerns than vengeance. The Lord and Lady of Fairytown agree on few things, but the Duchess tricked and humiliated them both. I've no doubt they sensed the termination of that centuries-old bargain." He bowed to Danielle and Armand. "Fairytown will be in your debt."

"As they will be in yours," Danielle said, smiling. Whether that debt would be enough to earn Trittibar his former place as ambassador, she couldn't say, but she intended to push Fairytown to do so. It was just one of many topics she planned to discuss, along with revisiting Malindar's Treaty and sending Jakob to visit the fairy courts to learn their ways when he was older . . . and the Duchess was no longer a threat.

She watched Trittibar depart, then turned to Father Isaac. "Now remind me, please. What are the formalities for annulling a marriage?"

Palace business kept Danielle occupied for the rest of the day. It was well after dark before she was able to slip away to help her husband herd Jakob into bed. Nicolette had gotten him ready, but ever since his return from Allesandria, he had insisted on seeing his mother and father before settling down to sleep. It was a demand Danielle was happy to oblige, especially on this night.

Once Jakob was finally tucked away, she slipped quietly into the hall with Armand.

He offered an arm. "How goes your day, Queen Danielle?"

"Very long, King Armand." Danielle managed a weary smile as she slipped her hand through his arm. "I've mediated a dispute between the Fairy Church and the Church of the Iron Cross, met with Lord Garbarin of Eastpointe over the upcoming marriage of his daughter—"

"Isn't she the one who ran off with a dwarf?"

"The same," Danielle said. "And then I had to stop at the gardens to lecture the rabbits. They've been driving poor Leonard to distraction." She shook her head. "Your parents did this job for more than twenty years?"

"You heard my father when I accepted the crown. I've rarely heard such an evil laugh."

She kissed him. "Have you seen Talia or Gerta? There's one final matter I need to take care of tonight."

"Try the southwest tower."

She should have guessed. Gerta enjoyed the view from the towers. She often snuck away to the western towers to watch the sun set. Danielle started to leave, but Armand tugged her back. He kissed her again, more deeply this time, and said, "Don't be too long."

Smiling, she made her way through the palace, doing her best to greet and acknowledge all she passed while fending off further requests for her time. By the time she finally reached the tower, she was seriously considering asking Gerta to cast some sort of illusion or disguise that would allow her to move about in peace.

She found them standing atop the tower, looking out over the waist-high walls toward the ocean and arguing about Fairytown. Danielle leaned against the door. "Aren't there supposed to be guards up here?"

"I sent them away," said Talia. "Will you please tell Gerta how many times Fairytown has used loopholes in the treaty to—"

"It's in their nature," Gerta countered. "Might as well ask a bird not to fly, or an Arathean not to be so stubborn."

"I'm not saying we shouldn't reexamine the treaty," Talia said. "Only that our first priority has to be the protection of our people."

"Most fairies have never raised a hand against humans. Would you imprison them all to protect us from the threat of a few?"

"Fairytown is hardly a prison," Talia shot back.

Danielle cleared her throat. "Speaking of threats . . ."

Both of them turned to face her. Danielle suppressed a smile when she saw how close they stood to one another. She started to speak, but stopped to stifle a yawn.

Gerta and Talia exchanged knowing looks.

"A rough day, Your Majesty?" asked Gerta.

"The hardships of royalty," said Talia.

Gerta clucked her tongue. "It must be difficult, having your every meal prepared by an expert chef, your gowns handmade by the best tailors in Lorindar, your room tended, with servants hovering about to fulfill your every wish."

"Be fair," Talia said. "The kingdom's treasury isn't endless. Why, I doubt she could buy more than half of Lorindar, at most. She's practically living in poverty."

"The poor thing."

Danielle gave them both a decidedly unqueenlike gesture, earning a delighted laugh from Gerta. Even Talia grinned.

"So what's the threat?" Gerta asked, slipping her hand into Talia's. Talia appeared a little self-conscious, but didn't pull away.

"Have you heard the tale of the girl with no hands?" Danielle asked.

"From Najarin, right?" Talia pursed her lips. "Her father made a deal with a devil. He cut off his daughter's hands, and in exchange the devil rewarded him with tremendous wealth. The story says she eventually replaced her lost hands with hands of silver, and went on to marry a minor king."

"That's the story, yes."

"You've heard otherwise?" asked Gerta.

"Rumors only, so far. A woman with silver hands was seen in the southern isles off the coast of Lorindar. Five people have been found dead. Four men and one woman, all wealthy."

Gerta's lips pursed. "Her father mutilated her for gold."

"So now she punishes the rich," Talia guessed.

"For their greed." Danielle pulled out the note she had received. "I've spoken with Najarin. The girl's father was her first victim. She killed thirteen other people before fleeing."

Talia whistled softly.

"A mermaid named Nallinix claims to have witnessed the last murder. She says the woman's hands absorbed magic, reflecting it back at her caster. A single blow from her silver fists was enough to crush bones. So be careful."

"Define careful," Talia said.

Danielle smiled. "It means you do whatever it takes to return home safely. That's an order from your queen."

"Not my queen," said Gerta. "I'm Allesandrian, remember? I don't recall swearing fealty to Lorindar."

"Come to think of it, I don't think I ever swore an oath to our new queen, either," said Talia.

"You leave in the morning." Danielle gave Talia a mock glare. "Don't keep Gerta up too late. Some of us need our sleep."

Gerta tugged Talia closer. "Sleep is overrated."

The setting sun made it difficult to be certain, but she could have sworn Talia actually blushed.

Danielle turned her head, hiding her smile. "Good night, my friends."

Author's Note

I REMEMBER SITTING IN A RESTAURANT with my friend Trey and his wife Adelia back in 2004. It was the last day of Windycon, a Chicago SF/F convention, and I was babbling on and on about this nifty new idea I had for a different kind of fairy-tale retelling.

It was my daughter's fault. She was going through a princess phase, and our house had been taken over by princess-themed movies and merchandise. I wanted to provide an alternate take on fairy-tale princesses, one that went back to the older source material while putting the princesses squarely in charge of their own stories. And I wanted it to be fun. Sort of a Brothers Grimm meets *Last Action Hero* thing.

A lot has changed since I first started playing with these ideas. The first version of Snow White's character was blind, relying on her mirrors to see. (I've posted a deleted scene with her at www.jimchines.com.) She went by the name of Lina in that first book, which was originally titled *The Stepsister Plot*, and then *The Stepsister Conspiracy*. She and her companions rode unicorns across Fairytown, which led Lina to make all manner of off-color remarks about virgins. And then I started planning book two, *The Mermaid Mysteries . . .*

Snow Queen was the book that gave me the most title trouble. My editor rejected more titles than I can count, including *The Snow Queen's Scourge*, *Shards of the Snow Queen*, and *Godzilla vs. The Snow Queen*. I finally went to my blog and begged my readers for help. Huge thanks to Arlene Medder and Lara (a.k.a. Miladygray the Internet Muse), who both suggested what would become the final title for the book.

Snow Queen was challenging in other ways, too. It's one thing to finish a book, but this time I needed to bring closure to an entire series. How the heck do you end a series that's all about what happens *after* the "happily ever after"?

I blame Talia. Back in '04, I was planning to write a more episodic series, something like James Bond for the Fairy-Tale Princess set, which would allow me to write book after book, make millions of dollars, and buy Hawaii. There would be no multi-book arcs, and no need to write a true end to the series. Then Talia had to go and fall in love, and I realized I couldn't just leave her hanging. Either the relationship needed to go somewhere, or else Talia needed to move on. And it wasn't just Talia; all three of my protagonists had to grow and change. Suddenly I wasn't just writing episodes, but larger character arcs and stories.

Ultimately, I believe that made the series stronger (even if I didn't get to buy Hawaii). I'm proud of these books. I love the characters. I love their stories. I love their strengths and their flaws. I love their struggles. And I've done my best to be true to the characters and their stories, and to find the endings that felt honest for each of them . . . even when that was hard to do.

Especially when it was hard. My beta readers told me they got choked up while reading the final few chapters of this book. Well, good! Because I had the same problem while writing them, and I'd hate to be the only one.

Thank you to everyone who has read these books. Thank you for joining me for these stories. Thank you for your letters and your e-mails. It makes my day to hear from someone who loved one of my books, to know that something I wrote connected and resonated with that person. Thanks also to everyone who told their friends about the series, or posted reviews. The bottom line is that without all of you, I'd have no writing career. And I really, really like my career!

As long as I'm thanking people, I have to give a shout-out to www.surlalunefairytales.com. This is a wonderful resource, and includes annotations and research information for a ton of fairy tales. I've used them a great many times over the past six years.

Thanks also to Sheila Gilbert, Debra Euler, and everyone else at DAW Books. To my agent Joshua Bilmes. To my friends and fellow authors Stephanie Burgis and Seanan McGuire, who read a draft of *Snow Queen* and helped me pound it into shape. To my cover artist Scott Fischer. To my family, who put up with me and the emotional roller coaster that is my writing process.

One thing I've learned from this series is that the line between ending and beginning is a thin one. I hope you enjoyed the final (at least for now) book in the Princess series. If you need me, I'll be in my office beginning the first book of the *Magic ex Libris* series. That book is tentatively titled *Libriomancer*. What will it be called when it comes out in 2012? Your guess is as good as mine . . .

—Jim C. Hines

Once upon a time...

Cinderella, whose real name is Danielle Whiteshore, did marry Prince Armand. And their wedding was a dream come true.

But not long after the "happily ever after," Danielle is attacked by her stepsister Charlotte, who suddenly has all sorts of magic to call upon. And though Talia the martial arts master—otherwise known as Sleeping Beauty—comes to the rescue, Charlotte gets away.

That's when Danielle discovers a number of disturbing facts: Armand has been kidnapped; Danielle is pregnant; and the Queen has her own Secret Service that consists of Talia and Snow (White, of course). Snow is an expert at mirror magic and heavy-duty flirting. Can the princesses track down Armand and rescue him from the clutches of some of Fantasyland's most nefarious villains?

The Stepsister Scheme

by Jim C. Hines

978-0-7564-0532-8

"Do we look like we need to be rescued?"

DAW 130